'Golden's book is the template for a score of books that have been published in the years since its publication. Many of those books have been bestsellers. Reading *Of Saints and Shadows* again, I was amazed how many elements now familiar in the vampire and thriller genres appeared in *Saints* first. Golden's imagination and expert plotting wove these elements into a startlingly original book, as exciting to read now as it was when it first appeared on the rack.'

Charlaine Harris

OF SAINTS AND SHADOWS

Christopher Golden

POCKET
BOOKS

LONDON • SYDNEY • NEW YORK • TORONTO

First published in the USA by Jove Books, 1994 and by
Ace Books, 1998
First published in Great Britain by Pocket Books, 2010
An imprint of Simon & Schuster UK Ltd
A CBS Company

1 3 5 7 9 10 8 6 4 2

Simon & Schuster UK Ltd
1st Floor
222 Gray's Inn Road
London
WC1X 8HB

www.simonandschuster.co.uk

Simon & Schuster Australia
Sydney

A CIP catalogue record for this book is available from the
British Library

ISBN 978-1-84739-924-3

Printed in the UK by CPI Mackays, Chatham ME5 8TD

This novel is dedicated to my wife, Concetta Nicole Russo Golden, without whose love and support it might never have been conceived, and certainly would not have become a reality. In a world where the daily horrors are more terrible than any fiction, our life together has given me the strength to stand on principle, to hope for the future, and to pursue our destiny with tireless passion, optimism, and confidence. Indeed, fools rush in. May we always be fools.

Acknowledgments

Like many other books, especially other first novels, *Of Saints and Shadows* took years to write. Over that time I've accumulated a long list of people whose contributions, or simple support, were invaluable not just to the evolution of the book, but to my evolution as a writer. Some of them are mentioned below, but a whole host of others were just there for me when I needed them to be, or shared my enthusiasm at a critical time. I thank you all for that, and hope you realize who you are without my having to tell you.

Special thanks to my wonderful agent, Lori Perkins, and to my equally wonderful editor, Ginjer Buchanan.

And to my family: Connie, Mom and Peter, Jamie, Erin and Eileen, Nana, Mom and Dad Russo, Julie and Michael, Veronica, Nona, and all the Goldens, Pendolaris, and Russos, aunts, uncles, cousins, in-laws, etc. With gratitude to my good and loyal friend, my nephew Carlos Westergaard.

Acknowledgment and thanks are also due to:

Clive Barker, Steve Bissette, Jay Cantor, Georgina Challis, Matt Costello, Steve Eliopoulos, Jeff Galin, Craig Shaw Gardner, Ray Garton, Glenn Greenberg, Rick Hautala, Nancy Holder, Albert Jimenez, Pam Jungling, Joe Lansdale, Alan Lebowitz, Betty Levin, George Marcopoulos, Rex Miller, Stefan Nathanson, José Nieto, Philip Nutman, Lisa Scarlett, Mark Tillinger, Elissa Tomasetti, Bob Tomko (for help and contributions far beyond the call of duty), Steve Williams, Doug Winter, the Cairns and Plumer families, and all my amigos at BPI (is there a *Doctor* in the house?).

I hope you're all proud of the monster you helped create.

Prologue

MANNY SOARES WAS GETTING JUST A LITTLE sick of pushing the damn broom. Twenty years in the secretary of state's office, and he was *still* pushing the broom. He let it fall with a clack to the tiled bathroom floor. He needed a smoke.

Manny lit up as he walked into the word-processing area—he would never smoke in one of the private offices. The lights were off, he had finished the room an hour ago, but it wasn't completely dark. There was light from the stars and the bright moon—a beautiful clear night, and tomorrow it was supposed to snow, but who knew, with the track record of Boston's weathermen. His only comfort on the job was that row of windows. Looking out, as he often did, Manny thought more in five minutes than he did for the rest of the day. Damn beautiful.

He stubbed out his cigarette in the ashtray on Tara's desk. Cute girl, that. He wondered if Roger was still in the office, and went into the hallway. Sure enough, the lights still burned in the corporations department, and Manny was not surprised. Roger Martin. Now there was a man who did not know the meaning of the phrase "quitting time."

"Am I gonna have to clean around you again?" Manny asked, leaning against the door.

1

"Not tonight." Roger stood and slipped on his jacket. "It's time to go home. Though I could sure use a drink before facing the wife."

Roger picked up his briefcase and moved some papers from his desk to Sheila's; she was the department manager.

"Have one for me," Manny said as he shook out another cigarette.

"One of these days they're going to bust you for that," Roger said, motioning toward the pack the maintenance man was slipping back into his shirt pocket.

"The hell with it. Nothing they can do. It's not during work hours. Want one?"

"Love one, but I'm trying to quit. I don't know why, I don't really want to. Peer pressure, I guess." He laughed.

"Suit yourself," Manny told him, and lit up.

Which was Roger's cue to leave.

Roger whistled as he rode the elevator down. He was trying to decide whether he would actually go out and get a little drunk before heading home. Home had not been a place where he liked to be sober lately. It was not that Julie and he had been fighting, though they did their share. It was worse. It was *cold*. And they didn't know what to do about it. Life at home was basically pretty tense.

Aw, to hell with it. Why shouldn't he go? It had been a while since he had been out after work. Downstairs and out onto the street, swinging his briefcase without noticing it, Roger continued to whistle, and to think.

He turned left at the courthouse, and the Publik House was two blocks away. A young couple came out, arms around each other, steamy laughter visible on the air. God, was he envious. It had been a long time since he and Julie felt as comfortable in each other's arms as those two kids did.

Kids. *Right!* They had to be twenty-two or -three. So what did that make him? Hell, thirty-three was young.

When he met Julie, Roger fell completely head over heels, shit-eating grin, fool-for-your-stockings in love, and they got married a year later. They laughed and worked, made love and worked, lived and worked. Then they tried to have kids, and that was the one thing that didn't work. He and Julie had not had sex for two months. He very badly wanted a drink. Things change.

When he pulled open the oaken door of the bar and grill, Roger thought, not for the first time, that maybe he'd find something more in the Publik House than a cold one. He had never cheated before, and had never imagined he would be ready to start. Things change.

Behind the bar there floated a young woman with beautiful green eyes and long auburn hair. Her name tag identified her as Courteney MacGoldrick, which Roger thought suited her.

What little light existed within the small, Colonial bar and grill was supplied by small candles on the tables that looked like they were supposed to keep the bugs away, and a lamp on either end of the bar. It was romantic all right. And dark enough so that you could sink into a corner if you really wanted to. Usually he did, but tonight he made a beeline to the bar and, on an inspired whim, ordered a Guinness.

Miss Courteney MacGoldrick, bartender extraordinaire that the little lass was, brought it to him right away, and served it with a beaming smile. A smile that elicited a strange reaction in Roger.

He completely lost his nerve.

In fact it was a half hour, and the top of the third Guinness, before he got up the guts to strike up any semblance of a conversation with her. He noticed she had a lull in her work, and he had been watching her compact form move back and forth behind the bar for long enough. He mustered up every ounce of courage in his gradually numbing body and spoke.

"So," he said. "How's it going tonight?"

And as she opened her mouth to reply he prepared to leave promptly before her words cemented his belief that he had made a complete ass of himself.

"Not bad," she said cheerily. "How 'bout you?"

Oh, my sweet Lord in Heaven! Small talk. One of America's greatest inventions.

They talked for quite a while. After about five minutes he started to get nervous again. A couple of guys sat down at the end of the bar, and he realized she would have to serve them in a few seconds. Now or never.

"So," he began again. "Can I buy you a drink when you get off of work?"

A heartbeat.

And another.

At least the damn thing was working.

"Do you think your wife would appreciate that?"

"My . . ." he began, and then felt rather than remembered the ring around his finger. Feeling about as stupid as it gets, he laid a twenty on the counter, picked up his briefcase, and without further ceremony scurried out of the bar with his tail between his legs.

Outside, he began to smile. Just the corners of his mouth at first, and then it broke into a wide grin.

A chuckle, a snicker, a giggle, and then laughter.

It felt good to laugh, even if it was at his own expense. Courteney MacGoldrick, without even knowing it, had probably just saved his marriage.

Fuck it, Roger thought, *we'll adopt.*

On his way back to the garage, he stopped for a moment to grab a cup of java in the Capitol Coffee House. Then he was on his way, blowing into the hole torn from the plastic cover. He unlocked the garage and went in. He was whistling again, a song that had been bludgeoned to death by Boston radio, and he still could not remember the name of it. That was Julie, she was great with stuff like that. He walked up the paved slope toward his car, one of the few left in the garage. It was a Honda Accord.

He often told Manny that all the expensive cars left early. Manny always laughed.

He was still whistling as he put his coffee down on the roof of his car so he could reach the keys. He unlocked the door, tossed in his case, and climbed in. He let the car warm up for a moment and turned on the radio. He smiled. It was that same damn song, a good omen, he thought. But it was ending, so he still could not catch the title. He began to fiddle with the dial again, when someone rapped on the driver's-side window, scaring the shit out of him. He banged his knee on the underside of the dash.

At the window was a man all in black, except for the white square at his collar.

A priest?

Also interesting was the cup the priest was holding out to him. Not the "cup of my blood" to be sure; this one had stylized letters on it that read CAPITOL COFFEE HOUSE.

His own coffee, which he had left on the roof of his car. Feeling foolish for the second time that night, he rolled down his window.

He took the cup (gave it to his disciples) and said, "Thank you, Father."

And then he saw what the priest held in his other hand. It was pointed at his head.

When Manny stepped out into the garage, he saw the man in black standing next to Roger's car. Roger was in it, and the car was running. He started to walk toward them. Manny's car was beyond Roger's and he could say good night. He did not recognize the other man. The tall man, all in black, who lifted his arm.

His hand held a gun. His finger pulled a trigger.

At point-blank range, the bullet's entry was fairly clean, but its exit was as messy as they get.

"NO!" Manny screamed, and cursed himself for it.

The man whirled, and Manny stood in shock as he glimpsed the patch of white amid the black garments. A priest. The guy was a priest, or dressed like one.

The good father pointed his gun at Manny's chest and put a bullet in it.

The killer began to walk toward the maintenance man's prone form, but the sound of an engine filled the garage. It was a car coming up from the lower level. Time for him to go.

Later, when the police arrived, Manny was still twitching, not as dead as the priest would have liked. In the late Roger Martin's car, blood and coffee settled into the upholstery.

It was going to leave quite a stain.

1

HIS MEMORY IS LIKE A TORNADO ACROSS time, touching down to pick up a single event or person and carrying it away until it is dropped in favor of something else. Most of the events are catastrophes, most of the people are dead. When he wants to think of something pleasant, he has to concentrate. But such is the nature of memory, and of time.

His name is Octavian. But it isn't, really. Or at least, it was not always. He has been a prince, a warrior, a monster, a murderer, a wanderer, and a thief. Now he can only observe and remember.

And sometimes he can help.

The radio alarm clicked on at 9:30 P.M., but Peter Octavian had been awake for almost half an hour. He hit the snooze with none of the annoyed reluctance that usually accompanies such an act. He was in a good mood. He had something to do tonight. Not as if he usually had trouble finding something to do, but he always preferred that it find him. Often the nightly news was his only source of entertainment, and that he loved. It amused him so to see the bickering between nations and individuals. He had become quite good at predicting events long before they happened. One of his favorite observations was that "history repeats itself."

Everyone said it.

So how come nobody was intelligent enough to be able to put that axiom to use?

Ah, well, they never had been.

Change. The more you fought against it, the faster it came. Inevitable as . . . well, as taxes anyway.

Peter stood up from bed and walked in darkness to the shutters that hid the outside from him, and him from it. He opened them and looked out. The moon and the stars were very bright, effectively illuminating the street eight floors below. He opened the window a bit and let the cold air in, sucking it into his lungs. Snow; tomorrow, maybe tomorrow night.

He left the window open and walked to the bathroom. Eyes shut, he flicked on the overhead lights. He yawned and stretched. Already naked, having slept that way, he stepped into the shower and pulled the curtain. He loved the steam and the hot water, and the chill that he knew would run up his spine when he got out. He had left the window open for that purpose. The shower was a strange thing for Peter. He hardly sweated, so he never smelled particularly bad. His hair looked clean without washing. But this could not prevent his hair from becoming disheveled as he slept, so he washed it.

He rinsed his long brown mane and stepped out, anticipated chill giving him a shiver. He toweled dry and went to the mirror, blew dry his hair, and pulled it into a ponytail, slipping an elastic around it. As he brushed his teeth, shining the smile that had won thousands of hearts (but when was the last one?), he could hear the radio in the other room. The snooze timer had given up, and the deejay was yattering about something.

"Just about a quarter to ten in the city, and a chilly thirty-one degrees right now outside WZXL. Here's a little reminder from yours truly that you'll be in big trouble if you don't pick up some sweets for your sweetheart. And, with a little reminder of their own, here's the Spinners with 'Cupid.' "

He rinsed his mouth and glanced up. The mirror image checked him out. He looked pretty good . . . for his age.

He smiled at his own joke. The same jokes seemed always to amuse him, and probably always would.

He stepped out of the bathroom, still naked, and shut off the radio. The phone rang and he began to get dressed as the answering machine picked up on the third ring.

"Octavian Investigations. No one is here at the moment, but if you leave a message and your telephone number, someone will get back to you as soon as possible."

"Peter. Frank. Just calling to check in. I spoke to Ted Gardiner earlier, but the cops haven't got a clue. If you need anything from me, please call."

Peter pulled his brown leather bomber jacket over the blue cotton oxford shirt, effectively hiding his armpit holster. Inside the holster was his .38. If it was good enough for Spenser . . .

Really, though, it was for show. If he had to hurt somebody, it was just as easy, and generally more satisfying, to do it with his hands. The part of him that craved that satisfaction frightened and revolted him, but he refused to deny its existence.

To overcome something, he knew, one must first accept it. So he did. But he kept a tight rein on that atavistic urge. *Very tight.*

Tonight he was on a personal job. Frank Harris was a friend, one of the few Octavian could claim, and his only daughter had disappeared. Peter knew better than most what it was like to lose someone, he'd lost plenty over the years, and he'd do whatever could be done.

Frank had given him little enough to work with. Janet Harris worked for a big Boston law firm as a paralegal. Six days earlier—that would have been Wednesday— Janet left work at her usual time, went to her usual bar with her usual friends, and left early with an unusual but far from extraordinary headache.

Six days was a long time. Trail could be awfully cold by now.

The cops, as usual, had done no more and no less than what was mandatory and then gave up the girl for lost. They figured she had run away with the milkman, or some such, and had unofficially quit on Monday night.

It was Tuesday, and Frank and Peter had spoken three times during the day. Normally, Octavian would have been up by 5:30, but he'd been out of state for a few days—and out during the day—and he'd needed some rest. He probably would have woken up earlier if Frank hadn't kept interrupting his slumber. But how do you explain such an unnatural need for rest?

Now it was 11:00 P.M., and Peter walked into the Publik House, the last place Janet Harris had been seen.

The first things to draw his attention were the eyes of Courteney MacGoldrick, which were giving him a very vigorous appraisal. Caught in the act, she blushed slightly, but did not look away. He kept his eyes locked on hers as he crossed the room and gave her a long-practiced, lop-sided grin.

The grin won her over, but it wasn't the only thing she noted. His eyes were gray, flecked with silver, which gave them a slightly hypnotic quality. His six-foot-four frame was wiry, and he carried himself like an old western gun-fighter. His face was ageless, but most people's best guess, and Courteney MacGoldrick's, since she happened to be thinking about it right then, was that he was probably in his early to midthirties.

"What can I do for you?"

"For now just a glass of white wine, and maybe a couple of answers."

"The wine's coming right up. The answers depend on the questions."

As she poured his wine he reached into his pocket

and retrieved his ID and a photograph. He laid both on the bar.

"Pretty self-explanatory," he told her when she returned, and he began sipping his wine.

Courteney recognized the picture right away.

"Janet came in a lot. Flirted a lot, a nice, funny woman. But she left alone, always. Only once talked about a guy at work she was attracted to, I don't remember his name. The night I saw her last, she got a headache after two beers and left, I already talked to the cops, but I'm sure nothing will come of that."

"That's *all*?" he asked.

"That's all," she answered.

Peter got up to go.

"Come back and see us sometime?"

"It's a date," he promised.

Out the door and into the street, on his way back to the State House parking lot, where he had left his car, he thought of her, and then forgot her, storing only what she told him. He had driven tonight, which was rare, but he was in the mood for music and had picked up the latest Seal disc. He hoped there was no ticket on the Volvo.

The night was quiet; and then it was not.

Sirens pierced the air and Peter winced. His ears were sensitive. An ambulance and police car sped past, rounded the corner, and stopped in front of the garage beneath the secretary of state's building. Peter was right behind, following on foot. He couldn't help it. He survived by curiosity and a sort of prescience that told him which things deserved his attention. This was one of them.

Two cop cars were already there when this latest arrived with the ambulance. The paramedics were getting out their gurney and wheeling it inside. He hoped that Janet Harris would not be on it when they returned. It seemed he had spent several lifetimes delivering bad news, and he was tired of it.

"Octavian." The voice belonged to Ted Gardiner, a

lean, black plainclothes detective with few manners but a lot of charm. He smiled at Peter. They weren't good friends, but there was respect there, and that was about as close as Peter usually got.

"What a surprise," Gardiner said. "Chasing ambulances now?"

"Thought I'd get a look at your next unsolved mystery," Peter quipped, a trait the cop brought out in him.

"Come on in." Gardiner ushered Peter through the door. "It's actually pretty interesting. I . . . Hey, you know, you need to get out more. A little Florida vacation. You need a tan."

"Are you going to fill me in on what you've got, wise-ass, or should I guess?"

Ted smiled. He knew about Peter's aversion to the sun, a medical thing, he'd been told, and he was just sarcastic enough not to care whether it upset the PI or not.

"Touchy, touchy. Just concerned about your health, Peter. You look like a fucking vampire."

"Asshole," Peter said, laughing at Ted and with him, "I *am* a vampire."

Ted smiled at him and then mustered up his serious face, which was rare. They had arrived at the scene, and the paramedics were bagging the body. Peter saw that the car door was open, and a lot of photographs were being taken of the interior. He looked at the corpse with the back of its head gone.

"Martin, Roger Francis," Gardiner informed him. "Age, thirty-three. Occupation, yuppie. Cause of death, pistol fired approximately six inches from the victim's forehead. Clean shot. Roger was nice enough to roll down the window for the guy. Motive, definitely not robbery—cash and credit cards still in the guy's wallet. Unless, of course, there was something of significant value in Roger's briefcase, because it seems our man rifled through that particular piece of baggage. The other ambulance had come and gone by the time you showed up."

"Other ambulance?"

"The janitor walked in on the thing. From what we know, he probably saw the guy who did it. But he won't be talking to anyone for a day or so. Bullet in the chest can do that to a guy."

The paramedics were about to zip the black bag holding Roger Martin's body.

"Mind if I take a look?"

"As long as these boys don't mind." Ted motioned to the paramedics, who stepped back to allow Octavian access to the body.

He bent down, looking closely at the wound, and took a deep breath.

Ted raised an eyebrow. Was this guy *smelling* the corpse? God, that was gross. But then, everything Octavian did was peculiar.

"What time did Martin leave work?"

"No idea. Why?"

"He's only been dead about an hour and a half, which puts the murder somewhere between ten and ten-thirty," Peter answered. "He smells of beer. If you check his work area, and don't find any trace of alcohol, then he must have gone somewhere local to drink and come back here afterward. Find out where he went, and what was in the briefcase, and you'll be that much closer to finding his killer."

Peter zipped up the body bag and stood to face Ted, who was looking at him with a sort of bemused smile on his face.

"You always give me the creeps when you pull that Sherlock Holmes thing."

"Elementary," Peter said, and winked. He was wondering whether or not to get involved, and decided against it. If he was supposed to be involved, the mystery would follow him until he paid attention to it. But just in case . . .

"Ted, do me a favor. Call me tomorrow and let me know how this thing turns out. And while you're at it, scoop me a copy of the missing-persons file on Janet Harris."

"Man, you don't miss a trick. I would have called you right away, but I thought you were still out of town."

"Got back this morning."

"Yeah, sorry. God, it's awful. Frank's been holding up, but just barely. And officially, I'm not even supposed to be on that case."

"Well, you can unofficially snag me that file and keep your ears open. I'm sure I'll need your help on this one."

"Sure thing," the cop said. "Have a good night."

"I'm working on it."

He walked to the lot where his car was parked—there was indeed a ticket—and decided to see if Janet Harris's roommate, Meaghan, was still awake. It was twelve midnight, exactly.

2

AS PETER DROVE HE THOUGHT ABOUT THE city. He would probably have to move on soon, and it would not be easy. Boston had been his home for ten years and he had come to care a great deal for it and its people. Sometimes it seemed like he had wandered through every major city in the world, staying in each only as long as it was healthy. Then he would drift into another city, perhaps in another country and under a different name. But this city was so much warmer than New York, London, Paris—than any of the cold, flashy cultural centers of the Western world. And the Eastern world was not the safest place for his kind.

Buildings of the future stood side by side with buildings older than the nation. It was a city with a small-town attitude. It was a political city, but the politics were old-fashioned baby-kissing politics and didn't show a sign of change. Networks of acquaintance crisscrossed from the highest office to the lowest shop. Even so, you could always hide away in the hustle and bustle if you wanted to, or needed to, as Peter did from time to time. A small, quirky, contradictory city, but it had taken in an orphan of the world, and he was grateful.

Peter parked the Volvo in front of an old house with a new coat of pea-green paint. Getting out, he looked

15

up at the second story, where Janet Harris and Meaghan Gallagher shared an apartment. There was a single light on.

The house was off of Huntington Avenue near Northeastern University. It was a far cry from the city's best neighborhood, but it wasn't bad. Trees lined the road, bare this time of year, and streetlights cast a ghostly light across small but well-manicured lawns and the cracked and potholed pavement. The silence and the cold of the night combined to lift him, energize him.

The wind brought the smell of fireplaces not too distant, and a major snowstorm coming in from the northeast.

Peter let himself into the foyer and scanned the few names on the battered black mailboxes. Three apartments in the house, and the middle label read HARRIS/GALLAGHER. He pushed the buzzer.

After a few moments he pushed it again, this time holding the button down for a few seconds. Still, there was no answer, so he buzzed once more and turned to leave. He had the outside door open, but paused a moment. His hesitation paid off when he heard a sleepy female voice.

"Hello?" it said. "Who is it?"

Peter let the door shut again behind him as he answered. "Hello, Miss Gallagher? My name is Peter Octavian, I'm a private investigator, a friend of Frank Harris. Janet's father?"

When the voice did not answer immediately, he added, "I realize it's late, maybe if I come back early tomorrow evening?"

"No, that's okay. I'm sorry Mr. Octavian. I was kind of vegetating for a sec. Come on up, I was having trouble sleeping anyway."

She buzzed him in, and on the way up, Peter thought about that voice, wondered what she looked like. That scratchy, sleepy tone had been kind of sexy.

He smiled, inwardly laughing at himself. It had been far too long since he'd had sex, and even longer since he'd had a relationship. There was always something more important to do, but he was beginning to feel the itch again. Unfortunately, now was not the time, and he was glad he had more pressing matters to attend to.

He knocked twice, softly, and he could hear first the chain and then a dead bolt sliding back. A pair of chocolate-brown eyes peered around the door at him.

"Please come in," Meaghan said, swinging the door wide and then closing and locking it after him.

Peter had made his way inside and taken his jacket off. When he turned around, he noticed her scrutinizing him. She smiled.

"You don't look like a detective," she said.

"Really? What do detectives look like?"

"Oh, it's not that you don't look the part. Only that most of the real-life cops I've met are . . . well, they're nothing like the ones in the movies, that's for sure."

There was a moment of silence as her amused smile— corners of the mouth turned up slightly—met his lopsided grin head-on. Peter shook his head, chuckling.

"I guess I'll take that as a compliment," he said.

"If you like," Meaghan countered.

They both laughed, easily and comfortably. And then Meaghan sobered.

"Any news on Janet?"

"None yet, but I'm just getting started."

Peter looked her over. He thought she looked charming. An old-fashioned word, but it fit. She stood there in her tattered blue terry robe, a couple of sizes too big, and what looked like a man's button-down oxford shirt underneath. The apartment had hardwood floors, and she wore sport socks to walk around. Her auburn hair was wild from the pillow, and she brushed the last of the Sandman from her eyes.

She took his jacket.

"Please, sit down," she said, and gestured toward the couch. Peter glanced about the apartment: two bedrooms, one bath, kitchen, living room, dining room. The place was attractively decorated in white with soft blues and pinks, and the furniture definitely had a New England feel to it, sturdy yet elegant. Full bookshelves almost completely covered one wall, and throw rugs decorated the floors. Framed prints adorned the walls, from Monet to completely indecipherable modern art, as well as a large photograph of whales with their tails out of the water. Old-fashioned iron radiators stood in several places around the living and dining rooms, but it was a bit chilly in the place. He liked it.

They sat down, he on the couch and she on an armchair across from it. It took him a moment to notice she was looking at him expectantly.

"Um, I . . ." he mumbled. "I'm sorry, it's been a long night."

"No problem."

"I figure you've already been a few rounds with the cops, so I'll try to keep the questions to a minimum."

"Whatever you need to know to find Janet. The cops sure aren't gonna do any good."

"Okay. Miss Gallagher . . ."

"Meaghan." She smiled, and he returned it.

"Yes, Meaghan. First things first, I guess. Would you mind if I had a look around Janet's room? It might give us a clue."

"No problem," she answered, getting up again.

"It's the back room," she added, and Peter got up to follow her.

The room was spartan, but elegant. One bureau, two night tables, each adorned by a lamp, and a wicker chair in the corner. A large brass bed, a small TV set, a good-sized throw rug on the floor. A floral print hung over the bed. Janet Harris's only real vice seemed to be clothes. She had a huge walk-in closet filled with them.

"She's a snappy dresser, your Janet?" he asked.

"You've never met her?" Meaghan seemed surprised.

"Not actually, no. Her dad talks about her all the time, though."

"Frank's a sweetheart. Right now I'm almost more worried about him than about Jan."

"Why's that?"

"I don't know. I guess it's just wishful thinking, but I have this feeling she's okay." She paused. "So, how long have you known Frank?"

"Almost ten years. Since I stopped some kids from breaking into his restaurant. After that he gave me the run of the place when I needed to take clients out."

Meaghan sat down on the bed, one leg drawn up under her, and hugged herself tight against the chilly room as Peter glanced around.

"I'm surprised I've never met you."

"It's not too surprising actually. I only go in there once in a while, and even then it's very late. I always work at night, that's when the bad guys come out."

"And you're a good guy, eh?" she asked with a pleasant laugh.

"Yes, ma'am," he returned in a cowboy drawl. "An official member of the Fraternal Order of the White Hats . . . at least most of the time. I've been considered a bad guy once or twice, but then again, who hasn't?"

Her smile was warm, and then she was serious again. "I suppose we ought to get down to business?"

"Well, unless you intend to stay up all night."

"Would you like me to leave the room, let you concentrate?"

"Actually, if you don't mind, it's better if you stay here. You'll be able to help me find things."

"You know something, I must have really been asleep when I answered the door. I never even asked to see your ID."

Peter started to reach for his wallet.

"No, Mr. Octavian." She was smiling again. "Don't

bother now. I guess if you had wanted to have your way with me, you'd have made your move already."

She was flirting, but he figured that was healthy right about now. "Don't be so sure about that. And call me Peter, okay?"

She shook her head yes as he pulled out his wallet and tossed it to her.

"Just to make it official. Don't make fun of the picture."

"Come on," she said, after pulling it out. "This isn't half as bad as the picture on my license."

"Look at *my* driver's license," he said as he continued his search of the closet.

"Ugh. Now *that's* bad!"

He stood up and put his hands on his hips in mock consternation. "Give it here, you. I told you not to make fun of the picture."

She tossed it back to him and sat for another moment as he began going through the left nightstand.

"I need something hot. Would you like some coffee?"

"Actually, tea would be great if you have it."

"Oh, tea sounds great. I've been drinking too much coffee anyway."

She got up to fix the tea and turned around when she heard a sharp buzzing sound. Peter was holding up a white plastic vibrator with a glowing tip, which he had just pulled out of the drawer next to Janet's bed.

"Well," Meaghan said with a laugh, covering her mouth. "If she *did* run away, she probably isn't alone."

Peter laughed and dropped the thing back in the drawer, and Meaghan went to the kitchen to put some water on. He continued his search, which had so far proven fruitless, moving to the night table on the opposite side, but his mind was elsewhere—on Meaghan Gallagher. An unusual woman, he thought, independent and intelligent, with an ironic sense of humor, not to mention attractive. She was outgoing while at the same time Peter could see an extremely private streak in her, and secrets behind her eyes.

He shook his head in amusement. It really had been too long.

He knelt and began to search under the bed. He was starting to get the idea that this whole thing was a dead end, but he wanted to be thorough. Meaghan came back in.

"Water's on. How's it going in here?"

"Almost done. I'm trying to figure out if I've missed anything. Let's take a break for a minute. Tell me about Janet—how you met, that sort of thing."

"Sure, hardest question first." She smiled. "It's sort of a strange relationship, because we were both pretty much loners—a little too individual for the 'in crowd' in high school, so we kept to ourselves. I speak for her from what she told me, 'cause we first met in college, Introduction to Political Science with Schmelter. We started talking one day early in freshman year, the way girls do when they're looking for friends. I could see that like me, she was a pretty private person, and neither one of us had any close friends. So, by default really, we ended up with each other.

"Then, unfortunately, her mom died."

"How?" Peter asked.

"What's that?"

"How did she die?"

Peter noticed a small crease of pain by Meaghan's eyes.

"Cancer. Sucks, huh? Anyway, she came to me then because she didn't have a shoulder to cry on. Her dad needed support himself, and she didn't want him to see her weakness. I lost my parents in a plane crash a week before the surprise sweet-sixteen party they were throwing for me. Janet and I had a lot to talk about.

"After that we stuck together, facing the horrors of college as a team. We did everything and went every-

where together. Come sophomore year, we started room-
ing together, and as you can see, we still are. I don't know
how healthy it was for us to be so close—it certainly didn't
leave much room for others. There were rumors flying
around that we were lovers."

She stopped and gave him a funny smile, shaking her
head. They both heard the whistle from the kitchen, then.
It had been going for some moments before either noticed
it.

"I'll get the tea," she said, and turned quickly to go. "If
you're almost done, we can have it in the living room?"

"Fine. I'll be right in."

She got up and went to rescue the screaming kettle,
retucking and tightening her robe on the way. He stood
up and looked around Janet Harris's bedroom. He ran a
mental check on any place she might have personal things
that he hadn't checked. There was one place left. He'd
almost forgotten.

He stood at the foot of the bed and lifted the mattress
up off the box spring. Holding one end of the mattress up
with his right arm, he used his left to retrieve the one thing
that was hidden there. Janet's diary.

After returning the mattress to its normal position, he
went into the living room, diary in hand. He could hear
Meaghan moving around in the kitchen, and he thought
about what she'd said.

She came into the room with a tray and put it down on
the coffee table in front of him. She did not notice the
diary in his hands.

"Were the rumors true?" he asked.

"Pardon me?" she said, feigning ignorance, obviously
hoping he'd retract the question.

"Were the rumors true? Were you and Janet lovers?"

Meaghan simply looked at him for a moment, expres-
sionless. "What a terribly blunt, and completely unsubtle
question."

"If you'd prefer not to discuss it, that's okay with me.

But you might want to read this before I do."

He put the diary down on the table. From the look on Meaghan's face, he could see that she hadn't known Janet was keeping a diary.

"I haven't looked through it at all, but there might be something in here that can help me. Maybe, maybe not. If you want to read it before me, that's fine, but if I'm supposed to be finding out what happened to Janet . . ."

He left it at that.

She was very quiet. She picked up the diary and simply stared at the cover for a moment. She opened to the first page, then shut it again, closed her eyes, and rested her chin on her hands. When her eyes opened, she had made a decision.

"Let's get this straight, Mr. Oct—Peter. I do not consider myself a lesbian, though then again, I have nothing against those who do."

"Hold on," Peter interrupted. "I don't care what you are or aren't, and I'm not trying to put you on the defensive. I'm not judging anybody. Now, please. Relax."

She looked a little embarrassed, and a little nervous. She took a deep breath and continued.

"I'm telling you this because I would never tell the cops and I figure I can trust your discretion. You never know what could be important in finding her, so someone should know the truth.

"What I was about to say is that I don't consider myself a lesbian, but I would have to say I am bisexual. Though I've only been with one woman, and it was a long time ago, I don't think it's something you can stop being. You're right that the woman was Janet.

"I'm not worried about myself. There's nobody in my life I need to hide things from. I just don't want Frank to find out; it would kill him. He's an old-fashioned kind of guy, and Janet's situation is different from mine. She's far from promiscuous—as I said, she's a private person. But of the lovers she's had since I've known her, there have been at least a couple of women besides myself, as recently as last year. This is a little hard to talk about to a stranger. I've only ever told a couple of people."

She stopped short, looking at him. Something in his eyes, on his face, told her it was okay to continue. He projected an acceptance that was unique in her experience. There was an *understanding* that radiated from him that would have been impossible to explain. It was, in a way, like the attitude of people who are truly old, who have lived it all and understand your feelings better than you. She was calm now.

"We were lovers for almost a year—God, that's hard to say—beginning over the summer between freshman and sophomore years, right after we moved in together. The next summer we talked about one of us moving out, but realized it didn't matter. I don't really want to explain it to you, but that part of our relationship stopped. We went on being good, loving friends and constant companions, but there was nothing physical about it. We double-dated, set each other up on blind dates, the whole deal. Every once in a while, when one of us got badly hurt, things might happen, but . . .

"By the time senior year rolled around, we each had a full-time boyfriend. I really thought she was going to marry Simon, and I think she did, too. Then he got a job as a photojournalist down in Central America, and she stayed here. Things didn't work out with Max and me either, so Janet and I ended up where we started.

"I know she's had a couple of other women since, but she was the only woman I was ever with. I've never been attracted to any others. I don't know why it happened. . . ."

"You should be glad it did," Peter said, startling her into silence. She seemed almost to have forgotten she was revealing so much of herself, and now her candid speech shocked her.

"Really, you should be glad. Very few people ever really love someone. . . ."

She waited for him to continue, but he did not.

"She's my friend, Peter. We have our differences, like any people who share space. I love her, and I hope you can find her, but now I don't think I want to talk about this anymore. Thank you for being so understanding."

"Let's hope I can do more than that."

It was obvious to Peter that Meaghan felt a need to defend her actions, and he felt for her. Clearly, she and Janet had been there for each other when things were hard and life was more frightening than usual. And just as clearly, they had evolved to a point where they were more like sisterly coconspirators than anything else, still braving the world together. He hoped that Janet was still alive, and more than anything, he hoped Meaghan did not feel as though he'd forced her to reveal her secrets.

Seeing her depth of emotion, her depth of character, he was even more attracted to her. "Now," he continued, "back to business. Any men in her life?"

Your life, he'd almost said.

"She's funny, charismatic, good-looking. She attracts a lot of men when she goes out, but she rarely brings them home, and she hasn't for eight or nine months. It's even more difficult these days to find a compatible woman, and like I said, that's been over a year for her. We're becoming a couple of spinsters, really."

"I find that very difficult to believe," Peter said seriously.

"She's afraid to get involved, you know. She's been hurt, just like everyone else, even with all her precautions. She doesn't let anybody in except for her dad and me."

Peter was starting to think that Janet's personal life might be a dead end, and it upset him. If her disappearance or, if it came to that, her death, was a random event, he might never find her.

His eyes began to wander as Meaghan chatted happily about a couple of the guys Janet *had* brought home at some time or another. He glanced around the room and something caught his eye. A slim black woman's briefcase.

Remembering the missing briefcase at the murder scene earlier that night, he spoke on impulse. "What kind of work does Janet do at the firm?"

"Huh?" Meaghan was confused. "At the firm? She works in corporate, same as me. We used to work for the same firm, but I couldn't deal with the politics. Anyway, she works on organizing and dissolving corporations, on bankruptcies and stuff. Why?"

"No reason, really. A hunch with no backup. There's so little to go on that I'm wondering whether her disappearance has something to do with work rather than her personal life. It's worth looking into. You say you used to work with these people?"

"Uh-huh."

"Could you do something for me? I need to know exactly what Janet was working on before she disappeared. Maybe three or four days' worth of stuff. Can you get me that information?"

"Well, they're not supposed to do that, but I think I can get what you need."

"Great."

The conversation had come to a natural conclusion, and he got up to go. He was pulling his coat on and she followed him to the door. Once there, she handed him the diary.

"You don't want to read it first?" he asked, quite surprised.

"Nah. I checked the date of the first entry. There's probably nothing juicy about me in there anyway. Well, maybe a little nostalgia, but nothing more than what I've already told you."

They looked at each other, and Peter chuckled. She had told him the whole story because it might be important, maybe because she needed to tell someone. He had feared she had told him because she didn't want him to read it in the diary, but it wasn't in there and she'd known it. He was glad.

"So, if I'm going to help out, does this make me a deputy or something?" She smiled again.

"Or something."

She kissed him, quickly, on the cheek. "Thanks for being one of the good guys."

He apologized for keeping her up so late and told her he would be by the following night at about eight. He took her hand as they said good-bye.

"You don't get too many friends," he said. "We'll find her."

"Thank you," she said, but he was already halfway down the steps.

Outside, the night was brisk and silent and comfortable to him. The smell of coming snow was even stronger in the air, along with a taste of salt from the ocean a few miles distant. Winter was his favorite season.

As he opened the car door he heard the loud fall of feet on the pavement. Looking up, he saw a short man walking toward him, all in black with a white spot at his throat. An elderly Roman Catholic priest, bundled up in his overcoat, trudged past him.

"Late night tonight, eh, Father?" Peter said pleasantly.

"God's work is never done," the priest said without smiling, and continued down the street, away from him.

Peter got in the car and started it up. An omen, he thought, though whether good or bad he couldn't say. His kind had not had a good history with the church.

A few moments later his mind was back on Meaghan Gallagher. He had a feeling it would keep returning to that fascinating young woman.

Peter had gotten home fairly early, about 3:00 A.M., and had stayed up reading for quite some time. He wasn't very tired, but it was wisest to be in bed on time. His clothing came off piece by piece, and each item was put away neatly in its place.

In his underwear, he went quickly to the door and slid the dead bolt home, then checked to see that the rubber lining under the door was in place. It wouldn't do to have a space under the door.

He went to the opposite wall and tested the apartment's two windows. They were locked, but now he closed and bolted the solid wooden shutters he himself had installed on the inside. These fit perfectly into the window frames and had the same lining as the door.

The apartment was sealed.

The hunger had been creeping up on him all night, as it did most nights, and now it sang to him from his belly a wild song, an animal song. As he had become engrossed in the book the hunger and its song had receded. But the moment he put down that book, it returned, more powerful than before, the song virtually a hymn.

He stood in front of the open refrigerator like a child who can't decide what to eat, but for Peter there were no parents scolding him for wasting the electricity, and after all, he didn't have much of a choice in meals. He was surprised to find only four bottles left in the fridge. He would have sworn there'd been at least eight before he'd gone out of town. Not that it would have been the first time he'd fed without remembering.

Well, he'd have to call George when he woke up that night. He'd known George Marcopoulos, his best friend, since he first came to Boston. Many years earlier Peter had become a thief in order to end his career as a killer. This new career forced him to move from city to city fairly frequently. No matter how good you were at burglary, if you kept it up, eventually you got caught. Peter wouldn't be caught, but he might be discovered, and so he'd moved.

To Boston. That night he'd been truly starving and he'd actually paused to drink a pint before making good his escape. Had he left right away, he might have missed the other burglar in Boston City Hospital that night. But he didn't. He saw the tall white guy, all in black, slip quietly through the door to the morgue.

Against his better judgment, Peter had slid up to the door and opened it a crack, watching as the thief opened drawers and checked toe tags on bodies. Maybe he wanted to say a last good-bye to a loved one, but Peter doubted it. Before he could do anything, an older, white-haired doctor had come around the corner only to knock over the thief, falling on top of him.

George Marcopoulos, the medical examiner at Boston City Hospital, was on his back with a rather large, serrated edge knife at his throat before he had a chance to call out.

"Look at it this way," the thief growled as Peter looked on, "you're probably not the first guy to die from working late."

As the knife bit into George's throat Peter moved, dropping the bottled blood he carried. Before the bottles shattered on the floor, Peter had the would-be body snatcher on his back. But the guy was quick, for a human. The point of the blade came out of Peter's back, had passed dangerously close to his spinal cord, and the guy was pulling up with both hands.

With a howl, Peter had transformed.

The rest hadn't taken long, but when Peter took human form again, he was in rough shape, terribly weak. George might have killed him then, had he really tried. But he didn't. The old Greek knew without asking what Peter was, though he'd never believed in his life that such creatures might exist. In moments he was back in the morgue with blood to replace the bottles Peter had dropped.

"Okay, what do I do?" he asked as he approached cautiously.

"Feed me," was all Peter could say at first, and George did. Afterward, to speed the recovery process, Octavian poured a pint of blood directly on his wound. George stared as it closed of its own accord.

Once Peter was feeling better, the two had cleaned up the morgue. They talked while they did so, George almost in awe. Peter was quite impressed as well. The thief was in a condition that would have been hard to explain to police, and Peter was surprised how easy it was to hide a corpse when one was the coroner at a major city hospital. Of course, it didn't hurt that it was four in the morning.

On that night nearly a decade ago, he'd told George of the bloodsong.

"Ah," said George, smiling, "the children of the night, what music they make."

They had no choice but to be friends.

And now he stood in the open refrigerator door, feeling the cold but not really *feeling* it, making a mental note to call his friend, who would come to the rescue as he always had, making certain Peter would not be driven back an immortal evolutionary step. Making certain that the bloodsong could be sung without death, without destruction, without the hunt. Sometimes he missed the hunt, but sometimes he missed life, and he certainly didn't want to go back to that.

No, tonight the first pint went down fast and smooth. As it rushed into him he bit his lip and arched his back; a shiver ran through him as the music within him grew into a symphony, its rhythm speeding up.

He took his time with the second pint, savoring each drop, and the song built into a crescendo. When the second bottle joined the first in the trash, he was slowly coming down. His brain and his stomach nestled in a warm, too familiar place.

The song had subsided, but it was always there, a sexual throbbing rhythm that demanded one thing only: satisfaction.

The bloodsong's ecstasy had screamed within him, loudly proclaiming his power to any creature brave enough to approach.

"This is the King of the Jungle here," he whispered to himself, his eyes shut tight.

My God, he thought, as he did every time, the real thing gives ten times the pleasure, ten times the power. Then the bloodsong carries you on its melody to the next night, and the next.

Yes, he reminded himself. If you keep feeding it.

He pushed the thoughts away, the feelings away, at the same time struggling with the knowledge that Karl would be disgusted with him.

Or, more likely, that Karl is disgusted. Surely, he thought, his old teacher knew what Peter had been up to since they last parted company. And just as surely, he was repulsed by the philosophy that had lowered his warrior prince to a shadow thief and a servant of humans. Karl was most certainly ashamed to know that his old pupil and friend stole by deceit what he no longer felt comfortable about taking by force.

But that was Karl, Peter thought. He misunderstood completely. Peter could not follow the old German's belief that power allowed them the privilege to do what they wished. Rather, he felt certain that true power lent itself only to real responsibility: responsibility to seek knowledge, to experiment and experience, and to share . . . especially that.

His hunger satiated, he lay down on his bed and drifted into sleep as lazily as a feather falling to the ground. The growing certainty that student would soon have to become teacher weighed heavily on his mind.

Outside, the sun was coming up, the darkness was burning off, and all the things of the night were hiding away. Inside, Peter was fast asleep, sealed off from the day. His alarm was set for sundown: shadowtime.

3

HENRI GUISCARD TURNED UP THE COLLAR
on his overcoat. It was a chilly day, and the cardinal
wasn't getting any younger. He pushed through the revolving door of the Park Plaza Hotel and turned toward Beacon Hill, walking briskly. He was feeling his age again,
but doing okay in spite of it. He looked over his shoulder
from time to time, but it didn't appear as though he was
being followed. Of course, he thought, an elephant could
be hot on his tail, and he probably wouldn't notice.

Ah, he sighed, it's probably nothing. But after what
happened in Rome, he wasn't willing to take the chance.

He glanced over his shoulder again.

Throughout his life and his career serving the church,
Henri had been an outspoken and well-respected man of
God. Now, he hid in silence from the very establishment
he had served, paranoid, angry, and confused.

Guiscard could feel a storm rising to the north. As he
walked he let his guard down slightly and his mind began
to drift back past the events that had led to this moment,
to this time and place, past his days as a parish priest. He
thought about his childhood in Sicily.

"You're a Guiscard!" his father said, as he often did.
"You've got to fight back."

He had been beaten up once again by a group of older boys, and his father was angry with him. Within him roared the blood of one of history's greatest warriors, his father said. The Norman Robert Guiscard and his sons had been the bane of the Byzantine empire for a century. Guiscards would still be attacking the Byzantines, his father insisted, were it not that the family had outlasted the empire itself.

All of this was fine in theory, but when it came down to it, Henri did not feel much like a warrior. On the contrary, he felt like one big bruise. He was a frail boy, and though he tried to be proud of his heritage, he often wished he could tell his father that he was afraid. But that was out of the question.

Instead, at his father's insistence, he developed a sense of false pride, of bravado, and had been beaten by the others all the more frequently because of it.

"Careful, Father."

There was a tug at the cardinal's sleeve and he looked up at the young businesswoman pulling at him. Before he could ask her, crankily, what she was doing, he noticed the concern on her face, and then the traffic started to speed by. He had been about to step into the street as the light changed.

Smiling now, he thanked the woman and muttered under his breath at himself. He was nervous and afraid for the first time since he was a little boy, but he was also angry. He turned and looked at his reflection in the window of a restaurant. Bennigan's, he saw it was called. He was still skinny at sixty-four; over six feet tall and fairly healthy. He stared at the ghostly transparency of his own silver-maned, leathery face, into his own crystal-blue eyes. The ghost's forehead was furrowed and angry looking, and with good reason, he thought. He couldn't allow himself to be careless; there was too much at stake.

An attractive young couple having lunch on the other side of the window looked uncomfortably out at him, a very angry-looking priest staring in at them as they finished their cheeseburgers. He smiled again and chuckled, amused by the scene.

"Sorry," he mouthed to them, shrugged his shoulders, and walked on.

The whole, ugly thing began to play itself out once again in his mind, and he knew it would continue to do so until the situation was resolved—one way or another.

The little, perpetually bruised Normannic-Sicilian boy had become a humble and intelligent young man. Imbued with his father's staunch Catholic beliefs and thirsting for more than the precious little education with which he had thus far been blessed, young Henri decided that the only practical path was the priesthood. He still believed it was the best and most important decision he ever made. The church provided him with an education, with responsibility, and with a divine mission. As the priest of a small parish just outside Palermo, he continued to educate himself, learning French, Latin, and then English. He was stationed in Paris when he was made a bishop, and finally, five years ago, was named cardinal.

Rome was everything he had wished for, needed really, at the time. The comings and goings of bishops and cardinals, kings and queens, presidents and the pope himself had enchanted the man. His years in Paris had proven to him that the church was just as rife with corruption as any organization policed by man. It depressed him to realize how few of the Catholic powerful still had any faith at all. He knew that the power struggles that had endured for centuries were still going on, but in a far more clandestine fashion. Indeed, the church had sacrificed awe and wonder for earthly, material power, and at times Guiscard was nauseated upon meeting those to whom the collar was naught but a symbol.

But Rome was different, for some reason. The city reassured him, overwhelmed him really. It returned to him some of the magic of faith. He steeled himself against the cynicism of the outside world and again devoted himself fervently to study, despite his advanced age. He spent his days sharing new insights into modern theology with his brethren, and at night he pored over every volume the Vatican Library had to offer, digging ever deeper as time passed.

Except—and it had not bothered him at first, not until his studies became feverish, obsessive investigations into such complex things as truth and reality—there was one room he could not enter. What was more aggravating was that he had no idea what it was he was being kept from. Only with the consent of the pope could one enter that wing of the library, and in his time in Rome, he had never seen or, in truth, heard of anyone entering that room. Curiosity, though it was hardly as innocent as the word sounds, became a daily burden for him.

On that night he had been, as he most often was during waking hours, reading and doing research in the library. It was quite late, though this was not unusual, as he rarely got more than five hours sleep each night. It had been a particularly unfruitful evening and he was tired. His fingers pushed back his glasses, and he wiped the sleep from his eyes.

The light was low in that oldest among old rooms. He sat at a long oak table, in a typically uncomfortable high-backed wooden chair. Everything about the room was dark, old, and uncomfortable, seeming to confirm something he had suspected for some time now: that this truth-seeking institution cared not a whit for the truth, only for the semblance of truth, and discouraged anyone interested in looking past the veneer of modern faith.

No wonder the Dead Sea Scrolls have been decades in the translation and revelation!

Of course, he couldn't blame them, really. Nobody wanted to know the truth, only to believe what they were "supposed" to believe and be done with it.

But here in the low light, among the thousands of

ancient volumes, and seated on uncomfortable furniture, Henri Guiscard wanted to know. He wanted to know everything that was knowable, even if he could not understand it. Let them enjoy their stagnation, he thought.

Ah, old and cynical. He'd known it would come to that eventually.

He was tired and cranky and his eyes hurt from straining in the light. He was in the oldest wing of the library, which housed the most ancient books. The only thing that appeared to be older than those books was the oaken door behind him, the door to that room that so infuriated him. He put his head down for a moment and his eyes closed. He let them rest for a moment as his mental complaining subsided. Only later, when it was over, did Guiscard realize he had fallen asleep.

The intruder had entered the Vatican unseen by police, undetected by alarms, had made his way down long, darkened echoing halls, past the private quarters of cardinals and priests, had avoided discovery while descending into the bowels of the Vatican—a trip that took the better part of ten minutes when secrecy was not a factor—somehow walked right by the three attendants in the first section of the library without being seen, and had finally passed within two feet of the sleeping form of Henri Guiscard to stand in front of that forbidden door. Had he not been asleep, the cardinal might have applauded.

He did not know what woke him, but whatever the reason, he did indeed wake. He did not drowsily raise his head, rub his eyes, and yawn, nor did he snap awake, his eyes wide open. No, in his usual fashion, his head still down on his crossed arms on the table, he simply slid easily into conscious thought as if he had never left it.

He did not move for a moment, though completely unaware that anything was amiss. When he finally picked up his head, he removed his glasses and shut his eyes tightly before opening them again.

No, he reminded himself, it's not tired eyes . . . just bad vision.

He rubbed them anyway, put his glasses back on, and began picking up his things. He placed the book he had been reading on the shelf nearest the table, where he could find it again the next night. He prepared to go and turned for one last hateful glance at that eternally closed door.

Which was open. *Wide open*. He rubbed his eyes again and blinked twice, voluntarily. The door remained as it was. His first move was instinctual; he stepped nearer the small alcove framing the door. The possibilities sped through his brain. Those people allowed in the room, if they did indeed exist, might only come there very late so as not to arouse interest in others. But the presence of his sleeping form would then surely have deterred them. Number two, there could be an emergency of some kind, but in this case, there would most certainly have been a great clamor. Finally, whoever had opened the door could be there without consent, in which case he should find a library attendant.

He had decided not to enter the room, and was about to search for an attendant, when his eyes caught a glimpse of metal in this room of wood and leather and paper. The dim light of the library was reflected off some kind of silver metal above the door. He had looked at that door so many times, had studied it the way he had studied the books; he knew there was no metal.

Without knowing he was going to move, he found himself standing in that small alcove only inches from the open door, examining the metal strip that ran the length of the frame above it. It was a hole about an inch high and two inches deep, and propped against the door frame was the piece of wood that had been perfectly fitted into that hole. The wood had disguised more than metal, however. Inside the hole were a number of different-colored wires, and Guiscard could see that some of them were cut, along with a row of numbered buttons, similar to that of any alarm system.

They didn't trust anybody!

Guiscard had naively thought that a simple order, especially coming from this high in church hierarchy, would have been enough to deter even the most curious. Even in his most obsessive moment, he would never have dared to defy a direct order from the holy father. Upon closer inspection he realized he must be one of few so innocent. It appeared that the entire door frame was metal on the inside, the wood merely a facade. The whole thing was a huge, mechanized locking system.

He started, not breathing for a moment.

Yes, a mechanized locking system, but who had broken that lock? Was the intruder still inside?

He could breathe again, but did so as quietly as he could. Overwhelmed by his need to know, by his curiosity,

(killed the cat)

he pushed lightly on the door and soundlessly it opened wider. Over the threshold into the darkness, and he was standing still, heart pumping, pushing him forward, brain stalling, tugging him back.

The wall on his right continued on about twenty feet into the dark, while the wall on his left disappeared into the abyss of this mystery three feet from where he stood. In this little alcove, he made a conscious decision that would change his life, and many others as well. It was not impulse or accident, but choice.

He stepped forward.

The room was about twenty by fifteen with no windows. What little light there was emanated from a small lamp—almost a night-light like the one in his bathroom—that was plugged into an outlet next to the only piece of furniture in the room, a short glass case whose top now stood open. Tools beside him on the floor, the intruder reached into the case with both gloved hands.

Conjecture became conviction became fear became

regret and Guiscard struggled to force himself to withdraw from the room. Wanting only to be gone, he turned
too quickly, his shoe scraped the floor, his pants rustled
softly.

The intruder's head snapped around as if twisted by an
unseen force, and the cardinal stared at him, frozen by his
terror and yet fascinated by it. Expecting attack, he tried
to brace himself for flight, but just then the burglar began
to sway. Slowly swaying back and forth, he clutched at his
chest and then, without a sound, fell on his face, hitting the
marble floor with a loud smack.

Minutes passed before the cardinal had the courage to
approach the body of the stranger lying before him, and
when he did, it was carefully. No pulse. He turned over
the corpse, far from the first he'd seen. The body was
heavy and the man was old; he knew he ought to call
someone, but here was a mystery, right before his eyes. A
number of mysteries in fact. Knowledge and information
were old friends to him by now, but in his most private
of thoughts, he had always wished for a real mystery. An
almost perverse pleasure swept through him and he tried
to fight it down—disrespectful of the dead, you know.

And what was our thief stealing? Guiscard wanted to
know. He went to the case and removed its contents; a
single, leather-bound book. Though it was in good condition, he knew instinctively that it was even more ancient
than the library's oldest volumes. Opening the book, he
read the Latin title page, which identified the book as *The
Gospel of Shadows*, though the title itself seemed to have
been written far more recently than the other text, and the
Latin was more modern. He began to read and was at once
seized by a feeling unfamiliar to him, an uncontrollable
and incredibly powerful emotion it would take weeks for
him to identify.

Dread.

The feeling grew in proportion to his awe and anger and
the minutes passed and he delved ever deeper into the vol-

ume of forbidden knowledge before him. How could the
pope keep such insane things on sacred ground? Did he
actually believe them? Didn't the mere fact that the book
was hidden mean that the holy father of Rome believed
them to be true? And didn't he know, in the pit of his
stomach, didn't he himself believe it to be true?

God in heaven, if it *were* true, what should he do?

But no heavenly reply broke the predawn silence in
that city of ancient secrets. Enough. The cardinal chose
his own course. He had perhaps ninety minutes before the
sun rose, and he would need every one of them. Book held
tightly in his arms, he closed the door gingerly behind him.
He arranged his discovery among his other things, went
upstairs and across the courtyard, up to his room without
notice. He packed a few pieces of clothing, identification,
all the money he had, and the book.

No one questioned him on his way out. When the
theft was finally discovered, Cardinal Henri Guiscard was
already on a plane bound for New York. His world no
longer existed, and he was running headlong into the
void.

A week later he was in Boston, and now, nearly three
more weeks had passed and he had set in motion a series
of events that he hoped would accomplish the impossible.
He plotted the destruction of the Roman Catholic Church.
Foolish it might be, he assured himself, to think one renegade priest could do that kind of damage in a world
where the faithful believed what they wished.

Two young women passed by, hand in hand, and he
silently wished them luck. A burly man proudly bore a
cross on his chest, and Henri shook his head with pity.
Down the sun-starved alleys of this old city, the homeless
thrived in ever-increasing numbers, and they were the only
ones who had escaped the machinations of church and
state. The dark-suited and skirted businesspeople strut-
ted by, strong in their belief in their own freedom—yet

it was painfully obvious that their government had been manipulating them, lying to them for decades.

He should talk, though, eh?

He had readily swallowed deception, had taken faith like a miracle elixir that does nothing but confirm your illness, inspiring further consumption.

"And who is the fool?" he whispered to himself. The greatest fool is the one who sees the truth and still believes in his own free will and power to act.

But act he had, and he was certain he had not gone unnoticed. The keepers of the book would surely be on his trail, might even now be tracking him. He looked around from time to time, but nothing seemed amiss.

As if he, an old man who'd seen one too many Alfred Hitchcock films, would actually know if he was being followed. He smiled at himself. Better, of course, to be as cautious as possible. He knew well the tendrils of Vatican power that snaked around this Earth.

Another block of hotels and restaurants, screaming horns and shouting cabdrivers. Brakes squealed as those dark suits hurried toward lunch meetings, and Guiscard heard bits of nonsense conversation as they rushed past.

The buildings created a valley through which the icy wind whipped, angrily buffeting the crowd with their backs turned toward it. Henri's eyes watered and his teeth clenched and he shivered as he brushed the hair from his eyes. Above him, the sky was swollen and gray, a warning of the storm to come.

He walked down a block, then turned and made his way back to the Park Plaza. He had made one huge circle, walking in the direction of Beacon Hill, then doubling back in an amateurish attempt to smoke out any predators.

Inside, patrons and employees of all religions gave him a kind of deference that had always fascinated him but that he now found repulsive. It was the collar, he knew; it had once meant something to him, and for these people

it symbolized the fact that something else was out there.
That there was a plan and therefore a being or beings who
had devised this plan.

Well, he had good news and bad news for them. The
good news was they were right. The bad news was they
were right. Never wish too hard for something or you
might just get it. He had heard that statement several
times and only just recognized its humor.

Across the lobby, doors opened into Legal Sea Food,
where a hostess led him on a winding path through an
ocean of business lunches, to arrive at a table where Daniel
Benedict sat. The attorney had arrived early enough to get a
table in the busy restaurant, and Henri was glad to sit down.
Time for business, though. Daniel's face was grave.

"Your waiter will be along shortly," the hostess chirped
before gliding away.

"Good afternoon, Your Eminence."

"Please, Dan. I appreciate the respect and your sense of
propriety, but it is unnecessary. Call me Henri, or Father
Guiscard if you must."

"Sure, Father, sorry. To business then?"

"To business," he affirmed, but paused when he noticed
how distracted Benedict was. "What's wrong, Daniel?
Something gone wrong with our business plan?" he asked,
though he could see it was something more serious.

"No, Father, nothing like that." He sighed, letting his
breath out slowly, so slowly. "A good friend of mine—
you've met her actually, Janet Harris, the paralegal who
works with me—she's disappeared. Just gone. Thin air.
And nobody knows where to even begin looking."

"How awful."

"I'm sorry, Father, I guess the collar brings out the con-
fession in us old Catholic-school boys."

That damn collar again!

"It's not like we were dating or anything, but, well, I
was pretty taken with her. Sorry, I'll shut up now."

"No, Daniel," he said sincerely. "Please don't shut up

on my account. You've every reason to be upset."

"Well, let's get to work so I can stop thinking about her."

The waiter arrived, giving Henri a chance to take a good look at his friend. He was overworked and under stress, but a good man. He began to wonder whether this business would cause trouble for Dan, but his involvement had been unavoidable. After all, how much trouble could there be in setting up a nonprofit church organization? Of course, that might depend on what that organization was preaching . . . or publishing for that matter.

"What can I get you, Father?"

"Hmm?" Guiscard smiled up at the waiter. "Oh, I'll have whatever he's having."

The hostess led Liam Mulkerrin to his table, two away from the renegade Guiscard and the lawyer Benedict. He sat with his back to them.

Benedict's appearance was deceiving, he thought as he sipped his water. The man was of medium height, only about five-eight or nine at the most, yet stocky and muscular from lifting weights, and his sandy blond hair was clipped in almost military fashion. His smooth skin would have given his face an almost boyish appearance had it not been for his square, jutting jaw and gravely serious eyes.

He looked like a man of action, Mulkerrin thought. But looks are nearly always deceiving. He had been following the man for several days, in court, in bars, listening to him argue and simply converse. Benedict was a thinker, a general among common soldiers.

Which made it necessary to kill him as quickly as possible.

The cardinal, on the other hand, had to be kept alive at least long enough, just long enough, to reveal where he had hidden the book. Though Mulkerrin had sworn his fealty, it was not the wishes of his Vatican superior that nurtured his dedication. No, more his own power, his own plans. These were pushing him on. He was the only living being to have mastered the skills taught from that book, to have memorized its every word. Certainly there were others who had begun to train, whom he had begun to tutor, but they had far to go and the older masters were long dead.

His acolytes, his pupils, his disciples (if he allowed himself that small sin) must finish their training. He could not by himself command all the forces described in the book. But by commanding his disciples, who in turn would command the darkness, he would be power. Power incarnate.

The Blessed Event, which he had so carefully coaxed his superior, Garbarino, into orchestrating, was only the beginning of Mulkerrin's plan. The prelude to the Blessed Event was already taking place in many locations around the world, but before that wondrous day arrived, he had to recover the book.

As he waited for a waitress to take his order, his fingers drummed a soft rhythm on the table. Any of the restaurant's patrons, glancing at him, would have seen a man deep in thought. And indeed, he was concentrating, but his appearance was a facade. Mulkerrin listened very carefully to the conversation two tables away.

Much of what he heard he already knew, but he was still angered by it. Guiscard's plans were moving faster than he anticipated. Benedict was partly to blame; in a nation of idiots, Guiscard had found a competent lawyer. Mulkerrin reminded himself of the need for expediency in the attorney's termination.

Perhaps the mist-wraiths, he thought, and smiled to himself. Sorcery, it once was called, but that was when the world believed in such things.

By the time Mulkerrin had finished his lunch of bay shrimp and salad, the conversation at the next table had long since turned personal. He lost interest as Guiscard and Benedict talked of family and friends and offered opinions on politics and the weather. He was elated by the knowledge that the lawyer lived alone.

He noticed that neither man broached the subject of religion.

He paid his bill and sat sipping coffee without tasting it as the two men rose and donned their coats. As they began to walk away Mulkerrin put down his coffee, and followed quickly after them.

A mother scolded her little boy for not finishing his lobster. The boy smiled violently at her, and she shut up quickly, unnerved. The friendly hostess was being harassed by a couple complaining about the long wait, and as Mulkerrin passed she suggested they fuck off and die.

He barely paid attention to the hostess as he went through the door. He stood in the Park Plaza and watched as Benedict and Guiscard said their good-byes, the cardinal heading for the elevator and Benedict crossing the lobby toward the door. Liam started after him.

Outside, the wind had died down a bit and snow was falling silently. Not much had accumulated in the hour since it had begun, but the sky was bleached white, promising quite a storm. The lawyer was headed toward Government Center, back to his firm, Claremont, Miller & Moore, and Father Liam Mulkerrin followed with practiced nonchalance.

The snow became heavier, the flakes huge and falling fast. Two blocks from Benedict's destination, Mulkerrin began to weave the spell. His hands moved in small jolts at his side, his fingers pointing and bending, drawing circles in the air. He whispered a few guttural words under his breath. Though complicated, the spell had become simple for him. A block from the building it was complete; when Daniel Benedict entered the building, Mulkerrin was there. Though a small part of his conscious mind stayed with his body, standing there on the street corner with his eyes closed as the snow fell in his hair, it was there only to alert him if anyone disturbed his corporeal form.

The rest of his mind rode up the elevator with Benedict, concentrating on the job at hand.

Looking out through Daniel Benedict's eyes, Liam Mulkerrin saw a pretty woman approaching; through the lawyer's ears, he heard her say hello. What Mulkerrin most enjoyed about this spell was that the host had no idea he or she was being violated. He could intrude upon a person's life for hours, and only the most spiritually attuned would ever feel the invasion. His only regret was that being inside a person's mind did not allow him to read it.

Mulkerrin relaxed in Dan Benedict's mind. He was looking for anything; any bit of information could be the clue to the book's whereabouts. The woman was in her thirties, jet-black hair and gray eyes.

"Martina." He waved. "What's up?"

"I've been looking for you, Danny."

"If it's a problem, I don't want to hear about it. I'm cutting out early. I need to get some rest."

"It's about Janet," she said, and Mulkerrin felt the lawyer start.

"What happened?" he asked, the hope in his voice undisguisable.

"Well, it's sort of weird. It seems her father hired a PI, and he's got Meaghan helping him out.

"Meaghan came in today and wanted a rundown on Janet's recent cases. I gave her some stuff—files, notes, Jan's calendar. But I told her you were the lawyer on most of those cases and she should talk to you for details. She left her work number on your desk."

Dan was silent for a moment.

"I hope that was okay," Martina added. "I mean she said she'd have the stuff back by Monday."

"Huh. Oh, yeah, that's fine. Thanks."

Mulkerrin was angry. This mission was starting to get complicated and he hated complicated. As Benedict headed for his desk the priest contemplated his next move.

On the desk, Dan found Meaghan's number and picked up the phone as he dropped into his leather chair. Mulkerrin memorized the number immediately. Benedict was nervous and dialed too quickly, making a mistake. On the second try, it went through.

"Chaykin and O'Neil."

"Meaghan Gallagher, please."

"I'm sorry, Meaghan's left for the day. As a matter of fact, we're closing due to the storm. Is there someone else who could help you?"

"No, no. I'll try her tomorrow."

The lawyer hung up, then spun through his Rolodex, stopping at *Janet Harris: 685-2033*. Mulkerrin memorized this number as well, and out on the street, snow blanketing his hair, a sneering smile crossed the priest's face.

Benedict wrote the number on a piece of scrap paper and put it into his right-hand pocket. He grabbed his briefcase and left. He had never removed his coat.

Mulkerrin let himself drift out of Benedict's head and blinked as his vision came back into focus. A young man smoking a cigarette stood and stared at him as he opened his eyes. Obviously he had piqued the man's curiosity.

A few moments later Benedict came out. He began to walk away from the building in the heavy snow. Mulkerrin watched him go, frustrated. Now he would have to dispose of this private eye, whoever he was, and this Gallagher woman. He had no idea what they knew, but there was no room for security risks in this situation.

As he watched the lawyer disappear into the blinding white, he smiled in spite of his annoyance as he thought about what was in store for Daniel Benedict later that evening.

4

IT WAS STILL EARLY MORNING, YET PETER
Octavian sat up in his bed. He stared into the darkness, not
seeing his apartment but something else. He was not truly
awake, yet neither was he dreaming.

Through the darkness of his room, across the city and
the ocean and halfway across another continent, his mind's
eye looked upon a small room in southern Germany. A
room in which his friend and onetime mentor, Karl Von
Reinman, slept peacefully. Across his chest lay a young
female Peter had never seen before.

Octavian had first met the German on the night of his
own death, well over five hundred years earlier. Truth
be told, Karl was his murderer, though it had been the
result of a contract between the two men. Afterward,
Peter became part of Von Reinman's coven, following
him all over the world with the other eleven. It was Karl
who named him Octavian, the eighth.

Gradually something began to change between them.
Peter was learning and growing, and though born to the
life of a warrior, he had grown tired of it. He abandoned
the coven in Boston on the eve of the twentieth century and struck out on his own to learn as much as
he could about their kind. He did learn, and changed.
He tried to convince Karl that he and the others were
destroying themselves, that they were both far less and

far more human than they cared to believe . . . or were able to believe. But it was hard for his old friend to listen. Though his mind had forgiven Peter, his heart still felt that betrayal.

Now Peter sat completely still, staring blankly at the walls of his Boston apartment, entranced by this vision of an old friend. He and the German shared a psychic rapport, a consequence of Peter's initial transformation. He could see exactly what Karl was doing at any time, if he cared to look. This time, however, he had not looked. This was being shown to him and he had no idea why. He was a helpless witness.

It wasn't a question of waking up. One moment Karl was asleep and the next he was simply wide-awake. He had sensed, far too late, the presence outside the front door. An ax crunched thick wood, the door. Quietly, he tried to wake the girl, Una. She was replacing number one, who had been brutally killed less than six months ago. But the new Una, formerly Maria Hernandez, had been transformed less than a week earlier. Now she was too blood drunk to wake, and Karl's silent prodding was useless.

He left her there.

There were no windows in the bedroom, a safety measure. If there was but one intruder, he need only wait in the dark room and kill them as they entered. But he knew instinctively who they were, and was certain they would not be foolish enough to send only one or two.

Karl grabbed the bedspread that was balled up at Una's feet. He threw it over his head, wrapping it around his face like a cloak. Just in case. He ran into the front hallway. The ax fell again, letting a stream of daylight into the house. Light stabbed across the room and a flaming scar appeared on Karl's face. He moved quickly from the spot.

What had Octavian told him, half a century ago?

Believe, he had said, and you will burn.

It was difficult to concentrate. In the hall he put a hand and foot on either wall and scuttled up a few feet. He pushed up on the wooden square that served as a door to the attic and moved it to the side. Quietly, he pulled himself in, and slowly replaced the trapdoor as a larger portion of the heavy front door splintered away, allowing a hand to reach in and work the locks.

Poor Una.

As he heard the invaders make their way into the house, he turned to the attic window. Bars inside the glass, shutters outside. He crept toward it, completely silent as he had taught all of them to be over the years. He thought again of Octavian. Believe and you will burn, he insisted. Karl tried to convince himself he did not believe in Christian legend, in myth. It was so hard to know what was true when you were a part of that myth.

Somehow, some way, Octavian claimed, the church had fabricated the legendary physical constraints of the immortals and had somehow convinced these poor creatures, his ancestors, that those constraints were real. Hence, though they were capable of wonderful and terrible things, they were also capable of their own destruction. Self-immolation, a sort of suicide.

Believe and you will burn.

The screaming began below. It seemed Una was awake, and unfortunately she believed in the legends. He moved over the bedroom. The light fixture in the bedroom, an old thing with a slowly rotating fan, had been installed by someone with very little skill, and there was space around the fixture through which Karl could see the goings-on in the room.

He wished he hadn't. Una's flesh was singed and scarred—the scars the shape of the silver cross wielded by a black-haired man. As others held her back with their own crosses, the man held the Christian symbol against her eyes, each in turn bursting in her skull. Her breasts were next, the nipples with their delicate pink areolae charred black by the crucifix, and if Octavian were to be believed, her own faith in its power.

Believe and you will burn.

Karl wanted to go back down and destroy them, make them suffer as she now suffered. But there were too many of them and who knew how many more might wait outside?

"We know you are here, thief and killer. Why not come out and we will free the girl? Come out before we do something irreversible to her."

Karl held back the urge to answer, exercising more control over his rage than he had ever been able, ever been called to before. Then the cross continued its assault on her legs and belly. Two of the men grabbed Una's ankles and forced her legs apart, and the silver cross was thrust unceremoniously between them. The black-haired man, the speaker of the group, held the cross with both hands and stirred hard, as if churning butter. There must have been six inches of silver inside her, burning and tearing, destroying everything it touched.

Una's screaming stopped and she began to vomit blood.

Karl smelled kerosene and realized they were about to torch Una and the bed and the house around her. The only way to end her suffering was right behind him.

He went quickly to the window and as soundlessly as possible tore the bars from their place. The noise was partially obscured by Una's retching, but nevertheless they heard him.

"The attic!" one shouted, as if none of them had considered it before.

Karl Von Reinman barely had time to consider Octavian's advice. If he were to survive—if there were any way to save Una—he must accept his old student's claims. His eyes fluttered closed for a brief moment, and he concentrated on his disbelief. He backed up four steps, ran at the window, and crashed through, the noise of the breaking *glass and shattering shutters enough to tell them immediately what he had done . . . the last thing they had ever expected.*

He crashed to the ground amid the shattering glass, trying desperately to keep his concentration. He wished he could metamorphose, but he was certain the change would be strenuous, distracting, and therefore deadly. If he allowed himself even for a moment to become frightened, if he became even momentarily disoriented, he might fall back on his centuries of belief in the Christian myth of his own existence. And then he would burn just as surely as if he were at the center of the sun.

He smiled as he got to his feet, and if he could have spared the energy, he might have laughed. Octavian, his bastard son, had been right all along.

He glanced toward his front yard just as three men, led by the one with the ax, rounded the corner and began to approach him. Though they were not dressed in their ritual garb, he knew them on sight, the way the mouse knows the cat, regardless of its breed. Vatican men. They were clergy!

Well, he supposed he shouldn't really be surprised. It was only that he hadn't expected retaliation so soon.

He sniffed the air—two more had come out the back and were behind the house and there was one on the roof. The roof! Was he Santa Claus, that they thought he might climb out the chimney? No, they knew exactly what he was, and they were here to execute him. What Una had suffered would be nothing in comparison to what they must have planned for him.

The clergymen were almost upon him and he prepared to fight, his mouth set with grim determination and a dark silence forced upon him by his need for total concentration. Though he was not burning, the sun beating down on him still hurt. Its pressure bore down on his back, driving spikes of pain from all over his body to his brain.

The man on the roof dropped down onto Von Reinman's back with a net of some sort as another ran at him clutching a silver dagger. Looking at the dagger, he felt the vulnerability of his heart the way he had felt it in his eyes and testicles centuries ago as a human. He moved far faster than they, and had thrown off the net and its owner with one swift motion as he tossed the owner of the dagger to the ground yards away. The man with the net was scrambling to his feet as Von Reinman lashed out with his leg, his foot caving in the back of the man's head. The skull gave way easily under his strength, and there was a slight sucking noise as he withdrew his foot.

The smell hit him immediately, and the previous night's feast raced through his brain, reminding him of poor Una. He could smell them now, their blood; he could hear their hearts beat. It beckoned him, that smell, that sound, called to him to come and slake his thirst, to relieve himself of his desire, his hunger.

Karl looked up to see the man with the ax and another clergyman standing, unmoving, yards away. The priest who wielded the silver dagger and whom Von Reinman had hurled to the ground was up now and charging his back. His mind seethed as he realized this fool thought to take him by surprise. At the last moment he turned, a guttural snarl and the hate in his squinting eyes the only outward signs of his rage and pain. These priests and monks, these pathetic, overconfident children, were insignificant. Yet the threat they posed was not. At a subvocal level, he chanted to himself, "You do not believe, you do not believe."

And it was working. In a blur of motion he moved from the dagger's path, grabbed the hand that held it, and pulled, removing the arm at the shoulder. The man's throat erupted in bellows of pain as his fresh wound spurted gouts of blood into the air. Karl pulled him close, driving the silver dagger into the man's belly with such strength that its tip exited the back and Karl's hand was buried in his guts. With the claws of his other hand he dug into the man's face and pulled, tearing away much of the skin, leaving bone and muscle visible beneath.

Von Reinman grabbed the dead man's neck and crotch, lifting him easily above his head, and heaving the corpse at the one with the ax and his companion, who still stood idly by.

And then he realized what it was, the other smell that the bloodlust had blocked from reaching his brain: it was fire.

His house. His house was burning down. Those assholes around the back hadn't attacked him yet because they'd been busy setting his house on fire so he couldn't get back in, torching a century's worth of treasures and the corpse of Una along with it.

Now he was really angry.

The two who had ignited the house now rushed at him from the back and he spun to face them, worried about turning his back on the man with the ax. These two didn't look like much, he thought, and was ready to disregard them when one stopped still and, lightning quick, threw another silver dagger straight for his heart. He was so taken off guard that he barely moved in time and the knife plunged into his chest only millimeters from his heart . . . and he screamed.

Lord, it hurt! The blade seared his flesh as he removed it, all the while inwardly cursing himself. It did not hurt, he told himself, yet he wondered. Octavian had never mentioned silver. Was that, too, a part of the brainwashing his people had undergone, a deadly hallucination? He was getting confused now, his concentration slipping. What was real and what was not?

I do not believe, his mind chanted, and finally the pain began to fade. Far too late, though, as the four men converged on him.

Worried about the shiny ax blade that might have been silver, Karl lashed out instinctively with the dagger, slicing deeply into a neck. The ax man's head rocked back on its stalk, then spilled over, hanging from the spinal cord as the decapitated priest stumbled a few steps and then finally fell over.

He struggled with the three remaining clergymen, noting that the men looked strangely alike. Ah, these must be the Montesi brothers, he realized, the pups of the late sorcerer Vincent Montesi. Karl fought on, but he was confused, distracted, a little scared perhaps. Surely the destruction of the heart would be a logical way to destroy his kind, but the silver had hurt so badly. Perhaps that was true, and if so, what of the spikes of pain being driven into him now by the sun? What was real?

The man on his left was reaching into his coat, and Karl refused to allow another dagger to be brought into play. But it was a distraction, as the man on his right brought a large silver crucifix up in front of his face. A thousand questions stampeded through his brain, but before any of the answers could come, the cross was laid against his forehead and he was screaming.

It burned. Burned so that he could smell it over the smoke from the pyre his home had become, the pyre they'd been dragging him toward. He could smell his own flesh on fire from the cross, and he stumbled and fell, dragging the priests down with him, on top of him. A dagger was plunged into his back at the precise moment that he gathered all his immortal strength and tossed them away. He leaped to his feet, disoriented, and looked up at the sun. He howled as his face blistered and smoked. His clothes began to burn and his eyes withered and blackened in their sockets. His hair and face were aflame as well.

In a blast of heat and ash, Karl Von Reinman exploded, leaving nothing but burning shards of cloth and a fine black powder.

The three monks crossed themselves, muttering a silent prayer. One of them produced a small plastic vial in which he collected some of the ash that had been the German vampire, to keep the remains unwhole. The three dragged their dead over to the house and threw them into the flames. Another prayer was said, and then they turned and began to walk back the way they had come.

"I never thought he would be that difficult," Thomas Montesi said.

"Nor did I," his brother Isaac continued. "He was one of the old ones. I was sure he would still believe."

"Ah," said the third and youngest, Robert Montesi, "but he believed in the end. That's what counts."

"Still," argued Thomas, "His Holiness will surely want us to investigate further."

"Yes," agreed Isaac. "He'll want to know how this old one discovered the truth. It means a lot of work for us."

"Perhaps," Robert said, and smiled. "But only if we tell him. Besides, when he returns from his quest, we will all have more than enough to do."

And then they were all smiling, and soon they began to whistle, the three of them, a song they had heard in a Bavarian inn the night before.

Peter Octavian woke with the smell of burned flesh in his nostrils. It was not suddenly, as if from a nightmare, or slowly and leisurely, as if from a long and profound slumber. He simply woke. One moment he was paralyzed and the next he could move and think and his eyes began to focus in the darkness of his room. Disoriented, he attempted to pull together the reality of what had happened. Even when he had made such psychic connections with Karl of his own accord, they had never been so vivid, so clear. He had been unable to analyze what he was seeing, only to react. And now that he could think it over, one thing remained clear. Whoever had done this to his old friend must pay with their lives.

The problem was that already the details were beginning to fade from memory. He knew the assailants in his vision were from the Vatican, but their faces were losing

shape in his mind, as were, thankfully, the more grue-
some details of the battle. Only the bare facts remained.
Karl was dead, presumably murdered by the church. The
Vatican rarely went after his kind unless a particular creature had directly challenged their authority.

He hungered for revenge and could not help but be
angry with himself. He knew he could have done nothing,
but a terrible guilt still hounded him. Perhaps if he hadn't
abandoned Karl and Alexandra and the others that New
Year's Eve almost a hundred years before, perhaps Karl
would still be alive. Ah, but such fancy was idiocy. The
question now was what to do about it.

As he got up and paced around the room, coming back
to sit on the bed before getting up again and repeating the
circuit, he realized that for now the answer was, do nothing. Though he mourned his longtime friend, he knew that
there were others, still members of the coven, who were
far closer geographically to Karl, and they would have to
begin the investigation without him. He had business to
take care of here in Boston. He only hoped they would
not begin the revenge without him, even though he knew
they would not welcome his presence. One way or the
other, though, he would make sure Karl's death did not
go without retaliation.

The phone rang, and he realized he was still panting
with his fury. He took a couple of deep breaths to try to
calm down and answered it on the third ring.

"Octavian."

"Yeah, Peter. Ted Gardiner."

"Uh-huh. What's up, Ted?"

"Um, listen, have I caught you at a bad time? I could
call back."

His voice had betrayed the anger he felt, but it was not
time to share it. "No, I'm fine. Go 'head."

"I've got the file on Janet's disappearance for you
whenever you want to pick it up. There isn't much in
here, but I'm sure you can do more with it than we can.

Also, you asked me to call about that garage killing last night. Roger Martin, remember? Anyway, it seems he'd been working late on a rush job for his manager, not uncommon according to her."

"What was the job? What corporation?" Peter asked, more out of habit than interest.

"Some church thing is all I know. Anyway, he went to the Publik House for a drink after work, which his wife says is unusual. He was coming back for his car when he got hit. We'll know more about it when the janitor comes around. The docs are pretty sure now that he will."

"Thanks, Ted. Keep me posted."

"Peter? You okay?"

"*Fine*, Ted. Maybe a little tired. Sorry."

When he hung up the phone, Peter was much more relaxed and genuinely sorry to have been so short with Ted. He was in a bitter frame of mind as the alarm clock buzzed, startling him. He swore and knocked it from the bedside table. Its plastic window cracked as it landed, and he cursed again.

Stop it, he told himself, and forced his lungs to draw a deep breath, hold it, and let it out slowly. He fought to contain the emotion that was overwhelming him. Rage and fear and grief gnawed at his heart. Steeling himself against these emotions, he walked to the window and opened it, swinging the shutters wide and breathing in the cold night air.

The night air? The alarm had gone off. He knew his vision or whatever had come to him in the early hours of the morning, not long after he'd gone to sleep. It seemed so immediate. And even though he didn't really need to sleep, or at least very little, he still felt tired somehow.

He smiled grimly. *No rest for the wicked.*

He turned back into the room and surveyed his art collection, his eyes perfectly capable of clear sight in the dark room. The paintings were incredibly dissimilar, not a repetition of theme or style in the room. Some were calm and sensual, others angry and violent, and the sculptures showed the same variety. Away from it all, standing on a marble base in the corner, was a traditional bust. His father, he had once explained to a young woman amazed at the remarkable resemblance he bore to the subject of the sculpture. Now, today, he thought, he would have to claim it was his great-great-great-grandfather.

The Publik House. That was the last place that Roger Martin had been seen alive as well as the last place Janet Harris had been seen. A coincidence, almost certainly, but something to store in his mind.

He stood there staring about the room for quite some time. Then, feeling calm but with a heavy heart, he went about preparing for the night. He had to meet Meaghan at eight o'clock and he was running late. He hoped that she had done as he'd asked.

Peter stood by the window watching the snow fall. He was dressed and ready to go, but the snow, though beautiful, had him worried about traffic—it must be bumper-to-bumper in the storm. He looked at the cracked clock face and saw that it was a quarter to eight. It would take him at least twenty-five minutes to reach Meaghan's place if he had to fight the storm and Boston's own brand of intimate traffic relationships. Even in a raging blizzard, many a Bostonian would be happy to roll down his window to let you know that you "fuck ya muthaa."

Only because he counted on Bostonians to be less well armed than residents of Los Angeles or New York, Peter felt comfortable flipping these pleasant folks the bird, or when he was in a particularly cynical mood, rolling down his window to shout back, "You're an excellent judge of character."

No. No traffic tonight; he couldn't deal with it right now. With all that had happened already that day, he might just lose control. He zipped up his jacket and went out, but rather than take the elevator down, he walked the three flights to the roof, stepped out onto the windswept surface, and closed his eyes as the snow flew in his face. He could feel the cold, but it didn't bother him.

As the storm screamed around him he walked to the edge of the roof and surveyed the city he called home. It was the kind of night in the kind of city where you'd really have to go out of your way to attract attention. Peter didn't want attention, he just wanted to be on time for his date . . . appointment with Meaghan. And he wanted to fly.

Of course it was quite painful—excruciating in fact—but hey, what's five hundred years of living do if it doesn't heighten your tolerance for pain?

The metamorphosis began as painfully as ever, and Peter tried to keep his concentration on the city lights and heavy snow. It was an effort not to voice his pain, and he set tight his lips against the urge. Neither he nor Karl nor anyone he had ever met truly understood the nature of the thing that was happening to him now. He only knew that it must be magic pure and simple, for now his clothes were changing with him and the pistol in its holster, and when he returned to his human form— a much less painful process—he would be dressed just as he'd been when he left his apartment.

Ah, the pain again. Over the years he had waited for it to go away, for his body to grow accustomed to the change. It never happened. Though it was often worse, it was never better.

And then the metamorphosis was complete, the pain was ended. Until next time.

It was nearly eight, now, and he flew quickly, manipulating the high winds, using them to bolster his speed. Though he knew it was nothing but a myth he could not completely thrust from his mind, the initial transformation always made him feel somehow unclean. Riding the winds was a relief—soaring, cleansing.

• • •

Meaghan did not mention his lateness, nor did he apologize. Her mind was on Janet and, more and more, on Peter. There was something about him that was at once incredibly strong and amazingly gentle, something . . . unnaturally natural, if that could be. The only word she found to describe him was human. He seemed a prime example of what people want to be, of humanity. And yet he scared her as well, as if somehow, being around him might lead her to some self-examination she wasn't entirely prepared for.

What the hell, she'd been in lust before. He'd probably turn out to be an asshole after all.

"So what did you find out?"

"Well, I went to Claremont," she began with a toss of her head and a cascade of auburn that she could see had pleasantly distracted him.

"That's Janet's firm?"

"Right. Claremont, Miller and Moore. I was able to get most of the stuff she was working on, but the lawyer I needed to talk to, Dan Benedict, with whom Janet worked quite a bit, was in a meeting or some such thing. So I left him a note. I figure Dan would be able to give us an idea whether any of these cases might have put Jan in danger. And that about covers it."

"Have you started going through the papers at all?"

"No, I figured I would wait for you. I didn't want you to miss the fun."

Peter made no reply other than to nod his assent, and Meaghan suddenly felt like an intruder in her own home. The night before she had felt slightly uneasy in his presence, but it had been a nervous kind of feeling, her stomach telling her she was about to begin something whose outcome was far from certain. She still felt that, but this was different, more personal. He meant no insult, she was sure, but he was all business.

"I had the best lunch today, at this little place on Beacon Street," she began, trying to lighten the mood as they dove into Janet Harris's private files.

Peter nodded on occasion or mumbled a resigned uh-huh to show that he was listening, though she could see he was not. Finally, she tired of blabbing about herself and backed Peter into a corner about his own life.

"I don't like talking about myself much," he answered coolly.

That irked her.

"Peter, I know it's really none of my business . . ." she started, and perhaps because of the sound of her voice, he finally looked up.

". . . but I've already bared my soul and all my secrets to you, so if there's something you'd like to talk about?" She left it at that.

Peter saw the concern, the slight annoyance, and the discomfort in her face. "A friend of mine, an old and dear friend, died today," he said.

"I'm sorry," Meaghan said slowly, feeling very selfish. "Do you want to . . ."

"No," he said a little too firmly, and quickly added, "I'm fine, really. Sorry I'm so quiet."

He gave her a reassuring though weak smile and a pat on the knee and she felt slightly better, though still uneasy.

"Let's get back to work," he said, and they bent again to the piles.

"Do you think we'll find her?" Meaghan asked after a while. "You don't have much hope at all, do you?"

"Of finding the answers, yes, I do. Of finding Janet. No. To be honest with you I don't have much hope at all."

They worked in silence for a while, scanning every scrap of paper in Janet's files. To Meaghan's surprise, Peter made several casual inquiries as to her interests in music and the arts. Though neither mentioned it, they both noticed a careful avoidance of any extended discussion of

Janet. By the time they finished, it was after midnight and they had found nothing. As Meaghan got up to make a pot of coffee, Peter noticed a stack of files he hadn't seen earlier.

"What are those files?"

"Oh, those are nonprofits. Mostly tax shelters."

"We should go through them."

"I guess I figured they wouldn't have too many secrets to hide," she said, and paused a moment before a goofy grin spread across her face. "Probably just the opposite, right? I guess Dr. Watson must have made some pretty stupid assumptions in the beginning, too. Right Holmes?"

"Watson made some stupid assumptions at the end as well, but he was always there to cover Holmes's ass," Peter said with a reassuring smile.

"And what an ass!" she said before she could stop herself. But it didn't matter; Peter only laughed.

"Back to work."

Ignoring the call of caffeine coming from the kitchen, she sat down beside him once again, and together they began to read each file. The manila folders were in reverse chronological order, and Peter picked up the third from the top. Something he saw there made him tense up, visibly.

"Peter," Meaghan said loudly, and he looked up, suddenly angry. She shrank back, but the look was gone so fast she had to wonder if she'd imagined it. "I asked you if you'd found something," she said quietly.

"Maybe," he offered, but she could see there was much he wasn't telling her.

"These corporations would still have to be recognized and approved by the secretary of state's office?"

"Of course."

"Janet took care of that stuff herself—the contracts and forms, I mean?"

"Yeah, why? Have you got something or not?"

He looked at the file, then shook his head. "I'll let you know." His expression was intense. "Listen, do you mind finishing up here? I just remembered some things I've got to take care of."

"At midnight?" Meaghan asked.

"Yeah. I'm sorry."

Suddenly he looked at her so benignly that she didn't want him to leave. He was again the art and music lover who enjoyed hot tea and friendly chatter. But she'd been exposed to a somewhat volatile side as well, and though she found him increasingly intriguing, his mood swings had left a chill in the air. She was trying to understand this man, and he did not seem willing to make it any easier.

When they said good night, he apologized for his rudeness, turned, and left. She was glad he was gone, but after a few minutes, she changed her mind. Peter Octavian was having a strange effect on her, and Meaghan found it frustrating. He was surrounded by an atmosphere of danger, which excited, even aroused her. She turned on the television set, knowing it would be useless at the moment to attempt to sleep.

Outside, the snow had stopped, and the fine white blanket was marred only by Peter Octavian's footprints. They led from the front step around to the back of the building, where they came to an abrupt end. High above, Peter was gliding through the darkness, breathing in the night air and wondering what he would find when he reached his destination. Once there, he would certainly need the talents he and his kind were notorious for, which had made him into a singularly capable detective.

∗

5

DAN BENEDICT WAS TRYING VERY HARD TO
relax, leaning way back in his beloved La-Z-Boy with his
feet up, arms behind his head, his old, ragged bathrobe
with a belt that didn't match pulled tight around him as
he huddled down into the chair.

It wasn't working.

He sighed as he wiggled his butt again, trying to shift
himself into a more comfortable position without disturbing his bathrobe or moving his arms. On his color
television was the late show, a black-and-white film that
had been colorized. Dan had tuned all the color out of his
set. You just couldn't watch Bogey in color, dammit. It
was un-American.

Max was curled up on the floor at his feet. His head lay
on his crossed paws, but try as he might, the big shepherd
couldn't sleep either. So there they lay, man and dog, staring intently at the action on the screen, unable to relax as
sense of dread settled on them both. Max emitted a low
growl for no apparent reason, and Dan silently seconded
the motion.

"You may have the falcon," the Fatman was telling
Bogey on the screen, "but we most certainly have you."

Dan scowled—this was his favorite part of the movie
and yet he could not enjoy it. He and Max had watched
the film more times than he could count, and until now,

it had never failed to entertain him. He reached out to the table next to him, sipped his Coke, and then put the glass back down, ice clinking. He huddled further in his chair in another futile stab at comfort. There was no draft, yet he shuddered. Had he been looking at Max, he would have seen that his pet twitched as well. Of course, Dan would have passed it off as fleas.

At the next commercial, Dan realized he had been unconsciously stifling his need to urinate, and as he jumped up to head for the john, the urge hit him almost painfully. He walked stiffly down the hall so as not to disturb his bladder, flipped on the bathroom light, shut and locked the door. He knew there was no need to do so, but habit forced him. As a child he had been terrified by the thought that someone might walk in on him while he was on the toilet.

His subconscious mind had already decided that, hey, since he was in here anyway, why not get the evening sit-down over with? So he sat comfortably on the foam-rubber seat, reading the *Boston Globe*. His mind drifted in and out, half reading and half wondering whether it would be too late to call Janet's apartment to see if Meaghan had any news. He continued combing through the *Globe*'s business section until he had forgotten the comfortable chair, Max, and *The Maltese Falcon*.

And then he heard the sound of Michelob's latest jingle wafting down the hall, snapping him back to reality. He dropped the paper, cleaned up, and was still pulling up his pants as he walked back to his chair. As he sat down Bogart came back on, and he realized he had missed fifteen minutes of the film. The dog hadn't moved an inch, and Dan realized he was either asleep or very close to it.

Well, he thought, at least one of us can relax.

Dan had just begun to be comfortable again when the next commercial break came. It was infuriating. They always seemed to stack up the ads near the end, when you're paying the closest attention. Now that he was comfortable, he really didn't want to get up, but his stomach

signaled to him that a snack was in order, and he had risen
from his roost without thinking about it. In the kitchen, he
snatched a bag of Chip-a-Roos from the cabinet above the
stove, carrying them back into the living room.

As soon as he broke into the bag of chocolate chips,
Max woke up. It wasn't Dan's plopping back into his
chair that roused the animal, it was the sound of the bag
crinkling open. The commercials seemed to run eternally
as he consumed cookie after cookie. Finally, the film came
back on und Dan reached for his Coke to wash down the
junk food.

Of course, Max wanted a cookie.

As Dan tipped back his glass Max jumped up, front
paws on Dan's lap and nabbed a couple of goodies.

"Shit!" Dan yelled as Coke spilled down the front of
his robe and into his lap, soaking what cookies hadn't been
salivated on by his hungry pooch.

He continued cursing down the hall to the bathroom,
where he pulled off the robe, soaked it for a minute in
the sink, then threw it in the hamper. Not that it was the
first stain on the old robe, and he sure didn't expect it to
be the last. Still—he was pissed.

"Dammit." This night had quickly turned into as nightmarish an experience as his day at work had been. He
knew it wasn't the dog's fault, but he had to stifle an urge
to kick his faithful canine companion right in the ass.

He'd missed more of the film, and any chance of enjoying it was shot to hell, but he swore to himself that he'd
finish watching the damn movie if it killed him. There
couldn't be any further interruptions, he told himself.
What else could happen? He promised himself that even
if another distraction did present itself, even if Santa-
fucking-Claus shimmied down the chimney, even if the
house burned down around him, he would not move his
ass from that chair until the last credit had rolled on
The Maltese Falcon. That shouldn't be too hard—there
couldn't be more than five or ten minutes left to the film.

He headed back down the hallway where Bogart flickered in the dark.

And then the power went off.

So that's what rage feels like.

"FUCKFUCKFUCKFUCKFUCK! Fuck."

Dan felt destructive for a long moment. Goddamn fuses, he told himself, and headed for the kitchen to find a flashlight, but on his second step he tripped over Max. The dog jumped up and moved away from him, wary of further injury.

As Dan stepped into the kitchen Max began to bark.

It was more like a growl at first, a low snarl building until it became a loud and angry bark at the shadows. Dan was spooked. It wasn't like Max to react so violently to such a minor event. He turned back toward the darkness of the living room and could scarcely make out Max's quaking figure in the moonlight falling through the windows. Max was standing in the middle of the room, circling first in one direction and then in the other, barking at nothing.

Dan moved quickly into the kitchen in the dark. He wanted to get the lights back on as fast as possible, and he rifled nervously through kitchen cabinets and drawers until his hand closed upon the flashlight. His eyes were finally starting to adjust, but he would need the flashlight to find the fuse box in the basement.

He had just reached the door to the basement when the barking stopped and the howling began. An urgent, alarming howl, practically a wail, filled the house and Dan's anger and frustration turned to fear. He stood listening, chilled as Max's howl turned abruptly into a quiet whimper. Slowly, almost against his will, he turned and walked back toward the living room.

Somehow, even the moonlight had disappeared.

Dan's pupils attempted to focus, to no avail. In the utter, unnatural darkness only his flashlight offered any illumination, and its light was strangely dimmed and condensed, so that it shone weakly in a very small circle as he scanned the room.

He heard sounds then, terrible, wet, slapping sounds, and he aimed the light that way. When it fell on the black-clothed back of an intruder, Dan's heart jumped and he sucked in his breath. Before he could become angry at the intrusion, he became frightened, and though he loved his dog, for a moment Max was forgotten.

Words backed up in his throat, building up pressure like water with the hose choked off, until they finally burst from him with no thought toward his own safety.

"What the hell are you doing in my house!"

The intruder didn't flinch at the sound of his voice, had obviously known he was there. He turned slowly, allowing Dan to see beyond him in the illumination of the flashlight, see what he'd forgotten.

Max.

"I am telling your fortune, reading your future," the trespasser said.

The dog lay on his back, his belly slit wide open, his guts spread on the floor in the dark. The intruder ran his fingers through Max's entrails with apparently clinical interest, yet when Dan turned the light on his face, a sickening smile told another tale. Only then did Dan see the clerical collar.

"My God, Max." Dan could feel the tears and the fear joining together within him to create something else entirely.

"Come now, Mr. Benedict," the priest said, wiping his hands on the carpet as he turned to face Dan. "The viscera of animals have often been used to divine one's destiny."

Dan snapped.

He dove toward the priest, flashlight held high as a weapon, ready to bring it crashing down on the maniac's skull . . . but there was nothing there. Instead he fell, outstretched arms and cheek sliding in a warm, wet mess that he told himself was not what he knew it to be, knew it must be.

Tears streamed down his face as he sat up, retching, cookies and the cold Kentucky Fried Chicken he'd eaten for dinner streaming onto the carpet in another mess. Seconds passed as he caught his breath, but the tears continued. His heartbeat was much too loud in his head and the taste of vomit and the smell of Max—oh, Max— overwhelming him. He'd always thought himself prepared for an intruder, a street mugging, any threat to himself, but he'd never anticipated such insanity, such terrible cruelty.

"Where the fuck are you?" he growled as he peered into the darkness with his flashlight.

Oh, I'm still here Daniel, the voice came, sounding slightly muffled but close by. *Don't you worry. I wouldn't miss this for the world.*

"Miss what, you bastard. I'll fucking kill you, you lunatic."

I think not.

As Dan watched, the beam of the flashlight grew shorter, and shorter still, and more narrow, until it barely illuminated a foot in front of his face. It did not dim, however. If anything, the light grew stronger. It simply could not penetrate the blackness around.

He blinked, and as he did so the claustrophobic, unnatural dark receded, and moonlight returned to the room. But that overwhelming blackness had not disappeared. In one corner, the maniac leaned against a wall. All about the room the darkness had solidified, coagulated really, into shapes which were only beginning to take on a distinct form. The intruder was forgotten.

Dan's eyes darted from shape to shadow as gelatinous, lifeless white eyes appeared and began to stare back at him. Gaping, toothless, useless mouths grinned widely. Easily a dozen of the creatures filled the room. The shadows undulated, their shapes constantly rearranging themselves. The head of the largest one brushed the ceiling. The darkness seemed to seethe within the creatures and tendrils of shadow snaked from one to the other, like an electrical current traversing a circuit.

For a fraction of a moment they were simply, silently, and ominously there—and then they dissolved.

The darkness flowed about him in a circle, creating a vacuum of which he was the center, a circuit he dared not attempt to disrupt. The whirlwind of blackness drew tighter and tighter around him with each passing moment. With the coiling shadow two feet from him on either side, it occurred to Dan through his blossoming madness that he had forgotten to scream. As he opened his mouth wide to do so, the darkness rushed in.

Suffocating, he fell to the ground. He attempted to close his mouth but found the task impossible as the darkness continued to violate him, beginning to stream in through his nostrils as well. His mind threatened to collapse in upon itself as he wondered where they were all going, how those huge creatures could fit inside of him. His brain screamed for oxygen and he began to lose consciousness.

And then it stopped.

He could breathe again, and did so in huge, heaving gulps. He sat up, turning away from the torn and broken remains of his dog, garishly illuminated in the moonlight. Dan sat completely still for a moment, still recovering his breath, and then, shakily, he stood. It was only a moment before he felt it. It began as a sort of nausea, the feeling of bile rising in his throat and the painful constriction of stomach muscles.

Then the shadows began their work in earnest, and the pain rocketed to every part of his body. He could feel it inside him, growing, expanding; the pressure in his head was intense, and he covered his eyes to hold back the agony that was building there. His scream was short, cut off by pain such as he had never dreamed possible, a pain that did not allow for screaming. His stomach ruptured as the darkness continued to expand.

Blood and shadows shot from his ears and nostrils, from his anus and the head of his penis. Flesh began to bulge and bubble all over his body, bones cracked, and he cried out to whatever gods would listen to end his pain.

He barely heard Liam Mulkerrin's laughter. The priest approached him, barely visible to Dan on a conscious level.

"The Lord may not hear you, Daniel," Mulkerrin said, "but his servant will be your salvation."

He lifted his hand and the silver pin glinted in the moonlight as he barely touched it to the lawyer's taut, bulging belly.

The darkness exploded from within him.

As Daniel Benedict's corpse fell to the ground his eyes burst, sending plumes of black smoke shooting from their empty sockets. As the shadows finally expanded to their full size, the lawyer's body was scattered about the room, mixing with the ravaged remains of his dog.

In the kitchen doorway, Father Liam Mulkerrin watched this spectacle with amusement in his bright eyes. A simple spell had shielded him for the most part from flying gore, though he needed to wash his right hand, which held the pin. The mist-wraiths he had called upon to assist him were gone in moments.

Liam knew that he ought to have stayed with simple, inconspicuous forms of murder, gunshot wounds and the like. But as each day went by he became more and more frustrated with this mission, and his only relief came from spectacular cruelty, unending pain, and extraordinary murder.

Some men played the piano, some painted. Liam Mulkerrin's art was death. His was a masterful talent, whose calling would not be denied. Simply shooting someone with a gun was like asking Chopin to play "Chopsticks."

6

A LETTER FROM FATHER LIAM MULKERRIN, Representative of the Vatican Historical Council, to His Eminence Cardinal Giancarlo Garbarino, Special Attendant to His Holiness and Chairman of the Vatican Historical Council.

Your Eminence:

Though there have been one or two unforeseen difficulties, I believe that the object we discussed should be in my hands within the week. Should any further complications arise, I will notify you at once.

Yours in Christ,
Liam

7

WINGS FLUTTERED, THE BAT SLOWED, hovering five feet from the ground. Across the street, Phil lay slumped in a doorway as a chill ran through him. He had passed out hours ago, and usually slept the night through.

But not tonight.

Tonight a shiver raced from his toes on up, and when it reached his eyes, they opened. He shuddered as he pulled himself into a sitting position, hugging his knees. Felt like the devil dancing on his grave, he thought, and began to dry-heave on the street. Phil, who hadn't been able to remember his last name since—well, since he could remember—shook his head to clear his mind and eyesight. He dry-heaved again and a surprised look crossed his face. He'd long since become immune to the bottle, so what the hell was this?

He turned over, trying to go back to sleep. And that was when he saw the bird. Big fucking bird, Phil thought. No, a bat.

Big fucking bat.

And then it changed. The bat's flesh started to pulsate as it flapped its wings—wings that began to stretch. But really the whole thing was stretching, wasn't it? Phil watched in terror and fascination as the transformation took place. The creature's eyes were scanning the area, and though he hadn't quite decided whether this whole thing was a hallucination or not, he knew for goddamn sure he didn't want the thing spotting him.

A moment after it had begun, it was over, and the bat was now a man. A hard-looking man, who moved strangely, fluidly, as if he were flowing along rather than walking. And the man looked right at him.

"Oh, my Lord Jesus," Phil hissed, for he'd once been a religious man. "It's a . . . it's a vam—"

The old drunk stopped midsentence, unsure of what to do, of what to expect. He half expected to die, almost wished it would happen, though he'd never admit it to himself.

And then the thin, dark creature lifted its right hand—or talon or whatever—put a finger to its lips, and said . . .

"Shhhhh."

And then it walked away, around the front of the building in front of him. Phil lay there, staring after the thing for a moment, and then reached for his bottle, muttering something half curse and half prayer under his breath. He would tell no one. Not just because he knew that nobody would believe him, but also because he was disappointed. He had witnessed something that he had always been told was only in stories, something that had terrified him as a child. And now that he'd seen it, knew it was real, in a way he felt let down because he was still alive.

To his credit, it never occurred to Phil to follow the thing.

Peter sighed aloud as he approached the entrance to the secretary of state's building. Allowing the old homeless man to see him had been careless. If Peter could slip once, he could do so again.

Must have Meaghan Gallagher on the brain, he thought.

Long ago, he would simply have killed the old man. Sucked him dry and laughed about it the next night. But times had changed, humanity had changed, and Peter

Octavian had changed as well. Conflict was foolishness, he knew, and it disturbed him deeply that more of his kind did not realize this, and certainly did not share his fondness for humans.

The Defiant Ones.

His people.

The barbarism and inhumanity that had made them truly human had seemingly become immortal along with their flesh. They had learned nothing in their centuries of unlife, as if their ability to reason had died along with their humanity. It shamed him to know that not long ago, he, too, had been a barbarian. But already his warrior's soul was giving way to enlightenment, and finally to peace. He no longer took life if it could be avoided, unless, of course, revenge were involved. Vengeance was one primitive emotion he could not overcome, nor did he want to.

No. The old man had not deserved to die.

Peter shook the clouds of philosophy from his head and set his mind to the problem at hand. He examined the glass doors to the building, with their alarm system hooked into the main lobby, and his course of action was plain: he could not open the doors without setting off the alarm, so he must go under them. At his mental command, his molecules drifted apart and a hot, wet cloud of mist slipped under the door. He had often wondered why this transformation was so painless and the others so excruciating. Not that he minded.

Frustrated, Peter leaned back in the late Roger Martin's chair, drumming his fingers on the dead man's desk, and began to wonder whether someone had beaten him to it. He'd been through every inch of Martin's desk, every file in the man's filing cabinet, and come up empty—not a single reference to the case that Janet had been working on. In the Rolodex he found Janet's and the lawyer Benedict's telephone numbers, but that was nothing he hadn't expected to find.

He was tired, suddenly, and cold. Hungry! He snickered quietly to himself, amused by his own stupidity. He had meant to go see Marcopoulos. His supply of "groceries" was low, and he hadn't banked on having to go out in the sun. He'd have to be at peak strength, and that was going to take more blood than he had on ice.

He picked up the phone from Martin's desk and dialed the number for City Hospital. The phone rang once.

"Dr. Marcopoulos' office," an unfamiliar voice said.

"Is he in?"

"No, I'm sorry, the doctor went home early tonight." That unfamiliar voice had an attitude problem, Peter thought.

"Could I leave him a message?"

"I *suppose*," she said with a huff.

"Please tell him that Peter called. That I'm having a barbecue tomorrow and I want him to bring the drinks."

"The drinks."

"Yes."

"I'll leave it on his desk." Her sign-off was barely a grunt.

And that's when it hit him.

Where do you put something when you're done working on it? On the boss's desk of course! Ted had said that Martin stayed late to finish something up. He could only hope that the government's slack working habits would hold up and that no one had worked on it yet.

He moved quickly around the room. Too quickly, in fact. Papers blew off desks as he slid by, though not before he had scanned each one. On the other side of the room was a desk with an engraved silver nameplate on it—SHEILA TIMULTY—SUPERVISOR. He picked up a pile of papers from the "in" box on the desk, and about halfway down, he found what he'd come for.

Nonprofit church organization. Cardinal Henri Guiscard. The name he had seen in Janet's files. Exact same case. Janet was missing and probably dead. Roger Martin

was as dead as you can get. Put two and two together
and you still have some gaping holes and one big fucking
question . . . Why?

What the hell was there about a nonprofit church organization that was worth killing for? Not that he thought the
church was innocent. Far from it; his kind had been through
too much with those slavers. But what could these people
possibly have done or known to get them killed? And who
else was on that list? This Guiscard, most certainly, unless
he were the killer. But he wouldn't be able to find the
cardinal until morning at least.

Benedict, the lawyer Meaghan had mentioned?

He was back at Martin's desk before the thought was
completed, the Rolodex was open, and his hand was on
the phone.

Only the work number, so he called information. He
figured these yuppie lawyer types all wanted to live in the
city, keep up appearances don't you know, so he tried that
out. The operator was kind enough to give him the address
as well: 14 Brighton Street. Three miles away and practically the damned suburbs. He went to the window and
pulled it open. The government must have realized how
dismal an employer it really is, because on the seventeenth
floor, the windows only opened about an inch. His flesh
steamed until only steam was left, drifted out into the cold
night air, and re-formed into an entirely new shape on the
other side. As he flew away, his thoughts were scattered,
searching for a focus beyond two corpses and a mystery
he felt he hadn't even scratched the surface of. Sure, he
knew who was behind the murders, but he had no clue yet
as to why.

"Shit," Ted grumbled as his unmarked car rolled onto Brighton Street. He was off duty, but he'd been on a
blind date with his sister's girlfriend Irlene. She was surprisingly pretty, but didn't have too much upstairs as far
as Ted could tell. It certainly wasn't anything out of "Love

Connection." He'd been right down the street when the call had come over the radio, but he damn well wasn't the first one there.

Ted rolled to a stop in front of number fourteen Brighton, where a yellow plastic police barrier already blocked the front door. Two uniformed officers were keeping at bay the few neighbors who had bothered to come outside when they saw the blue lights flashing down the street.

"Hey, Donny," Ted called out to one of the men.

"Hey, Ted." A pause. "How was the date?"

"How the hell—" Ted began, but stopped. He didn't want to give Wallace the satisfaction. "It was just fucking grrreeaat."

"That so, Tony the Tiger? Then how come you're here."

"Your wife sent me to ask what you wanted for breakfast, dickhead."

And then he'd passed Don Wallace, who couldn't think of a snappy comeback and probably would stay awake all night attempting to come up with one.

Ted heard an engine behind him and turned to see an ambulance pulling in quietly. They were in no rush, that was for sure. There was a rank smell coming from the doorway, and it puzzled him. Unless the guy had been dead awhile, he shouldn't be able to smell the poor bastard all the way out here. Especially with the cold.

"Save yourself the nightmare," said an old voice.

George Marcopoulos emerged from the doorway, his breath pluming as Ted's was into a light mist around his head. It could have been a halo.

"What?" asked Ted. He knew the man, but not well.

"I wouldn't recommend you go in there unless you absolutely have to. It's a real mess."

The ME looked ill, and Ted read that as a sure sign that his advice was best heeded. "What's going on?"

"Nothing I've ever seen before, or hope to ever see again," Marcopoulos whispered softly enough that Ted wasn't certain he was supposed to have heard. "Hello, Peter," the old man said.

Ted jumped. He hadn't heard Peter come up behind him. His curiosity was piqued. What the hell was going on around here?

"Peter. How'd you get here?"

"I rode in with George," the detective said, smiling at the old Greek. "Shall we go in?"

"No!" George nearly shouted, which Ted thought was pretty weird. "I don't think you need to see what's inside. Either of you."

"I'll just go in and see what the boys've got, but I'll try to avert my eyes. Okay, Doc?"

Ted went inside.

Peter had been about to argue when he smelled it. The stench of the blood hit him full force and almost brought him to his knees. The carnage inside must be extreme for George to insist that he stay out, but even out here the smell was overpowering. If he went inside, he might lose control. Better not to be tempted.

"Thanks for the cover," he told George. "I didn't bring my car tonight. And thanks for the warning—from the whiff I got of what's in there, I wouldn't want to see it even if I were human."

Peter smiled at his friend before he continued. He was happy to have a confidant, someone who knew his secrets, someone to share the truth with. He remembered the night that George first discovered his secret, and how afraid he had been of his reaction.

"He's been ripped apart, Peter. From the inside. It looks as though someone planted a bomb inside him and he simply exploded. The dog, too. But even if that were possible, we haven't found a single trace of any explosive."

There was no humor in the old Greek's eyes. "Whatever happened here, it's evident that your experience will be of far more use than mine in finding the answers. I was home when they called me."

"I figured. I called your office."

"They called me because they had never seen anything like it."

"Who found it?" Peter wanted to know.

"That's the clincher," George said, looking Peter in the eye.

"Fellow across the street. Williams, his name is. He's sitting on the john and has a clear view of Benedict's house from the window. He glances out at the house just as the lights go. He kept looking to make sure the whole block wasn't going to go, but it's just Benedict's house."

"Did he see anyone?" Peter interrupted.

"Patience, my friend. Yes, Mr. Williams saw someone leaving the house just a few minutes later. And this is what makes this whole thing even more bizarre. The suspect was dressed like a priest. Williams watched him walk to a car that was parked a short way down the block—too far for him to get any details, so don't bother asking—and drive away."

"So after a while," Peter continued for him, "the guy's curiosity is piqued and he comes over here."

"Calls first actually, and getting no answer, comes over to find this mess. There is another set of footprints besides Williams's, but the snow piled up so quick there was no way to get a good look at them."

What the hell was going on? Peter wanted to know. That branch of the Vatican, which was pretty obviously involved here, had not been so active in a century. And Karl Von Reinman's killing, though surely unrelated to these murders, must be Vatican work as well. What the hell were they up to?

"Why do you say 'dressed like a priest'?" Octavian asked Marcopoulos. "Perhaps he *was* a priest."

Janet Harris. Roger Martin. Dan Benedict. Did the killer know that Peter had been asking the right questions? Most probably, he thought. And so he might be next on the list. He was sure he could take care of himself.

Asking the right questions.

Meaghan had been the one asking the questions.

Ted drove. It had started snowing again.

Meaghan was wide-awake.

"Wide-fucking-awake," she mumbled angrily to herself.

She stared at the ceiling in a vain attempt to overcome her insomnia and shake the cobwebs from her head, cobwebs that held an image of Peter Octavian that, try as she might, she could not put into focus. In the madness of the last couple of days, the more often she had tried to thrust him from her mind, the more often she had been surprised by his intrusion into her thoughts.

He disturbed her. Not only tonight, when he had left so abruptly, but from the moment they first met. There was something about him that made Meaghan profoundly uncomfortable, as if for some reason, she did not belong. Or perhaps it was Octavian who didn't belong.

"So what's the biggie?" she asked herself quietly, a bad habit Janet had often chided her about. "You think he's a creep, right?"

Ah, there's the rub, she thought.

She didn't think Peter Octavian was a creep at all. Sure he made her nervous. But he also created a longing in her that did not originate between her legs. Not to say—she chuckled—that he wasn't sexy as hell (if you liked the type), but that wasn't the cause for this longing or for the fascination she felt for him. There was an empty feeling in her stomach when she thought of him.

"Christ's sake!" she said aloud, and rolled over, sighing heavily, to face the wall. "He's just a guy," she told herself. "No matter how peculiar he is, he's just a man."

Convinced that she had rationalized quite enough for the evening, Meaghan closed her eyes and attempted to sleep. It was only a moment before she felt it growing again, in the pit of her stomach, like a tear forming in her eye. She had been through it over and over since he'd left.

She wanted him, of that there was no doubt. But that was far from normal behavior for her. Normally, it took her a long time to make that kind of decision, especially now when taking a lover, male or female, could mean risking your life. And it was not like Peter had made any moves on her, beyond some very natural flirting. Her desire was a dark secret weighing on her mind.

Certainly, he had some special quality that had touched a chord within her. But what the hell was it? There was an aura about him that attracted her like musk, but she couldn't name it.

And then she could.

Finally. Wonderfully.

And maybe now she could sleep.

It was *danger*. Beyond the aura of mystery that surrounded him and the animal attraction she felt for him was a sense of adventure, an almost tangible atmosphere of danger. Tangible yes, and she recognized the electricity it produced. It reminded her of the wire-taut tension in the air the one time she had fallen asleep at the wheel, waking only to find herself hell-bent for the center guardrail, oncoming traffic heavy. She snapped awake, terror howled in her chest . . . and she could feel it.

That's the way she felt around Peter Octavian. Not that she was afraid of him, though there was an element of that as well. But the air around him, the room as he moved into it, crackled—no, bristled—with danger.

She felt much better, comforted somehow, that she had finally recognized her attraction. Now that she had, she could concentrate on wondering what it would be like to be with him. At last she was relaxed, sleep right around the corner, and like a naughty child, she hoped she would dream of Peter. . . .

Only when the buzzer rang did Meaghan realize she had indeed fallen asleep. She looked at the glowing numbers on the clock at her bedside; twenty-five to three. She'd been asleep for just fifteen minutes, but she felt groggy. The buzzer rang again, reminding her that someone was trying to get her out of bed at 2:30 in the morning. Under normal circumstances it would have spooked her; with Janet missing, it scared the living shit out of her.

Meaghan got up and threw on a robe. She had been sleeping in her night shirt—an old, faded man's oxford—and had her socks on, and even with the robe, it was chilly as she crossed the apartment. Before she reached the door, her visitor buzzed again, more insistent this time.

"Hello," she croaked, half-asleep, as she worked the buttons on the intercom.

Nothing.

"Hello?" she said again.

And now she was awake. What was going on? It wasn't the first time somebody'd buzzed an apartment at random as a prank or simply in error. But it was two-fucking-thirty in the morning and her roommate was missing and presumed dead by anybody who had half a brain.

"Shit!" She raced for the phone. No reason to take chances. Nine-one-one.

And then the knock.

"Jesus," she whispered, cursing herself for romanticizing danger. The emergency line rang for the second time. "Answer, you bastards," she cursed under her breath. "That's what you're paid for."

The third ring and the second knock came simultaneously. This time the knock was longer, more urgent, and she imagined the same for the ring. Almost immediately the knocking became a banging.

"Meaghan," the knocker shouted.

"Police department, you're being recorded," the emergency operator finally answered.

It was Peter at the door.

"Sorry," she said to the cop who had taken his time to answer the phone. "Wrong number."

Realizing that he would either wake the whole building—if he hadn't already—or break down the door, Meaghan ran to unlock it and flung it open.

Peter's eyes, and the eyes of the black man behind him, were wide with surprise and the detective's mouth was open as he was about to shout again.

"Would you mind keeping it down," she said, still shaking in fright. "I do have neighbors."

"Why didn't you answer?" Peter asked sheepishly as the two men came in.

"I was doing my nails," she said a bit icily, and then backed off. "I was sleeping when you buzzed. How come you didn't answer me when I buzzed you in?"

"Some guy was taking his dog for a walk and we just came on up. Not too bright, huh?"

His innocent face and raised eyebrows were too much for her, and she finally relaxed. She was scared, not angry, and now that the fear had gone, she was left with only amusement at the irony of his appearance here, late at night, with only this other tall, dark stranger to protect him from her advances.

Just kidding, she told herself.

"I'll put on some tea," she said, and dashed into the kitchen. He doesn't like coffee; she chuckled to herself. Already changing our habits for a man we've known for two days. Uh-huh.

She came back into the living room while the water was heating up.

"I'm glad you're okay," Peter said gravely.

"Well, you nearly scared me to death." She laughed, showing him that she expected no response. The tall black man seated by him on the couch was smiling, both in greeting and, she thought, in amusement.

"I'm sorry," Peter started, a bit uncomfortable. "Meaghan, Ted Gardiner, one of Boston's finest."

"Peter, though it was a nice thought, I'm sure you didn't get me up to introduce me to your friends." She smiled at Ted. "Nice to meet you, by the way."

Ted nodded as Peter stood up and began to pace and to talk. He seemed somewhat amused by the situation, by Octavian's nervousness, which he'd guessed might have a little more to do with Meaghan Gallagher than with crazed killers disguised as priests.

Meaghan's eyes were wide as Peter told her, brief-ly, about Roger Martin and Dan Benedict. He told her he believed that Janet was dead. For the moment she'd forgotten about her attraction to the man. Now she just wanted to know what the hell was going on.

"I asked Ted to give me a ride over here after I found out about Benedict. Meaghan, we could both be in danger. I'm sorry I brought you into this."

And there it was. Now the danger she'd felt was real. Perversely, it felt good.

"Don't be ridiculous. The killer, whoever he is, brought me into this when Jan disappeared. You've only tried to help."

"Ah, but have I? Helped, that is."

"We'll just have to wait and see, won't we?"

For the first time that night their eyes met, locked. She saw a depth in Octavian's eyes that was unfamiliar to her, but she sensed that it held burdens and struggles that had nothing to do with the potential danger they faced. He had demons in his soul.

And what a silly thought that was, she chided herself as the teakettle whistled in the kitchen. Only as she spun did she notice Ted fidgeting in his seat. Poor guy, she thought.

When Meaghan returned with a tray, Ted thanked her solemnly. She smiled at him. She felt an affinity toward Ted because she sensed that he, a policeman, was also made uneasy by Octavian, though both men were unaware of it. In the way he looked at Peter, Meaghan could tell

that Ted had a deep respect for him, bordering on awe.
The kinship she felt with him revolved around Peter. They
were . . . the only word that came to mind was disciples,
and she didn't like the image that conjured, or the power
that it gave Peter in her thoughts. He was just a guy, she
reminded herself for what seemed like the hundredth time
that night.

She realized she'd been holding her breath, and that
she was staring at Peter. She shook her head and spoke
to break the silence that held them all.

"So. Someone wants to kill us. What the fuck are we
going to do about it?"

Peter looked up, all worry gone from his face.

"Nothing tonight," he said calmly. "Tomorrow we'll
find the man who is the center of all this, and then we'll
get some direct answers. For tonight, if you don't mind,
I'll sleep on your couch, just to play it safe."

She wanted to be nervous; if it was serious enough for
Peter to want to stay here to protect her, she must truly be
in danger. And as much as that excited her, it frightened
her as well. But Peter was calm, and confident, so she
simply nodded her head.

"Peter," Ted said, making Meaghan realize how little
he'd said since the two men had arrived.

"Are you sure you want to go outside tomorrow? I mean,
if you want, I can find some time to track this guy down."
The policeman's forehead was knitted with concern.

"Thanks, Ted. I'll be okay. Besides if you were to
get too heavily involved, there'd be no way to keep the
department out of it, and we don't want them involved
just yet."

"Okay, if you're sure. Let me know if you need anything."

Meaghan was incredibly confused, and Peter could see
it in her face. He answered her question before she had
time to ask it.

"The sun," he said grimly.

"My skin can't endure direct sunlight for long periods of time, which is why I work almost exclusively at night. I know this sounds like a bad joke, but I suffer from a rare skin disease similar in some ways to albinism. It does no damage but causes intense pain. I'd like to explain it to you, but I don't really understand it myself. Fortunately the doctors do, and they've developed a treatment that significantly diminishes the pain. Which is why we've got to go to Boston City Hospital in the morning."

"God," she said. "That must be terrible."

"It's been this way for almost as long as I can remember, so in a way it doesn't seem quite as bad as you might think. Only a few people know about it because frankly I don't like to draw attention to myself and I can't stand pity. I'm only telling you because you'd find out in the morning anyway."

Meaghan wanted to know more, but Peter began to speak to Ted. Obviously, as far as he was concerned, the subject was closed.

"I'll call you first thing," Octavian said, and the two men stood up and made their way to the door.

"And Ted," Peter concluded just before shutting the door, "remember what I said about not bringing the department in just yet. Their involvement would only serve to get a lot more people killed."

Ted nodded. He was about to leave when he seemed to remember something.

"I'm an idiot."

"No argument," Peter said, and smiled a tired smile.

"I forgot to tell you that the janitor, the one from the Martin murder—he's awake. I'm sure you'll want to talk to him. I'll set it up."

Meaghan lay in bed, listening to Peter get comfortable in the next room. If she had been confused before, she was completely baffled now. There was no denying the strange effect he had on her, or the now tangible aura of danger around him, around them both. But she was afraid. Afraid of whoever might be waiting out there to harm her, to kill her, and a little bit afraid of Peter. That, she definitely didn't understand. She felt bad for him, yet he scared her; he scared her, but she felt safe when he was nearby. And now she was cold; she had turned up the heat, but it seemed colder now than when Peter had first arrived.

Cold and afraid and confused and insomniac—before she even knew she was going to do it, she was up and walking to the door of her bedroom. She opened the door and Peter looked up at her as she was standing in the open doorway in her nightshirt, socks, and underwear. She wanted to run, to hide under her covers, but he spoke to her, and then she knew she could not.

"What's wrong?" he asked. His voice was calm and quiet; she was entranced. Meaghan walked across the room and knelt by the couch, where he lay with his head propped up on his hand.

"I'm just a little scared, I guess," she heard herself say, though she'd wanted to say that nothing was wrong. But she knew that he would know, perhaps did know, exactly what was wrong.

"There's nothing to be afraid of," he said, and smiled at her as if she were a child come to her parents' bed to hide from the thunder.

He knew.

She was sure that he knew that she was not only afraid of the killer. That he knew exactly how he made her feel inside, and that it scared her as much as anything else. It was unbelievable, out of control, that she could be so drawn to someone she had known for just under thirty hours.

"Trust me," he said. "There's nothing here, even in the dark, for you to be afraid of. Nothing to fear in the shadows. In broad daylight, *that's* where the terror is."

His hands moved through her hair and the words no longer made sense to her, though the sound of his voice soothed her. He was kissing her forehead and she was happy. She felt desire come upon her as his lips brushed her cheek, and her lips. She tasted his mouth, strangely cold, and his tongue met with hers. Not since her first night with Janet had she wanted someone so much, so quickly. His head moved down and his lips began to caress her neck.

He stopped. *Abruptly*.

He took a deep breath and then slowly let it out. She wanted desperately for him to continue, but he raised his head, his eyes closed tightly, and spoke.

"Perhaps," he said, opening his eyes. "Perhaps you should get some rest. It's almost morning and we've got a busy day ahead of us."

She smiled to hide her disappointment, as if that were possible. He had had second thoughts. He was speaking kindly and trying to comfort her, and he had, after all, come here to protect her from whatever danger she might face. But he had dismissed her, at least for tonight, and it stung. She felt foolish, but she still wanted him. She promised herself that there would be another time.

When Meaghan had retreated to her bedroom, Peter let out a breath and relaxed. "Too close," he whispered under his breath.

He would see George Marcopoulos first thing in the morning. His "medicine" couldn't wait until the afternoon.

✳
8

VENICE... SEVERAL HOURS EARLIER

They called it La Serenissima, the Most Serene, and in the winter months it was easy to see why. Ethereal light from the moon, the city, and the stars lit up the sea mists that drifted in from the larger canals. The chill night air kept even the pigeons out of the piazzas, the birds huddling instead with the gargoyles that looked down from the crumbling facades of the city's grand palazzos.

Tonight, though, carnival was not far off, and she could feel it in the air. The pulse, the beat of the city's heart, was quickening, if only slightly, in anticipation. Its blood ran a little faster now, through arteries, alleyways, deep with the shadow of a growing passion, not stilled by the cold. Barroom doors exhaled light and noise, attempting to rouse the sleepy city from its winter slumber. When carnival arrived, it would awake indeed, even if only for a few days.

Alexandra Nueva sat astride a gilded bronze horse, itself one of four that stood atop the Basilica di San Marco. Naked as the day she died, her deep brown skin glistening in the ghostly light, she silently watched the couple beneath her in the Piazza San Marco. They waltzed in the drifting mist. No band played, no radio blared. Even with her acute hearing, Alex could detect only one rhythmic

sound, that of the lapping of the canal as it spilled over
onto the flagstones, gondolas bobbing at their moorings.

It was to this music, Alex thought, whether they knew
it or not, that the couple danced. And she liked them for
this. They moved to the same wordless tune that led her
and her kind through the night, guided them through the
darkness. She closed her eyes and listened to the music,
broken constantly by the distant din of the Venetian youth,
yet overwhelming, even absorbing these other noises into
its rhythm until all became harmony.

*And suddenly she is mist, floating to the music. Floating
after the young American couple. North they move, out of
the square, and she drifts after them, the light penetrat-
ing her as it does the sea mist. After all, she is only a
part of the music. She does not mind leaving behind the
basilica, with its campanile, the bell tower she loves so
much for its history of debauchery and death—a history
in which fifteenth-century clerics, those who deserved it
the most, were suspended in wooden cages and left to
die from starvation and exposure, fed just enough to keep
them alive for months on end. She does not mind leaving
behind the beauty of the basilica itself, its beautiful horses,
or the Doge's Palace, filled with extraordinary works of
art from some of history's greatest creators, as well as a
vast dungeon and torture chamber.*

*Beauty and pain, the double-edged sword that is life,
the sword that led Alexandra Nueva to her death and now
rules her unlife, these things are no distraction to her for
this sweet moment of drifting.*

*The couple stops on a short bridge to look south,
where, several buildings down, the Bridge of Sighs
stretches across this narrow canal. They kiss. And
the kiss deepens and the blood pounds first in their
hearts and then in their heads and then in their
loins.*

And the music of the shadows stopped, was overcome
really, by this new music that pulsed in the veins of the

lovers, misty-eyed to match the misty light rolling through the city in waves. Though she was still mist, Alex felt carnal now, felt a lust that, though not the same, matched the lovers' in its ferocity.

She had watched them the night before, to no avail. But watching them, hearing and feeling them now, she knew that tonight would be different. They crossed to the other side of the bridge and entered the Hotel Atlantico. Alex knew just where their room was, right on the first floor, the window only six feet from the water. Gondoliers passing by could see right in and would shout to the woman if they saw her in the window, then go on poling through the canal, singing loudly, hollering even louder to warn any other that might be around the next corner, lantern clanking in the dark.

Of course, this time of year the gondoliers were few and far between, and dressed for the cold when they *were* out. And this late at night, there were none. So there was no one to see Alex as she took form again, in answer to the stirring she felt within her, on the ledge outside the lovers' window. She stood well back in the shadow of an outcropping on the side of the stone building and watched while they . . .

Entered laughing, not out loud but in their hearts, and she could hear them. They smiled at each other, passion in their eyes and barely contained mirth threatening at any moment to burst from lips stretched taut to hold it in. Instead, sounds of contentment came forth from those lips as the lovers fell to the bed, nuzzling and caressing, hands roaming under clothes until the clothes themselves magically disappeared over the side of the bed. The window was open just a crack, but the shades were thrown wide and the lights were on. Half of Venice could have seen them, Alex figured. They didn't notice, or didn't care. His head was between her legs and her voice rang out. Then she was on her knees and he was behind her. Alex watched as the young man . . .

Entered her, sliding his penis into her with a slow and steady rhythm—a rhythm that could not disguise from Alex the wilder pumping of their blood, the beating of their hearts, the laboring of their lungs. She could practically smell the blood as it rushed to their loins—as it rushed to *her* sex as well. She felt her wetness and could no longer keep her hands from herself as she watched the couple pleasing each other. In her heat the cold air went unnoticed except by the moon, whose light glinted off her deep purple nipples. The lovers began to shout as they rocked to the music of the night, and Alex could stand it no longer. With one hand she pushed open the window; with the other she brought herself to a wailing orgasm along with the woman in the room. Taking a deep breath, yet still shuddering, she . . .

Entered the room, practically floating to the floor. The man in the room saw her first and was struck dumb. Then the woman opened her eyes and was about to speak when Alex raised a finger to her lips.

"Shhh," she said.

And what could the two say to this beautiful naked African woman who had appeared from the cold Italian night?

"Let me love you both," she said, but neither replied. They knew they didn't have a choice.

After all, they *had* volunteered.

Venice was similar to many other European cities in that visitors to its canals and alleyways came primarily to explore. Certainly shopping and history were also a draw, but it was adventure that was the true attraction.

Of course, in the colder months, the number of visitors to the labyrinthine city decreased dramatically. With one exception. In the days leading up to carnival, people began to flock to Venice again, anticipating one of the largest parties in the world, rivaling Mardi Gras in New Orleans,

Carnivale in Rio, and other celebrations around the globe. Each year, beginning the Friday before and lasting until the wee hours of the morning of Ash Wednesday, locals and tourists alike became part of the event, a part of the tradition and the legend. They lost themselves behind masks and costumes.

But this year they weren't alone. Behind masks and costumes, behind the revelry, the tradition, and the legend, others also hid. Some of these others were human, and some decidedly not. The humans posed as tourists, staying in hotels and inns, shopping during the day, even as their masters slept on in cellars and basements, darkened hotel suites, and luxurious private homes. They weren't there for carnival. The humans had come for another celebration, masked by the Venetian festival, a gathering of their shadow masters, the Defiant Ones.

Like many such gala events, there was to be a feast.

Yet, if all of the Defiant Ones who attended these events were to feed on the local community, the results would bring immediate attention from the international media, a startling and painful spotlight that no amount of political manipulation could turn away. To avoid such attention, the shadow dwellers flexed a worldwide muscle of conspiracy and control, created a network that brought together, over the course of each year, the humans who attended their gathering in the guise of tourists.

In reality, they were volunteers, there for no other purpose than to serve their masters, their gods. Imagine, if you will, a consensual agreement between humans and their cattle, an idea both ridiculous and sublime. This was the nature of volunteers. More devoted than any cult, only half of them lived to return another year, and those only so that they might proselytize, beginning the cycle anew.

Of course, such an extraordinary operation was impossible to hide, or would have been had it not been for one factor.

Humanity never notices that which it does not wish to see.

Corruption, conspiracy, and death.

Beneath the surface of the revelry of carnival, in the shadows created by the extra light such excitement throws on the city, death lurked, barely acknowledged. Locals and tourists alike felt it, and it bred a cautiousness that was absent the rest of the year. People traveled in large groups and kept off the streets in the early-morning hours. They fought to rise above the feeling waiting there in the shadows; they turned away or closed their eyes if those shadows were momentarily illuminated. They refused to see. This year it was Venice. The year before, New Orleans. Before that, Milan, Rio, so many others.

Venetian authorities, and those of other cities that had experienced the gathering, were forced by circumstance to overlook and often cover up the mass disappearances. To their nervous, yet grateful relief, most of these disappearances were noted only by hotel managers, whose clients never checked out. Only rarely were inquiries made by governments or families of the missing.

For the volunteers, who hoped so deeply that they would die in Venice, carnival was a religious experience, a time of worship, a pilgrimage to Mecca. Oh, to be chosen, to be among those worshipers handpicked to serve the needs of the Defiant Ones . . . but of course, not all of those who turned up missing were volunteers. . . .

"I come all the way to fuckin' Italy, an' I can't get away from the fuckin' slants," the burly man said, just a little too loud.

The club itself was very loud, Euro-dance music pouring from the speakers mixed with American R&B. Venetian youth rubbing elbows and other extremities with visitors from around the world. The club was very loud.

And yet this dickhead was talking loud enough for Shi-er Zhi Sheng to hear him even over the noise.

"I'm telling you, Marco," he insisted to his tablemate, who was obviously a local, "people say there's a difference. There's so many different kinds now, y'know. You got your Thai and your Vietnamese. Your Cambodians, Koreans, Filipinos. You got your friggin' Eskimos and Hawaiians, who are Americans, fer chrissakes. And of course, you got your plain old Japs and Chinks. They're all friggin' slants. Lyin', cheatin' economic goddamn terrorists, bringin' the U.S. to ruin. Jesus, and once I thought the blacks and Spics were had. America would be a paradise if it was just them we had to worry about! No way, man. Ferget about movin' to the States. Hell, the rest of the family may end up movin' back here with you."

The bigot paused for a breath, then his eyes zeroed back in on Sheng, the motivation for this diatribe.

"'Course, if you keep makin' the same mistakes we did, Italy'll be crawling with the yella bastahds soon enough. And then where the fuck are we all gonna move to?"

Yes. Shi-er Zhi Sheng heard every word the bigot, whose name was Richie, said. And this was a big mistake on Richie's part. As a matter of fact, it was, by any standard, the biggest mistake in Richie's life.

Richie, who didn't even need a last name, was well over six feet—though Sheng couldn't tell exactly how tall while the jerk was sitting down—and weighed approximately two hundred and seventy-five pounds. He had definitely lifted weights at one time, and though he wasn't fat, his muscles had become sheer bulk.

Sheng, on the other hand, was roughly five-foot-five. The hair at his temples was gray and his build was slight. It was all he could do to keep from leaping across the crowded bar and tearing the man's head from his neck.

It wasn't just the man's bigotry and ignorance that spurred him on; he was distraught over the death of his mentor, his blood father. In turn, it wasn't just the presence of the crowd that held him back. After all, he had others to worry about. Within the space of days there would be thousands of the Defiant Ones gathered here, and he could not be, *would* not be, the cause of their undoing.

And yet he couldn't just sit here. He had to feed. And after hearing the drivel of this American ox, he knew that he would have to feed on this man. Not for hunger; for pleasure. He wanted this one for no reason other than the joy he would feel at bringing about his death.

The hell with it. Even these Italians have seen a lame Bruce Lee movie on "Kung Fu Theatre," or whatever they called it in Italy. Either that, or they'd probably seen that foolish old David Carradine TV program. He could have all the fun he wanted, and because he was a "slant," no one would think to wonder. Alexandra could vent her grief over Karl's passing in her way, and Sheng would mourn in his.

"Hey, fella!" Sheng shouted, without any trace of accent.

Richie turned around, eyes wide, completely taken aback at being addressed by this, the object of his hostility.

"Richie, right?" Sheng asked, grinning like a fool and sticking out his hand for a shake.

Richie shook, too dumbfounded to respond.

"Since you seem to know everything there is to know about us slants"—he paused—"I'm going to give you a chance to leave this establishment in one piece."

Richie was still stunned, but now he did grin back. It was a nasty grin, one that took a fierce pleasure in any call to violence.

"You have three guesses to figure out exactly what kind of 'yella bastahd' I am. If you have not guessed correctly by then . . . well, in terms with which I am certain you are familiar, I'm gonna beat the living shit out of you."

The dancers near them stopped moving and a crowd began to gather. Richie could not believe that this little gook had called him out. He didn't like to start things, but if the scrawny bastard had a death wish, he was more than happy to oblige. He could feel the adrenaline rush that always accompanied the onset of violence—the muscles in his back tensed, he stood to his full height, and a quiver of anticipation ran through him.

"Fuckin' Jap," he said softly, still grinning that meat-hungry grin at the man only a foot and a half from him.

His fist whipped through the air in a lightning-fast roundhouse—he'd done this before—and connected solidly with . . .

A beer glass. Which shattered. And if it hadn't, it might have been broken by the sound of his shrieking.

The guy had brought up his mug to meet Richie's punch so fast the big man hadn't even seen it. He had aimed at the guy's face, but when his fist got there, the Asian's head had moved. Fast.

"Wrong," the short man said softly, and now the fighters were drawing a crowd. Though many of them spoke little or no English, the sound of Richie's wailing as he cradled his bruised and bloody knuckles did not need translation.

"I'm not a Jap. Two more guesses."

And he smiled. It was the smile that got to Richie.

"Chink!" Richie screamed as he flew across the few feet that separated him from his prey, only to belly flop on the wooden floor of the club, knocking the wind out of him.

"No," Sheng said, sitting calmly back down on one of the barstools. "I am not a 'Chink.' One last guess."

As Richie got up, sucking air back into his lungs, he was more shocked by the Oriental's balls than by his speed. It took guts to turn your back on a tank like him, no matter how fast you were.

It was humiliating. Not just what the guy'd done to him, but this little peckerhead turning his back on Richie. That just didn't fuckin' happen. Never would happen back home, nobody had the stones.

He stomped up behind the shrimp, expecting him to turn around any moment. But he didn't! He kept ignoring

Richie like he wasn't there. He was dead.

"Vietnamese gook cocksucker!" Richie screamed, and reached for Sheng's head . . . and the next thing he knew, his own forehead was bouncing off the hard wooden bar.

Richie slid to the floor and lay there for a moment. His vision wavered, black spots in front of his eyes. He scanned the crowd: the bimbos and the dancing fags, MTV on screens you couldn't see through the smoke, drinks tipped back. And here came his worst nightmare, gliding over to him as if floating. A goddamn gook who could whup his ass.

Shi-er Zhi Sheng leaned over the fallen man and whispered in his ear, "Wrong again, friend Richard," then dragged a long fingernail across the man's cheek, cutting deeply. The blood began to flow.

Richie's vision began to waver again, yet he could see the crowd part for Sheng, the men especially keeping a respectful distance. The dancing resumed as Richie watched, hatred growing and raging, as the man disappeared among the bodies. He wanted to stand up, to call back the dirty fighter, have a fair chance at taking him apart, piece by piece.

Of course, he didn't dare.

Over an hour later the blood had crusted over on his head and the crowd had dissipated. He knocked back the sixth and last shot he'd had since he'd lifted himself up off the floor. It would be dawn soon, and Venice's only all-night club would be closed. It was only open this week because of the upcoming carnival.

He slid off his stool, paused for a moment to steady himself, and headed out the door, wrapping his coat around him.

It was cold. They said Italy was always warm, but that was tourist bullshit. It was just as cold in Venice as it was anywhere in New York during the winter. And even though the sun would be up soon, it was still black as sin outside. It's always darkest . . . whatever. He couldn't see a damn thing, could barely read the names of the small alleys he stumbled down. And the mist didn't help any. It swirled all around in the dark, clouding what few lights there were and making it impossible to see to the next corner.

"Actually*ly*, it wasn't a fair*fair* game*game*," came the voice, drifting out of the mist from everywhere and nowhere.

"How could a fool*fool* like you*you* have guessed the Yun Ling*Llng* range, separating Tibet*bet* and Sze-Chuen?"

Richie spun around, and around, like a dog chasing its tail. He wasn't listening to the words, only the voice. He'd never been very smart.

"But then*then*," the voice came again. "You were nev-er*ver* supposed to guess*guess* correctly*ly*."

And the wet mist swirled around his head.

It had teeth.

"*Everyone's* here this year," Alex said, her eyes communicating her disbelief. "Shit, I just saw Genghis and he's the oldest I've ever met."

"There are older," Sheng said quietly, turning his face away from his lover's so that she would not see the concern there.

"I know that. I'm not an infant."

"I'm not suggesting that you are. What I'm saying is that there are older members of our race here, in Venice, right now." He turned to look at her, and though he tried to hide his feelings, she could easily see how disturbed he was.

Alex went to him, a tall statuesque naked black woman comforting a short, thin, apparently aging Asian—a strange sight to be sure, though no mortal eyes could see in this darkened basement that to them was bright as day. They lay down together on the soft mattress, next to the stone wall. Outside of that wall a canal flowed. Though they had nothing to fear from it, the proximity of the water made them shiver, cold in a way no chill wind could ever make them.

"Why?" Alex asked, hoping he had an answer. "Why are they all coming this year?"

"It's Karl."

"Karl wasn't that old, they couldn't all have known him!"

"No," Sheng said, finally looking, really looking at her. Finally addressing the concerns they both felt. "They're here because they're scared, just like we're scared. I wouldn't be surprised if Aurelius showed up, and maybe one or two—maybe a dozen others we've never even heard of. They're afraid because of what happened to Von Reinman, and to Barbarossa and to Franco."

"They're still not sure about Franco," Alex insisted.

"You get the point."

They were quiet again, lying together, mourning the loss of their father, friend, and mentor, Karl Von Reinman, whose death they witnessed through their mind's eye, and whose killers they had recognized unmistakably.

Shi-er Zhi Sheng broke the silence. "How deeply must that traitor Octavian have affected Karl for him to think he could survive in the sun?"

"But he did survive, for a time," Alex reminded him.

"Testimony to his strength and age, but he should have stayed in the house." Sheng shook his head.

"He would have died along with Una," Alexandra said with feeling. "What good would have come of that?"

"He died anyway!"

"But at least he died trying to escape," Alex said.

"Bullshit," Sheng snapped. "He died pulling a fool stunt because Octavian filled him with lies and that load of drivel about a 'moral code for our kind' or some such. If Karl had stayed in the house, he might have had a chance. But Octavian had him believing he could survive outside.

Dammit! We should have killed Peter when we had the chance. Almost a hundred years later and he's still causing problems."

"It's not Peter's fault and you know it," Alex said, getting annoyed. "You're projecting your anger at Karl's death onto him. If you want to blame any of our kind," she growled, becoming angry now, "blame Cody October. I'll bet his pulling that renegade shit was what centered the Vatican's attention on us again. If it weren't for him, Von Reinman would still be alive today, Barbarossa would still be alive."

She was crying now, and Sheng wiped the bloody pinkish tears from her eyes with his fingers, pushing the hair away from her face and kissing her forehead. Alex lay her head on Sheng's chest.

"This is the first time"—she sniffled—"since Karl brought me to this life that I've cried. I didn't think I could do that anymore . . . didn't think *we* could do that."

"Me either," Sheng said, thoughtful for a moment. "Listen," he continued, "I don't even know if Cody's still alive, but if we find out he is, believe me, we'll hunt him down and get some answers, and we won't be the only ones on the trail. But right now we've got more important things to worry about. The assassinations are getting more and more frequent. I don't know how the church is finding us, but finding us they are. Over the next few days we network, have a good time, make contacts with the eldest among us, see who's here. We let everyone enjoy carnival, enjoy Valentine's Day, but when Tuesday's over, we call a meeting. We've got to either go underground or go to war, and it doesn't look like going underground would help much."

"So it's war, then," Alex mused, shaking her head. "I never thought I'd see the day. I never thought the church would chance it. And I find myself wishing Peter were here, and I sure as hell never thought I'd say that. He was the best of us when it came to this life. A warrior prince he was born, and as much as it seems to have left him, I doubt he's able to betray his own blood, his heritage, as easily as he did the coven."

"That's the truth"—Sheng nodded—"though I'm loath to admit it. And if that book holds in its pages what Karl believed was there, we'll need Peter even more."

"He didn't even call when Karl died," Alex said.

"Bastard."

9

IT'D BE A FEW DAYS BEFORE OLD MANNY
Soares would be able to start pinching nurses' butts, but
in the meantime, he was determined to get an eyeful. Ever
since he'd woken up several hours earlier, he'd been floating between drug-induced nirvana and a very special kind
of pain. The kind that doesn't fool around but comes right
on up and says, "Hey, fuckhead. You're not from around
here are you?"

Manny turned his attention back to the TV set. Unfortunately the injury to his left hand prevented him from
adjusting the volume or changing the channel. The nurses
had to do that for him, on top of everything else. Which
wasn't that big a deal, considering how much he slept.
He supposed that at this wee hour of the morning, his set
wasn't even supposed to be on, but Carmela, the night
nurse, liked him, and knew he'd be floating in and out
all night. He wasn't really sure of the time, but Cary
Grant played the dapper businessman in glorious black-
and-white on TV38's late late show. Also, he didn't like
the room to be too dark. Darkness led to thoughts of Roger's murder, and the guy he'd seen, the bastard who'd shot
him. The flickering of light from the late show broke the
darkness, sapped its strength, and kept his mind off the
nasty thoughts. For the moment.

His attention span was about ninety seconds, and he

began to slide again. Down, down into that liquid plane where the brain floated and the eyes sank. He was about to drop anchor in that softly rolling ocean when he heard it.

At first he ignored it, the clattering sound in the hallway, which he of course did not recognize as anything but a disturbance in the water. But when it came again, it could not be ignored, followed as it was by the click of the door handle and the turning of the knob.

This time there was no buzzing at the door, only an insistent knocking. This time she did not drift slowly out of sleep, but snapped immediately awake. This time it could not be Peter at the door, because he was on the couch *(rejected you)*. This time Meaghan was worried, but not scared. Even if Peter had rebuffed her advances, his presence lent her an assurance that was invaluable to her at this moment.

They had found Janet's body. She was certain of it. She could think of no other reason why someone would be knocking on her door at five o'clock in the morning. Not only that, but wasn't this the way she had envisioned it from the moment she realized that Janet was missing. Janet, the only person in the world she had ever been in love with, disappeared without a trace, and so of course it's only natural that the police would show up at five o'clock in the morning to tell her they'd found the body so she wouldn't learn about it on the morning news.

At least Peter was here. At least there was that. Even though he had turned her away, in her heart she knew that he had not done it for lack of desire. She could feel that there was something else holding him back, and as soon as she found that something, she would destroy it, leaving him open to whatever their obvious lust for each other might bring.

And maybe now that she knew the worst possible news awaited her at the door, maybe now she needed the glimmer of positive thinking that Peter represented.

She wiped sleep from her eyes as she entered the living room. Peter was already on his feet when she came in, reaching for the holster draped over an armchair and covered by his jacket. He looked at her, worried as well, though she didn't see her own certainty at the knocker's identity mirrored in his eyes. Rather, she saw a fierce curiosity. She shouldn't wonder, though; it had been a long night for both of them, but especially for Peter. And one way or the other, it was about to get longer.

Though she didn't realize it, her lack of sleep had put her in an almost trancelike state, so that when she went to draw back the dead bolt on the door and Peter slapped her hand away, she actually looked at him with wonder on her face, about to ask him what the hell he thought he was doing.

His look stopped her. And brought her to reality.

"No buzzer," he hissed.

That's right, Meaghan thought, you stupid bitch. No fucking buzzer and here you are sliding the dead bolt back when it could be just anyone, including the guy Peter was supposed to be here protecting you from.

She took a deep breath as the knock came again. Peter clicked off the safety on his gun and held it pointing toward the ceiling as Meaghan had seen detectives do in so many movies. Ah, another piece of TV myth confirmed. But I'm stalling, she knew, and only spoke when urged to do so by Peter's silent exhortations.

"Who's there?" she asked in a loud voice, louder and stronger than she would have expected. And the knocking ceased.

"Meaghan?" came the voice from the other side of the door, soft and feminine, almost a whisper.

Peter shot her a questioning glance.

"Meaghan, let me in," the voice came again, pleading in that low whisper. "It's cold out here."

"Holy shit, it's Janet."

She and Peter exchanged shocked looks as Meaghan

slid back the dead bolt, though she couldn't help but note that Peter's hands were still wrapped around the pistol he held in the air.

She pulled open the door, wide-eyed as she took in the figure standing in the deep darkness of the hall.

"Janet?"

In the moment between regaining what passed for full consciousness for him these days and the opening of his hospital-room door, Manny had felt an overwhelming sense of dread seize him. He felt cold, colder than any drugs could make him, colder than his Anita's feet would get on a winter night.

And then the door opened and in walked Carmela, backlit by the harsh lights in the hall, and that cold started to turn back to a dull throbbing heat. Though he barely noticed it, the chill did not disappear entirely.

"Manny," came her beautiful voice, silken, with an accent that was, in itself, enough to warm any man.

She carried a metal tray upon which sat a plastic bed-pan and water pitcher, as well as what appeared to be the medication for several patients. "I'm sorry about that noise. Had a little accident. Then I figured it prob'ly woke you up, so I thought I'd come in and say hi."

She bent over to fluff his pillow and gave him a long view down the front of her uniform.

"Hi," he said weakly.

"You like that peek?" she asked, and smiled a naughty smile. "I can see that you do." She laughed aloud as she motioned to the erection under his sheets. "If you're a good boy, I'll let you get a better look."

He was stunned into silence for a moment. "As soon as I'm a little better healed, I might take you up on that offer," he said, though he was finding the possibility pretty tough to believe.

Carmela picked up the TV remote control from the bedside table, clicking off Cary Grant. Now the dreadful darkness was broken only by the wan moonlight spilling through the windows, just enough to see Carmela by, which in itself was enough to keep the nasty thoughts at bay.

"Why wait?" she asked him, and a few buttons later, with his jaw dropped onto his chest, he found out that she didn't wear underwear.

"Janet!" Meaghan yelled.

And the young Miss Harris came into Meaghan's out-spread arms with all the vigor of someone who'd been lost and was now found. Amazing grace, Peter thought as he clicked the safety back on his pistol and shoved it into the waistband of his pants. He closed the door and slid the bolt back into place.

"Oh God, I thought you were dead!" Meaghan sobbed, sniffling into Janet's coat. "Jesus, you stink. Where the hell have you been?"

"Your dad's been half out of his mind," Octavian said, his eyebrows furrowing as he looked at her.

"Oh, Peter," Janet said without even turning around, "you're such a silly goose."

She giggled, and it came out an awful gurgling noise. Meaghan laughed right along with her, looking up at Peter with smiling eyes, so happy to have Janet home. He knew then how deeply Meaghan felt for the other woman, and that disturbed him even further. Try as he might, he couldn't force the pieces of the puzzle where they didn't fit. And there were a whole bunch right in this room that didn't fit.

"Where have you been?" Peter asked her, and this time she did turn around.

Even in the dim light that streamed from the hallway and Meaghan's room, Peter could see the hollow look in Janet's eyes. Her experience must have been traumatic to create such a haunted gaze. But even that observation didn't ring true. She looked around her like a blind person looks, turning her head to direct conversation to a person or to signal her attention, but not following anything with her eyes. And she did smell, that was for sure.

"I was lost."

"Lost?"

"Just lost. That's all I can really say."

In the back of a garbage truck, Peter was beginning to think, and the stains he could see on her dark jacket didn't do anything to kill that theory either. Of course, all of these things added up to about nothing. Here was the woman herself. In the flesh. Of course she'd have a story to tell, and might be hesitant to tell it with him standing right there . . . but that was the kicker, wasn't it?

That was why he knew something was way off with this whole situation. Several hundred years of watching people gives one a unique observational ability, but that didn't mean squat compared with the blatantly obvious.

Janet hadn't looked at him as she came in.

She hadn't turned around the first time he'd spoken to her.

She had known who he was immediately, recognized him right away out of what could only be the corner of her eye. She had felt comfortable enough with his presence to act like he wasn't even there, comfortable enough to call him by his first name. She didn't seem at all surprised that he was in her apartment at five in the morning.

Recognized him right away. Her father's buddy, the detective. No problem. Understandable, right?

Wrong.

Peter rarely let his picture be taken, and he was certain that that Frank Harris had never had any photo of him.

And they'd never met.

Manny Soares was still struck dumb with awe as Carmela walked, naked as a jaybird, to his door and turned the lock. When she faced him again, her grin was almost too wide for her face. Her hands ran over her body as she strolled to the edge of the bed.

"Baby, look at that," she whispered with obvious pleasure at the sight of his erection, which had become even harder (if that were possible) under the sheet. She pulled down the hospital whites and looked longingly at his groin.

"I don't think I'm up to this," he said, shocking himself with how truly he meant that statement. He was in no condition to handle a real fucking. A gentle blowjob, maybe, but not much more.

"I'll be nice to you, Manny. Very nice."

One hand started to jerk him off, real slow and deliberate, like she was truly enjoying the feel of him in her hand. Her other hand went between her own legs, and he could hear the damp, sucking noises her fingers made as they pumped in and out.

God, he thought, she was so wet already.

Carmela climbed up on the bed and straddled him, being as nice and gentle as she'd promised. Though the movements of the bed caused him pain, the drugs helped, and she moved awful slow. When Carmela eased down onto his cock, Manny was in ecstasy.

There was a little more pain as she held on to his arms to steady herself over him, but he fought it back easily now. Being inside her was overwhelming, and his only regret was that even if she hadn't been holding them down, his arms didn't have the strength to reach up and caress those amazing breasts. She raised and lowered herself on him very delicately, and that in itself was bringing him to the edge.

Carmela reached down and pulled up his johnny, which was simple, as the hospital gown was open in the back. She drew it up to reveal the wound, nicely closed by the doctors and covered with bandages. He worried for a moment that their activity might open the wound . . . but only for a moment.

Then Carmela stuffed the bottom of his gown into his mouth, returning her binding hold on his weak left arm as he tried to reach for it. *What the fuck?* This wasn't a part of the plan. His muffled yelling was weak to begin with; with the cloth in his mouth, it was nearly inaudible. Carmela kept riding him with that slow, hot rhythm, but now he'd had enough. He was afraid, and with his fear, the pain returned.

Only then did he see, stepping from the shadows by the window where he was sure there'd been nothing only moments before, the priest.

And his smile was the widest of all.

Normally Peter would have looked and looked for some kind of logical explanation for Janet's reappearance, bizarre behavior, and instant recognition of a man she'd never met. But this was different. Not only could he smell it, he could feel that something was wrong. It became more tangible by the moment as he became more awake, and now he looked even more closely at the stains on her jacket, especially a huge stain in the middle of the back, which appeared somehow to be growing.

He moved toward the overhead light as Janet whispered something softly to Meaghan, and the two of them laughed a lovers' laugh. Meaghan was obviously happy to see her friend, though the smell had moved her a few inches farther away than when they'd first sat down on the couch. His hand was on the switch.

"Janet?" he asked.

"Peter, what is it?" she said with a huff as she turned toward him, her hand firmly holding Meaghan's arm.

He turned on the light, Meaghan yelled, and he drew his gun as they realized, simultaneously, the source of the stains and smell.

"Bad move," said the thing that had been Janet Harris while it was alive, and Meaghan screamed as the thing stood up, pulling her, struggling, with it.

Peter aimed his gun at the thing's head. Though he'd never killed one before, he'd heard from some of his kin that the movies were right. There was but one problem.

"Not that that gun could hurt me, but if you don't put it down, I'll rip her head off," the thing said, and Peter's new knowledge of its nature allowed him to truly hear for the first time the hollowness of its dead voice. The stench of it was far worse than before, and now it occurred to him that all of its actions, its words, were not its own—that no undead creature could so resemble life without direction through some other agent. That's why it had seemed like a blind person. Somehow the thing was being controlled by a second party, and now Peter had a pretty good idea who, though he did not have a name for the priest.

His actions were not a matter of choice, but necessity. He dropped the gun.

The moment it hit the floor the creature's jaw was dipping toward Meaghan's neck. She screamed and struggled.

"This isn't real!" she screamed, though at that moment she realized those three words wouldn't make much of an epitaph.

And then she screamed again. No words this time, only agonizing wails. She looked down to see the furrows torn in her arm, bleeding freely on her carpet, and then shook the mist from her head as she realized that she was no longer captive. She turned, holding her wounded arm, to see Peter struggling with her insane roommate on the floor, her conscious mind attempting to deny what was obviously, impossibly true.

Peter's fist buried itself in the dead thing's stomach, coming up with something rotten, torn from the inside. The creature's hands ripped easily through Octavian's shirt, and Meaghan nearly fainted as she saw chunks of flesh ripped from Peter's bare back. She turned away.

"No, No, No, NONONONONO!"

She could not watch this thing.

And then the growling began, and at first she thought it was the thing, the creature, the dead woman on the floor.

But it wasn't.

The sounds of struggling slowly ceased as the growling increased and now Meaghan *had* to look.

No, she wanted to look. The hysterics were over. She had been waiting her whole life for something to happen to her. If she was going to die, she wanted to see whatever this thing was.

If she was going to live—well, she still wanted to see it.

She turned.

The wolf was enormous, the largest Meaghan had ever seen, though she'd never seen one outside of the zoo. It used that bulk to hold down the still slowly struggling corpse it stood astride. Its muzzle was buried in the dead thing's neck and its teeth were obviously worrying bone.

There came the snapping sound of something both wet and dry breaking, and the thing under the wolf stopped moving. The huge, gray animal turned its head from its kill and vomited up whatever of the dead thing it had swallowed, whether it had done so intentionally or not.

Meaghan could only stare; her thought processes had stalled entirely.

Finally the wolf moved away from the body of Janet Harris, her friend, her lover, her would-be murderer. The wolf looked up at her, and in that moment she knew exactly what was going on, and exactly who was looking at her.

Meaghan did the only thing she could. She turned and went quietly to her room, shutting the door behind her. She wrapped her freely bleeding arm in a wet towel that had been hanging on the standing mirror in the corner. She pulled out her metal wastebasket. It had a pretty yellow-and-red floral print on the side, but she didn't think about that at all as she puked into the can.

How? That was all she could think about.

And, of course, opening her bedroom door at some point.

• • •

Now Manny was well and truly screaming behind the gown stuffed in his mouth. And struggling as well as his body could. Fuck the wound! A valiant thought, but his struggles ceased after only a moment. He was spent. The priest was there, smiling. Carmela was there, smiling, riding him still with that steady rhythm.

"What others call cruelty," the priest said softly, "I define as the highest and purest form of art."

And then the true pain came, and Manny had not the voice to shout.

His eyes bulged with his agony as he watched the smile fall from her lips and her face turn into a rictus of her own pain. The nurse's stomach bulged and those gorgeous breasts heaved and sweat poured from both of their bodies.

Manny realized he was crying.

Carmela's stomach continued to bloat further outward, obscenely pregnant, until Manny heard a tearing sound and looked down to see her ripping apart, to accommodate an unnatural birth. The thing that appeared from inside her was dark green, almost black, and boiling with pus. Its body was a small mass of rotten flesh, with only two malformed limbs. Its head was larger than the main body itself and had two long, thin hornlike protrusions of a lighter green and a mouth, filled with razor sharp teeth, which were in turn attached to Manny's penis, as if it were some freakish umbilical cord.

Carmela's body slumped back, sliding off the bed, already dead as the thing she had spawned finished gnawing its way through Manny's cock and swallowed it without chewing. Though he knew the priest was still there, he could not take his eyes off the thing, off the wound it had left. The pain was worse than he had ever experienced, and he was certain that if he had not had heavy drugs in him, he would have fainted before now. He should've been so lucky.

The demon used its meager limbs to drag itself up his chest. As it reached his wound the little demon paused, tearing away the bandages to reveal an already reopened hole. Manny hadn't even felt it, and that, more than anything else, sent his voice soaring behind the gag, shrieking at its peak, which was barely as loud as his normal speaking voice at this point.

The thing bent its head, and what had first appeared to be horns now proved to be feelers of some kind, as they wavered and moved toward Manny's wound. They plunged, stabbing into that wound for but a moment, and when they withdrew, even over the sounds of his own shrieking and crying in his ears, Manny could hear twin sucking noises, one coming from his chest, the other from the demon's horns.

It moved yet again, farther up his body, and he realized it was coming for his face.

His hand, as completely helpless as he was, began to inch up his side. He had to get the thing away from him before it reached his face. No matter what else he endured, he didn't want it near his eyes.

The feelers caressed his mouth and nose; they were sharp, somehow, and yet did not cut him. He strained with energy he did not have, that he had borrowed from some reserve, from faith perhaps, and grabbed hold of one of the demon's arms. He had to keep it from his eyes.

But then the priest was beside him, and he was too weak to resist as the killer tsk-tsked and pulled Manny's arm away from the creature. He was finished, without the energy to resist, to cry out, to struggle.

The demon's horns plunged into Manny's eyes, bursting them, and then into his brain. The thing tensed for a moment, and then relaxed, settling onto his chest as the sucking sounds began in earnest.

Father Liam Mulkerrin stood by, smiling. With a flutter of his hands, the creature, the *penangglan*, burst into a blue flame, which seemed to burn in on itself and was quickly snuffed. It was as if the creature had never been there. Such minor shadows, Mulkerrin mused. It amazed him to think that the Malaysians had once thought their kind akin to the Defiant Ones, the only shadow race that had withstood the call of Rome.

He'd been feeling a bit guilty for going so overboard with the lawyer.

But he had enjoyed it so. And now . . . he did not care. Let them find the nurse, the dead man.

He looked at the janitor's corpse one more time. He smiled.

"A true artist never leaves a work unfinished," he said.

10

"NEVER...NEVER WISH TOO HARD FOR something," Meaghan whispered as she lay, curled in a fetal position, on her bed.

For the first ten minutes she'd sat there staring at the wall, rocking herself back and forth. When Peter stopped the soft rapping at her door, the quiet pleading for her to open it, that was when she lay down. She'd been alternately silent and then talking to herself as she heard him make a phone call, then take a shower—*he's in my shower*—and now she could hear him puttering around the kitchen.

"FUCK!" she grunted as she sprang to her feet, pacing now from east to west. All her life she'd been waiting for something to happen to her, something exciting, something dangerous. She'd dreamed she'd meet an exciting guy and run off to Europe.

Oh, she met a real exciting guy. Handsome and charismatic, the kind of guy you lose sleep over. The kind of guy your thoughts drift to when you're soaping up in the shower. Definitely hot.

And he's a goddamn werewolf!

Meaghan heard the teakettle whistle, and that sent her over the edge. *Lon Chaney making fucking TEA in my house!* She opened her door, not knowing what to expect, not knowing what to say.

But the last thing she expected to find in her living room was a kind-looking old white-bearded gentleman eating Vienna Fingers and flipping through her copy of *Cosmo*.

That stopped her cold, and she took in the zipped body bag just as Peter stepped into the room with a tray of tea for three.

She was stunned speechless, and so could only stare as Peter came in and put the tray down on the coffee table, all without looking at her. He opened his mouth to speak, but the old fellow shook his head and beat him to it.

"Meaghan," he said, and she let out a breath she hadn't realized she'd been holding. Some barrier had fallen, and she felt for the first time on the verge of tears.

She wouldn't cry, though.

"I'm afraid you have me at a disadvantage, sir."

"I'm sorry. I'm George Marcopoulos. It's a pleasure to meet you." He stuck out his hand.

Meaghan could not have begun to explain how surreal it felt to be observing such formalities with a bona fide monster in the room, but she took the man's hand by reflex. He held it softly.

"I'm a doctor, a friend of Peter's," and that's when she pulled her hand away.

"Then you're . . . are you . . . oh, shit," she said softly. And then she couldn't help it; she turned her back as she sobbed quietly.

Suck it up, Gallagher!

She did, quickly, and turned back to the doctor, careful to avoid Peter's eyes, for when she glanced at them just for a moment, she saw a fear and a pain there that called to her, made her forget for a moment what she had seen.

"No," George said finally. "I am not one of Peter's race. I'm as human as you are, and the day that he saved my life, much as he did yours tonight, you can believe I was just as frightened as you are right now."

"But"—*sniff*—"he's a werewolf or something. Jesus, what the hell am I doing here?" She wanted to tell herself it wasn't real, that it was a dream or something, but she'd gone way beyond that.

"No, he's not. A werewolf, that is. Nor is he a monster. He's just not human."

"Oh, well, that explains it. That makes it all just hunky-dory, Doc! Thanks for getting me up to speed—"

"Meaghan!" Peter finally spoke, and she wanted to cover her ears, but would not.

"No!" she said, looking straight in his eyes for the first time. "You just shut the fuck up for now, buddy. I am not an idiot and I'm not one of these silly bimbos you see in the monster movies. God knows I never thought things like you were real, but sittin' in the movie theater, I always promised myself that if I ever found out there were Martians, or werewolves, or goddamn bigfoots, that I'd deal with it rationally. And that's just what I intend to do once I'm through being scared and angry.

"Again, I am not an idiot. If you'd wanted to hurt me, or eat me or suck my blood, you've had plenty of chances to do it. Jesus Christ, I *offered* myself to you a few hours ago, and you turned me down. And here I was wondering why you didn't want me.

"Then—and oh this is the precious part—then my room-mate, probably the only person I've every really loved in the world, shows up after being missing for nearly a week, and she's a zombie. And she's ready to eat me like I've never been eaten before. And that's where you come in."

"Miss Gallagher—" George began.

"And don't think I've forgotten you, good Dr. Van Helsing or whatever your name is. I'm in the middle of what I only wish was the Twilight Zone in not much more than my underwear and you've got the nerve to tell me that your 'friend' Peter is a *good* monster. Well, fuck that and fuck you. Since this is the day when reality takes a breather, I can say that to you, a kind old gentleman. I can say I wanted to have sex with your fanged buddy here, I can say I was in love with a woman in front of a man I've never met who's probably old enough to be my grandfather. I can say whatever I want, 'cause all bets are off."

By now she had a smile on her face, while Peter and George were slack-jawed and staring. She could see that whatever they'd expected of her, it had not been this. Her smile widened and she took a breath to calm down, adrenaline pumping.

"So," she said calmly. "You were saying . . ."

Ted Gardiner stepped past doctors and nurses on his way to Manny Soares's hospital room. He was a little grumpy, and a little worried. A little grumpy because he hadn't had much sleep, and because once again, he was the last one on the scene. A little worried because he was the investigating officer and he didn't have a clue what was going on. A series of bizarre murders without one damn thing to link the victims other than coincidence. The captain was going to start kicking some butt if they couldn't come up with something soon.

And then Ted was pushing past the family of the victim, and the family of the dead nurse, families the other boys in blue were having trouble keeping away from the site of the murder. Suddenly Ted didn't feel so sorry for himself. Suddenly he wasn't worrying about losing sleep or about the captain.

Just what the hell was going on here?

He was surprised when part of an answer came. He didn't know what was going on, but he knew someone who might . . . Octavian, of course. This shit was right up the spook's alley. He respected Peter, even liked him nine times out of ten, certainly often enough to call him a good friend, but he had to admit that the PI sometimes gave him the willies.

And he seemed to know a bit more about all of this than he was letting on.

It turned out that Soares had ID'd Roger Martin's killer as being dressed like a priest, and Daniel Benedict's neighbor had said the same about the lawyer's murderer. It didn't take a genius to connect them. Of course, Janet Harris worked with Benedict, so her disappearance could be easily assumed to be a part of this whole thing. Ted expected her corpse to turn up on his doorstep at any time.

But Octavian, smarter than the average bear, had been one step ahead of the cops all the way, and Ted really ought to fill the captain in on that lead. But dammit, he'd promised Peter, and Ted had a thing about promises. Besides, he probably had a better chance of finding this guy through Peter than he did with the jokers with whom he shared a uniform.

Finally, and unfortunately, Ted got a really good look at Soares. He stumbled to the adjoining sanitized hospital bathroom. He hadn't been the first one there.

George was smiling. Yes, Peter had told him the woman was strong-willed, but he'd also said she was smart and pretty, so he didn't think much about it then. But this went far past strong.

She wasn't hysterical, she was just pissed off, getting all worked up as a reaction to her fear and disbelief. And he could see in her face that she found it exhilarating.

"What I was saying," George went on, the two of them smiling at one another as if they were sharing a joke. "What I was saying was that some years ago, I would have died if not for Peter's intervention. And though it is nearly impossible for him to die, he nearly did, that night, in saving me. He's my best friend, and being a doctor, I supply him with what sustenance he needs so he doesn't have to take it from unwilling donors. We all have our secrets, and what are friends really but the people we share them with?"

George watched her as she took it all in, but she was digesting it fine. It was almost as if once she accepted the reality of the situation, logic only dictated that she see the sense of the rest of it.

"And he *is* a detective?" she asked.

"Oh, yes, certainly," George answered.

"An investigator," Peter added, speaking for the first time since she'd shut him up.

But she didn't shut him up this time. No, this time, as George opened a bag he had brought and began to disinfect and then bandage her arm, she smiled right at him and George thought he saw something being born in her eyes right then, a spirit he had never had. It was George's turn to be quiet.

"So, who are you then, really?" Meaghan asked Peter, and at first he seemed not to understand the question. And then he sat a little higher in his seat before replying, his eyes still quite serious.

"I'm sure after all this there's very little you won't believe, so the truth will do as well as anything. I was born May twenty-ninth, 1420, in the city of Constantinople, capital of the Byzantine empire. Once the capital of the world. My birth name was Nicephorus Dragases, and I'm the bastard son of Constantine the Eleventh, Palaeologus, the last Byzantine emperor.

"So, if you want to get all technical about it, you could say I'm the last Prince of Byzantium. Technically."

And, finally, he was smiling, but now George was not.

"You never told me that."

He'd known of Peter's past, even his real name, but not of his lineage.

"You never asked," Peter answered, still smiling.

And now George looked at Meaghan, who seemed mesmerized by the whole thing. He could read it in her face—the undead she could accept, monsters and death were no problem, but a living piece of history sitting on

her couch sipping tea? George knew how she felt. His
ancestors would have knelt at Peter's feet, for Byzantine
they were.

"Ah," George grunted in mock disgust, "a tidbit he
holds on to for use in impressing girls."

Carnage!
Mulkerrin loved the carnage, loved the absolute destruction of a human life. His passion for the massacre was
unmatched by any other emotion he had experienced.
In many ways, it made the fact of his celibacy a
moot point.

Yes, he had a gift. Unfortunately, his superior expected
him to separate the art from the work. Get the job done
was the only criterion, ignoring the quality of the work in
favor of the efficiency of the job. But he didn't want to
be a hack painter mass-producing landscapes, he wanted
to be a true artist.

And he did have the talent.

But sometimes it got in the way. Sometimes he lingered
a bit too long before forcing a point, waiting perhaps for
just the right slant of sunlight for the shadows he felt
compelled to portray. Sometimes he messed up.

This was one of those times.

Wasn't it enough that the janitor had survived his
first attack? Wasn't it enough that the lawyer had gotten involved, and the other girl and the detective? And
yet it could all have been taken care of. No one would
have complained that he had waited too long to savor his
art, too long to force Guiscard to give up the whereabouts
of the book. As long as all the loose ends had been tied
up, and he had been confident that they would be, before
he retrieved the book and returned to Rome to prepare for
the Blessed Event.

No. Nothing would have come of it. Another job well
done, Garbarino would have said, and he would have
retained his artistic integrity.

But that would have been too easy. The detective was the scourge of the earth, a Defiant One, and the human woman probably nothing more than his fatted calf. Had he known in advance, he could have destroyed the creature easily. Even now, with the Defiant One alarmed, he could almost certainly destroy it. But time was running out. More important, there could be no possibility of the creature getting its hands on the book.

That would spell disaster.

But Mulkerrin reassured himself, the cleanup had already begun. Once he'd realized, on his way out of the hospital, exactly what had happened in the Gallagher woman's apartment, which events had caused Liam no small amount of physical pain due to his link with the corpse, he'd begun the cleanup right away. No more dillydallying for Father Mulkerrin.

A visit to Daniel Benedict's office, through doors whose alarms he hadn't allowed to sound when broken open, revealed that the police had been through Benedict's things and, not finding anything of interest, obviously not knowing what to look for, had left everything pretty much as it was. Even Benedict's Rolodex was still on the desk. Mulkerrin found such inefficiency amusing and appalling at the same time. He would never put up with it from his own men, but he almost expected it now from others. Corruption, stupidity, and just plain laziness were the order of the day. As far as the cops were concerned, any clues to be found in Benedict's office would not be easy to find, therefore it was not worth the trouble of finding them.

But the Defiant One, Octavian, he would look more closely, and Mulkerrin couldn't allow that.

The "lightning bug" Liam conjured had done the job nicely. A common demon, an easy spell, but oh so efficient. With a flutter of his fingers and a jumble of words, he had caused the thing to appear in Benedict's office. One more word, and the creature had flared, its explosion destroying not just the office, but a rather large portion of that corner of the building. All Mulkerrin needed was a couple of days' uncertainty as to the origin of the fire. He'd be long gone by then. Not as if they could trace it to him in the first place. Not as if they would if they could.

No. He was covering his tracks. He would love to get rid of Octavian and Gallagher, but he would have to come back for them. The book was of prime importance. Any longer and he could jeopardize the efficiency of the Blessed Event, and that would be the ultimate transgression.

No, he had to get the book back to Rome within forty-eight hours, which gave him one day and night to accomplish his task.

And Guiscard. Oh, Guiscard would definitely have to die.

Ted Gardiner drifted slowly off to sleep, hoping desperately that he would not dream of the hospital. He was pleased with himself. Just minutes ago he'd called in for messages and been told about Dan Benedict's office exploding. His eyes fluttered open one last time and he grinned sleepily as he looked at the rectangular piece of cardboard on the nightstand.

Wouldn't Peter be surprised. Two could play that Sherlock Holmes game, he'd tell his friend when they met at noon to start the hunt. *The game is afoot*, he'd say, waving the card in Peter's face. His little trip by Benedict's office earlier had probably saved them hours of legwork.

His fellow officers had left everything in the office intact, but Ted had slipped that one rectangle into his pocket. His conversations with Peter had made it stick out like a sore thumb. After the explosion, Ted had realized they were probably far closer to the end of this thing than any of them knew.

It was a card from Benedict's Rolodex. On the card was a name, a number, and a hotel.

Octavian wasn't the only one who'd be surprised.

*

11

"HOW DID IT START?" MEAGHAN ASKED, HER eyes squinting with concentration, with fascination. "How did you first meet Von Reinman?"

George looked up, first at Peter, then at Meaghan. He was still amazed at the level of acceptance she had reached in such a short time.

"Memory is a strange thing for my kind," Peter said, sipping his tea. "Humans lose many things in the haze of time, but we lose weeks, months, even years. Recall is active, rather than passive. An exercise, if you will. But what memory I do have is clear as crystal, as if I lived it only moments before. Fortunately, my first meeting with Karl is still with me."

"Sort of like having it on video," Meaghan said, and George smiled.

"Not really," Peter answered, smiling as well, "but if it helps you to think of it that way, it's close enough."

There was a moment of silence then, and Peter's face relaxed, a slight smile still on his lips and the look in his eyes very far away.

"Tell us," George said, only now realizing how little he truly knew.

"It was Thursday, the twenty-fourth day of May, the year of the Lord fourteen hundred and fifty-three. The Turks were at the wall. Indeed, they had been at the wall for what seemed like forever to us then. 'Us' meant myself, Gregory, young Andronicus, and an Italian sailor named Carlo."

"Your friends?" George asked.

"Yes," Peter said, sipping his tea once again. "My old friends."

It was impossible not to notice how much he missed them.

"We were soldiers in the service of Lucas Notaras, the megadux, but we'd been assigned to assist the German, Johannes Grant, in preventing the Turks from tunneling under the city walls. Half the time we wasted covering sections of the wall supposedly protected by the troops of Minotto Bocchiardi, the Venetian—there were a lot of Italians, mostly sailors, and other Christians there, defending the city. Mainly we dug countertunnels by the Caligarian Gate on the Blachaernae Wall, dropping down on the Turks and the Serbian silver miners they had pressed into service.

"While the sultan surrounded the city's fourteen miles of wall with more than eighty thousand men, inside we numbered less than seven thousand. We'd had few casualties, but there were many wounded, and supplies of food and arms were running low. Even so, we might have held out until help could arrive; the Venetian captain Trevisano had held the Turks in the strait of Bosphorus and the Sea of Marmara; they could not pass the boom which guarded our bay, the Golden Horn. But the Turks did the impossible—they moved their ships *overland* into the Horn.

"So now we dug countertunnels and fought each new siege against the wall, knowing that the city's fate had already been decreed. That day, the twenty-fourth, had been very strange. As we worked, a procession passed us carrying our holiest icon, of the Mother of Christ, to whom the city was dedicated. Every man, woman, and child who could be spared from the walls had joined the procession."

"And they dropped it," Meaghan said. "I read about this, but I can't believe you were there."

George said nothing.

"Oh, yes, I was there," Peter continued. "Not only did they drop it, but for several moments after, they could not lift it up. *Could not lift it*. Period. Eight men tried to do so. Not only were people terrified that Mary had forsaken them, but the icon had landed on one of the men, shattering his leg, and they struggled to free him. That went on for several minutes, the statue impossible to move, and then it did, returning to its usual weight, light enough for four men to comfortably march with it on their shoulders.

"Needless to say, the procession was over. But as the people scattered, matters worsened. The sky literally split open and water poured from the heavens like nothing I'd ever seen before or have ever seen since. A flash flood washed through the city, taking several lives. Our saving grace was that rain fell on the Turks as well; otherwise that might have been the end right there.

"That night, when we had time to ourselves, my friends and I sat in the grove, drinking and sharing our fear. There the strange events continued, and that night I met Karl Von Reinman. . . .

It was a warm, bitter wine that tasted the way Nicephorus imagined the urine of oxen might. But it was all they had. The wine was passed around in silence, the four men lost in their own thoughts. Women and children and the men assigned to the task after nightfall worked steadily to repair the damage done by cannon fire during the day. Where these four sat, the light of the full moon filtered through tree limbs above them, where nightingales sang.

"Strange, isn't it?" an unfamiliar voice asked, and the four turned to see a stranger approaching.

"What, besides yourself?" Nicephorus answered.

The new arrival raised an eyebrow and smirked as if

amused and leaned against a tree. When he spoke, it was with an accent they all recognized as German. After all, they worked with Johannes every day.

"The nightingales. You would think, especially in light of what will happen here fairly soon, that they would have migrated with all the other birds. But they are still here, and they continue to sing."

"Why should they not?" Gregory asked. "Do you think they feel an obligation to the emperor, and that is why they stay? They stay because they wish to . . . who can know a bird? And they sing because that is what birds do."

"Perhaps," the stranger said, a wistful smile on his face.

"Besides," said Andronicus, "what makes you so certain the city will fall?"

At that, they all looked at him with tired eyes. He knew enough to be quiet.

"You know what else?" the stranger continued, almost as if he hadn't heard their statements. "The roses. It simply amazes me that they're in bloom."

"Roses?" Nicephorus asked.

"Yes, the roses, can't you smell them?"

"All I smell is the dung of oxen," Carlo answered, with some finality.

"All the sadder for you," the stranger said, actually looking at them all for the first time, his gaze finally resting on Nicephorus.

"Could I join you?"

"The wine is almost gone," Andronicus said, though they all knew it to be a lie.

"I am not a wine drinker," the stranger said.

After a moment of uncomfortable silence, made even more unsettling for Nicephorus by the way the stranger seemed to stare directly at him, Gregory finally spoke up.

"Well then, by all means sit down and introduce yourself."

The stranger accepted the invitation.

"I am Karl, from Bavaria," he said as he sat, and the others introduced themselves to him.

"How do you find yourself dying with Constantinople?" Nicephorus asked.

"By no will of my own, I assure you. I was passenger aboard a Venetian ship, en route from the Black Sea to the Aegean. This was in November, when the sultan had first warned he would sink any ship in the strait. Of course, he was not believed."

"Rizzo's ship?" Carlo asked.

"Yes, that's right. She was sunk, and all hands who survived and didn't make the city walls were beheaded. Of course, Rizzo was impaled."

"It surely seems," said Carlo, "that sailors have taken the hardest blows in this siege."

"That it does," Andronicus said, anger rising. "But we showed them in return. Two hundred and sixty Turks were executed for the forty-odd Christian crewmen from Rizzo's ship who were murdered. In any battle, that's a fair trade."

"No, 'Droncus." Gregory shook his head. "That's not a trade. That's three hundred lives destroyed for greed, for power."

"For life! For freedom! For God!" Nicephorus was angry now. "I won't hear another word from you, Greg. Friend though you may be, we fight to the death for the glory of God and I hope we kill every last one of those heaven-forsaken devils. We fight for all that we are, so fighting becomes what we are. If that is how it is to be, I welcome it! Let them come and see what they have made us through their evil lust."

They were all silent again, eyes on the ground, brooding and angry and afraid. All except one. Karl looked at Nicephorus Dragases with a wide smile on his face, his eyes bright with admiration.

"Well said."

Nicephorus decided he liked the stranger, whether or not his tale was a true one.

"Only faith can save us now," Gregory insisted, "the power of Christ and the Holy Mother, and the good will of Saint Constantine the Great."

"Then we're dead," Nicephorus said, for a black mood had come over him since the night before. "Heaven itself has turned against Constantinople. Greg, you remember the prophecies. Andronicus, do you?"

"The last Christian emperor of Byzantium will share his name with the first, Constantine, son of Helena," Andronicus answered, eyes downcast. He was the youngest of the group, and not afraid to show his fear.

"Wasn't there something about the moon?" Carlo asked hopefully.

"That the city may not fall under a waxing moon," Andronicus answered, hopeful for a moment.

"And last night the moon was full," Nicephorus snapped back. "Now we can hope for nothing."

As the men spoke a heavy fog, highly unusual for this time of year, had rolled through the city, and just as quickly departed. Nicephorus and the others heard citizens by the wall, wailing that the fog was a veil hiding the Holy Spirit as it abandoned the city.

"Nonsense," he told his friends.

"Ah, but they all believe it," Andronicus answered.

"They believe a lot of things," Nicephorus said. "Most of them ridiculous. I'm getting tired of the superstitions."

"God is not a superstition!" Gregory said sharply.

"You know that's not what I meant, Greg."

"Well, now the fog has lifted, the moon is full and bright," Carlo pointed out, and they all looked up.

"Up here!" the voice of the sentry came down to them, sudden and urgent.

"What is it, George?" Andronicus called back.

"Lights!" the voice came again, and they were all scrambling for the ladder.

Once they were at the top, no words were spoken. The sentry merely pointed east, across the Golden Horn, where in the countryside, far beyond the Turkish camp, the same strange green light could be seen glowing in several spots.

"Do you think," George began, "that it could be Hunyadi, the Transylvanian prince, come to our aid at last?"

There was so much hope in his words that Nicephorus was loath to answer. "Perhaps," was all he said.

"Somehow," Carlo added, behind him, "I think not."

They all stood on the wall, gazing toward the strange lights, but Nicephorus held back, thoughtful.

"My friend." Karl's voice came in a whisper. "I think we should talk."

"About what?"

"Revenge. The future."

"We have no future, here," Nicephorus said flatly.

"My point precisely," Karl said, and now Nicephorus looked into his eyes and saw a pain and hate burning there alongside the intelligence he had already sensed in the man.

"Let's go."

They descended the ladder together and were silent for the half-mile walk to Petra, where Nicephorus had a temporary dwelling. There was a small grove behind the building, and it was there that their conversation began in earnest.

"Do you wish to die?" Karl began.

"No man does."

"Do you wish to kill?"

"Turks. The sultan."

"Do you wish to leave here?"

"If I don't do one, and excel at the other, I will leave here, yes. There is much of the world I would like to see," Nicephorus answered, and then looked more closely at his companion. The questions were upsetting him.

"What if I could promise you that you would not die, would kill many Turks, and would see all of the world you desire? Would you leave here with me tomorrow?"

"How can you promise such things?"

"Answer the question," Karl replied, amused, not impatient.

Contrary to what Karl may have thought, Nicephorus Dragases had indeed left Constantinople many times. He had traveled to Serbia, to Wallachia, to Venice, to Rome, to Russia. Despite his lack of true education, he was a very intelligent man. He knew what he faced.

"Vrykolaka," Nicephorus said with utmost certainty.

"Come now," Karl chided, "I heard you say earlier that you were tired of the superstitions."

"So I did, though I didn't know you were listening at the time."

"You were not meant to know."

"Of course not. However, I am a man who knows the difference between superstition and legend, and that most legends exist for a purpose, to represent something."

"Just so," Karl answered smugly.

"You are vrykolaka," he said again, without a trace of doubt.

"To use your logic, I am one of those who has inspired the legend."

"Well, we have established what you are, and what you offer me. Why do you ask me, and what is the price?"

"The price is precisely what you think. You die without dying. The sun is your enemy as is the Roman church, eating will become difficult, but there is plenty of sustenance in the blood of Turks, and you lose your name."

"I do not understand what it is to 'die without dying,' " Nicephorus answered. "I have ever preferred the night, and the Roman church is already my enemy. I cannot imagine not needing food, yet spilling the blood of Turks obviously appeals to me. As to my name, it is nothing. Again, why do you ask me? There are many soldiers here

who would kill Turks with you, vrykolaka."

"Yes, but how many are the son of Constantine? How many are warriors born, as you are? How many would have the courage to willingly meet death to return to the battlefield as death itself?"

There was silence as the light of the full moon tore through the trees overhead and the two beings stood face-to-face, watching each other's eyes. Nicephorus had spent his life nurturing an anger that was well hidden beneath the guise his fellows know. As often as he returned to Constantinople, he wanted to leave again. He sought something he had found nowhere in the world, something he had not been able to name. A courage, a knowledge, a power, an answer that would free him from the questions in his head, the search for a purpose, the release of the anger. The answer was clear.

"How many would have that courage?" Karl asked again.

"One."

"And that's how it began," Peter said, finishing his tea as George and Meaghan visibly relaxed, letting out breaths they had been holding.

"But there must be so much more," Meaghan began.

"Which will have to wait for later," Peter said. "We've got far too many other things to worry about for now. Another time I'll tell you what came later, and about the coven."

"But what about the sun, and the tea, and the cross, and all that garbage?" Meaghan asked.

"Well, to the best of my knowledge—"

"Whoa, back up there. What do you mean 'to the best of'?"

"If you'd allow me a moment"—he arched an eye-brow—"I'll explain."

She apologized with a scolded look and an encouraging shrug of the shoulders.

"I don't eat. I can, but I always throw it up later. Delicate metabolism, you know. I can drink most substances that aren't too strong or too thick. As George said, he supplies me—"

"How do you get away with that? Aren't the stocks so well guarded these days?"

She's right on top of this whole thing, George thought, smiling in wonder. He really admired this girl.

"It's easier than you would think. Peter can—are you sure you want to hear this?"

She nodded. George looked at Peter, who didn't appear to object.

"Well, as long as the cadaver hasn't been dead too long, I can always take a little. If the poor soul lost a lot of blood, it's even less likely to be noticed. I keep it refrigerated, and when my assistants ask, I say it's for comparative analysis. Also, Peter is unaffected by tainted blood. Alcohol and drugs in the blood are disagreeable, but disease-contaminated blood is okay. He doesn't even notice. When donors test positive for HIV, the blood is supposed to be disposed of. I get my hands on it."

Now Meaghan seemed really confused, and Peter was starting to look a little uncomfortable.

"But I thought it had to be, um, y'know, fresh?"

"It doesn't have to be," Peter said quickly. "It's much better that way, and the *(bloodsong)* . . . let's say the high is better. But it is sufficient.

"Don't be fooled, Meaghan. In many ways I *am* the monster of legend. I was born a warrior, and died a warrior. For the first four hundred and fifty years of my immortal life, I took my sustenance the way the majority of my kind do. From humans. Some of them offered it and some of them did not. For a time it seemed much like hunting wild animals. I enjoyed it."

"Why did you stop?"

Again, George was surprised. Meaghan was not stunned

by Peter's revelations, or the tone of them, only more curious.

"For several decades I had thought more and more about the hunt, and it began to hurt me inside. It was an ache of the spirit, and then I thought, perhaps the ache was in my soul. I didn't know, even as a boy in a land which had been a center of Christian faith for a millennium, even there I did not know if the soul truly existed. And now I found myself wondering again. Did such a thing exist, and if so, could such a creature as myself retain it through this dark metamorphosis?"

The three were silent for a moment, Peter gazing out the window, Meaghan at Peter and George at his shoes.

"But that's all another part of the story. I don't really want to talk about this anymore." He looked back at Meaghan. "I want you to trust me; in all honesty, I want you to like me. But I really don't want to talk about this anymore right now."

George continued to look at his shoes, but from the corner of his eye, he saw Meaghan take Peter's hand. The moment lasted until it became more than a moment, and then it was broken by the ringing of the phone.

George looked at his watch to see that it was 6:30 in the morning, and Peter picked up the phone on the second ring. He had to step over Janet's body to get to it, and that drew Meaghan's attention to the black bag. She curled up a little then, drawing her knees up under her. As Peter listened and grunted in reply to what he heard, George slid over next to Meaghan on the couch and held her hand in his, the same hand that had reached for Peter's.

"I'm sorry for all of this. We'll have her out of here soon," was all he could say, and she looked at him then, grateful.

"Thank you. If you hadn't been here, I would have thought I'd gone crazy for sure, and I probably could've convinced myself of it."

"Peter called. How could I say no? He knew I was the

only one you could talk to, and besides, he was . . ."

George left the word unsaid, but he could see in Meaghan's eyes that she heard it anyway.

Starving.

Peter hung up the phone. The news was bad, but it confirmed everything in his head.

"Meaghan, you look like you're doing much better than George or I could have expected with all this. I'm glad. But this thing is far from over. The man who killed Janet is still out there, and he used her to try to kill both of us tonight. It's obvious he didn't know of my nature, but surprise only works once. He killed Roger Martin and Dan Benedict, and that was Ted on the phone telling me that the janitor from Martin's building is dead and a nurse at the hospital also. Ted said it wasn't pretty.

"We don't have time to waste. If you hadn't noticed, the sun's going to be up very soon, and we've got to find this man before he has a chance to come back for us. All three of us need sleep and we're going to get it between now and eleven, when the hunt begins.

"The man we're looking for is a priest. Not dressed like a priest—he is a priest. The circumstances of Benedict and the janitor's deaths confirm for me that what we're dealing with is a representative of an arm of the Vatican which hasn't been known to be active in years. This man is a sorcerer."

He could see both of their mouths begin to open, to question.

"Yes, magic is real, demons are real, and we'll talk about them later. This man is very powerful and very dangerous, and no, I have no idea if the pope knows about him or not." He knew Meaghan's head was spinning, but it would do no good to let up.

"What it comes down to now is not revenge, not solving the crime or the mystery. Those things often involve patience. It comes down to getting him before he gets us. You follow?"

"Yes."

And he could see that she did. Couldn't understand it, but could see it.

"Any questions?"

"Plenty, but they'll wait until morning—until eleven. Even with all this, I don't think I'll have any trouble falling asleep. This is as close to an all-nighter as I've pulled in years, and certainly the longest night of my life."

"They can be very long," Peter agreed.

"What about . . ." Meaghan began, glancing at Janet's covered corpse before turning away and falling silent.

"You go to bed now," Peter said. "George will fill you in on the arrangements later today."

Meaghan stood and walked to the bag. She did not bend to touch it and her eyes did not linger on it. Instead, she looked back at the two men, one old and one infinitely older.

"I loved her," she said.

And the two men could not help but avert their eyes until she turned again and walked to her bedroom. When the door was closed, they went about their business, though they could hear her sobbing, finally.

After a few minutes the place was quiet.

✳

12

A LETTER FROM FATHER LIAM MULKERRIN,
Representative of the Vatican Historical Council, to His
Eminence Cardinal Giancarlo Garbarino, Special Attend-
ant to His Holiness and Chairman of the Vatican Historical
Council.

Your Eminence:

Things do not go well at all. For each loose string
I eliminate, two more seem to appear in its place. Last
night I discovered that one such string is a Defiant
One. I know not how he came to be involved with
the renegade cardinal, but he most absurdly poses as
a detective. He has apparently lived under this guise
for the better part of a decade.

Obviously, he and the woman he protects must be
eliminated. However, at this juncture, knowing that
the Blessed Event we have been working toward and
which the German Defiant One and the renegade
unwittingly conspired to postpone, knowing that the
date of that wonderful exercise is imminent, I must
take drastic measures.

I know Your Holiness would prefer that I wait for
your instructions, but I cannot. I pray to our Lord
and all those at his command that you understand.
I must act.

Today, while the Defiant One must sleep, I go to the hotel where the renegade hides. I will force from him the location of the book and kill him once I have obtained that most sacred of tomes. I will then leave Boston behind, along with two, the "detective" among them, who have some knowledge of these events which have transpired. After the Blessed Event, I will return here to Boston and dispatch these two, as well as any who might have been made to believe without the book as proof.

I realize that all of these actions are in direct conflict with your orders, but whatever punishment may come from my insubordination, I will gladly accept so that the Blessed Event may come to pass as we have planned.

Yours in Christ,
Liam

✳
13

JOE BOUDREAU HAD BEEN COLLECTING books since he was a teenager. He'd started with Ian Fleming, and now, at thirty-two, had become completely enamored with Andrew Vachss's *Burke* and Walter Mosley's *Easy Rawlins,* a hell of a long way from Bond. He'd always wanted to be a writer, had even sold a short story in college, but he didn't have the patience.

So he sold books instead. Sure, he had a college degree. He'd graduated from Boston University with honors, an English major, of course. And then he'd done what he thought he'd always wanted to do (ever since he gave up the notion of being a writer). He taught literature to high-school kids.

He quit that, too.

Yep. Joe Boudreau had earned himself quite a reputation as a quitter. Had taken guitar lessons as a kid. Quit. Played Pop Warner football. Quit that, too. Took a job in high school scooping cones at Baskin-Robbins. You guessed it. Then there was the writing, of course. No questions in his folks' mind where that would end up, and truth be told, it was sort of a self-fulfilling prophecy for him. His grandparents, his aunts and uncles, his parents, even his second cousins—they all figured Joe for a quitter.

Which of course he was.

So when he started teaching high school, everybody expected him to quit. The first year was great. He had a couple of troublesome kids, but for the most part, they were okay. He had confidence, he had passion, and he had a girlfriend, Martha. On their first date Martha had told him that she'd always said when she was a little girl that she would grow up and become a teacher, and that she would marry a teacher. They were made for each other. She shared his interest in modern writers, not just the classics like so many other bookworms.

But the kids only got worse, or Joe got tired of their disinterest, or of them, or all of the above. Martha was going for her master's at BC; she wanted to teach college.

Joe quit teaching, and Martha quit Joe. Their moonlit talks about Philip Roth and Robert B. Parker, Michael Herr and William Gibson, their love of Harvard Square, their favorite TV shows, the dog they never got around to buying (his name was Rusty), the favorite ice cream they shared when they couldn't resist it anymore, none of it mattered. It seemed Martha had put it all behind her like a drunken one-night stand, and all because he'd quit.

Not to mention the fact that she'd fallen for Paul Wilson, a tenured English professor at BC.

From that moment on, though Joe remained slavishly faithful to the family that had always made a big joke out of his lack of motivation, his only real loyalty, his only real passion, his only real friends, were the books. So there, in Harvard Square, where he and "the ex" had enjoyed so many bottles of Italian wine and viewed wonderful films in French that would later be made into terrible American films, there he opened up his own place . . . the Book Store.

And that's what it was. New and old, used or not, hard or soft, romance, horror, science fiction, mystery, and even those works of fiction with the dubious distinction of being called "mainstream"—he carried them all. But only fiction. What interested him were stories, and if he wasn't interested in something, he couldn't sell it to someone else. So no Madonna bios or nudie books, no art books, no how-to books, none of that. Just stories in the Book Store.

He did a booming business. In less than two years, it was the most popular bookstore in Harvard Square, where the only type of retail shop more popular than bookstores were ice-cream shops. (Funny, Joe didn't eat ice cream anymore.) Now, a full five years after he'd opened the store, he was a legend in the area. He'd never been happier and it had never, but never, occurred to him to quit.

Until today.

He hadn't even opened the book that lay in the locked drawer behind the cash register, but he'd seen the cover and the look on his cousin's face, and he didn't want to look inside. He'd always said he didn't want anything that wasn't fiction in the store, and he had hated to make an exception. But the guy was his nana's nephew, his mother's cousin, so what was he to say? No, he didn't want to open that book. But for the first time he'd thought about quitting.

Thank God for the children, then. For that's what saved him. Nothing gave him more pleasure, especially in light of the guilt he felt for abandoning his former students, than selling books to kids. Teenagers especially, were terribly hard to reach, and Joe took a special pleasure in recommending books to them, or helping them to locate or special-order something.

Today it was a boy he'd never seen, only about twelve years old, sandy blond hair and blue eyes. He might have been the all-American boy of yesteryear, that bizarre myth, but he was not. He was the urban-American boy of today, with torn blue jeans, high-top sneakers, a black concert T-shirt, a ring through his nose, and a skateboard under his arm.

But what he wore wasn't important.

It was what he said.

"Got any James Bond books?"

Ever the cynic, Joe gave the kid the once-over. No "excuse me," not even a "hey, mister." Just the question.

"Sure," said Joe. "The latest John Gardner is over on the espionage shelf."

The kid's eyebrows knitted then, like Joe was an idiot or something.

"No way, man. I want the old stuff. The ones they made the Connery movies from. All the other Bonds are lame. D'you got *Goldfinger*?"

Now Joe was smiling. He chided himself for ever having thought about quitting.

Eleven o'clock and all is well! At least that's what Meaghan wanted to bellow as she rolled out of bed. She had lived through the longest night of her life. Out her window she could see that it was another chill, overcast winter day. She wondered if that would make it a little easier on Peter.

Poor Peter.

She knew how crazy her thoughts were, but she couldn't help them. She'd been through it enough times since she'd woken up and lain there thinking. He was not human. Some kind of creature of legend but he was here, real . . . sleeping on her couch.

And she loved it.

She still hurt, no question about that. It would be a long while before she got over Janet's death, and not just her death but the manner of it. Something truly unnatural was happening around her, really happening. And yet, with reality as seemingly fragile as it was, Meaghan felt freer than she ever had to let the truth break loose from its moorings.

The truth. The truth was she had loved Janet more than she had ever loved anyone, and she no longer cared who knew that. They'd been lovers, but so much more, and it was Peter who helped her to see that. The truth was that she'd been waiting all her life for something to happen to her, something violent, something to which she could react with the passion and energy she had been saving like a virgin for the wedding bed, ever since she could remember. Since she'd been a little girl. Now that chance was here, that excitement was real.

And Peter was responsible for that, too.

The truth was that she and Peter and other new friends like that cop Ted and Dr. Marcopoulos were all in danger of losing their lives. They were the target of a lunatic unleashed by the Roman Catholic Church, the faith in which she'd been raised. Obviously, some of their secrets were about to be released from *their* moorings. Some truths about to be told. Only they weren't going to enjoy it as much as Meaghan was enjoying her own release.

The truth was that in one form or another, every horror story she'd ever read had a grain of truth, and everything she'd ever known about the church was a lie. Oh, ever since high school she'd thought of it as a hotbed of hypocrisy, ever since she'd walked in on her ultra-uptight religious mother ramming a vibrator between her legs only a year before both her parents were killed. But this was different. Peter didn't say there was no God.

"As a matter of fact," he'd said before she'd gone to her bedroom last night, "I can almost guarantee his existence."

She wondered about that. Wherever He was, He wasn't in church. Sure, Peter had said it was only a small sect of the church, but he'd also said it had been there since the foundation of Christianity. So maybe the pope and all the rest of the clergy who weren't involved were somewhat faithful—that didn't mean that these other guys didn't have influence when it came to matters of dogma. That would certainly explain a lot. Like why the church was still in the Dark Ages.

But of course, all of the little hypocrisies, labeling music and rerating films, all of it added up to nothing

when you factored in evil. True evil. Capital *E*. And for all
the centuries they'd been warning you against it, teaching
how to avoid it in a tone that said they were all too familiar
with it, with true Evil. And, well, they were.

Eleven o'clock and all was not well. There was a lot
happening that she didn't have a handle on. Though she
knew it would be unrealistic to think she ought to. A lot
of people were dead.

She shivered. It still had not really sunk in what had
happened with Janet. She'd seen it, pretty close up, too.
But her mind was still trying to convince her it was
a nightmare. It wasn't working. She couldn't help but
wonder how George was going to "take care" of Janet's
corpse, while also guaranteeing that she get a proper bur-
ial. Then again, he was the medical examiner.

Now as Meaghan pulled out clothes to wear—Levi's, a
man's shirt, and a cotton sweater—she looked at the clock
and realized she'd been wrong about both things.

It was also not eleven o'clock.

She carried her clothes with her as she tiptoed past a
sleeping Peter to the shower. When she was done in the
bathroom, she pulled on the shirt and pants and walked
softly back into the living room. Peter was still sleeping,
but she figured it was time to wake him up.

She stood over him for a moment, looking at his face.

Peaceful. So peaceful it was hard to imagine the savage power that lay within his sleeping form. And yet she
believed every word he'd said, and still felt a powerful
attraction between them. It was ridiculous. She kept telling
herself she ought to be scared or disgusted, but she wasn't.
Just fascinated.

Meaghan looked at the clock and saw that it was indeed
time, then bent over to shake Peter awake. Before she
could touch him, he was sitting up on the couch so fast
they almost bumped heads.

"Eleven o'clock," he said flatly, wide-awake.

"You startled me!"

"Sorry, good inner time sense."

"Good? I wish my Bulova was that accurate."

"Time to get to work."

Meaghan went to open the blinds.

"Whoa. Not yet. Give me a few minutes, okay?"

And she saw it all in that request, everything he had explained to her became clear with those few words. The pain and the struggle to learn a new existence, and then the triumph over generations of blind faith. The pain of that triumph and the courage it must have taken to make that first step, to test his theories for the first time. There were no guinea pigs for that kind of experiment.

"Whenever you're ready," Meaghan finally said, and she hoped that Peter read in that sentence all the things she had intended. She hadn't wanted to look in the refrigerator, knowing what Marcopoulos had put there for Peter, just for today's excursion. But she knew then, looking at him, that she would go to the fridge and feed it to him if that was necessary.

And suddenly she realized that it wasn't just the danger that drew her attention. It wasn't his charisma or all the stories she knew he must have lived and never told. She admired this creature . . . no, this man. Meaghan admired Peter Octavian. He had already triumphed over insurmountable odds. She only hoped that his luck, that his perseverance would hold out.

And then the phone rang, and she couldn't look at him anymore, so she had to answer it. It was Ted. The news was very good.

Father Liam Mulkerrin didn't get much pleasure from the daytime. Sunshine did not bring a smile to his face, and the mere thought of summer made him cringe—with its forever days and whiplash nights and a heat to blister even the coldest soul, summer was anathema to him.

Even now, in the winter in New England, with the sky overcast, promising snow, and a wonderfully chill wind slashing violently along the nearly empty, prelunch streets, it was still day. When he returned to Rome tomorrow, it would be much warmer, and though it could never be, he wished for a moment that he could stay in Boston. *(Finish the job.)* He'd been born here after all, though a lot more time had passed than was visible on his face, and he knew he'd been born at night. A cold winter night, New Year's Eve.

Liam Mulkerrin had never gotten much pleasure from the daytime. Never.

He appeared to be in his twenties as he walked into the Park Plaza Hotel. Oh sure, he still looked like Liam, but he looked like Liam had at twenty-three, the map of Ireland on his face and Irish eyes a-smilin'. When he approached the registration desk, the young woman behind the counter took notice. Her eyes lit and her chin tilted up in greeting before she noticed the collar and deflated just a bit. He read it all. It was so easy looking this age.

"Pardon me, miss," he said, complete with Irish brogue, "but would you be havin' the room number of me good friend, his Holiness the Cardinal Henri Guiscard?"

"Yes, Father." She smiled and emphasized the word "Father," a bit coquettish even though he was a priest. Liam knew all of these tramps had seen *The Thorn Birds* on TV.

"It's Room 624," she said after consulting her computer.

"Thank you kindly. What's yer name, lass?"

"Candy."

"Aye." Mulkerrin nodded and turned away. "'Twould be."

And enough with that accent, he thought, though he did not dispose of his youthful guise.

At the door to Room 624, he paused only a moment to mutter a spell as he turned the door handle hard clockwise. On the final word of the spell, the knob turned and he pushed, a grin glowing on his face as he considered the joys of forcing the book's location out of his traitorous brother clergyman. It would take a while. As long a while as he wanted.

He shut the door behind him and turned expectantly, but the questions, the disturbance, the fear he expected did not materialize. And neither did Guiscard.

He'd gone out.

"No," Mulkerrin said flatly, and smashed the lamp from the bureau. Its shade bounced off the wall, but its ceramic base shattered, sending shards all across the carpet. This was not a part of the plan. There were to be no complications. But Mulkerrin was not a fool. He knew that his anticipation of this moment had clouded his judgment enough that he hadn't followed up before coming to the hotel. He had checked not half an hour earlier to be sure Guiscard was there.

Now he was gone.

But, perhaps, it still wasn't too late.

Mulkerrin picked up the phone and dialed the desk. "Hello?" he said. "Candy?"

"No, I'm sorry. Who's this?"

"Ah, hello, this is Father Flanagan, I'm visiting with Cardinal Guiscard today. Candy was very helpful earlier and I thought you might be her but—"

"I'm sorry, Father, Candy's with room service. She was just filling in for me while I was on break. This is Lisa, how can I help you?"

Liam was annoyed. He knew he could have gotten what he needed from Candy. This girl was an unknown. No matter, sorcery would prevail where the simple force of his personality could not. He told Lisa that his esteemed friend was lying down for a nap, but that he had been asked to pick up the cardinal's messages for him.

"I'm sorry, Father, but I really can't—"

Mulkerrin spoke softly, several words that weren't in English, but Lisa couldn't help but understand them.

"I have the cardinal's messages right here," she said, and began to relate them.

But then Liam remembered Lisa's comment of just a moment before.

Room service.

"Thank you, lass. I knew you'd unnerstan'. But the cardinal asked me to fetch him a bottle of wine for when he awoke. Please send the messages up with the wine. 'Twill save me havin' to write them down and I'd be much obliged. And make sure it's Candy that brings them, won't you, now?"

"Certainly, Father," Lisa replied, and after she'd given her instructions to room service, she forgot she had ever spoken to a Father Flanagan.

When Candy knocked, Mulkerrin had already searched the room several times, just to be certain he would miss nothing, pages ripped from the book and held as security for instance. There was nothing. He pulled closed the door to the bedroom, to suggest the presence of the supposedly sleeping cardinal, picked up the pieces of the shattered lamp, and grabbed the two glasses from the bathroom. He placed them on top of the television.

"Ah, Candy, is it?"

"Yes, Father."

So demure. So acquiescent. She handed him the messages and he thanked her.

"You're welcome," she said, smiling. "Usually we don't deliver messages, but the manager wants to keep the cardinal happy, that's for sure."

She fidgeted, enjoying his presence in a manner most inappropriate, though she probably didn't even realize it. All of these Catholic-school girls soaked their panties around a handsome priest. Ever since grade school, girls like Candy had secretly hoped the wooden paddle would land on their behinds. Unfortunately, the paddle had been retired.

Candy showed Father Mulkerrin the label of the wine.

"Thank you," he said again, "would you mind pouring?" He motioned to the glasses, and though she seemed at first a bit uncomfortable, knowing she had to get back to work, she also smiled. She wanted to do this for him. Candy began to work the corkscrew into the top of the wine bottle.

And now the messages. From Claremont, the firm the lawyer Benedict had worked for before his untimely demise. From New Age Press—ah, Guiscard had been working quickly. From someone named Joe Boudreau, with a number.

Mulkerrin went to the phone and dialed as Candy poured. He glanced at her as the phone rang and caught her looking at him. She blushed and looked away. Her attraction was obvious.

"The Book Store," a voice answered.

"The what?" Mulkerrin inquired, almost forgetting his accent.

"The Book Store, not a tough concept. Can I help you?"

And then it was obvious.

"Where are you located?"

"Right in the middle of Harvard Square, man. Next to Strawberries and diagonally across the street from Grendel's."

"Thank you." He hung up and turned to look at Candy, who was standing, almost at attention now, waiting like a good little Catholic girl to be excused.

He stepped back toward her and picked up one of the glasses from the top of the bureau. He had something to celebrate. What had for a moment seemed a major roadblock had become simply a more public display of art.

"Please, have a sip with me."

Her surprise was undisguisable.

"Uh, Father. I'm sorry; I can't. I'm not supposed to drink on the job. I've really got to get back."

"Please. I insist." It took only a muttered phrase as he looked directly into her eyes. After all, it was what she really had wanted. What they all wanted in their secret hearts.

"Take off your clothes."

By the time Father Liam Mulkerrin left the hotel, Candace Dunnigan had been violated many times, by the wine bottle, first whole, then broken and jagged.

Certainly not a breach of his vow of chastity.

———————— ✳ ————————

14

JOE COULDN'T STAND IT ANYMORE. IT HAD been an unusually slow day thus far, and nobody had come into the store for more than twenty minutes, even to browse. As long as the customers had been coming in, he could keep his mind off that book. But with no distractions, it was all he thought about. It held a strange attraction for him, called to him somehow. He had never been particularly susceptible to curiosity until now. And yet, something inside of him realized that his growing pre-occupation with the book might not be entirely generated from within him.

Still, though, he couldn't take it. He pulled open the drawer and opened the book about a quarter of the way through. It was gibberish. Well, not precisely gibberish, but he was disappointed nonetheless. No, it was an almost indeciperable Latin, a dead language despite its status as the basis for English and the Romance languages, and one with which he had no more than a passing familiarity.

Joe stared at the page for a full two and one half minutes before beginning to read aloud what was writ-ten there. Halfway through the third sentence, he felt it.

A breeze blew through his store, though the door was closed and there were no windows to open. There was a smell on the breeze that he could not quite place, but that he disliked nonetheless. Somehow, it reminded him of all the times he'd failed, and the time when he was six years old and had gotten sick worse than ever before or since. The wind reminded him of that.

And then it stopped. For a moment there was silence. Then the first book, *Buffalo Girls* by Larry McMurtry, jumped off the shelf and hit the floor with a bang. After a moment several other books seemed to jostle about, but did not fall.

And then they all moved.

Tolkein and King slammed together and landed in a heap on the floor. Ludlum and Heinlein drifted slowly across the aisle and took each other's place. Every other Agatha Christie jumped off the shelf, turned spine in, then slid back into place. Danielle Steel, Jackie Collins, Sidney Sheldon, and so many more circled up one aisle, down the next, and around again at an ever-increasing speed.

Joe was nailed to the spot, finger in his cousin's book, jaw agape, and a single tear on his cheek.

A bell rang; he had a customer. His head swiveled from the books for but a moment, and his jaws clacked together when he saw his visitor. His cousin the cardinal, Henri Guiscard, whose own mouth now hung open.

Then the complete Sherlock Holmes slammed into Joe's skull, and he went down, behind the counter. As he sat up, rubbing his temple where blood now ran, he heard Henri's voice, raised in anger or hysteria.

"In the name of Jesus Christ, I command you. Leave this place."

Joe pulled himself to his feet to see that nothing had changed. The tumult continued unabated.

"By God, in whom I yet place my faith, I command you."

The books froze in place, whether feet or inches from the ground.

"Leave this place."

And they fell, in a pile.

Now his cousin was stomping over to him, and Joe was afraid again. The look on the cardinal's face was one of disgust, of rage. But then Joe saw something else there, a combination of fear and a sorrow so deep it warranted another name, yet had none. Henri slammed the book shut and spoke through gritted teeth, sounding more in pain than angry.

"I thought. I told. *You*. Not. To open. This book," he growled, thumping the book with the last two words.

Joe didn't know what to say. Take the guilt a family member can instill, then add the guilt a clergyman can inspire. He wanted to be sick.

"I don't, uh, suppose there's something in here that could, um . . . put them back?"

He could see the anger rise again in Henri's eyes. He'd tried to lighten up the situation—never mind that the situation was impossible, and therefore had never happened. Now he was getting shit and all because he agreed, against his better judgment, to do a favor for a relative.

"Are you so completely . . ." Henri began, and then rolled his eyes heavenward, turned, and walked toward the books on the floor. "Come on. Four hands can do the work faster than two."

And the work began, painstaking alphabetizing and categorizing. It would take a while, even with four hands. But one book would remain without its rightful place in the Book Store, Joe Boudreau knew. Whatever it was, it didn't belong there, on that counter, in that store.

Really, it didn't belong anywhere.

Peter was extremely happy to be out of the light, but even inside the hotel, he kept on the dark sunglasses that hid his perpetual squint from Ted and Meaghan. George was at work now, at the hospital, probably asleep at his desk. That's what Peter would do if he actually had a desk to speak of.

Instead he'd made an odyssey across town, in the noon-day sun *(mad dogs and Englishmen)*. Yes, it was overcast and cold, but to him daylight was daylight. Certainly, thanks to Ted's timely phone call confirming their des-tination as the Park Plaza Hotel, the journey was a hell of a lot shorter than it would have been.

"But the day ain't over yet," Peter muttered under his breath, prompting quizzical looks from Meaghan and Ted.

Meaghan had been wonderful, simply walking along-side him and only noting his discomfort by touching him on the elbow from time to time to share a look of encour-agement. And even that he couldn't believe, after the evening they'd shared the night before. She was either totally in control, and had a lot of class, or she was out of her mind. Either way, Peter figured, she was one of a kind.

On the other hand, the gravity of their situation not-withstanding, Ted had not stopped talking since they'd rendezvoused with him nearly forty-five minutes earlier. Ted alternately cracked jokes, some actually funny, and inquired quite seriously about Peter's health; what his behavior amounted to was a constant reminder to Peter that he was, indeed, exposed to sunlight. Luckily, Ted didn't require more than grunts and uh-huh's in response, otherwise Peter would have had trouble ignoring his every word. Certainly, he had overcome something that to his knowledge, none of his kind had triumphed over in many centuries, but that did not mean that there was no concen-tration involved, or that he didn't still have that nagging voice in the back of his head saying, "You ought to have blown up by now, you stupid asshole."

And of course, more than anything else, there was the fact that it hurt. Oh, yes, did it hurt. But that was to be expected. Until he could completely wipe that program-ming from his head, the pain would still be there. And he knew that the day would come, just as the day had come when he did not feel weakened by the sun's rays; one day the pain would be gone. Or almost gone, and in this one instance, almost would be quite close enough.

But now he could take a moment to breathe, and when Ted spoke, he could actually give a cogent answer.

"Your show, Peter. What's the deal?"

"We're just visiting, buddy. Unless there's a problem," he answered as they approached the portly Asian man a sign declared to be the concierge.

"And then?" Meaghan asked.

"Then we're all business."

The three of them must have presented quite a sight to the concierge, Peter realized. A tall, thin, scraggly-looking white guy with a ponytail and sunglasses; a handsome, muscular clean-cut black guy; and a pretty white woman whose every movement declared her status as a business-woman used to getting answers. The man must be baffled, indeed.

Peter also enjoyed the astonished look on the man's face when he discovered just who this strange trio were visiting.

"What room is Cardinal Guiscard in, please?" Meaghan asked in a practiced tone, cordial yet demanding, and smiled coolly at the concierge, whose name tag proclaimed him to be Jim Lee.

"I'm sorry," Mr. Lee replied, as polite as can be, "but the cardinal has asked not to be disturbed for the rest of the day. It appears he isn't feeling at all well."

"I see," Meaghan said, smiling again. "Well, we won't disturb him just now, but I would still like to know his room number for future reference."

"Ah, well, you understand it is the hotel policy not to give out the guests' room numbers. Rather, we connect visitors by house phone and leave it to the guests to give their visitors their own room numbers."

"But you've said we cannot disturb the cardinal, which would, I suppose, include a call to him on the house phone to establish his room number. Correct?"

"Just so," said Mr. Lee.

"Um-hm," Meaghan said, raised an eyebrow, and looked at Ted. "Theodore . . ."

As Ted flashed his badge and received the cardinal's room number in response, Meaghan looked at Peter and smiled.

"I'm enjoying this."

And he could tell she was. But he had a feeling the novelty would be wearing off pretty quick.

"I'm sorry if I was, uh, short in any way. Seems one of my employees has abandoned us in the middle of her shift. The, uh, cardinal is in Room 624."

They rode the elevator in relative silence, pondering the connection between a serial killer and a Roman Catholic cardinal. When the doors slid open, instincts bred through lifetimes of danger (with one lifetime considerably longer than the other) moved Peter and Ted in front of Meaghan before even they realized they were doing it. They got off the same way and began walking down the hall toward Room 624 with her trailing behind.

After Peter had rapped on the door three times without an answer, he suggested Ted return to the lobby to see if Mr. Lee could be coerced into admitting them to the cardinal's room without a search warrant. As Ted turned to go Meaghan gave the door a knock of her own, a furrowed brow the only sign of her annoyance. With the impatience of someone refusing to accept that a light is out, a phone rings unanswered, or a door is indeed locked, she jiggled the doorknob.

And looked down in shock, for truthfully, the impatient never really expect the light to work, the phone to be answered, or the door to be unlocked . . . and yet it was. Ted abandoned his quest for the concierge.

"Is there a problem for you coming in here?" Meaghan asked Ted.

"No can do without a warrant," he answered, confirming her suspicions.

"Which . . ." Peter began.

" . . . doesn't prevent *us* from waltzing right in," Meaghan finished, then smiled at him and started to walk in.

Peter's left hand was powerful, and when it landed on her shoulder, she stopped in her tracks. She turned around to see him draw his gun with his right hand, then slide past her.

"Me first," he said. "I've got a very bad feeling about this, and if I'm right, we might have reached a dead end for the moment."

When Meaghan saw the mutilated corpse of Candy Dunnigan, the novelty indeed wore off.

"Oh, shit," was all she said, and covered her mouth with her hand. Not to keep from vomiting, but to keep from screaming. After all she'd seen thus far, usual and impossible, the sight of the poor young girl before her aroused in Meaghan an emotion she had never truly experienced, something she only now discovered herself capable of: fury.

For the first time in her life, and the hell with questions of morality, she knew without a doubt that she could kill a man. Just as unconsciously as she took her next breath, she could end the life of the creature responsible for the atrocity before her. And it wasn't the fact of the murder. It wasn't the waste of a young, beautiful girl's life. It wasn't the mutilation or the savage sexuality of the attack.

It was the pleasure. The obvious pleasure the killer had taken in his work; that is what aroused the seed of vengeance in Meaghan's soul.

"And he's a priest," she whispered as Peter knelt beside the girl's body, touching one of the few clean spots to establish body heat, then sniffing the blood.

"Ted," Peter said, quite softly actually, and certainly not loud enough to elicit the speed with which Ted entered the room, took in the scene, and picked up the phone. The two men had known each other for several years. Communication came easy to them.

"Less than twenty, maybe fifteen minutes," Peter said.

Ted called in the corpse, then called the lobby and asked specifically for Mr. Lee.

"This is Ted Gardiner, Boston PD. I'm up here visiting the cardinal. I think you ought to get the manager up here right away. And you'd be doing your other guests a service if you were to come quietly and unobtrusively."

"Ted."

"Hold on, Mr. Lee." He turned to Peter.

"The phone."

"Mr. Lee, please call up on your computer all phone calls made within the past hour from Room 624 . . . no, I don't have a warrant, but if you don't bring them up, I'll throw you in jail for obstructing justice. A murderer is escaping while you jabber on the phone. Just do it. Now!"

Returning the wandering books to their rightful places in the store hadn't taken as long as Joe had expected, just more than a half an hour, really.

The priest had walked in just as they were finishing, and Joe had seen his cousin visibly stiffen at the presence of the other clergyman. He couldn't help but wonder at the cause of this reaction, though certainly the book had something to do with it.

The young-looking priest nodded a good afternoon to the two men and began to browse—had been browsing, actually, for ten minutes or so. Apparently, he had no connection with Joe's cousin the cardinal, yet the older man had not relaxed since his colleague had entered.

And now the young priest was approaching the counter, empty-handed.

"Having trouble locating a book, Father?" Joe inquired in his usual tone.

"Actually," the priest replied, "yes, I am."

"Well, if you know the author's name, I can probably help."

"There were many authors, really," and now the man smiled, not at Joe, but over his shoulder, and Joe couldn't help but look over that shoulder to find his cousin the cardinal answering this other priest's stare with his own wide-eyed version.

Curiouser and curiouser, he thought.

"Well"—Joe broke a silence he hadn't even noticed had fallen on the small shop—"if you'll tell me what genre of novel you're looking for, I can look up the title for you."

"It's not a novel, really." Still looking over Joe's shoulder.

"Not a novel? It's nonfiction, then?"

"Oh," and now the priest paused and did bring his gaze down to meet Joe's. "Yes. Most assuredly, yes."

"Well." Joe sighed, relieved now that he could get rid of this strange person, holy man or not. "That solves that puzzle. I only carry novels, Father. Just stories. No nonfiction at all."

Mock surprise dawned on the priest's face.

"Oh, but surely you are mistaken," he answered. "Surely you have one book here that is not a novel, not a work of fiction. An old book it is, and by many authors, as I've said. Certainly it may take a while to find a needle in a haystack, if the needle were in there. But really it's hidden in a pile of needles, where nobody would think to look."

At this, Joe did not know what to say. He realized that he probably ought to tell the priest to leave. He opened his mouth, but was cut off.

"Brilliant, really," the priest said, and now stood back, away from the counter, and executed a short bow, obviously directed at Henri. "An excellent gambit, had you been playing with someone who followed the rules. But, it's all for naught, I'm afraid."

Joe turned now, to stare at his cousin, certain that the book the priest was looking for was the one in the top drawer under the counter. Henri had a stunned look on his face, which at another time would have struck Joe as quite comical. And then the older man stepped around the counter and stood face-to-face with the newcomer, anger and disgust replacing the shock that had so recently ruled his features.

"Your name?" the cardinal asked.

"Liam Mulkerrin. Quite pleased to make your acquaintance, I'm sure."

"Joseph." Henri addressed him now. "Leave us now."

Joe was no idiot. As a matter of fact, he was quite intelligent. Intelligent enough to recognize a perfect opportunity to exercise his finely tuned skills as a quitter. He moved from behind the counter.

With his left hand Mulkerrin drew several figures in the air, then pointed at the door. Henri and Joe both heard it lock.

"I think not," Mulkerrin said softly.

"What are you?" Guiscard growled, shaking his head with revulsion.

"A faithful servant of the Lord." Mulkerrin smiled. "Which makes one of us."

Mulkerrin must have seen the slap coming from miles away, but he did nothing to stop it. The report echoed throughout the store, but he only smiled.

"Bean sidhe."

Mulkerrin might have replied with more than those two words, but if so, Joe didn't hear the rest. As soon as he had spoken them, the shrieking began. A wailing, howling scream that tore at his ears had been born with a gale-force wind blowing through the store. He covered his ears as the combination of wind and shrieking nearly drove him to the floor. The bookshelves were swaying at first, and then the books started to fly off them, again! Mulkerrin simply stood there, seemingly unaffected, and Joe noticed that while Henri had initially fallen to his knees, he was now getting back to his feet, hands clamped over his ears.

Henri was able to take a single step toward where Mulkerrin was standing, and Joe saw that his nose was bleeding.

"In the name of God," Henri began.

And then the first book hit him in the forehead.

On the stairs, Peter began running, with Ted and Meaghan close behind. The door to the Book Store was closed, and as Peter tried the knob Ted and Meaghan covered their ears. It was locked, and Ted put his shoulder to the door.

"What the fuck is that noise?" he shouted to Peter.

"Something I haven't heard in a while," Peter shouted back. "Get away from the door."

Ted did, then saw what Peter intended to do. "Hey, man, it's not going to budge."

But the door did budge. More precisely, it cracked into several pieces, which promptly blew back against the outer wall, catching Ted in the left elbow and barely missing Meaghan, who crouched low and followed Peter into the room.

"How the hell . . ." Ted tried to ask her, but she was already inside.

"What is it really?" she asked Peter, and then froze with her hands tightly clamped over her ears to gape at the bizarre tableau before them.

On the floor, two indistinct human shapes, nearly covered with books, more of which violently struck the pile as the seconds ticked by. Several feet beyond them, a young priest, seemingly unaffected by the noise and wind. Finally, beyond him, near the window, a gossamer, translucent figure floated, its face barely visible. Its salient feature was its open mouth, and it was from that mouth that the shrieking issued.

"Jesus," Ted yelled as he brought up the rear.

The priest looked at Peter, and all three of them clearly saw the shock register on his face.

"But . . . it's daylight?"

"The better to see you with, my dear," Peter replied, and smiled despite the pain in his sensitive ears, happy to have caught the killer off guard.

"No matter," Mulkerrin said, yet it was clear that he was greatly disturbed.

"Peter," Ted yelled again. "What the fuck is going on?"

And Peter turned to his friends, finally, with an answer. *"Bean sidhe,"* he said. "Banshee."

"Banshee?"

And then they were dodging books, mostly unsuccessfully. *Watership Down* thumped Peter in the chest and he yelled again.

"On the ground. Both of you."

Meaghan listened, though she'd barely heard. Common sense sent her to the floor with her arms and hands shielding her head. Ted, on the other hand, had always been long on courage and short on common sense. And it took courage, Peter knew, to face that horrible noise and the wind that nearly stole the breath from their mouths.

Of course, common sense might have prevented Ted from being struck in the temple by a hardcover romance, which sent him to his knees again. His nose was bleeding as he pulled his pistol. Aiming was difficult against the wind, not to mention his injured elbow, but he managed. As Ted's finger pulled the trigger Mulkerrin glanced toward the Banshee and Ted could see his lips move.

Ted fired.

It was a hurricane. As he watched, the bullet slowed until it was visible, then built up speed in the other direction, back the way it had come. As the bullet punched through his lower abdomen Ted had a moment to wonder why Peter hadn't drawn his gun.

As he lay on the ground, clutching his wound, Ted watched Peter advance on the priest, winning the struggle against the riptide in the air around him.

"That's right, Mr. Octavian," Mulkerrin said, haughty, his confidence back. "Banshee. But they prefer to be described with the language of their homeland.

"Bean sidhe."

Just over Ted's left shoulder, as he tried to stand, a second Banshee appeared. He turned to face it, only inches away, and stumbled backward as its wailing reached inside his head. Blood flowed freely from his nose as he let go of his stomach to hold his head with both hands. With a sound like the bursting of a water balloon, drowned out by the shrieking, blood began to seep from his ears.

This time, when Ted fell down, he didn't get up again.

Even over the shrieking, Peter heard Ted hit the ground behind him and saw the smile spread across Mulkerrin's lips. Octavian knew then what he was facing, not simply a sorcerer, but *the* Catholic sorcerer for this century. He himself had been branded evil so often, he could not help but recognize the true thing before him.

For a moment he was afraid. He had lived too long not to be. Then he turned to see Ted's corpse slowly being buried in books.

Enough!

Too many times he had led those humans he considered his friends to their deaths.

He had only looked away for a moment, yet when he turned, the sorcerer seemed to be ignoring him. What arrogance! For Frank and Janet and Meaghan, for all the others, for himself and for all of his kind, for Karl, Peter needed to kill this man. For all his magic, he was human.

But first, Meaghan must be removed. He scooped her from the floor, knocking aside the books that had already piled onto her. There was blood on her face, though whether from external or internal injury, he couldn't tell. Seven long steps with the wind at his back and he unceremoniously dropped her outside the door. There were people at the bottom of the stairs, but so far, none had been brave enough to come up.

Reentering the store, he covered his ears again, searing pain crushing his skull. Next to him, the second banshee flapped like a sail drawn tight, and somehow the cacophonous siren call seemed to increase in volume, and finally the two large windows at the front of the store exploded outward, sending shattered glass rocketing into the street below.

With his great strength, Peter was having trouble standing, and so he could hardly believe it when one of the two piles of books moved. Paperbacks tumbled to either side as another clergyman emerged from the mountain of fiction. Peter knew this could only be Henri Guiscard. The man was bleeding from the nose, ears, and eyes. He held his obviously broken left arm across his torso, with the right protecting it, and he stayed kneeling, bent over as if to protect his stomach as well. A glance at Mulkerrin showed him opening drawers behind the counter, but he still paid no attention to Peter, giving the detective time to help the cardinal. Peter rushed to Henri's side.

"Guiscard."

The old man nodded. Peter tried to lift him, but the man motioned to be let alone. Peter looked at him for a reason, and he and the cardinal locked eyes. He could read his fear and determination.

"Don't. Let him. Take. The book!"

"What book?"

"This book!" Mulkerrin yelled, triumphant, and held aloft an enormous leather volume. *"The Gospel of Shadows."*

His eyes glowed and his grin was a razor slash of teeth.

He looked right at Peter. Right through him really, and Peter read the challenge there. *You never had a chance, Defiant One,* that grin said. It told him all sorts of other things as well, but the most important message it delivered was this: He needed to see what was inside that book. It was obviously the reason for all of this death, and he needed to know what was so important. The sorcerer had slaughtered innocent people, including Ted, and surely was the essence of evil. For that he deserved to die. But the book added another factor. Peter had to get that book.

Mulkerrin pulled from inside his collar a silver cross, holding it before him as he rounded the counter. He started to walk toward the door, confident that Peter would not take up the gauntlet, that he was in too much pain or was simply too frightened to attack. He was wrong.

Peter sprang the eight feet to where Mulkerrin walked, forgetting the pain in his ears and the power he knew the sorcerer must control. The cross was nothing, much easier to ignore than the sun, while the silver was a bit more of a nuisance, a poison to him, but only if it penetrated his flesh.

He began to shape-shift as he moved, the metamorphosis faster than the eye could follow. In moments he had become a huge wolflike creature, standing on his hind legs. His claws reached the murderous priest, tearing furrows down his cheek. Mulkerrin screamed in rage and surprise, but did not drop the book. Peter attempted to tear it from his hands, and they struggled. Mulkerrin was far stronger than the average human, and Peter knew this must be some magical augmentation, though he'd never encountered such strength in any being other than his own kind. Still, he himself was by far the more powerful physically, and Mulkerrin had not been prepared to lose his imagined advantages.

The two creatures slammed each other into walls and shelving, Peter using his claws to tear at the sorcerer to no avail. Mulkerrin began yelling something that Peter did not understand, though he could certainly hear it. When he looked up, though, he saw that an aura of black light surrounded Mulkerrin's closed left fist, a light pulsing with sickness and death. He knew then that he was in trouble, that they were all dead.

Then he saw his opportunity.

Amid the shrieking and the wind and the flying books, the two banshees had not moved, and the first one was still standing by the shattered window, screaming. Peter and his enemy had moved within feet of that banshee, of that window. Peter shoved the priest back, holding the left arm aloft. Mulkerrin stepped back, still clutching the book in his right hand, and screamed in agony as the left passed through the body of the spirit. In seconds, ice had formed on it and the aura had dissipated in a light blue mist.

Mulkerrin kept screaming and lunged at Peter, who side-stepped and grappled with him as he went past, increasing his momentum until it carried both of them out the window, into the cloud-diffused sunlight.

And they fell, immortal detective, sorcerer priest, and the book, toward the glass-strewn pavement of Harvard Square, where afternoon shoppers were just making way for the cops. Never one around when you need 'em, Peter thought as he plummeted, and the only good one was dead back in that room. Peter held on tight, digging his claws into Mulkerrin's back, the book in the priest's hands pressed between them.

He looked down, and waited. Milliseconds ticked by, and then Peter dissipated from his man-wolf form into ethereal mist. It frightened him somewhat to metamorphose in the daylight, but there had been no alternative, and having done it, he felt more confident than ever about his abilities. Now, as mist, he watched Mulkerrin hurtle toward the pavement, satisfied that he could grab the book and make good his escape before the cops caught on, hoping that nobody really got a good look at the "man who disappeared."

Something was wrong.

Mulkerrin wasn't screaming. His face was not a rictus of fear, of a new knowledge of his own mortality.

Rather, though his face held more than a trace of annoyance, he was smiling.

In mist, Peter saw two streaks, barely visible, emerge from the window of the Book Store accompanied by a horrible noise. The banshees moved to their master's aid at a speed no human eye could have observed. In only slightly more time, Mulkerrin had been swept away amid a shrieking that shattered windows for a block, hailing broken glass that sliced into tourists and students observing the scene.

The next day, most everyone would have a different version of what they had seen, and some would even deny having been there in order to avoid discussing what was clearly a mass hallucination. Falling people do not simply disappear.

Ah, but they do, Peter thought as he drifted back through the window in time to lie down among the rubble before the cops arrived. Meaghan was bent over Ted's corpse, her eyes hard but not crying, trying to dig him out of the books. At first glance Peter thought that Guiscard, also, was tending a dead man, but then the pile of books shifted, and Peter could see that the younger man was indeed alive. Even so, when the cardinal looked up, Peter could see only fear in his eyes.

"A cairn of books," he said softly, almost to himself. "That's what this almost was. I don't know what I'd have told his mother."

"I didn't get the book back," Peter informed him.

"I ought to have a cairn myself. The book is gone? Well, for me the damage is done. For you, though—whatever it is you creatures are calling yourselves—for you, with that book back with its owner . . . well, your troubles are just beginning."

✳

15

"MY, YOU ARE GOOD, AREN'T YOU?"

Cody looked up at the red-haired woman with the British accent and was pleased. Pleased not simply because he'd managed to avoid anything resembling hard alcohol, not because he was handily defeating the casino dealer at blackjack, and not just because the woman happened to be very pretty and extraordinarily well made. No, his pleasure came from the look in her eye, an unconscious look that Cody had come to recognize well over his century and a half.

She'd made up her mind.

It was a male trait, mostly. The moment a man looked at a woman, he'd decided whether or not he'd like to put it to her, given the chance. Anyone who knew what to look for, and had half a mind to look, could see it plain as day. A male trait. Mostly. Some women, like the British redhead, also got that look.

And it wasn't just the look, it was the voice, too. Not the way she said "you are good" or the rest. But the emphasis on that "my," almost as if he had just dropped his pants for her viewing pleasure.

One look made up his mind. He was getting tired of winning at cards.

"Actually, it's not much of a challenge," he said, smiling at her and moving down one chair so she could sit at his right, then looking at the dealer. "Hit me."

The dealer dropped a six of diamonds down on his eight of spades.

"Not much of a challenge?" She laughed with false yet instructive amusement. "This is Monte Carlo, sir."

"Yes, ma'am. But blackjack is a boy's game. Poker's the game for a man. Unfortunately, in your Monte Carlo, it's nearly impossible to beat the house in poker." He turned to the dealer again.

"Hit me."

"It's not *my* Monte Carlo."

The dealer dropped a three of hearts, and his total was seventeen.

"I'm sorry, you seemed so fond of it. No, of course you're English, aren't you Miss . . ."

"Thomas. Vanessa Thomas. You're not going to play off that seventeen, I hope."

"Hit me," he told the dealer, and got a three of clubs for his trouble. The dealer went over twenty-one, and Cody cleaned up again.

"Nicely done. Now, I've told my name. You are?"

"Tired of playing blackjack. Could I buy you a drink and lose my winnings on your favorite number in roulette?"

"Well," she said, and there was the face again, the voice, "the drink for certain, but I tend toward other types of gambling than roulette."

And so they avoided roulette. As they talked Vanessa sipped white wine and Cody nothing but seltzer. They wandered from table to table, observing mostly losers who could have won if they'd quit while ahead. Vanessa was charmed by the man's unaffected-looking, long brown hair and the beard he wore, both in complete contrast to his white tuxedo dinner jacket and the rose in his lapel, as if a cowboy had been hired to play James Bond. He had . . .

" . . . the nicest eyes."

"Thank you, Vanessa. Thank you very much. That's quite a compliment coming from a woman of your caliber."

She blushed, now, at the compliment so deftly turned in her direction. "You know, you haven't told me your name," she said, and the fingers of her left hand slowly stroked the stem of her wineglass.

"Cody. Cody October, but please just call me Cody."

"Ooh. That's a wonderful name. So American. It's like something from a John "

"A John Wayne movie, I know. So I've been told."

"Actually, Mr. October, I was going to say a John *Ford* movie."

"Well, thank the Lord, a woman who knows her Westerns! Things have surely changed since I was a boy."

"Come now, Cody, your boyhood can't have been that long ago. You don't look more than, oh, thirty-five or so."

"You're being generous, Vanessa. I think you'd be surprised at my age even if you weren't erring on the side of courtesy with your guessing."

And she certainly would be surprised. Actually, even Cody was surprised. Not simply because he hadn't aged since he died in 1917, but because of another, more radical fact. He had gotten younger. Even Von Reinman had never been able to explain that one. His death had come a month before his seventy-first birthday, and here he looked like he was just approaching his forty-first. Which reminded him—he did have a birthday coming up in a couple of weeks.

But hell, he wasn't going to complain.

"You're exaggerating," she told him.

"You'll find I have a tendency to do that."

She looked at him queerly for a moment. "And how will I find that out?" she asked, serious now, with an eyebrow arched and a bit of an Irish brogue slipping out from what had been a good hiding place.

"Well, darlin'," he said, and now Cody let his accent slip out, to make her feel a little better, and waved his arms like a bad actor. "There's a coupla ways you might find out more about me. First off, I reckon I'm sick to death of this casino and these clothes and drinking seltzer and the people, present company excluded, who frequent these establishments of ill repute, dens of iniquity, etcetera, etcetera. So what that means is, I've got to go, and soon, before I decide to start an old-fashioned bar fight just to spark some excitement for the folks here.

"The question, if I may put it so bluntly, all my cards on the table, so to speak, is whether or not I'm leaving here alone. Now, please don't think I assume too much, or anything, for that matter. However, I know one thing for sure and that's that I'd enjoy a walk by the water under the moon right about now and it would be far more enjoyable if I wasn't walking alone. Whether we're walking back to my ship or back to your rooms or just walking isn't the important thing. What's important is the company and the quiet."

All the while Cody was speaking, Vanessa's smile had been getting bigger and wider, and now she was shaking her head and kind of chuckling, down deep. She looked up at him when he finally took a breath.

"Well, Mr. Cody October, like most Americans you sure do talk a lot. A lot of words when a few would do. If I'm to understand you correctly, you'd like to take a walk with me. In reply to that, I can only say that I am a bit nackered myself and should be making my way back to my hotel. If you would like to safeguard my passage there, I'm sure I can't think of a more pleasant way to end an evening."

"Oh," Cody muttered as he held out his arm for her to take, "and Americans talk a lot."

"Well, you do!" She laughed as they walked toward the exit. "Where are you from originally, Cody?"

"Originally? I was born in Iowa, but I've lived all over.

You might say my soul was born in the American West. The Old West."

"Oh. A cowboy, huh?"

"Well, no. A million other things but never exactly a cowboy. Really, I suppose I'm an entertainer, a storyteller."

"Oh, well. That's more like it. I love stories. Would you tell me a story, Cody?" Vanessa asked just as they left the casino for the moonlit Riviera night and turned toward the water. "If you're especially good, perhaps we'll make it a bedtime story."

"Careful, Vanessa. This kind of story could keep you up all night."

"I'd bet on it," she purred, and snuggled close to him.

Well, this was one for the books, Vanessa thought. Winning a bundle, he is, and she walks over, smiles at him, and quicker than you can say "Bob's your uncle," she's walking him back to his yacht. Sure, of course the first thing she thought was he was probably some pervert. But no, the look in his eyes was a healthy lust, not one that told you he was a right bastard and a lying one at that.

Not a chance. She could read men and Cody was an honest one. The only lies he told were huge ones, transparent tall tales for his own amusement and hers as well, which did her no end of good in the laughs department. She hadn't had a good one in a while. No, this Cody wouldn't lie to you, just change the subject. And it wasn't in a rude way; no, it was rather skillful actually. The conversation would just seem to float away from topics he didn't want to cover, and if you weren't paying close attention, which she was, you'd never realize he had masterfully controlled its course.

No. This guy was one for the books. Even if it were just for one night.

First thing was, he was funny. Second, he was obviously smart and well enough off. Of course, there was the fact that they had a few things in common; they didn't want to talk about where they'd come from or where they were going, they were both hiding something besides an easily identifiable accent, and they shared strong desires and were not afraid to announce them.

And finally, the most important thing about Mr. Cody October (which name, she was certain, was as fake as her own teeth) was that his presence left Vanessa quite aroused. And it wasn't the money and it wasn't the smarts and it wasn't the fact that he was nearly bloody psychic as a cardplayer. It wasn't even the fact that he was so damned handsome, which he was in a most unconventional and old-fashioned sense—she'd never been one to go in for long hair on men, but it seemed right on Cody. She liked the beard, too. The eyes—not quite gray but with no better word to describe them—they surely had something to do with it. He was tall and that helped; thin, too, with a strong build, but not bulky all over, and she did so dislike those mutant musclemen on the television. He was handsome on the whole, but no movie star, that was for certain.

No, what had drawn her over to the blackjack table to watch in the first place was not just his looks, but something more, something that enhanced them. Though obviously just forty, his eyes crinkled at the edges and a light grew in them and lit his face with a fatherly amusement and grandfatherly wisdom that was concerned and dismissive all at the same time, as if he didn't need to care about his actions, but did so for his own purposes.

So all of that, put together, that's what got her over to the table. But what was it, to return to the important question, that aroused Vanessa so? What was it that inspired her to leave with him, to practically invite him to make love?

It was the same with all the men she fell for. It was the easy charm and the warmth of his smile and the nonchalant spontaneity of the man. The part of him that whispered to her, "You mean everybody isn't like this?"

that assumed that contrary to popular opinion, life was a game but a fun one, and it truly wasn't winning but how you played that was important.

And then it hit her. He'd spelled it out for her. He was an entertainer. A performer and a storyteller in a way that few British men ever could be, or understand. No, this gift Cody had was something purely American, and for the first time in her short life Vanessa envied the people of that nation. To produce such men, to whom constant good humor and easy laughter were not extraordinary, but rather the order of the day. To Cody, sharing the mood and the laugh and the tale was not serious business, but as natural and necessary to his being as breathing.

Vanessa thought all these things about Cody as they walked along the cement path rising above the rocky shore and leading to the pier. He'd been telling her stories from the moment they left the casino, with a short break when she asked if he really had a ship and could she see it. A man with class, he hadn't tried to hide his randy grin, but rather shared it with her in an intimate fashion it takes men in general years with one woman to master.

She didn't think she'd ever wanted a man more in her life, and here he was blabbing about having fucked the Princess of Wales.

"You slept with Princess Diana?" she asked incredulously, eyes wide.

He looked at her in mock surprise, his face the picture of innocence. "Well, hell. Hasn't everyone?"

They were approaching the pier now, the cement soon to turn to wood, and she balled up a little fist and socked him in the shoulder.

"Well, I haven't," Vanessa said.

"That's a shame," Cody replied. "I would have liked to've seen that."

She hit him again.

"Now then," he went on, "tell me a little bit about yourself. My tall tales are getting taller and I want to save the best, and the dirtiest, for later."

"Well, you know most everything I'd like to tell you, though I'll tell you what most women won't. I'm thirty-one, I weigh one twenty. My teeth are fake, but my breasts are my own. I know things in the States regarding breasts have gotten a bit dicey. I'm not from London, but I say I am because you'd never have heard of the town."

"You'd be surprised."

"Well, perhaps I would. You are a man full of surprises, but even so, let's say I'm from London. I have no parents, no family, I've been married twice, but I've never been faithful and don't intend to start. I have all kinds of hobbies, the most important of which you'll soon discover, and the rest of which you'll probably never know. That about covers it."

"Why were you at the casino? Doesn't seem like the kind of thing most people would do on a whim, jet off to Monte Carlo for a couple of days by themselves."

"Why, I should have thought that would be obvious Cody, love. I'm hunting."

Now his eyes perked up and his face took on dark qualities that were new to her. The entertainer was still there, but now there was danger in him, too. She wasn't sure how she felt about that. He said one word. It wasn't a statement. It wasn't a question. It wasn't truly aimed at her.

"Hunting."

"Come on now. I see it in your face and I knew it when I saw you. You're hunting, too, a predator. We're all out there looking for something, but only the aggressive ones, only the predators, are truly going to get what they're after."

Now he smiled at her again, and Vanessa returned the smile. She knew what he was thinking, that they were both going to get what they were after.

• • •

Cody was still sizing up the girl. Certainly she wanted him to give her a poke, but he'd wait until later to decide if she could handle his preferred method of penetration as well. He'd known plenty of women who couldn't, but an extraordinary number who could. He'd killed some in the early days, but eventually had regained his self-control. His whole life, even before Major North had pointed him out to Ned Buntline, the hack writer who'd given him his awful nickname, even before that, he'd been able to talk almost anybody into almost anything. And he'd much rather be offered what he needed than take it. Still, he wasn't above a little midnight theft when necessary, though still without killing. Of course, if he were defending himself, that was another story entirely.

No, he didn't like to kill for sustenance. He'd learned a lot since he'd scalped Yellow Hand in memory of that maniac Custer, and the most important thing was that killing folks is not only bad for the soul, but it's also bad politics and ends up causing no end of trouble.

Cody liked to think he was simpler than all that. Just a storyteller, he told himself. Even fifty years earlier his curse was that if he told his stories, the true and the not so true, he ran the risk of people believing him, and nobody was supposed to know he was still alive. These days, though, he talked incessantly and was never believed.

As he talked to Vanessa he began to sense even more strongly that she might be willing to do all sorts of "kinky stuff" with him. It had gotten easier since American "doctors" had started to publish books about people who drank blood for various reasons, from health to insanity. And hell, even if he decided not to go for the throat, so to speak—well, he'd have more than enough fun with this fiery redhead. And he liked her a lot, smart and pretty as she was. He'd always had a little soft spot for redheads, especially ones he could talk into bed.

So he'd give her a poke. Maybe even drink her blood. But he wouldn't kill her. She seemed like a pretty nice girl, after all.

"We're here," he said, and gestured at a beautiful ship. Not a huge yacht like many of the ostentatious vessels berthed here, and yet certainly of a size and condition that communicated stature, like its owner.

They turned onto the walkway. Vanessa could see the name painted on the side, and it was *Wounded Knee,* a strange name for a boat, to be sure. But Cody was a strange man.

For the first time, Vanessa noticed that she and Cody were holding hands. They'd done it instinctively, naturally. She looked at him and smiled. His smile was both warm and sad; a man who'd done things he shouldn't, and couldn't forget, yet who lived life with a rare energy. Every day, every conversation, every moment was a game to be won. Like blackjack.

In contrast, it usually seemed as if every thought that entered her own mind contained a but. Not this time. Cody may have been a little strange, a bit larger than life, but he definitely had style. Definitely one for the books. She squeezed the hand she held tightly and led him toward his boat.

"Cody!" The voice rang out from the deck of the boat, deep and full of the promise of violence. It was a tone Vanessa's first husband, Ian, had taught her well. She hated it.

But then another sound replaced it, one with which she was unfamiliar but quick to recognize. She hated this new sound most of all.

It was her companion, her new friend, screaming.

Damnation, it hurts!
Cody can't control his voice at first, the scream sliding out like far too much whiskey from an empty stomach.

A slow breath, like wiping that whiskey vomit from his mouth, he regains control.

"Cody!" the voice booms again, and it's all moving too slowly. "I don't want to have to tell you this more than once. Move away from the woman and she won't be hurt."

She won't be hurt? Hell, he's the one with a silver dagger sticking out of his back and they're telling him *she* won't be hurt? What kind of shit is that?

He moves quickly.

Cody can't see the man who'd been yelling to him, but as he turns there's no mistaking the trio coming down the pier, or the one only a dozen steps away, who must have backed off when he realized his silver dagger had missed Cody's heart.

"Pull it out," he says to a still-startled Vanessa.

"What? But I—"

"Do it!" and he's glad she's as tough as he thought she was, because she does do it, puts one hand on his back, covering part of his spine, and with the other, yanks the knife from the wound. Cody sinks fangs into his lip but does not cry out. The lip will heal almost instantly. The wound in his back bleeds freely and will take much longer, poisoned as it is.

"Now get in the boat," he growls as he sees all four men begin to move forward.

"But . . ." she says again, and he looks at her now, sees her fear just as surely as she must be able to see his anger, his pain, his intentions.

"Get in the boat, damn you. They're going to kill me and you're going to be a witness. You think they'll let you live?" He wants to save the girl, but he hopes she'll be smart and help him do it.

He knows who they are, immediately. He's surprised, actually, that it's taken this long for them to get to him. Von Reinman's death was a blow, and at first he'd wanted to go after his mentor's killers, but then, when reports of other assassinations began to trickle in, he'd realized what they were doing and decided simply to wait for them. Karl's death was just the latest in a series of tragedies that had proven to Cody that his friendship with other men was a curse for them. First his father, Isaac Cody, and then his brother, Sam, and then men who were like brothers to him; Dave Harrington, James Butler Hickok, Sitting Bull. Karl Von Reinman's death still rankles within him, but it is the cumulative effect of all of these untimely deaths, deaths he could not prevent, that drives his rage now, lends an old storyteller even more courage and strength than Von Reinman's blood had given him nearly eighty years before.

He is on his first attacker, the man who stabbed him, before the others can even lift their weapons. They'd been insane to attack him at night in the first place, so he knows they'll be packing whatever weapons it might take. That means silver bullets, and though the wound in his back is healing, silver hurts like hell and might kill him. He isn't about to let that happen.

He can hear Vanessa gasp at how fast he moves, a man who's just had a foot-long blade plunged into and then removed from his back. His would-be assassin is yelling in fear, though he's been trained all his life not to do so. Cody turns him to face his church brothers as they squeeze off their first shots, wasting silver as it thunks into his boat, the pier, and their no-longer-screaming associate. Still, Cody effortlessly holds the dying body up as a shield and pulls out his own weapon.

"My God!" he hears one of them shout. "He's armed."

And he is armed. Well armed. A nine-millimeter Beretta, semiautomatic loaded with hollow points, fifteen in the clip and one in the chamber. They aren't silver. They don't need to be. He was always a much better shot with a rifle, but it's hard to carry one under a tux jacket. But the pistol is enough. The last thing these guys expect is a gun.

"Shit." He takes a slug in the abdomen. It travels through

his human shield before it reaches him, so its entry is slow and painful. It will have to come out.

Though the slug in his belly made them difficult, two huge steps and a massive leap take Cody onto the deck of his boat, corpse still held tightly to him with his free left arm.

"Get below!" he yells to Vanessa, who doesn't listen too good.

Crouched behind the cabin of the yacht, he sees the men rushing down the pier. They must think the gun's just for show. Who the hell sent these guys? Obviously, nobody was doing his homework. Cody squeezes off one round, which punches a tight black hole through the forehead of the one in the lead and completely obliterates the back of his head in a chunky spray.

Ah, hollow points!

The two remaining men jump over their fallen comrade as they make for the momentary shelter of the boat itself, huddling against the yacht out of the line of fire. He can hear them scrabbling against the wood. Of course, they'd be trying to get aboard. Suicidal fanatical assholes.

"Cody!" the voice comes again, and this time he sees its owner, standing on the ship in the next slip, a huge cross held up in his left hand, reflecting the weak illumination from the pier, a pistol in his right.

"Resistance is useless. Your death is the will of God himself."

It hurts Cody to look at the cross, but he does so anyway. To aim. The man takes two slugs in the chest while a third ricochets off the cross. He gets off a couple of shots himself, but they go wide. Nonetheless, Cody chides himself for getting slow in his old age.

Three seconds is all the time it takes for him to turn the ignition key, starting the motor, and slip into reverse. He is moving backward, out of the slip, even as he hears the sirens of the police responding to the sweet song of gunshots. Monte Carlo, New York, Kansas all those years ago, that gun song remains the same as the sound that killed over four thousand buffalo for him, the sound of death.

One of the two remaining men is running down the pier after the boat, totally ignoring the fact that Cody's got this gun and is obviously a damn good shot. When the idiot realizes that Cody isn't slowing down, he plants his feet and starts shooting. Cody ducks and ignores him. It isn't these guys who killed Karl, but he knows where he might be able to find the men who gave them their orders.

And it's not just for Karl. It's for him, too. Not because they tried to kill him, but because he's insulted. They didn't even make a good attempt. They didn't do their homework, didn't bother to try to find out who he was before he died, whether he'd be a challenge even for so young an immortal. It was almost embarrassing.

Oh, and here's the last one, climbing up over the prow of the ship. He'd left one of his assailants alive on the dock, but Cody needs to have a word with this one. Curiosity is killing him. Looking over his shoulder to be sure the yacht won't hit anything as it backs up, he leaves it in reverse and hurries to where the monk is just pulling his legs up. The assassin doesn't have time to aim his gun before Cody slaps it from his hand and hauls him to his feet. He can see his own mad eyes reflected in the religious fanatic's frightened ones.

"Do you know who I am?" he asks in a clipped, unamused tone.

"The undead, evil Defiant One. The scourge of—"

"No! You fool. Who I was, who I was, who I was. Do you know who I was before I became the 'scourge'?"

The man stares at him in horror and with a complete lack of understanding. "No," he says.

"Idiot!" Cody says as he slaps the man hard enough to shatter his jaw. "Asshole!" And he slaps the monk's other cheek. "This is ridiculous. You come to kill me and you're completely unprepared. Doesn't the name mean anything to you? Cody, Cody, Cody! William F. Cody. Buffalo Bill, for chrissakes! I'm an American legend, you moron. You've never heard of me?"

"No," the man says truthfully.

Disgusted, Cody throws him overboard.

Only when he is back on deck, with the yacht finally moving from Monte Carlo toward Italy only a few miles distant, only then does he wonder what happened to the girl. Only then does he look around to see her dead and still bleeding on the deck from a wound to the throat. Only then does he curse himself for his pride. As long as he has been alive, pride and alcohol have been his downfall, not to mention a freeness with money that he couldn't control, a blind generosity that helped everyone but himself.

But tonight it is pride that concerns him. He goes to the woman's side and checks her pulse, certain she is dead before he touches her. He has ever been, directly or indirectly, the cause of death for those around him. Cody shivers at his shallow thoughts of pride. Certainly, he was still insulted and he could not help such foolishness any more than he could the pain of the silver bullet in his stomach. Yet he tries to push it back, away from him, tries to focus on the woman.

He'd meant to save her, but ego fed his anger and anger made him blind.

He would go to Rome. There was more to all of this than met the eye and he knew now that he had to investigate. It was the last thing he wanted. He'd grown accustomed to being the rebel, the troublemaker, the solo act, rather than the scout he'd always been at heart, the friend and boss and father figure.

But this woman's death hurt his soul, made it ache the way a broken heart does. What did it matter? She was just another girl. But she wasn't, because he failed to save her. And no matter what he'd become, what he'd done, in his heart of hearts Cody still thinks of himself as a hero.

He wants, no needs to drink, to feed, but he can't bring himself to feed from her. A few miles out he drops her body, wrapped in a blanket from the cabin, into the ocean. She is gone then, and he wonders about her, whether she would have given herself to him willingly. What secrets she hid, as so many humans do, as so many creatures do.

They drift with her on the open sea.

✳

16

CODY COULD THINK OF A MILLION PLACES he'd rather be than Rome. A billion he'd rather be than a rooftop overlooking the walls of the Vatican at going on three in the morning. But he was angry and more than a little curious.

Karl's death had been just the latest in a series of assassinations in the immortal community. It was all anyone was talking about, and they all knew who was doing the killing. The question wasn't even what they would do to exact retribution from the Vatican, but if they would do anything. After all, they were afraid. All but the oldest, and for the most part, they were the ones being hunted.

Or at least, that was the general pattern until Karl's murder. Certainly, Karl was old. As a matter of fact, Cody didn't know how old. But surely not much more than a thousand years. The Defiant Ones being murdered were older than that; the younger victims of these Vatican hunters were only bystanders, generally members of the covens of the oldest of the old. So what made Karl a target?

The book.

Cody didn't know how he knew this, but he did. All Karl had talked about the past couple of years was getting his hands on some book the Vatican had squirreled away since Christ was in diapers, and rumor had it that he had succeeded in stealing it.

No wonder they killed him.

But what was in the book, and more important, where was it now? And if that was their reason for going after Karl—well, what was their reason for going after him? Certainly he'd pissed them off almost as much as he'd pissed off his own kind with his complete disregard for secrecy and his flagrant affairs with some of the world's most celebrated women, allowing himself to be photographed with them. Still, he didn't fit the bill at all in light of recent events.

But such concerns would have to wait.

Now he was crouched in the darkness, a gargoyle, keeping watch over the nocturnal activities at the home base of his greatest enemy. He had to be out of his mind! But somehow he wasn't afraid. Perhaps it was insanity finally plunging its talons into his brain, but he couldn't be scared. Hell, most priests and nuns wouldn't know a vampire if one walked up and bit them on the nose. The pope himself wouldn't know what a Defiant One was if he sat on one.

But the others.

They were the ones to be worried about. The ones that scurried now, in and out of doorways, up stairs and across courtyards. Lights were on in windows that Cody guessed were not usually burning this late. Cars pulled up and priests and nuns and monks got out, and the cars pulled away empty. Where the hell they were all going was a good question, but the most important was, of course, why?

Why all the activity, all the arrivals in the wee hours of the morning? It looked like a bunch of clergymen getting ready to pitch a religious version of his old Wild West show. Hell, he wouldn't have been half-surprised to see Annie Oakley walking about if she hadn't been dead for decades. Of course, he wasn't one to talk.

But the activity *was* out of place; he didn't hang around the Vatican every night, but he didn't have to in order to recognize that this wasn't the norm. Cody began to feel afraid. He didn't have the answers to his own questions, but of the answers that were possible, none was pleasant in light of recent events. And with each moment that passed, more questions filled his head. He decided to move closer and investigate further—after all, he had come here for answers—but he was held back by one all-important piece of logic.

None of his kind could enter the sanctuary of the church.

So what now? He couldn't very well sit on the roof till the sun came up and hope somebody would shout out the answers. Nope. The answer was obvious. As soon as he saw somebody who looked like they might know what was going on here, he'd have to make a grab for that person before they could get inside the walls.

And no sooner had this decision been made than a black limousine pulled slowly up to the gate on the north side of the Vatican, away from the square but where Cody might have landed on them had he simply fallen from his rooftop perch. There was nothing on this limo to mark it out as different from any other. But at three in the morning, with this flurry of activity, Cody would have bet on it carrying somebody with answers. He was a gambler by nature, and he knew an easy bet when he saw one.

The door to the limo opened and the chauffeur stepped out—a large man in a long raincoat, red tie, and driving gloves. Six steps later one gloved hand pulled open the rear door, and Cody moved closer to the edge, preparing to descend and ready to move on both men if the driver waited for the passenger to go inside. He didn't. The passenger, a priest with an obviously heavy brown leather briefcase, stepped from the car and the driver shut the door and turned, without acknowledging his passenger, to get back into the limousine.

Cody was tensed and ready to spring, planning to change even as he plummeted from the roof, when he saw the man.

Another figure, a man with a ponytail wearing a long black coat—a classic duster, Cody thought—ran in a crouch from the doorway six stories below until he was stooped down behind the limo, waiting for the driver to pull away. Cody didn't know who this new player was, but he figured he'd better sit back and find out. Maybe somebody *was* going to shout out their plans before the sun came up. As the limo pulled away, Ponytail jogged after it, still stooped low and slightly to one side. As the priest unlocked the gate, entered, and shut it behind him, obviously locking it in place, Ponytail rushed to the wall only feet from the gate.

What now, partner? Cody thought. You fucked up, he's inside and you're not.

One minute Cody was watching ol' Ponytail, and the next minute he wasn't. Because the guy was gone. He turned into a cloud of mist with a speed even Cody wasn't used to and then floated right through the gate into the Vatican.

INTO THE FUCKING VATICAN!

Cody's jaw was agape in complete astonishment at what he had just witnessed. Over and over, he told himself it was impossible. But he had to know, and so he had no choice. Looking like a gargoyle himself, one with its mouth wide open, he stayed there, sitting atop a building in Vatican Square, waiting for answers to far too many questions.

"Giancarlo, brother, it is wonderful to see you," Liam Mulkerrin said as he entered the office of his superior Cardinal Garbarino. They despised each other as all men who ache for the same power must, yet they bit back bitter words with steel-trap grins in a rare show of wisdom for such lustful beings.

"Liam, please sit. I have been awaiting the pleasure of your company, though I had hoped it would be sooner and with better news." Giancarlo was displeased that Mulkerrin had left some loose ends in Boston.

"Don't worry a bit, Eminence." Mulkerrin's grin turned to a tight-lipped smirk. "I have things in Boston well in hand and shall return there the moment the Blessed Event is complete. Of course, I have returned with the object of my journey."

At this, Mulkerrin motioned to the leather bag he carried, which he set down on the floor next to his chair.

"And how goes the recruitment process for the Vatican Historical Council?" Mulkerrin asked, and it was the right question. Their mutual hatred would wait until the Purge was complete, for now they needed each other.

"The Vatican Historical Council, my friend, is alive and well, hundreds strong and growing. Nearly all of the clergy we had slated for recruitment were salivating at the thought, and the others will be more than willing to go along with the plan once they realize they don't have a choice."

Neither man noticed as a fine mist began to flow under the door of Garbarino's office.

"Wonderful," Mulkerrin said, eyes intense. "And my acolytes?"

"They have studied all they could without the volume you have retrieved. Certainly they have mastered what you had taught them before you were so rudely interrupted by that old fool Guiscard, but they could not have completed their training without the book."

"Well, the book is back and so am I. Give me a week to prepare them."

"Unfortunately, you lose track of time. We do not have a week. Rather, we should have moved the day after tomorrow. In reality, we can wait no more than three days to begin, to make the Blessed Event come to pass."

"It shall be done," Mulkerrin said, his eyes smoldering

as he thought of it, the glory, the Purge. He swallowed involuntarily and choked back a cry of manic joy. He looked at Garbarino and could tell that he, too, was on the verge of lunatic giggling at the thought of their ultimate triumph. The two of them would make real a goal the church had desired to reach for two thousand years.

As Garbarino turned to the credenza behind him and retrieved a bottle of red wine and two glasses, Mulkerrin quickly tried to regain some modicum of composure. It wasn't easy. Garbarino poured them each half a glass, then lifted his own to toast and Mulkerrin followed suit.

At Mulkerrin's right leg, a tendril of mist formed into fingers, then a hand, which closed about the handle of the priest's briefcase.

"To Venice," Garbarino toasted, and Mulkerrin hastily agreed, the glee creeping up on him again, threatening to distort the corner of his mouth.

But then a man appeared, standing right up against the side of the desk, Mulkerrin's briefcase in his hand. Both wineglasses went tumbling onto the desk, spilling red stains across weeks of paperwork. Garbarino's head snapped back as he took in their visitor with incredulous eyes, and Mulkerrin stood quickly, knocking over his chair and backing away from the intruder.

"Octavian," he roared, and it was pain, hatred, surprise, and self-loathing that poured forth in that one word. And the next word came on spider legs, almost a whisper: "How?"

"Assholes," Peter said, and the two, who had once thought themselves prepared for any eventuality, were so stunned that their sanctuary had been poisoned by the presence of this Defiant One that neither could react any further as he turned, the metamorphosis from man to huge bat happening quicker than their eyes could follow, and flew straight at the window.

Talons holding tight to leather, Octavian burst into the night, shattered glass glittering red as it exploded above the courtyard. He'd never flown so hard or fast in his life, even with the enormous weight of the book in its case.

He was angry, and now, for the first time in a long time, he was also frightened. Not for himself.

For his people.

Peter wasn't just running late, he *was* late. The train was five miles out of the station, moving east, when he caught up with it. Meaghan must be going crazy, he thought. They'd flown to Rome after making certain Gulscard and his nephew had the care they needed, not even waiting for Ted's funeral. That was what pained Peter the most, and yet he and Meaghan had agreed that time was of the essence. They could not afford to lose an hour, much less a day, and tonight had proven them right.

It still confused him that he had not argued when Meaghan announced that she would be accompanying him. Of course, he knew the reasons, but they were baffling. He felt like a teacher with a mad crush on his student, a guilty pleasure indeed, but the stodgy old professor would go out of his way to spend a few minutes of solo chitchat with the girl. That was Peter. He didn't know if he was falling in love with her. You'd think after centuries of women he'd know better than to let an acquaintance numbered in days have such an effect on him. So he told himself it wasn't love.

But it was one hell of a crush.

He landed none too gently on the roof of the train, tired from too much shape shifting and from flying so hard with the damned heavy satchel in his talons. His change back into human form was slow, almost leisurely, and when it was done, he stood, checking first for bridges (hell, if Wile E. Coyote had taught him anything, that was it), and tried to establish which car he stood atop of.

It was the third from the front, so maybe he wasn't as tired as he thought he was. Precariously near the edge of the roof, he glanced over the side and counted windows.

That was it, the third from the rear. He just needed to remember which side Meaghan was supposed to be on. It wouldn't do to be tapping on the window of the wrong berth on a train doing one hundred miles per hour at past three in the morning. Third car from the front, third window from the rear and on the left, that was what they'd agreed.

But what was the left side of the train? Left facing forward or facing backward? Well, forward was the logical answer.

Logic prevailed. A couple of taps on that window, holding tightly to the metal rail on the roof's edge, and Meaghan's face appeared at the window looking extraordinarily relieved. Luckily the windows on these European trains slid down more than two feet. Peter didn't think he'd have had the energy to transform again.

"Well, it's about time," she said when he'd crawled inside, and through the smirk on her face that broadcast amusement, he could see how worried she had actually been. He didn't blame her; they both knew what kind of power Mulkerrin had, and they had already wondered aloud whether there were more like him at home.

"It was easy," he said, earning a raised eyebrow. "No, I mean it. They were so completely taken aback by the fact that I was there, in the damned Vatican, that they could hardly speak, never mind try to stop me."

"Thank God," she said, making no attempt to hide her concern now, and Peter thought once again that his feelings for Meaghan were more than mutual. "But that's it, you know."

"What's it?" he asked.

"That's it, Peter. We'll never have a chance to take them by surprise again." She looked worried again.

"Oh," Peter said, by way of consolation, "we'll see about that."

Meaghan looked at him sternly for a moment and then giggled, a sound that was as alien, and as wonderful, to

Peter as the sound of her beating heart when she hugged him.

"You arrogant man. One would think half a millennium would teach you something, after all!" She sighed in feigned exasperation and hugged him tight.

Peter wished he was as sure as he sounded. In reality, he had no idea where all this would lead. He supposed it would all depend on—

"So that's it?" Meaghan said, breaking their embrace and glancing at the leather case. "The cardinal was so vague about its contents, yet the thought of its existence frightens me. It's terrifying to realize that everything you've ever known is a lie."

"It's not everything, just one church," he said, shrugging off his coat.

"Just the one in which I happened to have been raised," Meaghan added.

"Well," Peter said with a shrug, "I suppose we ought to have a look at the thing."

He picked up the case and went to turn on the light, but Meaghan's hand on his arm stopped him. She took the case from him and put it on the top bunk, then sat and patted the spot next to her where she wanted him to sit.

"First thing in the morning, I promise," she said.

"Meaghan . . ." Peter began while sitting; he was tired after all. "I don't know about—"

"Are you hungry?"

"No."

"Then shut up and kiss me, fool."

It was an offer he couldn't refuse. As soon as their lips touched, his exhaustion retreated. It didn't leave precisely, only took a backseat to observe the festivities. The first kiss was warm and soft and accompanied by a most peculiar feeling, that of energy leaving his body through every pore, and yet when it was gone, he felt better than ever.

Their tongues touched and Meaghan ran hers over Peter's sharp teeth. He felt a barely perceptible shiver run through her and she squeezed her legs together. Meaghan wore only a robe over her nightshirt and panties. The robe came off at the pull of her belt, revealing the bandage she still wore on her arm where Janet's teeth had torn the skin. Peter gently stroked Meaghan's breasts through the fabric as she unbuttoned his own shirt.

And then a knock came, and it wasn't on the door.

Peter and Meaghan felt complete and utter panic combined with terror and an anger neither would recall a moment later. They were up in half a second, staring at the window, Meaghan with her little fists balled to attack, Peter quickly obstructing her view of the window.

Though neither Peter nor Meaghan had ever seen the man before, they both thought he looked oddly familiar.

The two stared at the intruder, who smiled awkwardly, upside down, then slowly, deliberately, knocked again. Then he held one hand out, raising his eyebrows in an expression clearly meant to say, *Well, what exactly are you waiting for?*

Peter moved toward the window, cautiously.

"I'm going to let him in," he said.

"What else can we do?" Meaghan asked in response. "I don't suppose sorcerers knock before they enter."

The intruder pulled himself into the room as the night rushed past outside the window. Peter and Meaghan stood well back, she and the book behind him. They both saw the look of recognition that passed over the intruder's face when he got his first good look at Peter in the dim light.

"Nicephorus Dragases," the intruder said. "My distinct pleasure to make your acquaintance."

17

VENICE'S HOTEL ATLANTICO IS ONLY A FEW short blocks from Piazza San Marco, or St. Mark's Square, and its front windows offer an intriguing view of the Bridge of Sighs. Its guests can make love at night with the moonlight streaming in through the windows and the breeze carrying the voices of gondoliers calling to warn their comrades around the next corner that they're coming through. The gondoliers do sing; that's not a lie. It's quite romantic, actually.

On the lower floors, guests must change clothes in the dark and pull the curtains during the day. Gondoliers and their passengers generally have roving eyes. But then, who doesn't? If a picture interests you, you look. It's human nature.

Tracey Sacco and Linda Metcalf weren't there for the romance. They were there to worship, to be taken and used by their masters, the Defiant Ones.

They were volunteers.

Their room at the Hotel Atlantico overlooked the canal. Though they did not know it, it was the same room in which a young couple had offered themselves up to Alexandra Nueva only days earlier. If you looked out the window and to the left, you could see the Bridge of Sighs. Linda and Tracey were ostensibly friends, but they were very different people. Linda was too obsessed with the

Defiant Ones to notice the romance of the city. Tracey, though she dared not mention it to her "friend," failed in a miserable attempt *not* to notice it. She felt lonely, and afraid.

Linda had survived Venice, New Orleans, and Venezuela, each time paying the hotel bill of whomever she'd been sharing the room with, each time going home alone. She was sure that this time she'd be one of the chosen, she'd be honored. She was far from stupid. You had to be pretty damn smart to get as far into the circle of the volunteers as she'd gotten. But intelligence, in the long history of man, had never had a bearing on worship.

And she could not deny that worship was exactly what this was. Martyrdom, sacrifice, purification. Faith. Those were the principles of religion. Linda didn't think she had ever actually seen a Defiant One. She had no idea if they paid any attention to the sacrifices offered up to them.

But she had faith.

Tracey had faith in nothing but herself. That was the way it was and always had been. Tracey had never seen a Defiant One either, but that and the fact that she, also, was far from stupid were the only things the two of them shared. This was Tracey's first year as a volunteer, though it had taken her three to get into the loop and a fourth to convince Linda that she'd be the perfect roommate. The differences between them would have been substantial even if Tracey had been everything she seemed.

Which she was not.

In truth, she lacked not only faith, but religion. Oh, she believed all right, but she believed because of the things she had seen and heard, believed because she was terrified, and because it made good copy, and making good copy was her job.

Tracey Sacco worked for CNN.

"So," Tracey said with a quaver in her voice that she hoped passed for excitement rather than terror, "you're the expert, babe. What do we do now?"

It was 10:00 P.M. (yeah, ma, Tracey thought, do you know where your children are?) Linda had said they'd go out later, when the streets weren't quite so crowded, quite so safe. God, it was crazy. And yet it fit right in with the whole point of this thing. They were here to sacrifice themselves, after all. What the hell had she gotten herself into?

Only the biggest news story of the decade. An international cult operating around a community of dark, shadowy figures that the cult deified, worshiped, and to whom they attributed a wide array of magical and demonic powers, and she'd managed to get right into the middle.

When she'd first gotten wind of it, through an old friend whose sister had disappeared in a small town in Germany one year, well, she'd been a little skeptical. But as soon as she started doing her homework, she realized it was there. And she couldn't possibly be the only one aware of it; there were just too many disappearances, too many murders, too many patterns.

So why was it not public knowledge?

For very simple reasons. People with power didn't want it to be. Stories were censored around the world, facts blurred, homicide reports vague, times and dates of death adjusted and the media absolutely under control. It was done the same way government, especially the American government, keeps people in the dark.

Sure, JFK was killed with one bullet.

Sure, George Bush knew nothing about Iran-Contra.

Uh-huh.

As soon as Tracey realized the extent of this story—her story, she had started to call it—she had gone behind closed doors with her boss, Jim Thomas. When she was officially and very publicly fired from CNN, nobody asked why Jim's salary suddenly doubled. And there was no Mrs. Thomas to wonder why half that salary went into a bank account in the name of Terry Shaughnessy. Of course, Tracey Sacco had a passport that identified her as Terry Shaughnessy, and several with other names as well, just in case. Even Tracey Sacco wasn't her real name, but she'd been Tracey for so long that she was becoming accustomed to it, almost like a nickname. In her heart, she might still be Allison Vigeant, for that was her real name, but in her head she had become Tracey.

As far as Tracey and Jim knew, it was the deepest cover any investigative journalist had ever gone under. She risked her life every day. And now she wasn't just risking it, she was throwing back her head and baring her throat to the wolves—the Defiant Ones, they were called. She had to learn exactly what she was up against, and stay alive to tell the story. Nothing else mattered.

"Tracey!"

Tracey snapped back to reality.

"I'm talking to you!" Linda whined in an unattractive way that Tracey hadn't heard from her before. Her nose wrinkled and she realized it was also the first time she'd smelled perfume on Linda, never mind that it wasn't a particularly pleasing scent.

"Sorry, Lin," Tracey said, putting on her best smile. "I'm just so—I don't know—blown away by the whole thing. So, what are we doing first?"

"Well," and now Tracey saw a girlish excitement return to Linda's face, and her voice took on the mesmerized tone of a child reciting her Christmas list to a department-store Santa. "I'm just so nervous. We're invited to a party."

"A party? You never said anything about—"

"I know. That's because I never knew about it. I guess it happens every year, but only a few of us are invited. It's just such an honor, isn't it?"

"Sure," Tracey answered.

I'll bet it's a meat market.

"Why do you come to us?" Alexandra Nueva asked, brows knitted in a mixture of anger and concern.

They stood in a library of sorts, a collection of rare, museum-quality books on occult subjects. The library, and the house that surrounded it, were owned by the Defiant One who stood in front of them. A true elder, he'd been known by many names, the latest a millennium old.

"Yes, Hannibal. What exactly do you expect us to do?" Sheng pushed.

The tall man paused a moment, his mouth forming a question that would go unasked. He cocked his head to one side and studied Alexandra before answering.

"Well, I should think it ought to be pretty obvious by now that a pattern is developing."

"Obvious to anyone with an ear to the ground," Alexandra agreed. "Old bastards like you are being stalked by the church. They'll probably get to us eventually, but the pattern lies with age."

"Oh, they'll get to you eventually, I'm pretty sure of that now. But what about Karl? He was not nearly so old as the rest of those who've been killed."

"An error?" Sheng suggested. "Practice?"

Hannibal sneered, obscenely long fangs jutting from his mouth, his thin white hair flying across his blue eyes as he turned on Sheng. "Don't be flip with me. Von Reinman should have taught you to respect your elders. Of course, he was nothing, so we shouldn't expect much from his brood."

"Fucking pompous showboat, I'll tear your—" Alexandra started, thrusting herself toward Hannibal, her own fangs bared.

But Sheng held her back and kept his own mouth closed. It wasn't that Hannibal frightened him, per se, only that he knew what the creature was capable of. And it wouldn't do to have the animosity that existed between Hannibal's clan and what remained of their own coven become open warfare. Sheng and his brothers and sisters wouldn't stand a chance. They were too young, too weak, too inexperienced, and too few.

"Now." Hannibal fumed. "Let me tell you a little story. Last night I was in Monte Carlo. I'm not much of a gambler, but my companion, a human, enjoys it. When the Vatican killers entered the casino, I spotted them immediately. They were looking for someone, and because of my age, I automatically assumed it was me, even though I was not the only one of our kind there."

He paused for effect, all politician. "It was Cody October."

"You've seen him? He was there?" Sheng sputtered. "I can't believe he'd come so close to the carnival. Unless . . . well, unless he's planning on coming, but that would be crazy."

"He was always crazy." Alex shook her head in disgust.

"Regardless, it was Cody October. I, personally, have never understood what it was about him that so infuriated your group. Certainly his behavior is, shall we say, unorthodox, but his actions have been crude at best and no real threat."

"It's really none of your business," Sheng said coldly. "Get on with the story."

Hannibal only stared for a moment, then did so. These young ones were obscenely rude, and in his own home! He might have to kill them eventually just as an example.

"Cody was there, gambling. Winning actually. At the time I took his presence as a matter of convenience. It was nothing to have my companion stagger drunkenly up to him, slap him on the back, and loudly shout his name as if he were a long-lost brother. The Vatican men couldn't help but look his way and, of course, recognize him for what he was. That's what they're trained for, after all.

"Cody, on the other hand, was so engrossed with the game, and with a rather attractive young woman who joined him, that he barely registered my friend's greeting, didn't realize that he'd never seen the man before in his life. And of course, he didn't notice the assassins, even as they followed him out when he left with the woman. And I, of course, followed them.

"As I said, I thought they were after me, but now I'm not entirely sure." Hannibal returned from wherever his mind had gone when telling the story to find that Alexandra and Sheng were staring at him.

"Well?" the two said in unison.

"Well what?" he asked innocently.

"Did they get him, you idiot?" Alex nearly shouted at him. "Is Cody dead?"

Hannibal blinked.

"Cody? Dead? Most certainly not. The assassins never had a chance. It was really quite a show. Pity, though, the woman he'd picked up in the casino didn't survive."

Hannibal said all this very matter-of-factly, as if there was a point that Alex and Sheng were missing.

"So what does all this have to do with us?" Sheng finally asked, not wanting to sound stupid but tired of waiting for clarification.

"Well, that's the pattern we're discussing, child," Hannibal said, and Sheng bristled. "Only truly ancient members of our race have been assassinated thus far, with the exception of your late mentor. Now the Vatican has tried to assassinate a renegade member of your coven. It could all be coincidence, but I doubt it."

"Seems pretty circumstantial to me," Alex said.

"As it did to me until this morning."

"What was this morning?" Sheng asked.

"I had a call from a human . . . mmm, associate in Boston. It seems our friend Octavian has been investigating a strange series of murders involving a Roman Catholic cardinal."

"My blood," Alex cursed, "you have us all under surveillance, don't you?"

Hannibal's smile just then would have forced many reasoning creatures from the room.

"Not all of you, my dear," he said. "Only . . . the truly dangerous ones. Regardless, Octavian is on his way here, to Italy. More precisely, as far as I'm told, he is going to Rome—may already be there, in fact." Before they had a chance to react, he continued. "What I want to know is, why are he and Cody here? What special vendetta does the Vatican have planned for your coven? What are you not telling us?"

They looked at each other, trying to digest what Hannibal was telling them, but he wasn't finished.

"And one more thing. Octavian made travel arrangements on a commercial airplane." He looked at them expectantly, analyzing their faces, their reactions. "Much of his flight was to take place during the day."

For once, neither of the lovers could think of a single thing to say.

Giuseppe Schiavoni ran his gondola across the Grand Canal a hundred times a day or more during the tourist season. When it got cold, though, that meant fewer and fewer tourists, fewer and fewer trips. Less and less money. So he saved up to take a long winter vacation, letting the younger men bear the brunt of the cold winter for the few tourists and the Venetian locals who wanted to cross the canal. But wherever Giuseppe vacationed, he was always sure to be back by carnival time. Not only did the tourists come despite the relatively chilly weather, but it was fun. And an old widower like Giuseppe Schiavoni didn't have as much time for fun as he had in his younger days.

Now he ran his *traghetto* across the canal with pleasure, for he carried two beautiful young American women, not a man in sight. This was something of a treat, generally. But tonight, well, tonight was different.

"Ladies," he said to them, raising his voice to be heard above the chilly breeze, "it's cold and getting late. Are you certain you don't want me to take you back to your hotel?"

"But signore," Linda Metcalf answered, "you are not the usual gondolier, you are a ferryman, and this is your post. You can't very well abandon it to escort us home."

"I'm done for the night," he answered, nodding his head, "and I'll tell you, I don't want to stay out any later than I must."

"But how will we get back?" Tracey Sacco asked, a worried look on her face.

"Oh, there is a water taxi, every hour on the half until the day after carnival. But still . . ."

"What are you so worried about?" Tracey's eyes narrowed and she glanced at Linda, who was doing her best to ignore their exchange.

Giuseppe looked from one of the women to the other, opened his mouth to speak, and then realized that nothing he could say would make any sense to them. "I'm an old man," he said finally. "The older you get, the more shadows you see in the darkness. Humor me; be careful."

Now Tracey smiled at him. "We will."

"At least until we get to the party!" Linda said in that high-school cheerleader voice that grated on Tracey's nerves. "Then all bets are off."

Linda's eyes were glassy and she had a vague, almost delirious smile on her face. It made Tracey shiver.

And then they had arrived.

"Ca Rezzonico!" Giuseppe boomed, naming their destination as they pulled alongside a small dock. Then he leaned over to Tracey as Linda was scrambling out of the gondola and whispered to her.

"Be careful," was all he said.

Tracey followed Linda up onto the dock and to the stone street that ran in front of Ca Rezzonico.

"Ca Rezzonico," Linda began, loudly operating as tour guide for her roommate, "designed by the baroque master Baldassare Longhena. Construction was begun in 1667. Eighty-five years later it was finished, complete with ceilings painted by Tiepolo."

"Who the hell is Tiepolo?" Tracey asked, feigning interest but paying real attention to Giuseppe as he made his way back across the canal.

You be careful, too, she thought, and closed her eyes for a moment to push the wish across the water to the man. She said a mental prayer for all of them.

"Some artist, obviously," Linda answered. "I don't know, I checked this place out in the tour book before we left the room. I don't want to seem uneducated. This is a high-society thing, y'know?"

"You're a quick study," Tracey said, then looked up at the building for the first time.

The structure sat facing the Grand Canal, a monolith, its walls echoing back the lapping sound of the water from the canal and from the Rio di San Barnaba that ran along its southern face. Huge and beautiful, lights displaying its glories for all to see, the building stirred an appreciation in Tracey, as truly great art and architecture often did.

"Ca Rezzonico is home to the Museum of the Eighteenth Century," Linda continued as they walked down Calle Bernardo, and now Tracey tuned her out completely, for they were passing Ca Rezzonico and their true destination was coming into view.

For all that it was significantly smaller than Ca Rezzonico and not lit up like a Christmas tree, the home of their host was even more impressive. Though its stone face was impassive, it was brought to some semblance of life by the plants that grew and hung all around it, the vines that crawled over it. It was a singular sight in Venice, for while they had seen numerous potted plants and flowers, no building had appeared so completely overgrown as this.

It was clear that the party had long since begun. Where light normally streamed from the windows of a home, here music and revelry spewed forth in its place; and where the sounds of life were usually a dim undertone, an echo from within, so here the lights were but a shadowy flickering. It seemed almost . . . normal, the comfortably familiar scene of celebration.

But Tracey knew that whatever waited inside, it was far from normal.

"I don't know. . . ." she started to say, and then the door opened.

The two women both took an involuntary step backward as the music coming from the house climbed a decibel. Neither said a word, only watched as a strange couple came down the steps. A tall, exotically beautiful black woman and a shorter, dangerous-looking Asian man walked arm in arm toward the two women, leaning close together. The woman looked over her shoulder at the door, as if to satisfy herself that it was indeed closed.

"Do you believe any of this?" Alexandra Nueva said to her companion, just loud enough for Tracey and Linda to hear.

"Unfortunately, I do," Shi-er Zhi Sheng answered. "Indeed I do. And all it does is confuse me more. For the first time in a long time, I'm scared to—"

Tracey and Linda froze where they stood, face-to-face with the strange couple. As Tracey looked at the Asian man's face she felt her muscles contract and realized she was fighting to keep from wetting herself. For in that moment, staring into the man's face drawn tight in an animal growl, she thought he would kill her.

Even as his face softened, she did not relax. Her mind still held a terrifying picture of him.

"Where are you women going?" the man asked brusquely, and now Tracey looked away from him, at Linda, who still wore her strange smile, at the woman, whose face was even more stern than her man's.

"To a party," Linda told them happily.

"Go back to your rooms," the tall woman said, and now the smile finally dropped from Linda Metcalf's face.

"Will not!" she whimpered, like a petulant child.

"Why do people keep telling us to go home?" Tracey asked, looking at the man. She had been feeling more and more that this story wasn't worth it, and the deeper into it she got, the more frightened she became. She didn't think she wanted to know what the Defiant Ones truly were after all. "Why?" she asked the man again.

He approached her now, uncoiling his thick arm from that of his partner's and stepping up close. He grabbed her firmly by the shoulders and captured her eyes with his gaze. She stared into those eyes and was lost for a minute, drifting there in the moment before he spoke.

What the hell is going on?

There was something in those eyes that was far from normal.

And then he spoke.

"The only thing waiting for you inside that house is death," the man said, never taking his eyes from Tracey's.

"Then we've come to the right place!" Linda said, and now Tracey wanted to hit her, to hurt her.

But she could barely move, and when she spoke, it was a whisper. "But why do you care?" she asked, and incredibly, it was the woman, surely out of earshot, who answered.

"We don't. Be certain of that. But the owner of that house . . ." She gestured in disgust.

"And the host of your party," the man added.

"He's no more a friend of ours than he is of yours."

Now the man let her go and stood back. The tall woman came up to join him and Tracey again noticed how beautiful she was, statuesque. They walked away together as if the meeting had never taken place, as if she and Linda had just disappeared. It was damned unnerving.

"Let's go-ooh," Linda whined.

And something happened in Tracey's head as she watched the couple walk away, calmly strolling into the night yet with complete knowledge of whatever was going on in Venice. Something was born or something died, she wasn't quite sure, but suddenly she knew she was going into that house, to that party. She knew she would do whatever she had to in order to find the answers to all the questions in her mind. Not for the story, or a career, or anything so obvious. It was more simple than that. She just *had* to know. And she couldn't let fear stop her.

"Quit whining, you little twit!" she snapped at Linda, who looked at her as if slapped. "Just shut up and follow me and try not to look so excited. It's embarrassing."

Tracey went up the steps and Linda followed her, still staring but subdued.

✳

18

THEY'D BEEN INSIDE THE HOUSE FOR LESS than ten minutes when Tracey realized exactly what the Defiant Ones were. She almost said it out loud, but caught herself.

Inside the front door, their coats had been taken by a huge and silent Italian man. Tracey didn't know whether the man was silent because he would not speak or because he could not, but what good to ask him? As they made their way into the house few people paid them any mind. There were many rooms and practically a new spectacle in each. In one, people danced normally in the center while onlookers sipped drinks from a bar. In another, lit only by a flickering fireplace on one wall, an orgy raged on while Linda and Tracey paused in a failed attempt to connect legs to bodies to arms in their minds.

In the hallways, couples of all description held each other tight, opposite and same sex, different colors, different sizes, and in all stages of undress. Tracey gawked momentarily at the inhumanly large breasts of one woman before looking between her legs and spotting a huge penis dangling there. Cries came from a room upstairs where the crack of a whip kept Tracey from looking through the door. Linda, it appeared, had no such compunctions and mentioned to Tracey that she might like to go back to that room later.

They'd been handed drinks on the first floor, and they now made their way up the steps to the third. Their entire journey through the house had been accompanied by gropes and feels in the dark, spanks on the rump, tweaks of the nipples, hands sliding up their skirts. After a few moments it had seemed foolish to worry about, but now, on these steps, it was worst of all. They could not help but rub themselves on people as they squeezed to get through, to get up the steps, to get past the hands.

And why were they going up?

We're looking for something, Tracey knew.

Tracey was squeezing by a blond woman now, chest to chest, and she looked toward the top of the stairs to avoid making eye contact with any of these people. Before her brain even registered what was happening, the blond woman had a hand up her skirt, pushing her panties aside to get at her.

"God," the woman breathed at her, "you're shaved. I love it when they're shaved."

Tracey batted her hand away and used her elbows to shove the woman back. With people sitting on the steps, though, she lost her own balance, her drink hit the carpeted steps, and she came down hard on her knees. She took a moment to get a breath, reached for her glass before it could be shattered, and began to stand.

She looked up to see the face of a man, eyes closed in ecstasy as his lips massaged somebody's penis. Tracey couldn't see the face of the man receiving the blow job for the forest of people above her blocked her view, but it was clear from the way his knees almost buckled that the cocksucker was doing a good job. The man's lips curled back slightly from the huge penis in his hand, and a bloody red tear of saliva fell to the steps. Then another. And then Tracey could see a drop of blood, real blood, escape his lips and slowly drip down the side of the standing man's cock.

But the man wouldn't let it go. And he didn't even

need to open his eyes. His tongue snaked out, longer than
Tracey thought possible, and caught the blood before it
could drop. Then he pulled the cock from his mouth and
Tracey could see that it was covered with the bloody saliva. Once more the man opened his mouth wide to accept
the width of that penis.

Tracey saw his teeth. That's when she knew what the
Defiant Ones were, and more importantly, that they were
real and she stood here among them.

She stood up quickly, almost knocking down the blond
woman who looked as if she was ready for another try,
but scowled now as she saw the look of terror on Tracey's
face.

"Shouldn't have come," the blond woman said, misin-
terpreting her horror.

Now Tracey shoved Linda ahead of her, rudely knocking
people out of the way as they cleared the last few steps to
the top.

"Tracey, what the hell?" Linda yelled at her, but Tracey
came barreling up behind her, almost knocking them both
down when the stairs ended. There was more room up
here, but still too many people.

"Sorry," she mumbled to Linda, then spoke up. "I need
some air, Lin, I need some breathing space or I may fall
down."

Really she felt like she might throw up. "I've got to—"

"Perhaps I might be of some assistance?" the voice said,
silky smooth and sexy in a chivalrous sort of way.

Tracey looked at the speaker and knew immediately that
this white-haired man was one of Them. Somehow, now
that she knew what they were, that they indeed *were* at
all, she could identify them on sight. He offered his hand,
and for a moment she shrank back, then realized where
she was and what she was doing here and thought better
of it. She took his cold hand and allowed him to lead her
through the crowd. Linda followed with what Tracey now
fully realized was awe on her face. Awe that was mixed

with excitement, both sexual and frightful.

In moments the three were alone in a large bedroom, lit only by candles. There was a washbowl on the bureau, and Tracey used it, splashing her face and then drying it with the towel she was handed by this elegant . . . thing. Finally, she could not avoid looking at him. At it.

"You're feeling all right now?" he asked, solicitous and kindly, but something glittered behind his eyes and now Tracey remembered the eyes of the Asian man they'd met on the way in. She realized that couple must also be . . . inhuman.

"I'm fine," she answered, and heard Linda giggle behind her.

She turned to her roommate with a look meant to wither, but Linda only stared at the tall, handsome creature. Tracey turned back to him and realized that there was something mesmerizing about those green eyes.

"Let me introduce myself," the creature said. "I am the owner of this home, and your host." He executed a short bow.

"You may call me Hannibal."

Over the past several years Tracey had woken up many times having forgotten for a moment what day it was or just where she was. But this was more than that. As she came up and up and up from the depths of a dreamless nowhere sleep, she didn't know who she was, or if she was at all. She climbed up from that place not out of desperation or with any great difficulty, but slowly and steadily forward because she already seemed to have some upward momentum and it would have been an effort to prevent herself from drifting into the waking world.

It would have been worth the effort.

The horror grew around her in stages, her senses clicking in as if switched on one by one.

First her sense of touch awoke, shocked to attention by pain in her arms and wrists, and a tremendous ache between her legs, from some terrible violation. And her neck hurt. But before she could wonder about any of these things, her sense of taste warned her that her violation had not been confined to her vagina, or even her rectum. The unmistakable taste of semen filled her mouth, combined with the biting-on-aluminum flavor of blood.

Hers or someone else's.

Her sense of smell kicked in right away, picking up the same things in the air, sex and blood. The bloody smell was overwhelming the pungent odor of recent copulation, and she was reminded again of the pain at her throat. She reached a hand up quickly and found the wounds.

As she remembered just where she was alarm bells sounded in her head, and her ears worked again. She'd been bitten! And now she heard the grunts and groans of a man—it had to be one of Them—and the slapping sounds of intercourse. And yet there was one other sound, a hungry sound. The tearing sound of the feast.

Darkness finally cleared from her sight, all of these thoughts and sensations having come to her in a matter of seconds. Her head moved around, slowly so as not to tear the wounds at her throat, though she thought the bleeding had stopped. She saw him.

Hannibal, their host, the creature she and Linda had been warned about by the couple before coming into the party. His back was toward her, and she admired his well-muscled body for a moment. It wasn't only his eyes that were mesmerizing! She watched as he thrust again and again into someone *Linda* but her eyes were torn away from that body toward the sucking, tearing, slurping sounds coming from his mouth.

They were not kisses.

She knew this, and yet was drawn to the sight. Grunting as he thrust, and tearing as he grunted, Hannibal worried at the bloody gash at Linda's neck like a wolf at a carcass. Truthfully, though she tried to deny it to herself, his face had lengthened slightly, his nose and jaw protruding far more than was normal for a human, and now dipped into that wound with the enthusiasm of any such beast.

She had to get the hell out of there. From the sounds of his grunting—he had ignored her own retching—Hannibal would not be much longer with Linda's . . . oh, shit. The girl had been a pain in the ass and was totally screwed up about pain and death, but who knew how she'd gotten that way? She was only human, after all.

Hell with the clothes, Tracey thought. She didn't want to give him an extra moment. She was out of the room with no thought for noise, the party still raged on unabated, but now the orgy was almost complete. The stairs leading down to the second floor were not as crowded as they had been on the way up, and yet the creatures there, human creatures and the others, were lying down now, or against the walls, and attached in ways both sexual and violent. The carpet was splotched with blood where she could see it, yet it was for these splotches, like targets, that she aimed her steps.

Shaking off a dozen hands that reached for her, and batting away several that actually got hold, she thought she might make it to the second floor without incident. Halfway there, a leg moved quickly, in time with a screaming orgasm, bouncing with pleasure just as her foot came down on a bloody spot of carpet. But she struck flesh instead, roundly muscled flesh. Her weight was already forward on that leg, and down she went.

Tracey screamed as she fell into the mass of flesh. She just couldn't hold it in any longer. Linda had led her into the biggest news story ever, and into the middle of a hive of supernatural, undead monsters straight out of pop culture and ancient mythology. And now Linda was dead, her body violated by one of Them, and her own body had been violated as well, not only sexually but . . .

"NOOOO!" She screamed again, almost a growl, as her head hit a wall and her body tumbled down across hands that grappled her, legs and breasts and elbows and penises.

And there were fangs there, too, and that was what had made her scream. Was she one of these things now? She'd been bitten, and what did that mean?

She realized she knew nothing.

She realized she had to get out, that the truth had to escape with her.

Three steps from the bottom, she stopped moving. Hands wrapped around her now as mouths closed on her breasts, teeth biting down. She couldn't tell the sex of those around her or even if they were human, but when incredibly strong hands forced her legs apart and she looked down to see a beautiful redheaded woman lapping at her she knew for certain that *she* at least was one of Them. The pleasure was incredible, and she wondered for a moment just what the creature was doing to create such feelings, almost overwhelming her fear. Then she felt two sharp pricks in the folds of her labia, not unpleasurable in themselves, but terrifying because she knew what they were.

And yet she strained, not against those arms that held her down, but to push her crotch further into the redhead's face, to bear further on that tongue and lips, the teeth. It was terrible, and tears fell from her eyes, but it was wonderful, too.

Hands picked up her head and a penis aimed straight for her mouth, thickening and elongating as it reached her lips. That broke the spell, the imminence of that penetration brought back all that had happened and gave her the burst of strength she needed. Throwing herself forward, several people about her toppling back, she landed rolling on the second-floor landing, then stood up immediately, staring back up the stairs. Already the hole she had occupied had filled with flesh, and she'd been forgotten by all.

"Bitch," the creature with the growing penis growled at her. Not everyone had forgotten her. But at least he wasn't giving chase.

She looked at the top of the stairs, expecting Hannibal

to emerge at any second, and yet he didn't. But that meant nothing, for she knew he'd be after her in mere moments. Looking down the steps, she could see the first floor, and yet what should have been a hopeful sight was discouraging, and she almost fell to her knees in despair.

The stairs were covered, from about three steps down to the bottom, with bodies. For the first time she noticed that some of the bodies were not moving. There were corpses on the stairs! There was no way she could make it down those steps without being dragged down for good.

The answer was clear.

She made it down to the fourth step and could go no farther without being attacked. Then she jumped. The fall over the banister was no more than fifteen feet, and she was lucky enough to have her feet land on bare floor. Her luck was short-lived, though, as she felt her ankle turn badly, and her momentum carried her onto her side in a roll. She knocked into a trio of lovers, but for a change, none of them tried to drag her into their bloody sex play. Sprawled there, she could see into the room with the dance floor, which had become a sea of sweaty flesh. She ran through the house, and for a moment thought she might never escape the mixed smell of blood and sex and yet, God help her, she thought she might be getting used to it.

Finally, she found the door. She reached into the closet and grabbed the first coat she laid hands on, hoping it was long enough to cover her.

It was.

Out the door and into the street, she panicked when there was no gondola in sight. At first she thought she might just find any passerby, or a policeman, but then she realized the enormity of it. The people must know, the police must know, what was going on. Or at least, if they didn't really know, they knew enough to be afraid, to stay indoors, not to get involved. How was she to get back to her room?

She wanted to scream, but the only ones brave enough to come out at night now would be those inside the house she just left. And she surely didn't want their attention. Not, at least, until she had blown the whistle in the light of day. National—no, world news would be made when she tore the veil away from this madness, and then these things would be hunted down and destroyed. Forget any inkling of curiosity or morality here, they were monsters and they must be destroyed!

Where the hell was the *traghetto* boatman? She looked out over the canal, calm and freezing cold, the water lapping at the edge of the street. And then it hit her again that no one was out, that the boatman wasn't coming, that she was alone. The cold came up on her then, though it had been there all the time, and latched itself onto her body like an icy leech, ignoring the thick fur of the coat that fell to her knees, knowing, like an intimate lover knows, that she wore nothing underneath.

She had time to wonder which way to run before the third-floor window directly above her exploded outward, showering glass down onto the street and into the canal. Miraculously, barely half a dozen shards hit her, only two cutting the back of her neck as she bent to avoid the broken glass. Then the unmistakable, naked form of Hannibal shot out the window, transforming itself before her eyes, flesh flowing until a huge bat swooped low above her, out over the canal then back above the street, and changed again just as quickly in the moment that it lit upon the ground in front of the house.

"How rude," Hannibal said, with the air of a deliciously offended gossip. "I can't believe you left without saying good-bye!"

Tracey backed up a few steps, unable to look away from his hypnotic green eyes, the white hair snapping in the wind like an ivory flag as he stood there, naked and erect, bloody and flushed, but obviously not feeling the cold.

She took another step back and almost fell into the

canal, losing her balance for a moment and tearing her gaze away finally to be sure of her footing.

"No," Hannibal said, unsure, and she looked up to see that the smirk had gone from his face. "Get away from there."

She was uncertain herself, but any chance was better than no chance. She jumped.

She was under in a moment, and then her head bobbed up, but it was several seconds before she could take a breath. The cold had her in a crushing bear hug, her lungs fighting to continue their work. Her muscles twitched involuntarily and she knew she couldn't last long if she had to swim.

So did Hannibal.

"Such spirit," he said as he hunkered down by the water's edge, "but oh, so silly. Why, you're going to freeze to death, my little darling."

"Better . . ." she barely said, above the shivering, but couldn't continue.

"Ah, you think so. Well, you're right in assuming that I can't come in after you. That old wives' tale about crossing running water is simply rubbish. But swimming in it? Well, that's another story entirely. So you have two choices, both of which you think are death, hmm?"

Tracey just looked at him, his eyes drawing her out of the water but her muscles paralyzed by the cold. He couldn't make her move, and she would eventually get too cold to swim and sink like a stone. It wasn't deep, but she was in over her head, to say the least.

"Tracey, darling . . ."

When had she told him her name? For that matter, she didn't remember anything between being led into his bedroom and waking up there.

"Tracey, don't drift off like that, it isn't sleepytime. Why aren't you dead already? You know I already bled you, so why are you alive at all, have you thought of that?"

I was just getting to that, she thought.

"I'll save your icy brain the trouble, dear. I was saving you for carnival tomorrow night. You were to be my 'date.' Of course, you would have died the next day for certain. Now, though, I could easily sit here and watch you die and go inside and have my pick of the women in the house—it is my party, after all—but I would rather have you. You show such . . . passion, emotion.

"Let's make a deal, shall we? My word of honor on the throne of my forgotten homeland. If you come out, I'll bleed you tomorrow, but I won't kill you. As a matter of fact, I'll protect you from the rest of my kind. You'll be a kept woman until you die naturally or I grow tired of you and let you go. Of course, you will serve me with your blood and your body, until that time.

"But you'll be alive, and I imagine you'll have thousands of chances to escape. It might even be fun!"

He smiled at her, enjoying himself tremendously, and held a hand out over the water. She thought for a moment of pulling him into the water to see exactly what damage that would do, but she knew his strength was prodigious and what little she normally had was long since sapped away by the water.

She barely had the strength to grasp his outstretched hand.

19

"WE MUST ASSUME THAT OCTAVIAN IS aware of our plans," Father Mulkerrin said, fury seething in his mind, barely contained behind his eyes.

"I still don't understand how he was able to come onto holy ground," Cardinal Garbarino said, shaking his head. The man was still partially in shock.

"I told you, Giancarlo. The creature fought me during the day. In the sun! He should not even have been able to be outside, never mind being able to transform himself in the light of day."

"But how?"

"God knows. But you've read the book as I have. Somehow he's freed himself from the fetters our forebears placed on his kind those centuries ago. Why, that's the very thing we've been trying to prevent by killing the oldest of the Defiant Ones. But Octavian . . . he's a mere pup, barely five centuries old. He shouldn't be—"

"Well, that ought to do for now, Liam. We've got to forget about how and why for the moment and start to do something about it. We cannot wait. We must move out today and be in place to attack tomorrow at first light. And we've got to get that book back."

"But, Giancarlo," Mulkerrin said, worried now, "I told you we must assume Octavian knows of our plans, and that would mean he is headed for Venice as we speak, to warn the rest of the demonspawn. We can't wait another day!"

"What would you have us do? Attack them at night? Suicide."

And then silence reigned, and the two men realized they had been shouting at each other. It had been only twenty-some-odd minutes since Peter Octavian had stolen their most prized possession, their guidebook and bible, the reason for their very existence—*The Gospel of Shadows*.

They would have it back.

"Round them up," Garbarino said quietly. "At dawn, round them all up and get them moving. We have until noon, no later, and we must be gone. By ones and twos we'll leave, on foot, by car, however. And tell them—tell them all—we won't be coming back."

"We?"

"Of course we. I'm joining you. Oh, I've a couple of people I'll leave here, agents nobody knows are even acquainted with me. But I don't want the rest of the church getting underfoot, getting in our way."

"How will you prevent that?" Mulkerrin truly wanted to know.

"I'm going to pay a visit to His Holiness. By noon our brothers here will have more to worry about than where we've disappeared to."

There were four of them, three men and a woman. They were Mulkerrin's immediate subordinates, and through them he would command the Vatican forces when they marched for the final time against the Defiant Ones.

The three priests were Isaac, Thomas, and Robert Montesi, brothers whose father had been Mulkerrin's star pupil, a powerful sorcerer who'd been killed by an ancient Defiant One. Mulkerrin hadn't yet discovered which creature killed Vincent Montesi, but he had a description of the thing, and he would always search for it. Montesi had been the only being Mulkerrin had ever allowed himself to call friend.

The fourth of Mulkerrin's lieutenants was a nun, Sister Mary Magdalene. Mulkerrin had never known her by any other name. Her once-attractive face had been terribly scarred during an assassination mission years before. She had fought on, undaunted, as the creature had torn at her face, ripping her right eye from its socket. The lids were sewn together, but it was easy to see there was nothing behind them. And Mary refused to wear a patch.

All were skilled in the arts of sorcery. Skilled, but not masters. The book must be retrieved for them to complete their studies and for those under them to also continue to learn. As Mulkerrin explained their situation Mary's grave face became even more grim. Isaac and Thomas stood taller, preparing themselves mentally for what was to come. And Robert . . . Robert Montesi smiled.

Oh, what a weapon he is, Mulkerrin thought.

"How many do we have?" he asked them.

"Two hundred twenty-two," Robert answered, and even Mulkerrin was impressed with the number.

"Nearly half a hundred more in and around Rome," Mary added, referring to a group of women she herself had been training.

"And more than one hundred and thirty near Venice," Isaac said.

"One fifty," Thomas finished.

"More than four hundred! What a glorious event," and now Mulkerrin also stood taller, his eyes wide and his mind reaching to encompass the scope of their plan. Final victory was within their grasp.

"For the love of God," Mary intoned.

"For the love of God," the Montesi brothers repeated.

This put a damper on Mulkerrin's spirits. Certainly it was for the love of God. But it was for himself as well. *He* would be victorious. He would control all of the dark forces of the universe, as well as a powerful army of sorcerers. They would have to be away from the church for some time after the event. But in ten years, twenty, he would return and wrest control with whatever force, physical or magical, was necessary. He would be pope. And slowly the church would become nothing more than a magical extension of his will. His every darkest dream would be enacted. Garbarino and all others who purported to be his betters would be gone.

All of his enemies.

And then, of course, he would simply have to find new ones.

"Liam!"

It was Robert Montesi.

"Yes, Robert. I'm sorry, I was lost in prayer for a moment. I ask God to bless our endeavor." He paused. "You must pass the word down that today is the day. All of your soldiers must have their weapons and be gone from Vatican City before noon. Inconspicuously! By twos and threes and not to be seen as doing anything out of the ordinary if possible. Tell them . . . yes, tell them they will not be coming back and to be prepared for that. Regardless of the outcome, we cannot return here or we'll jeopardize all the church has worked for."

He looked at them, but they seemed satisfied with his explanation. They would know nothing of Garbarino's actions.

"All Rome personnel will board the train we have prepared at the train yard. Make sure they all know where it is, two-point-five miles from the station. Thomas."

"Sir?"

"Alert Venice personnel to our arrival. We will rendezvous with them at midnight exactly, just north of Santa Lucia station at the warehouse next to the Scalzi Church. At that time we will make our way into the city to take our positions so that we may move out at dawn."

"At night, Father," Isaac asked. "Aren't we sure to be spotted?"

"Of course some of us will be seen by our quarry, perhaps even killed. Nevertheless, we must be ready by dawn. Give instructions that no Defiant One is to be attacked at night. If one of our people is attacked, they may defend themselves, but in such a case they must not allow the Defiant One to escape to warn its fellows."

"During the attack, sir, what of the civilians?"

"We've been over this, Thomas. It shouldn't come to that once people see the monsters we're there to destroy. But if it does, you know the standing orders. Civilians are expendable. Property damage is expected and more than likely efficacious. Fire is one of our best natural weapons. "Any questions?"

"None at the moment, Father," Mary replied sweetly.

"No, sir," the Montesis answered together.

"Meet me back here in one hour with a full report and to receive additional instructions."

"In the name of God," they all said.

"In the name of God," Mulkerrin repeated.

It was strange enough that this familiar-faced intruder should interrupt Peter and Meaghan—just when they were starting to get better acquainted—by knocking on the window of a speeding train. But now that they had let the stranger in, not only had he apparently recognized Peter, but he had called him by his birth name, his mortal name, Nicephorus Dragases. When the surprise wore off, Peter got annoyed.

"You know me," he said, not a question.

"I reckon I do," the intruder answered.

"I don't recall ever meeting you."

"Oh, you haven't, but even so, I know you well, Nicephorus Dragases," he said, using the offending name again.

"How in hell do you know that name?" Peter growled, and the intruder retreated, hands up.

"Please, sir. I don't intend offense. We mourn the same tragedy, that of our shared friend and father, Karl Von Reinman," the intruder said, and lowered his head and his hands.

Peter was not convinced. "What is your name, brother?" he asked the stranger.

"Cody October," the intruder answered, with no small amount of pride.

Peter Octavian laughed. He shook his head to show Cody that he meant no offense, and laughed a bit more.

"Oh, shit, you scared us. I thought you looked familiar."

Now it was Cody's turn to look confused. "But we've just established that we have never met," he insisted.

"Much to my regret, sir, and it's an honor that we do so now," Peter said, extending a hand, which was promptly shaken. "I've been an admirer of your insubordination for years, and of your talents long before then."

Cody blushed then, if such could ever be said of an immortal, and executed a deep bow to the both of them. "I'm flattered."

"Uh-mmm." Meaghan cleared her throat, and Peter turned toward her, finally recovering from his nervous relief and genuine excitement at meeting this other creature, a fellow prodigal son to the same unnatural father.

"I'm so sorry. Meaghan Gallagher, meet William F. Cody," Peter said, and Cody bowed again as Meaghan nodded with an expectant smile. "Better known, of course, as Buffalo Bill."

Buffalo Bill? Meaghan smiled a genuine smile at Cody, then at Peter. "You gotta be kiddin' me," she said, her Boston accent making a rare appearance.

Cody grimaced.

"As uncomfortable as I am with the nickname, and as much as I've always preferred Will or just plain Cody, it is the label that made me famous. A mixed blessing, at best."

"Unbelievable," Meaghan said, shaking her head. "Who's next, Sitting Bull?"

"Unfortunately not," Cody answered, though it was obvious that Meaghan had expected none. "Thanks to a bastard named McLaughlin, my blood brother is far deader than I.

"Now, Peter," Cody continued, "unless of course you prefer your true name?"

"No more than you do your stage name."

"Well taken. I'm sorry to have interrupted your and Meaghan's, um, evening, but since I am here, perhaps we ought to have a look at that book?"

That brought Peter and Meaghan back to reality.

"How do you know about the book, and how do you come to know I've got it?" Peter asked as suspicion began to creep back in.

"Well, I certainly didn't just happen to guess you were on this train. I was watching the Vatican for an opportunity to grab someone who might have some answers. As for the book, I sort of assumed I knew about it from the same place you did."

"And where might that be?" Meaghan asked, still in the dark about so many things, and afraid, though she'd never show it, afraid of the dark.

"Well, from Karl, of course," Cody answered, frustrated.

"From Karl?" Peter asked.

"Certainly. He's been after the thing for years. I figured that's why Karl was assassinated, because he'd gone after the book. He wasn't nearly as old or powerful as the others."

"What others?" Peter asked, not really wanting to know.

"What the hell is going on here?" Meaghan said, mostly to herself.

Cody explained, what he knew anyway, about the assassinations, about Karl's interest in the book, about the attempt on his own life in Monte Carlo and his stakeout of

the Vatican. In return, Peter and Meaghan shared their side
of the story, Cardinal Guiscard's discovery of the book,
the murders that led to their confrontation with Mulkerrin,
the many coincidences that led Peter into the battle.

"You know," Peter finished, "I thought I would have
to put off my search for Karl's murderers until after I'd
solved this case, or leave it to the coven. But now . . . all
roads lead to Rome."

"You mentioned the coven again," Meaghan said, "but
you still haven't explained it, the setup, everything. If you
two are part of the same coven, how could you not know
each other?"

"There's more to it than that," Cody answered before
Peter could. "Karl Von Reinman brought me to this life
on my deathbed, because he knew me and didn't want me
to die. Only when Peter left did Karl bring me into the
coven, years later. Hence my name. 'October,' 'Octavian,'
see any similarity?"

"Of course, but . . ."

"Number eight, Meaghan," Cody continued. "Karl,
though I loved him, was an arrogant son of a bitch.
When he renamed us, he numbered us. Una was his
lover. Jasmine *Decard*, Louis *Onze*, Veronica *Settimo*,
Rolf *Sechs*. These were the members of our coven,
all numbered. It was one of the things that made
me leave so soon after joining them. And Peter's
reasons, if I may be so presumptuous, were also my
own."

"So when did . . ." Meaghan began, then redirected her
question. "Peter, why did you leave? And when?"

"Yes, Peter," Cody added, "I know why you left, but
Von Reinman wouldn't hear any talk of the circumstances.
What happened?"

Cody leaned against the window and Meaghan sat on
the bunk. Peter had been standing near the door, but now
he performed a minor foot shuffle, which in the cramped
space could have been interpreted as pacing. This went

on for a few moments before he turned his attention back to them.

"It was in Boston, on New Year's Eve, 1899. The turn of the century. There were thirteen of us, the coven. We were rarely all together, yet never very far apart. Bonds were formed, and animosity was born, and quite often the only thing that kept us from killing each other was Karl. A whisper was usually enough, when he was angry, to quell any furor. But that was an unusual night.

"We were introducing a new member to the coven, an Irish girl we called Shannon Twin. The tradition was to each tell our stories, to show the new member that we had nothing to hide, that we were a family. But New Year's Eve had always been a night for hunting, and as they say, the natives were restless. . . ."

"That's fine, Jazz," said Una, an older Brazilian woman who was Karl's lover. She was thanking Jasmine Decard for welcoming the newcomer, Shannon, with her story.

"Louis?"

She looked expectantly at the Frenchman, Louis Onze, who sat in a red-velvet-upholstered chair that matched the others around the room. Tastefully decorated in old European style, tapestries hanging from the walls, Karl's Boston apartment had been their New Year's Eve meeting place for five years. The locals were catching on, though, and the coven would have to find different hunting grounds for next year's gathering. As simple as it was to make immigrants disappear in Boston—especially Irish and Italians fresh off the boat—they couldn't get away with it forever.

"Louis," Karl said now as the Parisian had ignored Una's request.

"Enough," a voice said, and all eyes turned toward its source, Shi-er Zhi Sheng, a fierce little Oriental man, with his temper at boiling point.

"*Aren't you all a little tired of this?*" he said, aiming his remarks primarily at Alexandra, Trini, and Xavier, his current clan within the coven. "*I know that I, for one, was in favor of letting the second spot remain empty until the beginning of the year. The last thing we need is to be initiating a new member, lovely as she may be, at what has become for us, due to past actions here, the most dangerous city on Earth.*"

"*Sheng.*" Karl paused. "*Sit. Down.*"

He did.

"*Now, I can see that for whatever reason, the lot of you are less than enthusiastic about this initiation and introduction. I can only assume it is your urge to be down on the streets, among the thronging masses. You are forgiven, tonight. But two nights from now, we finish this process. Shannon will receive the same courtesies that you all received upon becoming a member of this coven. I will make absolutely certain of that.*

"*Now,*" he continued.

"*Let's hunt!*" Xavier shouted.

"*Hell, let's eat,*" Trini added.

Peter looked at them, scanning the room for some hesitation. He didn't find any. Trini and Xavier had the bloodlust in their eyes, Veronica and Ellen were still glaring at each other, but they were putting their cloaks on, getting ready for the stroke of midnight, the moment the new year would begin and a dozen lives would end. It had always been a baker's dozen, but not this year. Jazz and Louis played in a corner, the lovers batting each other about like savage kittens. Una comforted Shannon, who looked frightened at the prospect of slaughtering her own people. Karl helped the two on with their cloaks. Rolf, the mute German, hovered about, searching for something to do with his hands.

Alexandra Nueva and Shi-er Zhi Sheng stood to one side. Like Peter, they had not reached for their coats, and now the two whispered to one another, each in turn *glancing at Peter for a moment and then looking away. The most perceptive of the group, other than Karl of course, they'd seen it coming for months, and now here it was.*

"Let's go, children," Karl said, chiding kindly, "you've got to at least look human if you're to feast at midnight."

Alexandra and Sheng picked up their coats, looking at Peter with a mixture of anger and amusement. Peter looked away, unable to face them, though he knew in his heart he had made the right decision.

In my heart I know, he thought, but what right does a cold, dead heart have to feel such pain?

"Peter?" Karl said, asking many things in two syllables.

Why don't you have your coat on?

Why aren't you looking at me?

Have you finally decided to speak your mind?

Oh, yes. Karl had almost certainly realized several months ago that there was something going on in Peter's head. Something that might cause Karl to disown his favorite son. There was bad blood between them, and with their kind, such feelings could be avoided only for so long.

"I'm not going."

Their silence, the stares of his family, were more painful to him than the glare of the sun could ever be. He thought he might die right there.

"What do you mean, you're not going?" Xavier Penta asked him, the black man's eyes wide, his jaw open in shock.

"Just so. I'm not hunting with you tonight, or ever again."

He looked up now, directly into the eyes of his mentor, his true father, his best friend, Karl Von Reinman. He found them exactly as he expected, sad rather than angry like the others.

"You're too good for us now, Peter? Is that it?" Ellen asked, spiteful that another man would leave her. The story of her life. This time, though, she and Veronica were of one mind.

"No, Ellie. He just likes to slap his father in the face."

That did it.

"I will say this once, for the benefit of the entire coven, and especially for you, scared little Shannon," he added, motioning to the girl. "Do not ever attempt to question my relationship with our father. It is not your place to do so.

"As to why I will not hunt with you . . . simply put, I no longer hunt. Truly, I have not hunted humans in months."

Karl's sadness turned to shock. He had sensed Peter would be leaving, but this . . . They were all stunned.

"Now, Peter," Louis began, but Una interrupted.

"How can you live?" she asked, concerned for him now.

"I manage."

"Coward!" Trini yelled, stepping up to him now, right past Karl, who still had not said a word. "Weak, frightened woman, who are you to call yourself warrior? You shame your family!"

"Trini," Karl said, speaking up finally.

But Trini went on, shouting his hate into Peter's face, yet Octavian simply stood there. "You are not one of us, gelding. You spit in your father's face! We should hunt you ourselves, you arrogant, traitorous coward. If I—"

And Karl struck him down. As Peter watched, Karl's arm lashed out once and Trini crumpled to the ground, his next insult dying as it reached his tongue.

In the moment that followed, the heartbeat that intervened between that triumphant moment and the impending, heartrending pain, an awful tableau burned itself eternally onto the memory of Peter Octavian, he who had been Nicephorus Dragases until the father of his spirit and of his agony renamed him. Those he loved now despised him. Alexandra Nueva and Shi-er Zhi Sheng had been his closest friends other than Karl. He had purposely drifted away from them, intent upon freeing his spirit from the hell of conscience that had suddenly and irrevocably been born within him. It had surprised him, but they did not seem surprised at all by his actions now. It was their silent presence, as silent as Rolf, which made the picture so painful. They had said nothing, but their eyes radiated more hate than all of the others. His friends . . .

"Why?" Karl asked, finally, ending the moment, severing Peter's bond with Alex and Sheng forever. Now to destroy his bond with Karl.

"The humans," he said quietly, though surely they could all hear him. "It was different when we were warriors, and even then it was a slaughter. But we were almost always fighting for something. For decades now, it's been just killing and more killing."

"Peter." Karl shook his head, not understanding. "They're animals."

"You don't understand," Peter said, exasperated child to parent.

"Explain it to me."

"They're you! Don't you see?" Now he turned to the group, sweeping his arm to include them all. "They're you. That's why you kill them. Surely, you need the blood, but they don't have to die and you don't have to take it without asking. You kill them because you hate them. What are these humans whom we discuss as if they were cattle?"

"They are cattle!" Karl screamed, at last.

"No, my friend," Peter continued, softly still at first, then growing to a shout, "I say again, they are you. But not you. They are greater than we who can live forever, can take their lives at will. They have powerful spirits, the wonderful certainty of death, and warm, beating hearts. We hate them and kill them because they are us!"

Then, quiet again.

"And I cannot do it anymore."

Finally, Peter bent to pick up his long coat, slipping it on. He looked up again at Sheng and Alex, the tiny Oriental and his tall, black goddess of a lover. The hate was gone now, and Peter thought he saw a strange mixture of pity and amusement on their faces. He turned back to Karl, whose own face was a mask of sadness.

"Will I see you again?" his best friend asked.

"Not soon."

And he left.

As he told his story Peter turned away from them, fumbled for something to do with his hands. Meaghan felt for him. Peter knew he had done right, but the specter of betrayal still haunted him. She reached out and pulled him down to sit beside her on the bunk.

"And that was it?" she said.

"No. Later that same night I came upon Alexandra and Sheng attacking a pregnant woman, an Irish prostitute, on her way home apparently. I knew I could not stop them from hunting, but the infant was an innocent. I . . . stopped them. I took the woman to the nearest building which would open its doors."

After a moment of silence Meaghan spoke. "The woman died?"

"Yes," Peter said. "But I returned the next night and discovered that the child lived. A boy, he was taken to a church orphanage."

"Well," Cody said, turning back toward the window, "I wish they had let me go so easily."

"They didn't?" Meaghan asked, and she and Peter both looked at him.

"Oh, Karl told them to leave me be, but some of them didn't listen. I guess I just rubbed them the wrong way, eh? But that's a story for another time." Cody looked at Peter and realized he wasn't paying attention. "Peter?"

"Oh, sorry," Octavian said, shaking his head. "Just thinking about all of this, about Karl."

"It was awful," Cody said, and the two immortals locked eyes for a moment. Like all those creatures who had been made more than human by Karl Von Reinman, they had witnessed his death in their minds. "More than awful, as helpless as we were, but we will avenge him or truly die in the attempt."

In the silence that followed, a pact had been made. Cody wasn't the only one who fancied himself a hero, nor the only one who knew what honor was.

"All right, let's get back to the here and now." Meaghan broke the silence, recognizing the men's grief but not wanting to allow it to affect their efforts. "Let me see if I've got this straight. Von Reinman hired this Gypsy to steal the book, and we know that the guy just sort of up and died when Henri Guiscard walked in on him. Are we to assume this master thief had a weak heart?"

"I sorta doubt that," Cody said. "I'd be willing to bet Karl hypnotized the man, planted a mental time bomb in him that, in the event of his discovery, would cause his heart to simply explode on the spot."

Meaghan was horrified.

"Get used to it, Meaghan. Cody and I aren't innocent by a long shot, but we're about as innocent as our kind gets. The majority are devils, all right. There's a reason for every stereotype, and thankfully, an exception to every rule. But make no mistake when we get to Venice—Defiant Ones are, in the main, evil and vicious creatures. Forget that and it could kill you."

Meaghan took this as seriously as Peter meant it, and yet there was something about his words that just didn't sit right with her. Looking at the two that she had ever met, she found it hard to believe that the creatures could be evil simply by their nature.

"Well, why didn't Von Reinman go himself?" she asked, back to matters at hand.

It was Cody's turn to get quiet as he backed off and looked at them both more closely. "Yes, Peter," he said warily. "Tell Meaghan why Karl didn't go himself to steal the book."

"Simply that he couldn't," Octavian answered. He hadn't noticed the tone of Cody's voice. "Legend has told us that our kind cannot traverse holy ground."

"But, Peter," Meaghan countered, "tonight you—"

"Went in there yourself!" Cody finished for her. "How in hell did you do that, friend? I would never have believed it if I hadn't seen it with my own eyes."

Peter shook his head. "In a way, and this is not meant as an insult, I sort of expected more of you, Will. Of course, it took me more than four hundred years to figure it out, so I shouldn't act so high-and-mighty."

Meaghan had some idea of what Peter was talking about, but he'd never explained it to her in detail and she was fascinated. Cody, on the other hand, didn't have a clue, and this was obvious to both of them from the look on his face.

"It's all bullshit," Peter said.

"What?"

"Bullshit, Cody. It's a load of crap. The sun, crosses, holy ground, all of that stuff is pure shit, made up by the church to weaken us, to give us those handicaps, to control us. Everything except maybe for silver, which is poison in some way. Our race has been brainwashed. Don't you think there were Defiant Ones—don't you think there were *vampires* around before the church was there to call us 'Defiant Ones,' before the cross meant anything, or their version of 'holy ground'?"

"Well, of course, but—"

"Doesn't it stand to reason, then, that if the religious aspects of legend are not true that all other aspects of the myth must be called into question?"

"Yes, of course, but if all of this is true, well, I mean, how did you figure it out?"

"That night, the night I betrayed the coven, when I stopped Sheng and Alexandra's attack on the prostitute? I said I took her to the nearest door. Only when I was inside, laying her dying form on a table, did I realize it was a church."

Cody nodded in understanding.

"That night I realized that not only were we not what we believed ourselves to be, but that we have never known exactly what we are."

"Which is?" Cody said, stepping closer to them.

Peter looked up and the eyes of two noble men met in sorrow and wonder. "I truly do not know," he said. "Any more than I can discover what the church knows about us, and how they were able to play with our minds in the first place."

Peter smiled then. A clever smile that made the others smile, too, though they didn't know what for. He picked up the leather case within which lay the book that had been the source of their troubles and their questions.

"But I know you for a gambling man, Will Cody. And I'm willing to bet that the answers to all of our questions are in here."

"Well, then let's get to it!" Meaghan said.

"There's something else you both should know," Peter said. "Cody, you haven't asked where this train is headed, but if you think about it for a minute, I'm sure you can guess easily enough."

"Oh, shit," Cody said quietly. "Venice."

"That's right, brother. We're going to the family reunion, something I would guess neither of us has done in a long time. I can't imagine we'll be too welcome there."

"That's for sure."

"And yet we have to go. Meaghan and I had planned to go anyway, to see if we could find sanctuary and also because I wanted to know what was being done about finding Karl's killer. Now we don't have a choice. It's the only place we can go."

Peter's face was dark with anger, his eyes cold, and Meaghan knew she would never want to be the cause of that rage.

"What happened?" was all she said.

"Your assassinations, Cody? They're a part of a larger plan, a much larger plan. Something I overheard Mulkerrin and his superior referring to as a 'Blessed Event.' Time is short, they said, and they must move on Venice as soon as possible."

"So these killings," Cody picked up, "they're a smoke screen. Nothing more than a way to keep us off balance and unsuspecting of their real motives."

"Or a way to make sure that some of our most powerful will be absent when the attack comes," Peter answered.

"But in broad daylight?" Meaghan said.

"When better?" Peter nodded, a rueful smile on his lips.

"Speaking of which," Cody said, getting back to business, "we'd better put the rest of this off until later. Sunrise is only a few hours off and I want to get an idea of what this book is all about before we look for a place to sleep."

Peter looked shocked.

"What?" Cody said.

"With all due respect, um, Will," Meaghan began, "I don't think you get it. What Peter had said means these guys will be moving on your people as soon as they can get mobilized. You don't have time to sit out the day in some dark room or a hole in the ground. This train will roll into Venice well after sunrise, and when it does, we're all getting off."

"But I'll die!"

"Haven't you been listening? That's all garbage, and besides, from what I've been able to pick up, you're already dead. That much isn't part of your brainwashing anyway. We'll take an hour to go over this book, and then Peter's going to coach you a bit on what is and isn't true, and then it's going to be up to you!"

"But I—"

"Look, you're just going to have to trust us, okay! I mean if I can take all of this in and stay sane, then it's the least you can do to try to learn a little faith!"

Peter and Cody just looked at her, the former with a wide grin and a heart full of pleasure and pride, the latter in surprise and admiration mixed with a good amount of fear of the coming day.

"Faith," Peter said, putting his arm around Meaghan. "What a concept."

They took out the book and began to read.

✳

20

IN HER ROOMS, SISTER MARY MAGDALENE, to most known only as Sister Mary, prepared herself. She dressed in black, but in street clothes: slacks, a sweater, winter boots. It was to be the uniform of their forces upon arrival in Venice. She packed a change of clothing and two changes of her underthings in a black canvas bag, along with the silver dagger that was her only weapon. Of course, this did not include the weapon of her mind, her studies, her words. No, the dagger was for pleasure killing, for close-quarters dispatch of the hellspawn that had scarred her so. Certainly she had spells enough to do the job, but she enjoyed the physical struggle, enjoyed scarring them with hated silver in return for her own mutilation.

She had her orders, though; take no chances. Still, if an opportunity presented itself . . .

The Montesi brothers were also preparing. Isaac and Thomas packed their things, including a steel-reinforced silver sword, passed to them by their father and now dedicated to the purpose of eliminating his murderer, should they discover both his identity and his whereabouts. Though they didn't expect to find out the creature's name, they could be fairly certain of his whereabouts in the next several days. The two chatted eagerly about the coming battle, about where they would go when it was complete, and about the creatures they knew by name, whom they had been attempting to track but had not yet found.

Among them would be Peter Octavian, and almost assuredly this Cody October, who had popped up seemingly out of nowhere in Monte Carlo, distracting a team sent to find another one, a very old one. The team went after him and failed, and only one of them returned to tell of it. So he survived and the team did not achieve their goal, the discovery and death of the Defiant One called Hannibal.

"I knew I should have led the Monte Carlo group," Isaac said now, mostly to Thomas because Robert was ignoring his older brothers. Par for the course.

"You can't blame yourself," Thomas answered.

"No, he's right," Robert said now, and looked up from the map of Venice, where he'd been charting their strategy in minute detail.

"What?" Isaac and Thomas asked together, surprised that they had elicited a response at all.

"Truly," Robert said. "Or one of us should have been there at least. This can't happen again. After all, the Von Reinman thing went smoothly, clearly because we were there. Certainly we lost some good men, but the effort would almost certainly have failed if we had not been along.

"Actually," he continued, "we should be on all of these expeditions. Isn't one of the main reasons for these assassinations that each of us, and Liam as well, wants to find the creature that killed Father? Why, this one that they went after in Monte Carlo, Hannibal. He could be the one, and there, we've missed it."

"Yes, but our own thirst for vengeance is not the only, or even the primary reason for the killings," Thomas said, and they all were silent.

Robert cleared his throat and glanced around the small, spartan room, noticing for the first time the stale, sterile smell and the dull sunlight filtering through the window. He knew what his brothers were thinking, that even though Mulkerrin also wanted their father's killer found, he would not be pleased to find them making this their priority. In the larger scheme, they had hunted the older ones to lessen the chance that the Defiant Ones would discover and somehow overcome their mental bonds, as well as to thin the potential resistance in Venice. Von Reinman had been punished for his use of the dead Gypsy thief to attempt to steal *The Gospel of Shadows*. Robert shuddered to think of the book in the hands of Defiant Ones.

"All of this would have gone smoothly if it hadn't been for Von Reinman," he said. "Liam would not have been in Boston, and we *would* have been in Monte Carlo. Then we might have gotten Hannibal *and* Cody."

"And that's why Von Reinman died then, and not in Venice," Isaac said. "If only we'd known about this Octavian earlier."

"We could not have," Robert insisted. "There was nothing to indicate he might be a threat. We've been too confident."

"You're absolutely right," Thomas said. "After this purge, we're going to have to be extraordinarily careful tracking down those few who escape or who didn't come in the first place. With what we know this Octavian can do, and how clever the cowboy from Monte Carlo is, why, we've no idea what we'll come up against next. No, proceed with caution is the best course."

"And of course, the way we'll find Father's killer," Robert added.

Isaac and Thomas looked at each other then, because they'd shared thoughts about just that subject a short time earlier. They had wondered together whether it was finding their father's murderer that drove Robert so and gave him an almost supernatural energy, or whether it was simply the search itself.

Instinct told them both that their little brother was different. They were soldiers, assassins, and sorcerers in training; Robert was an artist. In that way, he was the most like their father, and like their mentor, Liam Mulkerrin. Certainly, Isaac and Thomas Montesi loved their work.

For their brother, though, it was lust.

They hadn't been able to read the whole book, not only because some of *The Gospel of Shadows* was in Latin so old even Peter could barely understand it, but because of time. They'd agreed from the start that there was very little of that commodity; they needed time to look at the book, a little time to rest, and Cody needed some time to get used to the idea that he was going to have to go out in the sun.

William Cody had always been an adventurous man, filled with strength and courage. In life he became a lovable braggart, but with a grain of truth in all his showman's tales. It had been a long time since he was comfortable admitting to anybody that he was frightened, but not far into their reading, he said just that.

"Lord, I'm scared," he said, and Peter nodded, confirming that Cody was not alone in his fear.

But they didn't have time to be afraid, or to read all the many reasons they ought to be.

So they skimmed.

When they had finished, a cold silence settled over them, then Meaghan stood up.

"Look, it's almost dawn and we've got about an hour and a half until we reach Venice. We should try to get some rest, hmm?"

"You're right," Cody answered. "Only thing is, this little berth is pretty cramped right now, never mind if we all try to catch a few winks in here. Why don't I find an empty berth? I'm sure there are a couple."

"What about the sun?" Peter asked, before Meaghan could voice the same thought.

Cody had started to walk toward the door, but now he turned, head down. It was a moment before he looked up at them, and his anxiety was plain.

"It's there in the book, Peter. I'll pull the curtains in the berth and come down the hall against the wall, away from the window. It'll be good practice for me before I have to be in direct light. When we have to get off the train, why, you'll get off first. I read the book—in my head I know it's all bullshit, but my gut isn't sure. Once I see you standing there in the sun, I think I'll be okay."

"You have to be," Meaghan said, a command rather than a plea.

"You will be," Peter said.

Cody turned to go again, but then looked back at them and laughed. "You know, it seems like such an extraordinary fiction. That damned book is so outrageous! Hell, I'm an undead, blood-drinking creature of the night, and *I* can barely believe it!"

Meaghan moved toward him, a hand on his elbow. "No," she said, "the outrage, the fiction, is what they've put in your head. Now you're just like me. All the things you thought you knew for certain are wrong, and you're going to have to have some faith."

"There's that faith business again," Peter said, putting the book away. "I never used to believe in God because of all the crooks who claimed to be His voice. But I've come to think he may be up there after all, watching the mess, pissed off at the poseurs and wishing He could start all over again."

"They can't all be poseurs," Meaghan said.

"Well, they're not all as bad as Mulkerrin and friends, even in Rome. We know from what we just read that *this* pope, at least, is in the dark. But nobody's got the whole picture right. If they did, what would be the point of God?"

"The New Church of the Undead." Cody laughed again, then shook his head. "Faith."

"You'll die without it," Peter said, and on that sober note, they parted for a rest.

• • •

Not surprisingly, none of them got much sleep. Cody spent the little time thinking more about the book and what the day and, more important, the daylight would have in store for him.

When Cody had left, Peter and Meaghan were quiet, comfortable together in their silence. Peter lay down on the lower bunk and put his arms behind his head, staring up at nothing and wondering where the hell all this was heading. His thoughts leaned toward another subject as well, one neither of his companions had considered. Just what kind of reception could they expect in Venice? It took him only a moment to decide that they would have to work fast. The arrogance and anger of the Defiant Ones, especially those with whom Peter and Cody had past relationships, could end up getting them all killed.

Meaghan went to the window and looked out at dawn rediscovering the Italian landscape. Peter assumed that she was attempting to digest all she had learned from the book, from him and Cody, and to prepare for the days to come as they upped the stakes even further. He was wrong.

In truth, Meaghan was much stronger than Peter, or even she herself, would have guessed. She had confronted his nature, the existence of his kind, the contents of the book that he had stolen back from its original owners, not to mention the idea that Buffalo Bill Cody, a hero half out of American history and half out of American myth, was there, on the train with them. She had come with Peter for so many reasons, not the least of which was simply because she wanted to. Certainly she wanted to do anything she could to get Mulkerrin, the man who murdered her best friend, her lover.

She recognized with a frightening mental clarity that she had stepped outside the realm of morality, but also that it was a morality upheld by the same systems that had created the religious beliefs she now knew were so much smoke and mirrors. She had no problem with the concept of killing Mulkerrin. That same clarity made it a simple thing to admit, and actually to embrace, the excitement, the solidly sexual thrill she associated with danger, with fear. She had entered a brand-new world, that almost nobody human was aware of. All her life she'd wanted more, and now she'd gotten it.

All of this she had realized, almost before they ever reached Rome.

And yet she knew for certain that her attraction to Peter was not based solely on these things, but on her knowledge of him. He was a hero. A kind, courageous creature whose instinct tells him to kill her, to drink her life essence, and yet who wishes nothing more than to have her, to make love to her in the way that a man, a human man, would. She could see that battle in his eyes and she trusted completely in his ability to win it, to control the darkness in him.

The Gospel of Shadows had completed something for her, a concept that had been yearning to be born in her brain, a puzzle that had at last gained a missing piece. Of all the creatures of the night, the demons and wraiths and their like, only Peter's kind had been able to fight back, to keep their freedom, to remain *defiant*. Now she believed with all her heart that the reason for this was a simple one, a spiritual one.

They had souls.

As a living, breathing, rational human, it was the only explanation which made any sense to her. They were able to fight for their own destiny because they had once been human, and that is human nature. The nature of the human soul.

At the beginning she had almost lost it, almost gone over the edge. But since that time, in her apartment, when she had started down this path, she had never looked back. She was a part of this thing, no matter what new insanity threatened them. Now only one question remained to her.

Where did she fit in?

She was human, after all.

What part was she going to play in the coming conflict? Would those gathered for carnival in Venice allow her to take part? Might they not simply kill her? Against such an enormous group, would even Peter and Cody be able to protect her?

No, she'd get no rest. Rather than worry about what was to come, she knew that there was business left unfinished. She turned and walked the few steps to the bunk, where Peter had been watching her for minutes, as the sunlight blossomed on her face.

She sat by him, on the edge of the mattress, and put her hand on his chest. "Make love to me," she said, though she didn't need to.

Peter reached out and pulled her to him, Meaghan's lips inviting him with more than just words. They kissed deeply, deliberately. They knew time was of the essence, and all the more reason to draw their time together out, to make it last until they must move on to the challenges ahead.

Meaghan's robe slipped easily from her shoulders as she helped Peter with his pants. Their kisses explored each newly revealed inch of flesh with a curiosity that was more than sexual. Peter had never been with a human woman who knew, truly knew, what he was. Meaghan was overcome by wonder and fear.

"Bite me," she whispered in his ear. "Taste my blood."

His rhythm didn't slow, but he frowned. "No. I don't need to."

She pushed him off then, onto the floor, so he was sitting there. Then she sat down on him, lifting his penis and guiding it into her again. They faced each other, sitting up, as she rode him, and now Meaghan looked directly into Peter's eyes, so he could see she meant it, so he could recognize the sincerity of her lust.

"It's not for you. *I want it.* I want you to do it. Bite me," she said, in time with the bouncing of her hips. "Taste me, just a little."

She kissed him, hard, then licked his lips. Peter kissed back, overwhelmed by her desire. His mouth moved down to her neck, but Meaghan stopped him.

"Not there," she breathed, her voice filled with the whisper of need. She pushed his head down, leaning back as he licked her left breast, taking it into his mouth. He ran his sharp teeth over her nipple, then moved on and, without pause, sank those teeth into the soft flesh of her breast.

As he did she moaned, deep and loud, not from pain but from the release she felt building. His ecstasy was equally clear as Meaghan's nails raked his back, digging furrows in the flesh that healed seconds after they were made. Again and again she scratched him as he sucked the blood from her breast, sliding on his cock, his hands gripping her ass.

He leaned back then, pulling his face from her chest, grunting and still slamming into her as he came in huge spasms within her. Peter's orgasm was joined by her own as Meaghan quivered, impaled on his penis, her legs twitching behind his back.

Covered with her sweat—for he didn't sweat—a small amount of blood smearing between them, they held each other close, still quaking slightly. She kissed him again as he withered inside her, and she wanted nothing more than that.

Then the train began to slow and they heard a knock, at the door this time, and then Will Cody's voice. "Venice," was all he said.

"Give us a minute," Peter croaked out, but certainly loud enough for Will to hear, then he smiled at Meaghan—a smile she had never seen before. She thought that must have been the smile of Nicephorus, a brave, young, passionate man.

Meaghan looked down at the twin wounds, so tiny, on her breast, then up at Peter. The smile was gone and he looked sad for a moment. But she shook her head, smiling herself now, touched her breast, the small holes, then put her fingers to her mouth tasting her own blood and sweat. Then she leaned forward and looked him in the eye again.

"Thank you," she said, smiling, kissed him, then slowly slipped off him.

She'd already decided what her role was to be. The only question left was how to explain it to Peter.

21

THE ROOM HAD BEEN BUILT FOR ROUGH play. Soft black leather filled with down and some other kind of padding beneath that prevented sound from escaping and allowed play to continue even if the walls were coated with whatever variety of human fluids could be expected to splash, drip, or smear on such surfaces.

Tracey looked around, taking in the instruments of pain/pleasure. Though she had some little knowledge of these sex games, she didn't recognize any of the room's furnishings. Monstrous things they were, and she turned away, back to her predicament. In the back of her mind a voice piped up, attempting to decide which of those torture machines would be the least painful and wondering how anyone could enjoy such things. Would she?

Certainly not.

Here she was chained, though most elegantly, to the wall. She sat on a black leather chaise, fully clothed, for Hannibal had given her back her things and asked her to get dressed before incarcerating her. In general she had no plans to cooperate with him, but she couldn't refuse to get dressed. She'd nearly frozen to death in that water, and even now was chilled to her bones. She knew that she must be getting sick. How could she not? The room itself was fairly warm, and smelled of something terribly sweet, like sticky cinnamon buns. And it was black, but for the lamp next to her, which was green and obviously not a part of the room's usual decoration.

Everything was black—the walls, floor, and ceiling, the machines, the door, even the chains. The one that kept her here led from a black metal plate on the wall to a shackle, padded on the inside, around her right ankle. The links of the chain between were invisible, the whole thing covered in a padded black leather sheath of some sort. The other chains in the room were not as forgiving.

For captured prey, she was being treated fairly well. She'd been fed, allowed to choose a book from the library, and was treated with deference by Hannibal's human servants, none of whom was shackled.

Now she sat, her throat raw, her forehead hot and her nose running like crazy. She was getting very sick and there wasn't a damn thing she could do about it. Of course, Hannibal had two quick and sure cures for her illness, but neither was terribly attractive to her. No, now that the sun was up—and she knew it was, for they would never have chained her if Hannibal was around to hunt her down if she got free—she pretended to read while her mind analyzed every escape plot she hatched, and rejected them all.

She had to get out! She had to call in the damn story. CNN had a bureau in Rome, but there was an outside chance that there'd be a team in Venice to cover carnival. Certainly there would be some reporters here, and even if CNN had to share the story or the tape, it would still be her story, and that's what mattered. Not only did the world desperately need to be warned, but she wanted—no, needed—to be the one to warn them.

Patience!

After all, they'd have to feed her.

"Look at me, damn you!" Peter yelled.

He and Meaghan were standing on the train platform, both urging Cody to step out from the shadows of the train itself. Will had stood aside as the other passengers had filed past him, and Meaghan had run to buy both men hats and sunglasses in the station. She was gone only minutes, and Cody had made a little joke about the hat. A man used to sombreros and cowboy hats, his dislike of its narrow-brimmed style was plain.

"It'll keep the sun off your face," Peter had said. "That's all you need to worry about for now."

But now he wasn't being quite so kind as the train conductor walked toward them, clearly curious as to why their fellow passenger refused to step down from the train.

"Look at me, Will!"

"I'm looking," Cody replied, exasperated. "Doesn't it hurt, at least?"

"Yes, it fucking hurts! It really hurts at first, like every inch of uncovered skin getting stung by bees all at once. But it doesn't last, understand. It wears off until it's just an uncomfortable ache, like a light sunburn. Surely you remember sunburns?"

"I hated them then, when they weren't likely to kill me, and I surely hate them now," Cody snapped.

There was a long pause, and the conductor was almost upon them. Meaghan knew he would tell them to shove off, and she didn't want to get into an argument. She turned to Cody.

"You damn coward!" she growled.

He looked like he'd been slapped, then began to stutter some kind of reply, but she was having none of it.

"Some hero you are! The noblest whiteskin, the great scout, the world's greatest showman. Sounds like a bunch of buffalo shit to me! You're supposed to be *the* man's man—gambler, lover, hunter, horseman, the best at everything, the symbol of the Wild West. But that's all crap, isn't it, because William Frederick Cody, the hero of children around the world, Buffalo Bill, is afraid of getting a sunburn!"

While Peter looked stunned, Cody's face went from shocked to embarrassed to angry, and the train conductor, who'd finally reached them, tapped his foot patiently and waited for her to finish, obviously recognizing Meaghan as a force to be reckoned with, and not to be interrupted. When she did finish, all three men fumbled for something to say.

Meaghan didn't afford them the luxury.

"Come on, Peter," she said, turning on her heel without so much as a look back, "let mama's boy ride the train back and forth until nightfall. It'll probably all be over by then anyway."

Peter looked after her, eyebrows raised. He opened his mouth, but nothing came out and she kept right on walking. He turned to Cody and shrugged, a guilty, silly grin fighting to break out on his face. Finally he shook his head and laughed, then followed after her, catching up easily. The conductor watched them for a moment, then turned to their reluctant companion.

Red-faced with fury and humiliation, not daring to give it another thought, Cody was out in the sunshine and hurrying after them before the first word was out of the conductor's mouth. He didn't understand Italian anyway.

"I know what you tried to do," he said to Meaghan as he caught up to them, "and it didn't work. I'm out here because I want to be, not because of your petty child-ish antics. Lord, woman, but you are a pain in the ass! And you," he said, turning on Peter now, "you'd better be right, 'cause right now I'm hurting like hell."

And indeed, his flesh felt like it was on fire. But, he consoled himself, at least it only felt like it.

"Don't you worry your pretty little face, Will." Peter laughed. "We've got more than enough worrying to do to keep your mind off of dying."

"You're right. I'm sorry, no more delays."

"Okay, look," Peter said, their conversation taking a sober turn. "The sun is our advantage—it'll keep us from being attacked by some of our friends who hold a grudge, at least until we can talk to them about what's going on."

"Fine," Meaghan said. "Now, where do we start?"

"I think I know just the place," Peter said.

It was just past eleven in the morning when Giancarlo Garbarino arrived for his appointment with His Holiness the Pope. As usual, the pontiff was late, and Garbarino sat in his parlor awaiting his return from Mass. A papal attendant brought him herbal tea, though what he would really have liked was some of that Viennese chocolate coffee. Unfortunately, with the pope's poor health, such things were too rich for him.

When finally he did show up, the pope seemed perturbed, barely acknowledging the clumsy bow and perfunctory kiss of the ring he received from Garbarino, disrespectful attempts at tradition that would have insulted a more prideful, less pious pontiff. He stepped into his internal chambers with Garbarino on his heels, then turned and stepped into the small library that served as his private office. This space was reserved for those around whom he felt comfortable. Garbarino knew the Holy Father didn't like him, but he also knew that the man respected him and his academic efforts.

The attendant who had served Giancarlo his tea—Paulo, he thought the man's name was—appeared immediately just as the pope was about to summon him.

"Tea, Your Holiness?" Paulo asked.

"No, thank you," the pope replied.

"Cardinal?"

"Yes, please, Paulo. And from the looks of it, though he said no, His Holiness will probably change his mind about the tea, so bring him a cup as well." He smiled at the young man.

The pope looked at Garbarino, ready to argue about the tea, but then changed his mind and settled back in his comfortable burgundy leather chair. "Paulo," he said, "please bring the tea and then do not disturb us. I am in ill humor today, and the cardinal better be here to cheer me up."

He smiled at Garbarino, then, but it had no effect.

Your humor is not what ails you, the cardinal thought.

"And why so cranky today?" Garbarino asked, as usual abandoning all pretense of propriety in addressing the pontiff.

"My back is acting up," the pope replied, "but more than that, attendance at this morning's Mass was frightfully low, and you know how that bothers me."

"Ah, well, don't fret. I know a lot of my people were going out today on the newest research venture, and that flu that's going around . . ."

"Yes, I'm coming down with it myself, I fear."

Paulo reentered then, setting his platter down silently in front of Garbarino, who shushed him away when he reached for the pot. He left the room, shutting the door behind him, letting Garbarino pour the water for tea.

As he placed tea bags in the cups a small capsule dropped from his palm into the pope's tea, its membrane dissolving immediately and releasing a clear, tasteless liquid that would mix with the tea within minutes. He had done away with John Paul I in the very same fashion.

He served the pontiff first, then himself, watching as His Holiness began to sip at the steaming cup. Garbarino began to smile and sip his own tea. With John Paul it had been important that he not be discovered. This time, however, nothing mattered. If they knew the pope had been murdered, if they knew he was the killer, such knowledge would be useless, for he'd be long gone, never to return.

Ah, but such a service he was performing for the glory of the true God, whose nature Roman Catholicism had only begun to grasp. It was control that mattered, mastery of all things, all creatures, natural and unnatural. This was what God had intended for man, and for His church.

He chided himself, as the pope sipped, not to become overwrought. After all, he was a soldier in God's army, a pious man, not a self-righteous, self-serving lunatic like Liam Mulkerrin. No, of the many things that caused Giancarlo Garbarino to commit the sin of pride, the foremost was this—he considered himself completely sane, something he couldn't say about many others.

"You know, Giancarlo," the pope said, putting down his cup after only a couple of sips, enough to make him ill surely, but probably not enough to kill him. "I've been wondering for some time about Cardinal Guiscard."

Now Garbarino perked up. Where was this coming from?

"Henri Guiscard was quite a scholar—is quite a scholar still, I should think. I never understood why you didn't want him on your Vatican Historical Council, unless it was simply that you didn't want to compete with another cardinal. Regardless, his disappearance concerns me, as does the disappearance of that hellish book."

"The book, Your Holiness?" Ah, all propriety now, aren't we, he thought.

"Well, I never got through the whole thing, only bits and pieces here and there, and of course the reports you wrote about it. But, well, we agreed that it was yet another example of misguided zeal along the lines of the Inquisition. I mean, vampires? Weren't witches and exorcists bad enough?"

"Quite true," Garbarino agreed, though in actuality the only portions of the book the pope had ever read were those Garbarino included in his reports on the subject.

"While many suffered and died for those false impressions, the church doesn't need any more bad press. We still haven't gotten out from under that Father Porter fiasco," the cardinal said.

The pope visibly shivered, whether from the poison or disgust, Garbarino couldn't tell.

"But why Guiscard?" the pontiff continued. "Not that I knew him well, but he seemed genuine enough. And more intelligent than most of us, for certain. Why take that book? If he had wanted to hurt us with it, which doesn't make sense in the first place, why hasn't he done something with it?"

"I can't honestly say, Your Holiness," *but it seems you might have become a liability even if you weren't needed as a diversion.*

The pope sighed then. "Well, I can't help but hold you partially to blame," he said.

"Me?"

"Well, if it weren't for your recommendations, I would have had the thing destroyed and we wouldn't have this problem, would we? I can't even brief the PR people unless the thing comes out, because if it doesn't, I'll have told them about it for nothing, and then it probably *will* get out. It's so frustrating."

"I'm certain it must be," Garbarino said, "and I'm sorry for whatever role I played in these events."

"Ah well," the pope said, "nothing to be done about it now."

He paused, his head bobbing for a moment. "And suddenly I'm feeling even worse. It appears the flu has caught up with me, after all."

"Drink your tea," Garbarino said. "You'll feel much better."

"No, thank you, though, Giancarlo, but I didn't really want it in the first place. That herbal flavor is simply awful, but I dare not tell that to Paulo, who has somehow been told it's my favorite. I'll just ring him now, to pick up the tray. If you're done with yours, that is."

The Pope reached for his intercom, but Giancarlo's hand stopped his before he could reach the button.

"I'm afraid I can't let you do that."

In two and threes they left, from all exits, and singly as well. Fathers and brothers and sisters, drifting out of the Vatican with no hint of shared purpose, no recognition of one another. Vatican police surely noticed a larger volume of clergy on their way to museums, to the airport, to shop, visit hospitals and churches, or merely to walk. The clergy who were not leaving, who were not aware of the sinister purpose behind this exodus, also noticed a larger volume of departures than usual in those morning hours.

Those taking their leave set off in many different directions, at different times, and purportedly for different reasons . . . while many may have thought the volume peculiar, none thought to remark upon it.

As they made their way toward the appointed meeting place, two and one half miles from the train station in Rome—some taking far more circuitous routes than others—they were joined by several dozen additional clergy members from the Roman community. Sister Mary and the Montesis had organized this exodus so well that it indeed appeared to be nothing more than coincidence.

Unless, of course, you happened to be standing near the train yard as Roman clergy filtered in, in threes and fours, and boarded the train. If you watched while some emerged in a new uniform of all black, male and female alike, without collar or habit, you would most certainly have been curious. If you had seen many of these people take gleaming silver daggers from the assorted bags and totes and briefcases that they carried and hide them in the folds of these new uniforms, or in the boots they wore, unlike anything you could have seen clergy wearing before, well, then you certainly would have remarked upon it to the first person who would listen.

And Vincenzo Pustizzi had every intention of doing just that, of stumbling from the train yard where he often slept and telling the first policeman he came into contact with. He would have done exactly that if Robert Montesi hadn't seen him first. If the youngest Montesi brother hadn't called upon something invisible, something awful, to crawl inside him and eat his heart, he would have blown the whistle for sure. Nobody in Rome would have believed Vincenzo Pustizzi, but he would have told them all right.

By noon, when Giancarlo Garbarino and Liam Mulkerrin left together, Sister Mary Magdalene and Robert Montesi were just getting the last stragglers aboard the train. Isaac and Thomas, meanwhile, were making final arrangements with their Venetian unit by cellular phone. They were aware, of course, that these phone lines were never secure, but it was taken for granted that their enemies were far too arrogant to believe they were in any danger. Certainly espionage was not within their range of skills.

When Garbarino and Mulkerrin arrived, just as the train was preparing to depart, both were smiling.

Brother Paulo had served the pope faithfully for several years, and the pope before him for the duration of his life as pontiff. Paulo considered himself a simple man, like his father before him, a man who asked very little of life and of God. A roof over his head, food to eat, warm clothes, and to serve God. He was well pleased and suffered himself the merest glimmer of pride with his work. His job, after all, was to care for him who was closest to God Himself, a man who had far more on his mind than what to wear and what to eat. Paulo considered himself far more important to the daily life of the pontiff than the pope's handlers, the men who made his travel arrangements and planned his public appearances. This man was responsible for the well-being of millions of faithful churchgoers, and the religious health of the rest of the world as well. Paulo had been made, through appointment as well as by default, the caretaker of this man's well-being.

Nothing else mattered. It did not matter that the pope could be an old curmudgeon like so many men of his age. It did not matter that there were certain things about which Paulo had become disillusioned since taking his post. It did not matter that the pope spent more time than Paulo felt was appropriate in baby-sitting the internal and external political factions attempting to exert their influence upon Catholicism. It was not Paulo's place to disapprove.

The Lord moves in mysterious ways, and always had.

It was with these things in mind that Paulo entered the office/library that had always been the pontiff's favorite room. It was common for the pope to fall asleep in his leather chair, reading a book or simply thinking, especially after tea. And he hadn't been feeling well, which made him much more likely to need a nap. After all, when all was said and done, he was still a mortal man, and, well . . .

"Non è che lui si faceva più giovane," he said under his breath.

He wasn't getting any younger.

Paulo knocked lightly, to be certain His Holiness was still asleep. Sure enough, there was no answer. He turned the knob and pushed, a blanket over his arm. He always covered up the old man when he was sleeping. One good draft could make his cold that much worse, and he refused to wear his slippers at night. It was frustrating.

Paulo was surprised by the darkness in the room. The shades were drawn and the lights were off. It seemed that His Holiness had made no pretense about falling asleep this time. He would rather sleep in his office than his bed.

Paulo smiled to himself and shook out the blanket. Quietly, he stepped across the room and pulled the curtains apart only an inch or so, enough to see by. He turned toward the desk where the pope had his head down, and at first saw nothing out of the ordinary.

Then he stopped. He tilted his head in an attempt to figure out just what was out of place about the sleeping form. Then he realized what it was. Rather than resting his head on his folded arms, as he usually did, the pontiff had let his arms dangle at his sides, his head at an awkward angle on the desk.

And there was blood.

"Madre di Dio!" he shouted.

He rushed to the chair, nearly slipping in the blood of the Pope of Rome, and could clearly see the terrible gash that had been sliced into the man's throat. A mortal man, indeed. The blood was everywhere, and Paulo couldn't stop the tears that came, harbinger of a scream that was building in him, that would escape in moments. He turned to run from the room, to call for police, but tripped and fell on the carpet. He reached in the semidark for what had tripped him, and his hand came back wrapped around a terrible instrument of death, a dagger in the form of a crucifix, the form of Christ, the life-giver, forged into a life-taking weapon.

He stood, dagger in hand, too confused and distraught to notice that others had come into the room. Too horrified to hear the words that they said, to realize what it was that *they* were seeing. The lights came on.

Only then did he see the note, pinned to the pope's robes, one word, an indictment of all that Paulo's simple life had led him to believe, scrawled in blood.

Philistine!

22

THE BASEMENT ROOM WHERE ALEX AND
Sheng slept had become a bit more crowded. Before
morning, they'd been joined by Jasmine Decard, Rolf
Sechs, and Ellen Quatermain. As the dirty Venetian canal
water lapped against the stone by their heads, the couple
made a valiant attempt to sleep while Jazz and Ellie made
quiet love to the mute German. It had been quite some
time since they'd seen one another, and they'd found it
hard to sleep the day away. Grief over their bloodfather's
death had soon led to physical comforts. Still, they were
quiet. Though Karl Von Reinman had owned this building, and surely one of them now owned it, the shopkeeper
who rented the upstairs might actually overcome his fear,
break his oath, and come down into the basement if he
were to hear the sounds of passion coming from beneath
his feet.

It was still daylight, just after noon the last time Sheng
had lifted his head to check the clock. No, it wouldn't do
to be disturbed.

"Where are you going?" The voice of the shopkeeper
drifted down to Sheng. Alex was still asleep and the three
lovers were distracted, but he heard the man's alarm quite
clearly. "You can't go down there!"

"I'll tell you what," whispered a woman's voice Sheng
was not familiar with. "Why don't you close up and get

some lunch? Come back in a couple of hours."

"I'll call the police!" the shopkeeper yelled at them; obviously there were no customers.

"No, I don't reckon you will," a man's voice said, and this time Sheng recognized it immediately.

"Up!" he hissed as he heard three sets of steps coming down the stairs. "Alex, wake up! You three, put your pants on! We've got company."

"What is it, *cher*?" Jasmine said dreamily in her sweet Cajun tones, though Alex was already up and alert. "It's still daylight, what harm can come to us?"

"It's Cody," he said, and they all looked at him.

"I don't know how, but it's Cody."

As Jasmine pulled on a pair of sweats and Ellie dismounted from the mute German's penis, a knock came at the cellar door.

"Knock, knock," the voice came again.

"Who's there?" Ellen asked with her clipped British accent. She was annoyed at having to be dressing so fast, and wasn't even sure whose clothes she was putting on. She didn't know Cody that well and wasn't sure how Sheng could be certain it was him. It was light out, after all.

"Oh, I think you know who it is."

"Damn right we do," Sheng said as he stalked to the door, threw back the bolt, and whipped it open.

"Sheng, wait!" Alex said, but too late, as weak sunlight came through the open door and singed his hair. He jumped back in a flash and Alex went to make certain he was all right. He'd forgotten there was a window on the landing halfway down the steps.

Though the light was weak, it was sunlight, and none of them had even seen it by choice in quite some time. It took several moments for their eyes to adjust.

It was Cody, after all, standing there in the sunlight, and he wasn't alone. Behind him stood Peter Octavian! The two creatures they hated most in the world had turned up on their doorstep, a strange enough event, but their presence defied more than logic. It defied all laws of supernature.

It was Alex who said it first. "How?"

"He learned by example," Peter said, speaking finally, "as you will all have to, my old friends."

"Traitor!" Sheng yelled at him. "You're worse than this foolish rebel," he said, pointing to Cody.

"No wonder you stay back, protected by the sun and whatever magic allows you to survive it," Ellen said, words dripping from her like venom. "I would take precautions as well if I had left my father to die!"

Peter moved, too fast for any of them to stop him, his right arm reaching almost inhumanly far in front of him to lift Ellen from the ground and slamming her into the stone wall so hard that plaster showered to the floor and stones moved backward to make room for her head. His eyes were locked with hers, his fury evident in his stance, in the savage change his face had undergone. For a moment he was far from handsome.

"Once," he growled, "nearly a century ago, I told all of you never to question my relationship with our father. Clearly, you've forgotten much!"

"And you've become as careless as the cowboy," Sheng said just as he, Rolf, and Alex pulled Peter away and threw him to the ground. "What's to stop us from killing you now?"

"How 'bout the cowboy?" Cody said, and waded into the darkened room.

"Five to two," Ellen said. "I like those odds."

The fight began in earnest. Peter and Alexandra were the strongest, yet she and Jasmine appeared to be holding back. Rolf worshiped Sheng and loved Ellie; the three of them fought hard. Claws lashed out and furrows appeared in dead flesh, then healed. Rolf was still naked and Cody launched a boot at his huge dangling penis and testicles. Peter threw Sheng the length of the room and the wall shook, plaster showering them again. Several of them began to change, to undergo a dark metamorphosis into other things, other creatures.

"STOP!"

They stopped, frozen for a moment in the midst of battle. Sheng suddenly remembered the woman's voice he had heard upstairs before Cody had spoken. They all turned to stare at Meaghan Gallagher, silhouetted in the dusty sunlight in the old stairwell.

"My blood," Jasmine breathed, "they've brought a human."

"Kill her!" Ellen said, rushing for the door.

"Wait," Sheng said, and Ellie was smart enough to stop.

"You're protected by the sun," Ellen said to her, "but the sun goes down eventually."

"No," Meaghan said, brows knitting, "I'm protected by your own ignorance."

"Cody," Sheng yelled, "this is your doing!"

"Afraid not," Will answered. "Just met her last night myself. Though I think I'm starting to understand what Peter sees in her."

Now Alexandra was shocked. She'd held back in the fighting because she and Sheng had once loved Peter, though Sheng's ego made him all the more hateful. She'd been hurt by Peter and had thought she wanted to hurt him back; now she was unsure. But this, this was . . .

"Unbelievable."

"What, Alex?" Peter asked, not unkindly.

"You're in love with a human?"

Peter looked up and Meaghan smiled at him, sharing the joke.

"That's not so unusual for us, is it?" he asked Alexandra.

"Yes, but it's never real for us. You wouldn't do it unless it were real!"

"True enough," Peter said. "But I think you're all going to have to rethink a lot of things. For starters, I don't think we're all as terrible as you seem to think we are . . . or at least, we don't have to be."

They all started talking at once, which made Cody nuts.

"Shut up! All of you just be quiet for half a minute. What the hell do you think we're doing here? Do you think we came for the company?"

"A good question," Jasmine said, truly interested. "What exactly are you doing here?"

"First things first," Peter said, a little hot under the stares of Ellen and Sheng. "Rolf, put some pants on."

At that, Rolf grinned. He had always liked Peter and only held a grudge because the others hated him so. Peter had always had the best sense of humor in the group. He put his pants on.

"Now," Peter continued, "you may blame me for what happened to Karl, but you might just as well blame yourselves. None of us were there, and if we had been, we'd probably be dead as well. Finally, what Meaghan—that's her name, by the way—what Meaghan says is true. It is not meant as an insult, only a wake-up call. Your ignorance keeps you here, and within the next twenty-four hours, it may very well kill you."

"What in hell—"

"Sheng," Alex interrupted. "Let him talk."

Sheng was red-faced with his fury and disbelief.

"It's fine if all of you want to kiss and make up with Octavian. Karl is dead and this traitor, always his favorite son, still lives. But how can you stand to be in the same room with Cody October, the creature that murdered your brothers? How can you?"

Peter was visibly stunned. "What?"

"Oh, he didn't tell you that, did he?" Sheng continued.

"Sheng," Peter said, "Shannon was killed for her stupidity and Veronica committed suicide. You can't blame Will for—"

"I'm not talking about them. Haven't you wondered where they are? Trini and Xavier and Louis?"

In fact, he hadn't. Peter had assumed they'd be arriving that night. He looked at Cody, who had backed off several paces.

"I would have felt it," Peter said uncertainly.

"No," Alex said. "Many of us learned how to sever that bond. We didn't want the strays like you two looking in on what we were doing."

Octavian walked toward Cody. "Is this true? You murdered your brothers?"

Cody only looked at him for a moment, then shook his head in disappointment. "You know much more about me than I do about any of you. I would almost expect it of the rest, Peter, but not from you. Our father commanded them to leave me be. Those three came after me. They died trying to kill me."

"You were bringing too much attention to our kind," Sheng yelled, and even Rolf glared at Cody with mute fury. "Your antics were inspiring too many questions and you were too recognizable, and you know that! That FBI man, Laurence—hell, he even believed in you!"

"That's my business," Cody said as he advanced on Sheng. "I was putting some things right that never were after my death. Karl knew that and you were all told to keep away. None of *you* were disrespectful enough to come after me, but those three did."

He turned to Peter. "Get to your demonstration already. As soon as you're done, I'm leaving."

"As you wish." Peter turned to face them all.

"Haven't you forgotten something?" Meaghan said from the doorway.

"I'm sorry, Meaghan," Peter said, looking pointedly at Sheng. "Please come in. No harm will come to you here."

"You're awfully sure of yourself, Octavian." Ellen said, but Peter ignored her.

"Meaghan Gallagher," he began, "Shi-er Zhi Sheng, Alexandra Nueva, Jasmine Decard—cover your tits,

Jazz—Ellen Quatermain, and my silent friend, Rolf Sechs."

"Pleased to meet you all," Meaghan said as she stepped out of the light and into the room, Daniel into the lion's den.

There was a tense moment, and then Alex stepped forward and shook her hand. "Welcome," she said, and when she saw that Meaghan didn't flinch, she realized that she meant it.

"Now," Peter began, and all eyes were on him, "for my demonstration. I'll need a volunteer from the audience. The bravest among you, please."

Rolf raised his hand like a schoolboy.

"Ah, yes, I thought you might volunteer, Rolf."

Peter moved toward the door, where the area of sunlight was as clearly marked as if its boundaries had been drawn. He motioned for Rolf to step with him up to its perimeter, and the big German did so.

Peter stepped into the light. Rolf and the others just stared. Even Cody still couldn't get over it and he'd conquered the fear as well.

"Magic," Sheng said smugly.

"Far from it," Meaghan said behind him, though he ignored her.

"Peter," Alex said, "we all knew that you believed this was possible. It's what you told Karl. And Hannibal's had people watching you. He *told us* you could do it. But I didn't believe it until now. How is it done?"

"Rolf," Peter said. "Give me your hand."

Rolf looked at him, his smile faltering. He searched Peter's face for some sign, and found nothing. His own chiseled features revealed doubt, his blue eyes narrowed with confusion. He was afraid, and he hated it. He shook his head and walked away from Peter's outstretched hand.

"It's okay, Rolf."

"I'll do it," Alex said, and Peter smiled again. Once he had loved Alexandra Nueva, and he had known that she was the bravest of them, though Rolf would surely be the first to volunteer.

Alex walked up, reached into the light, and grasped Peter's outstretched hand.

And she burned.

She didn't pull away, though, just looked at Peter's face as her hand and wrist blackened, then burst into flame. "Get to the point," she snarled through gritted teeth.

Peter let go and Alex pulled back, cradling her arm. Sheng went to her, glaring at Peter.

"What does that prove?" Ellen asked.

Peter ignored her. Instead, his attention was on Alex. "Why did that happen?" he asked her.

"What?"

"Why did your hand burn?"

"I put it in the sun, you idiot."

He smiled at her. "Wrong answer."

"Well, then," Jasmine said, intrigued, "what is the answer?"

"I tried to teach Karl this ages ago," Peter said sadly. "Obviously it didn't work. Alexandra's hand burned because she believed that it would."

"Of all the stupid . . . her hand won't heal for days!" Sheng said.

"That's where you're wrong. Have a little faith, won't you?"

"Not in you," Ellen said, but now even Sheng was listening.

Peter stepped forward, out of the light, then put only his hand back in. "Nothing happens because I don't believe it. But if I will it . . ."

His hand started to blacken just as Alex's had. When the flames began, he pulled it back.

"Ouch," Cody said.

Peter held his hand in front of them, and as they watched, it healed.

"I don't understand," Alex said.

"That's okay, darlin'," Cody told her. "Neither do I, and I can do it."

"Sheng," Peter said. "Turn to mist."

Sheng did.

"Ellen, become a wolf."

She did.

"Back to normal, both of you. Now just watch."

And Peter did something incredible. Cody couldn't have imagined it, but he did it. The other five immortals in the room just stared with jaws slack, but Meaghan screamed.

Peter burst into flames. In moments he was immolated, his body exploding in burning ash and cinder.

"My blood," Jasmine hissed. "He wasn't even in the sun."

Then an even more incredible thing happened. As they watched, the ash drifted together, of its own accord. The flames leaped higher and the cinders built on one another, and in a moment Peter was standing, bent at the waist, his face a rictus of pain. There was not a mark on him.

"That . . . hurt."

"Don't you see?" Meaghan said, as surprised to find herself speaking as the others were to hear her. "Don't you understand what he's saying? You turn to mist, you turn into any number of things, but you control it. Sure, it hurts, but what is pain to you? And if you can be mist, why not fire and ash? Why not water or earth, for that matter?"

"Hmm," Peter said, looking at her strangely. "I hadn't thought of that."

"You hadn't thought of that," Ellen said, almost panicked now. "This is insane."

"Oh please," Meaghan said, her voice loaded with sarcasm. "You've lived this life and you're still questioning these things? After all the things I've had to swallow, this should be easy for the bunch of you! No wonder the church is knocking you off. You can't feel the truth when it bites you on the ass!"

"Now just a minute," Ellen began, but Meaghan would not be stopped.

"You don't have a minute! That's why Will and Peter risked their lives coming here. You've been brainwashed for centuries by the church. They've been keeping you like dangerous cattle for a thousand years, culling the herd once in a while if you get too close to the truth because they can't *really* control you. That's why they call you the Defiant Ones. Well, they did the next best thing. They made sure you'd handicap yourselves with these superstitions. You're even more powerful than you think you are."

"Sheng," Peter said, "when I left the coven, you called me a gelding. That's what we *all* are. The church cut our balls off long ago, only they didn't really cut them off. They just made us forget they were there!"

Silence reigned. Then Alexandra spoke up: "Teach us."

"I'm afraid there's no time for that. You see, they are also much more powerful than we ever gave them credit for, and far more organized than we could ever have imagined. The black sorcery they have at their hands is extraordinarily powerful."

"Sorcery," Ellen said. "But they're the church."

"Don't be an idiot," Cody yelled. "Why do you think they call us Defiant Ones and only us. You know there are all kinds of dark things out there, but none of them have that name. The church controls it all. Do you think they could have done what they've done to us, and hunted us so successfully over the centuries, if they didn't have the darkness on their side?"

"Then we're not of the darkness?" Jasmine asked.

"If not," Alexandra said, looking around her, "well, then what are we?"

Peter's face became troubled and sad, and he looked around at what remained of his estranged family. That was the question that haunted him.

"I wish I knew," he said softly.

"The answer to that will have to wait," Meaghan said to them. "They've been holding back for years, waiting for the right time to destroy you all, and they've decided that now is that time. They've always known about carnival, about the annual meetings. They've been trying to weed out some of the old ones, some of the more powerful ones before this event to make it easier to take the battle to you."

"They can't possibly make some kind of mass attack on Venice," Sheng said, though he didn't know quite what to believe. "What about the media?"

"The church is coming just the same," Cody said. "And we've got to be ready when they get here."

"How do you know all of this?" Sheng asked, suspicious again.

"From the Vatican itself," Meaghan said, and held up the book.

"The Gospel of Shadows," Alex said.

"You know of it?" Peter asked, a little surprised.

"Karl had been telling us about that book for years," Ellen said. "If you hadn't abandoned us, you'd know that. He even had sketches of it from somewhere. But none of us thought it was real."

Alex explained to them Karl's plan to steal the book, and Cody nodded at Peter and Meaghan when his suspicions were confirmed. Karl had indeed given his Gypsy thief instructions that would kill him if he were discovered, and he was.

"We didn't know what happened with it," Alex said.

Peter explained to them the events that had taken place after the Gypsy was discovered, about Henri Guiscard, and about his own involvement through Janet's disappearance. He detailed what he had seen Mulkerrin do, and though many of them were aware of the church's use of magic, they were still surprised by the man's power.

"That's how you got the book? From this cardinal?" Alex asked.

"No," Meaghan continued. "Peter saved Guiscard, but Mulkerrin escaped with the book and returned to Rome."

"Then how do you come to have it now?" Sheng said.

"Simple really," Cody answered. "He went into the Vatican and took it."

Nothing could have pleased Cody more than the look on Sheng's face. Von Reinman's remaining children had a lot to think about, and even more to do, but with the animosity they felt toward him, he could not be a part of it. And further, they weren't the only ones who hated him. The majority of the immortals at carnival would want him dead. Venice was not a healthy place for him to be. Still, he had things to accomplish. There were ways he could help them, even if they didn't want his help.

He kissed Meaghan on the forehead and headed for the door, still smiling to himself at the contemplative silence that had fallen over the room.

"When will you return?" Peter asked.

"In time," he said, and left.

Upstairs, the Closed sign was in the window, but the shopkeeper had not returned. The police weren't coming either.

At the front of the train, Father Mulkerrin pulled Robert Montesi aside. He checked, with both his eyes and his mind, to be sure no one was listening before he issued his orders.

"Robert, you know I trust you completely, don't you?"

"Yes, Father," Montesi said with a smile.

"And you know that of all your father's sons, the children of my greatest friend and most powerful ally, only you have lived up to your father's example, only you have fulfilled the potential for greatness in the Lord's path."

"Yes, Father."

"I have a job for you, Robert."

Montesi said nothing.

"Giancarlo Garbarino is lacking in faith. He does not truly believe in our efforts. A less pious man than yourself, even I, might forgive him these sins. But we cannot afford any weakness—in ourselves, in our faith, in our strength . . . in any one of us. We do God's work, and such weakness is a hindrance to that work. You will take care of it."

It was not a question.

"At the first opportunity, Father," he said, and smiled.

"Vincent would be proud."

"Where is Hannibal?" Peter bellowed into the face of the elder creature's servant.

"Sir, please calm down. I have told you that the master is sleeping and does not wish to be disturbed."

The man was clearly rattled to be confronted by six Defiant Ones stepping into the house out of the bright sunshine of a cold February day. And he wasn't the only one who was rattled.

"Bloody hell, that hurts!" Ellen cursed.

"It'll go 'way," Jasmine said, "or at least dat's what Peter says. But I still don't quite believe it."

Meaghan had come up behind them, and now she took Jasmine's arm as Ellen shook off the warmth of the sun like a dog shaking off fleas. "If you really didn't believe it," she said, "you'd be dead."

She and Jazz locked eyes, then Jasmine smiled.

"You all right, girl."

Peter went storming about the house. "Wake him up then, Jeeves. I want to see him and I won't take no for an answer."

"Sir," the butler continued, "let me be quite frank with you."

"Oh," Sheng joined in with his usual sarcasm. "Please do."

"The master does not wish to be disturbed and he will not be. There is very little you can do about that. Even

if you should turn this house upside down, you will not
find him. Rather, he will rest peacefully, unmolested by
your group of rabble."

"Rolf," Sheng snapped. "Kill him."

As Rolf moved in Peter stopped him.

"No. Only kill when you must."

Sheng looked annoyed for a moment, but, remarkably,
let it go. Alex hugged him.

"I'm proud of you. There's too much at stake for egos,"
she said.

"Tell that to Octavian."

"All of you, search the house," Peter said, "but let's
respect our elders. Don't make too much of a mess.
Meaghan, stay with me."

It wasn't long before they started to drift back, unhappy. They'd found many things. A number of secret rooms
and a cold room with recent kills among them, but they
hadn't found Hannibal's sleeping quarters. Then Rolf
and Alex appeared, Rolf forcibly escorting an attractive
young woman with a leather-wrapped chain shackled
to her ankle. The other end looked as if it had been
pulled right out of the wall, and Peter imagined it
had been.

"Who are you?" Peter asked her.

"Why, don't you recognize me?" the girl snapped. "I'm
breakfast."

"Her name is Tracey," Alex said. "She's nothing, a
volunteer."

"A what?" Meaghan asked.

"They come here of their own free will and offer themselves to our kind," Peter said without turning.

"My God," she said.

"Yeah," Tracey said. "That's what I thought, too."

"You've got guts, Tracey," Peter said. "Why were you
chained?"

"I changed my mind."

"And smart, too." Ellen smirked.

"I recognize you, y'know," Tracey said to Alex, then to Sheng. "You, too. You're like him, like Hannibal."

"Yes."

"But it's daytime?"

"We're special," Sheng said, his nose wrinkling.

"I remember you now," Alex said to her. "We warned you to stay away from here. You should have listened."

"I wish I had."

"Alexandra, why don't we get that chain off her?" Peter said, and turned to the butler as Alex was tearing the metal away with her hands. "Jeeves," he said, "give her your coat."

"The master will not be pleased with your—"

Unasked, Rolf approached the butler and stripped him of his coat. He handed it to Tracey.

"Go," Peter said to her, and that was all. In seconds, she was gone, and just as quickly forgotten.

"When master Hannibal awakes, he will be quite angry, I can assure you," the butler sniffed.

"Well," Peter said, stepping into the living room and settling on a comfortable hunter-green sofa. "We'll just have to wait until he wakes up, now, won't we?"

23

TRACEY SACCO HAD NEVER RUN BEFORE.
Even searching the memories of her childhood, she
could not remember ever having run away from anything.
But then, she had never been driven by the singular overwhelming motivation that now propelled her: terror.

She had put up enough of a front to convince even herself that she was brave, that she was tough. And yet, faced
with demons out of ancient and Hollywood mythology,
whatever strength there was inside her reacted with a less
than human instinct. Every molecule in her body ordered
her to flee.

Certainly her brain knew that the creatures responsible
for her freedom, though out in the day, were the same as
the creatures who had terrified her the night before, who
had pursued and captured her, who had murdered Linda
and certainly many others. She knew that the short Oriental man and the black woman had almost commanded her
and Linda to turn away from the party the night before.

But it meant nothing. There was nothing but whim and
dumb luck involved in her freedom, and perhaps some sort
of internecine feud between these creatures. And she was
not counting on getting such a break again.

Down the steps she ran, nearly tripping, the butler's coat
around her little protection from the cold. She ran down
Calle Bernardo and past Ca Rezzonico, her eyes wide with

fear and shock. It was cold but bright and sunny, and the daylight itself served not to calm, but to solidify her terror until it had become something real, something tangible. She still wondered if she would be pursued. She didn't think Hannibal could come after her, but then she hadn't thought that *any* of these things could bear the sunlight.

At the canal she stopped short, looking out over the shimmering water, where she'd nearly frozen to death the night before. The *traghetto* man, Giuseppe, was nowhere in sight. Then she glanced to her right and breathed a huge sigh of relief. He was there, at the dock, letting out a young tourist couple, each of whom wore a baby in a sack on their chest. Her fear, which had seemed overwhelming, now presented itself as an obstacle to be overcome. She must get away.

She began to cry as she reached the dock, and Giuseppe Schiavoni recognized her right away.

"Signorina," he said, crossing himself, "thank the Lord you are safe."

That stopped her. He had warned them, clearly, but she had not recognized how sincere his warning had been. He knew. Maybe not a lot, but enough to be frightened and enough to be frightened for her. Enough to know that he would more than likely be safe, and that many of these tourists had come to Venice this year rather than another specifically because it was so terribly dangerous.

All of this went through her mind in the moment that Giuseppe saw her, and she wanted to talk to him, to find out what he knew and how he knew it. But she couldn't. All she could do in that moment was run to him, a kind old Italian man who looked more than a little stunned at her tears and her lack of proper winter clothing and the fact that she had thrown her arms around him to be hugged, to be protected.

The young couple bearing twins looked on in bewildered amusement, then walked off as Giuseppe hugged her tight for a moment, then held her away from him to look at her face.

"Girl," he said in his scratchy, accented English, "get in the gondola and we will leave the trouble behind. Your tears and those things you fear. Let's go."

She got in and huddled down low, as the wind off the canal was frightfully cold. Seeing this, Giuseppe took off his own coat and she pulled it up to her neck like a blanket.

"Thank you," she said, the first words she'd spoken since her facade of courage had broken down. There was courage there, no doubt. But it would take a while for it to return after her instincts had so completely overpowered it.

They made the trip across the Grand Canal in silence after that. Giuseppe looked at her from time to time with sad and nervous eyes, and as they reached the other side, and the Church of Saint Samuel, he bowed his head.

"Where is your friend?" he asked, hoping that the answer he received would not be the one he suspected.

"Dead."

"I should have stopped you," he said sadly.

She gave him a hard look, and then it softened as she thought of his kindness. "You tried," she answered. "There was nothing you could have done."

"But—" he began, but she interrupted.

"There was nothing you could have done then, but there is now."

"What. Only tell me and it will be done."

"Help me."

He looked at her strangely, as if he had not understood. "What can I do?" he asked.

"Well, for starters, you can tell me why you warned us in the first place. What do you know?"

"I will tell you what I can," he said, and was surprised at his words. He had always felt safe in this city, safe as long as there were enough people who wanted to be there, to be involved in the devilish events that took place every few years. And he had rarely felt guilt when he heard news of disappearances at carnival. These people had chosen to attend. The pattern had been established before he was born, and he had always assumed it would continue long after he was gone. As a ferryman, he had brought many people, some more dangerous than others, to carnival parties on Calle Bernardo. He had rarely carried them back. And yet, even the night before, he had sensed that unlike most of those special passengers, this young woman didn't really want to go. He could sense she did not belong. Regardless of her reassurances, he should have done more to stop her.

"The winter days are short," he said. "It will be dark in two hours or so. Where are you staying?"

"Hotel Atlantico," she answered.

She understood his concern and appreciated his unspoken offer. Tracey's terror had become an angry fear, a quiet determination. The reporter was back with a vengeance. She had the world's most useful tool, most powerful weapon, at her disposal. The media. She wouldn't rest until she had used it to blow this whole thing apart.

Along the Grand Canal to the Rio del Santissimo, Giuseppe took her. Then past the Venice Theater and into the tangle of canals that make up the true streets of Venice, and finally to the Rio Canonica Palazzo, where Giuseppe bumped the gondola up to the doorstep of the Hotel Atlantico, in sight of the Bridge of Sighs. Any other time Tracey would have found the journey incredibly romantic, though she was accompanied only by a scruffy old gondolier. Instead, it was painfully time-consuming as darkness approached. But she used the time well.

She discovered that Giuseppe knew very little after all, only myth and rumor and hints he had gotten from previous passengers. He certainly was not aware of the true nature of the Defiant Ones, and probably wouldn't have believed her if she tried to tell him.

Instead she quietly thanked him, assuring him that there was nothing more to be done, that she would leave immediately for home and never return to Venice for carnival. He apologized profusely for his impotence, and ironically, when he slipped away from the hotel, she felt bad for him rather than for herself, or even for Linda. Linda had gotten what she asked for, though certainly not what she deserved—nobody deserved that.

Once inside the hotel, as she showered and put on warmer clothes, Tracey began to plan. The first thing on her agenda was a call to her friend and boss, Jim Thomas, at CNN.

"What the hell do you think you're doing?"

"Now, Hannibal," Peter said with a gracious smile, "is that any way for a host to treat his guests?"

They'd been waiting for the sun to go down, but it was barely dusk when the host of the Defiant Ones' Venetian carnival awoke. Hannibal entered his living room to find it occupied by what was left of the rabble that Karl Von Reinman had once called a coven. It surprised him to no end to see Peter Octavian with the others, two of whom had professed only the night before to hate the man. And yet here they were, in his home.

"Get out, all of you," he said calmly, then turned to walk away, perturbed by their intrusion. "Robert," he said to his butler, "escort them out."

"He can try," Sheng said gravely, standing from his perch on the couch.

Hannibal stopped with his back to them, shook his head, and turned to them. "Von Reinman's pups were ever the riffraff of our kind. With him gone, the remains of his litter are no exception."

He left, and though Robert made a motion to usher them toward the foyer, none of them moved. Their wait was brief.

"Robert, where the hell is the girl?"

Though Peter had been all too happy to allow Robert and the few other daytime servants to put in order what little his friends had disturbed in their search for Hannibal, he had known that it would not be long before the elder Defiant One discovered that his "date" for carnival had gone missing.

"Master," Robert began, gibbering, "I . . . I tried to stop them, I told them you would be displeased."

"Displeased!" Hannibal yelled as he stormed back into the room. "Displeased is hardly the word I would use. Are you telling me that these . . . insects, marched in here and freed the girl?"

"And gave her my jacket to wear as well," Robert said quietly.

"Oh, did they?" Hannibal said, and stomped furiously to where Peter now stood, his smile replaced with a more serious look. "How dare you—" he began.

"Shut up," Peter said, and couldn't help a flash of self-satisfaction at the look on the elder's face.

"You would—" and again Peter interrupted him.

"Are we all, we Defiant Ones, as stupid as I'm beginning to think we are? Do we all have incredible trouble noticing the most obvious things? Do we all need humans to point out what is right . . . in . . . *our* . . . faces?"

As Peter spoke, his voice became louder and he moved closer to Hannibal until he was almost yelling in the old one's face.

"Octavian," Hannibal said quietly, his calm forcing Peter back several steps, "do you really think I am foolish enough not to realize that you all came here during the day, in sunlight? What you take me for I'll never know. Let me tell you that your presence here, though distasteful, is no surprise. I have been aware of your movements for quite some time. I am also not surprised at the presence of Miss Gallagher, though she is somewhat more attractive than I had been told."

Then it was Hannibal's turn to smile, and take a dramatic pause. Though Sheng and Alex knew he had a network of operatives out there who had been keeping track of them all, the apparent depth of his knowledge troubled even them. To Peter, it came as quite a shock. But it was a shock that didn't last.

"So you've been watching," Peter said. "But what do you really know? Do you know how it is that we're able to walk in the sunlight? Do you really know why I'm here?"

"As to the sun, not really. But I'm quite sure you'll tell me. As to why you're here, well, it has something to do with that book, does it not? The book which Von Reinman so badly desired from our friends at the church?"

That did it. At Peter's request, Meaghan had held her tongue, curbing her normally uncontrollable temper in such circumstances, and in the face of such arrogance as she found in Hannibal. But no longer.

"I was told to keep quiet," she began.

"With good reason," Hannibal commented, never taking his eyes from Peter.

"Obviously not. Seems to me this group has a hard time coming to the point."

"Which is?"

"Which is, you pompous ass, that Peter is here to save your hide. That sometime within the next twenty-four hours the Roman Catholic Church is going to descend on Venice for a good old-fashioned vampire hunt, and you're invited."

Hannibal finally registered some surprise, raising his eyebrows. "They wouldn't," he said.

"We've been through this," Peter cut in. "They would and you know it. You may have thought this had something to do with our coven, but you're wrong. It's all coincidence. They killed Von Reinman for the book. And you were wrong about Monte Carlo, too. They *were* after you and not Cody. But they're done fucking around.

They're coming here, now, for the final battle. We've got to warn everybody and try to make them understand why *we* can survive the sun. I came here because I thought you might want to help us. After all, it wouldn't be terribly good for your reputation if this happened at a party *you* were hosting."

"Indeed," Hannibal agreed, then sat on the sofa between Jasmine and Ellen, who were quite surprised. He leaned back, crossed his arms, and raised a hand to stroke his chin. "I don't suppose," he began with a smile as he turned his face up to Peter's, "you would consider replacing the young lady you *stole* from me with this one?"

The room was quiet, but Rolf, who was always silent, moved ever so slightly between Hannibal and Meaghan.

"Ahhh," Hannibal continued, "I thought not." He ran a hand through his white hair and leaned back, sliding deeper into the couch.

"All right, Octavian. Let's talk."

Tracey had left messages for Jim at every number she could think of, but she couldn't find him. Finally, she had reached his sister, who informed her that Jim had been on vacation and was flying home as they spoke.

Vacation! Tracey couldn't imagine.

She left her message again—it was Terry Shaughnessy calling and it was an emergency. She left her number, though she was certain Jim would get her messages at home before he talked to his sister. He'd know what was up.

But she couldn't wait around. It was already past dark and she knew they'd be out after dark. She didn't know if they'd come after her or even if Hannibal would know where to find her, but she was not looking forward to having to go out. If only she'd had a choice. She had to find out if CNN had a team there for carnival. Or if not them, anybody. And she knew where they'd stay if they *had* come.

Though dark, it was still early, there were people around, and her destination was only a few blocks away. On the corner of Calle de Canonica and Merceria de Orologio, overlooking St. Mark's Square, was a stone building that housed the Hotel Venezia. Though in the densest traffic area of the city, and one of the most expensive, the hotel had not been kept up as well as it might have. Eight years earlier, Tracey had been to Venice to cover the city's film festival, a small story to be certain, and she'd stayed at the Venezia. Back then it had been where all the media stayed when they came to town. She had purposely not stayed there in order to avoid the possibility of being recognized.

Now she hoped that it was still the hotel of choice for the media. She was counting on it. She needed a cameraman. It didn't really matter if that person worked for CNN or not; she had to find one. Words meant nothing in the modern world unless they were accompanied by pictures.

And she would need pictures. Legend had it that these creatures couldn't be photographed, but they seemed solid enough to her. Once the world saw them for what they were, in glorious color on a live television feed . . . well, they would be hunted down like the rabid animals they obviously were.

But they let you go, she thought, and then brushed it away. These were the creatures that had haunted the nightmares of humanity for centuries, their legend enduring when so many others had fallen by the wayside—and no wonder! No matter how powerful the fear of them, or how powerful the manipulators who protected them, or professed to protect the human race, by keeping their existence secret, it wouldn't matter, once the cameras were on.

A picture is worth a thousand words.

It would be several hours before Venice personnel arrived at the assigned meeting place, a large warehouse next to the Scalzi Church in the Cannaregio section of the city. In that time the Roman group would be organized, prepped, and armed. When the Venetians arrived, they would only need to be armed and assigned to one of the five squads before setting out.

Isaac and Thomas Montesi were responsible for the preparations, and all of their attention was given to these tasks. Robert, on the other hand, who did not mix well with the troops they had gathered, stayed back in the shadows of the warehouse, simply observing. He and Mulkerrin had barely shared a glance since their discussion on the train, but Robert was alert to every breath, every movement of his target, the Cardinal Giancarlo Garbarino.

And when that target slipped out the backdoor of the warehouse, Robert followed, certain not to be spotted. Garbarino was not without his talents, but Robert knew the man felt safe, secure in his position as the official leader of this expedition, and had not erected any magical or psychic defenses. A foolish man, Robert thought, and their mission had no room for fools—God had no time for them. He didn't even need his magic to keep from being detected. When Garbarino entered the Scalzi Church, Robert dropped all efforts to hide himself and entered after him.

The church called itself Sant Maria di Nazareth and Robert admired its Baroque construction and extraordinary artwork. Garbarino walked straight up the center of the church toward the altar, genuflected, then slid into the first pew on the right. Robert sat directly behind him, and only then did Garbarino notice him.

"Ah, Montesi," he said, "I see you also have come to pray for the victorious outcome of our holy mission. I had thought you would be preocccupied with the battle ahead."

"Too busy for the Lord? I think not."

Garbarino looked at him, searching his face for some sign of his intentions. Finding nothing but an obvious annoyance, he attempted to be affable. After all, the young Montesi had a reputation as something of a lunatic.

"Brother Robert, let me assure you I meant no affront. You do God's work, and he certainly understands if such glorious endeavors do not allow one time to worship in a formal fashion."

He turned back then, pleased with himself. Certainly the man could take no offense at his words, but must rather be pleased with such confident praise. He was a cardinal, after all.

A smile of self-satisfaction crossed his lips just as his peripheral vision registered a whisper of movement. Then the garrote was slicing cleanly through flesh and blood vessels and struggling through bone. In the two seconds before blackness took him forever, he looked up and saw, or imagined he saw, Montesi's madly grinning face looming over his own torso, spouting blood from its severed neck.

"God's work," Montesi said, and then there was nothing.

Robert thought he might have seen some glimmer of understanding in the cardinal's eyes as his head thumped to the floor, and then the light went out of them. He grinned at the head, thinking again what a pompous fool the man had been. Robert hadn't needed a single spell to kill him, though it shouldn't have been that easy.

"What in the name of God!"

Robert turned to see that a priest, likely the pastor of Sant Maria di Nazareth, had entered the church on his left, in clear view of the severed head and its former resting place. Robert was disturbed. He had meant to leave without cleanup of any kind. By morning all hell would have broken loose and the police wouldn't think twice about one decapitated corpse. But now, well, it was a slight annoyance, this distraction.

"Are you blind, Father?" he said to the priest, who had ceased his approach, and now took careful steps backward, toward the door through which he had entered. "Clearly this is *murder* in the name of God, as your death shall be."

The priest turned to run, but Brother Robert Montesi made no effort to follow. Rather he lifted his right hand and pointed his index finger at the retreating man.

"Dothiel ah-nul spethu," he said, and rocked back slightly on his heels as the power left his hand and flew, invisible, across the church, striking the priest and hurling him face-first into a beautiful fresco of Christ praying in the Garden of Gethsemane. It was said that Christ cried tears of blood in the garden, and now this aspect of the work was all too realistically illustrated.

He felt guilty for having used his magic on such a lazy spell—Mulkerrin had asked them to conserve their energy, but it had been reflex. And Robert Montesi was a magician, after all. Not a sorcerer like his superior, but he would be one day soon. Magic was the combination of spells of power and total control over the powers of one's mind. Only when he had added the ability to completely control the creatures of darkness, demons and other supernatural beings, would he be able to call himself sorcerer.

He longed for that day. The rest of this was but a prelude.

Feeling a bit sheepish, Robert walked over to the fallen priest, but the man did not move. His head was leaning against the wall, his body crumpled. The neck was turned at an awkward angle, forehead to the wall, and Robert thought it might be broken.

Best to be sure, though. He put his right foot on the back of the man's neck, then lifted his left and stomped down with both feet and all his weight. A satisfying crack told him that the neck hadn't been broken, and he was glad he'd taken the time to check. Not that anything the man might have said could have interfered with their plan, but Mulkerrin had taught him well. He didn't like to leave any job unfinished.

✳

24

"HAVE YOU GONE COMPLETELY CRAZY?"
Peter was livid.

"Exactly the opposite. I've never been more sane, or made more sense in my entire life," Meaghan snapped, exasperated.

"Meaghan, you don't understand what—"

"I *do* understand and I'm beginning to think I understand a lot more than any of you do."

The "any" she referred to had all gone, spreading the word and gathering together all of the Defiant Ones in Venice for a huge impromptu meeting scheduled that evening, Monday night, the night before carnival. They were alone now, in a huge and luxuriously appointed bedroom in Hannibal's home, which he had generously offered to Meaghan. She had had very little rest for several days.

"You all act like children," she continued, "with your petty arguments and feuds and your arrogant posturing—God, even the females do it—it's so frustrating. In light of what you've read in that damned book, you really have no idea of your power or the extent of it, do you?"

"Meaghan, I—"

"Do you?"

Peter looked at her, attempting an angry glare but barely succeeding at a frown. Meaghan almost laughed but didn't want to get off on a tangent. Peter did look cute, though, like a sulky child instead of a gun-toting outlaw from Cody's youth, which was his usual image.

"No," he said finally, and both of them relaxed somewhat.

"Listen to me," she said softly. "I know you don't want to hear this, but I'm going to explain it to you again, and this time pay attention.

"There are a lot of reasons I want this, some are selfish and some are practical. Let's start with the selfish.

"This is a life that my heart always wanted but my brain always told me was lost in the past, in history, if it had ever really existed outside of storybooks at all. Adventure, danger, romance . . . of course I never knew it would be combined with the childish antics of an entire race of undeserving immortals—"

"Well," Peter cut in, "you haven't met us all yet."

"A representative sample," Meaghan said archly, one eyebrow raised. She smacked him on the thigh. "Stop interrupting. What I'm saying, as goofy as it may sound, is that now that I've experienced this . . . life, that I always thought was impossible, well, I can't give it up. My second selfish reason is that I love you, and I can't give you up either."

They sat next to each other on the edge of the big bed, and Meaghan lowered her head for a moment, waiting as Peter's mind raced. He took her hand and kissed it, and continued to hold it as he spoke.

"I love you, and believe it or not, I understand how you're feeling about this life, if you can call it that. You know things nobody else does, you've been in constant jeopardy and survived, you've had contact with people more powerful than you ever dreamed possible. The world has, in a sense, been totally re-created in your mind. It's brand new, and you're learning more about it every moment. And the most exciting thing is, you know almost as much about it as the creatures who inhabit it, and are learning with them."

"You put it into words so much better than I do," she said, nodding and squeezing his hand.

"That's because you're at your most eloquent when you're angry," Peter answered, and gave a soft laugh. "But even though all these things are understandable, rational, admirable really, there is nothing which says you cannot simply go on participating in this new world as you are."

"You're wrong," she said flatly, and now her eyes narrowed. "You know what I'm going to say, so I don't know why you don't simply give in. I am human, vulnerable, and therefore a liability for you because you care about me. I am incapable of earning more than a grudging respect from your kind because of this vulnerability.

"All my life I have been complimented on work well done, and yet the majority of these compliments were delivered with an unspoken, usually unspoken, addendum. 'For a woman.' Do you understand that, Peter? I did a great job *for a woman.*' Only now it's 'for a human.' I'll never escape that feeling around the Defiant Ones, because this time they'll be right. Certainly they are no more intelligent than I, though many have lived my life hundreds of times over, but they live their lives and play their games on a plateau I can never hope to reach.

"I'm not really *in it*, am I? Though I've been involved in the most important discovery your people will probably ever make, I'm not a player in any sense except as your Achilles' heel. I can't live with that."

She looked at him, such fierce emotion in her eyes that he had to turn away for a moment. When he looked back, he seemed to have reached a resolution.

"Okay," he said.

They undressed each other slowly, and their lovemaking was equally deliberate. They savored every moment, every caress, every inch of one another. Meaghan rode him, her hair falling in his face. After several minutes she looked down and noticed that he cried bloody tears.

"What is it?" she whispered.

"I've never done this before," he croaked, and met her movements with a yearning thrust of his own.

She smiled then, her heart happy and light and confident.

"I'm glad," she whispered. "I love you, Peter."

"Love you, too," he said, then sank his sharp teeth into her breast and drank deeply of her.

Meaghan moaned and leaned into him, feeding him, giving herself over to him even as they made love. After a few moments their movements sped up. Peter withdrew his mouth from her breast, and she felt a loss there similar to the feeling of his penis drawing out of her. He pulled her down toward him, and she felt her breasts press against his chest as he pushed her face to his own throat.

"Bite me," he said.

And she couldn't, couldn't tear into his flesh.

"Fuck me," he said then. "Hard."

They moved together, faster and deeper. She slid her sweaty breasts across his cool body and gripped the pillow behind his head. She felt her orgasm coming seconds before it arrived, building to a crescendo of ecstasy.

And then it stopped. With his extraordinary strength Peter held her down tight on him, filling her deeper than she'd ever been filled, but not letting her move, not letting her reach that peak. She felt as though she couldn't breathe.

"Now," he said, *"bite me!"*

Her head dipped to his neck and she clamped her teeth down on his flesh, tearing into the softness there. Blood spurted on her face before she caught it in her mouth, an ejaculation of life. At the first swallow her orgasm began, and then Peter's hands were gone and they were pounding at each other again. She felt herself exploding again and again, the taste of his blood bringing a tingling, no, a screaming excitement that was completely new to her. She drank deep, and just as her orgasm began to subside, Peter climaxed, pouring himself into her and moaning under her. The predator, she held his powerful arms down at his sides as she lapped at the wound on his neck, which was already healing.

Exhausted, she lay on him as he dwindled inside her, drifting slowly toward badly needed rest. She barely grimaced as his teeth sank into her own neck, then smiled as he began to drink of her. It was a pleasantly sexual feeling, especially in the afterglow of such wonderful lovemaking.

As Peter continued to feed, Meaghan fell down through sleep to another place, a place of waiting and decision. But her decisions had all been made, and the smile was still on her face as she fell farther still, out of the realm of life.

Arriving at the Hotel Venezia, she went to the desk and introduced herself as Tracey Sacco, from CNN. She asked what rooms she might find her coworkers in, planning to mumble something about being in the wrong hotel if nobody from the network was there. Then she'd have to figure out how to track down someone from ABC or CBS.

But that wouldn't be necessary. The CNN "team" was apparently one person, with a room along the front of the building, and Tracey went up to the fourth floor with her fingers crossed.

Five minutes of determined knocking left her satisfied that nobody was there, but she kept knocking another minute anyway. She knew it wasn't realistic to think they would have sent an earth station, never mind a flyaway, but that was what she was wishing for. A live broadcast would be that much easier, and she wouldn't have to worry about getting any tape to Rome. She knocked again, but she didn't have time to wait. She would go to the lobby and ask about ABC, and if she couldn't find anybody, she'd have to come back up here and try to break in, hoping there was a camera in the room.

Just as she turned to go she heard the doorknob rattling behind her and turned to see the door opening and a sheepish-looking young man emerging. He was adjusting his belt.

"Sorry, I was, uh, indisposed. Can I help you?" he asked, innocence and embarrassment combining to redden his face.

She wanted to yell, but he had no way of knowing what was going on. She resolved to keep her cool.

"Tracey Sacco, I work for Jim Thomas in Atlanta," she said, hoping he didn't recognize her. "And you can start by letting me in."

He did.

"I'm Sandro Ricci," he said, without any trace of an Italian accent, then turned to her expectantly once they were in his small but comfortable room. "What's up?"

"Sandro," she said, "that's an unusual name."

"Not around here." He laughed. "It's short for Alessandro."

"They send you out here alone, Alessandro?"

One side of his mouth rose in an unhappy face, and Sandro nodded.

"I'm a cameraman, really, and originally they only wanted footage. Now, though, they want me to set up the camera and do a lead-in myself."

He sat on the edge of the bed and urged her to take the comfortable-looking chair in front of it. Tracey was ecstatic. The guy was by himself. She would still have to get tape to Rome, but at least she wouldn't have to waste time with some dorky field producer.

"That's why I'm here," she said, and he raised an eyebrow.

"Come again?"

"I was on a story in Rome and ready to go home when I got instructions to head here and do your reporting for you."

Sandro was silent for a moment, studying her. She wondered what he was thinking. Then he smiled.

"Yeah, I thought I recognized you," he said, and she was worried then that he might know she'd been fired. "What was your name again?"

"Tracey," she said, and sighed relief. "Tracey Sacco."

He stuck out his hand. "Nice to meet you."

Now, how to get him and his camera where she needed him to be. According to her lie, she was there to help him, and he wouldn't go where he didn't want to go.

"You don't sound Italian," she said, very friendly.

"I grew up outside Rome, but my family moved to the States when I was in junior high school. I spent high school in Baltimore and college in Chicago," he explained.

Sandro got up and began to unpack his camera. "We ought to get started," he said, and Tracey decided that she might as well just jump in.

"Listen, how would you like to make your career?" she asked. "I mean tonight. Wanna be the world's most famous cameraman?"

"What've you got?" he asked, doubtful but not sarcastic. He was too young for that, and Tracey was grateful.

"I'll make you a deal. We'll shoot the footage we need for the carnival story, with whatever setup and lead-in you want, and we take a trip to a house I was at earlier today.

"It's the biggest story ever, period." She smiled, though she was cringing at the thought of going back to Hannibal's house. But then, where else could she start?

"Okay with me as long as we get this stuff in the can first. I hope you're not going to get me in trouble."

"Oh, come on, do I look like the kind of woman who gets into a lot of trouble?" Tracey smiled at him, though Sandro did take another look at her when she asked the question.

"By the way," she added, "you don't happen to have a crucifix around here anywhere?"

Two hours later they had plenty of footage of carnival. More than enough film, with colorful intros by Tracey, of Venetians and tourists decked out in outlandish costumes and intricate uniforms. A light snow had begun to fall, which was uncommon for the season. It was a beautiful night, filled with music and wonder, and quite a number of drunken revelers as well.

Tracey was not happy. The longer they stayed out without coming upon anything out of the ordinary—for carnival anyway—the more nervous she became. Adrenaline had carried her earlier, but now she was tired and becoming frightened again. When they reached the Grand Canal, Giuseppe Schiavoni was gone, and another man was in his place.

"Where's Giuseppe?" she asked the man as they boarded the *traghetto* (though Sandro didn't want to take his camera on the gondola, she didn't leave him much choice).

"Left for Sicily," the man said. "His sister is ill, he said."

They rode the rest of the way in silence, Tracey becoming ever more nervous as they approached Ca Rezzonico, and the host that she knew lay beyond it.

After they disembarked and paid the man, something she had never thought to do earlier when Giuseppe had been kind enough to run her halfway across Venice, they made their way up Calle Bernardo very slowly. Tracey expected to hear the noise of a party, and was surprised to see the house in darkness. From her vantage point she could not see a single light burning inside.

"This is it," she said.

"This is what?" Sandro asked, and she could tell by his tone that he was tired and wanted to get home.

"You want to know? Roll tape," she said, and then the camera was running.

"My name is Tracey Sacco," she began, "or at least it has been for several years now. But it's not my only name. Terry Shaughnessy. That's another name I've used recently. My real name is Allison Vigeant, and some of you may remember me from before I went undercover. That's where I've been for four years. And now I'm breaking that cover to bring you this story. I'll start by telling you about my involvement in it, and before we're over, my cameraman, CNN's Sandro Ricci and I will show you how it affects all of you."

She went on, quickly describing what led her to investigate the Defiant Ones, her arrangement with Jim Thomas, and then giving a detailed account of the previous twenty-four hours. Through it all, Sandro's eyes grew wider and wider, until the end.

"Tonight, ladies and gentlemen, myth and legend become real. Hollywood horror leaves the screen and creeps into your living room. Tonight you will call into doubt everything you've ever known, or thought you knew. There are *vampires* among us, and this home behind me is owned by one of them. A savage monster named Hannibal," she concluded.

"Oh shit," Sandro said, shutting off his camera. "I'm dead. I'm going to get fired for certain. Look, lady, what is this, 'Hard Copy'? I don't need this!"

He pulled his bag onto one shoulder and started away from her, away from the house.

"Wait a minute," she called, needing his camerawork but also not wanting to be so close to the house alone.

Against his better judgment, he did wait.

"Everything that I said happened to me really did, and in that house," she said, pointing. "I know you don't believe me, but look at it this way. You're already out here, you've already got all that on tape, and I did help you out with your job tonight. Just bear with me a little while longer. Even if I'm completely out of my mind, I can prove I was held captive in that house, and probably a lot more besides. It's still a hell of a story. If I turn out to be a nut, the story's all yours."

He looked at her, weighing his options. He *was* already in it, but . . . "No," he said.

"Gutless," Tracey said, and that got him.

Nobody answered the door, though she rang the bell several times. She started to knock then, but gave it up after just a few moments.

"Must have given the staff the night off," Sandro said, and Tracey nodded agreement. She'd been certain there would be a whole group of them there, celebrating carnival. Now she realized they must have another location in the city, and that gave her pause.

Why stop at two? She'd known that the Defiant Ones rotated their annual . . . reunion, from one carnival to another. But who was to say exactly how many of these creatures were in Venice, and how many buildings they might inhabit?

Nevertheless, it seemed nobody was home at this address. She knocked one last time and then tried the knob. The door opened!

"Don't even think it," Sandro said, but she was already over the threshold. This was what she had wanted all along, but she'd never thought it would actually happen.

"It was open!" she rasped in a half whisper. "It's not breaking and entering, only trespassing. And besides, no one's home."

"Only tres . . . oh, boy."

"Roll that tape and get in here," she whispered, and though he knew he might go to jail, Sandro's gut told him there was a story in that house. He went after it.

They moved slowly and as quietly as possible. Sandro did not believe in undead monsters or any of that bullshit, but he was beginning to believe that something had happened to Tracey in there. Just what he didn't know, but the way she crept through that house, glancing back at him to reassure herself that she was not alone, well, it surely wasn't an act.

Plus she knew her way around the house.

It wasn't long before Tracey found the room where she'd been held, on the basement level, and it was just as she'd described it, right down to the hole that had supposedly been ripped in the wall when she was freed. Sandro now felt certain that there was a story here—the story of a woman held captive by people so cruel, so completely inhuman, that they somehow drove her mad enough to believe they were vampires.

He felt sorry for her.

Tracey screamed.

"What?" he yelled back. "What is it?"

"Jesus," she yelled, ahead of him, and then began to retch.

They'd gone on through the basement, checking inside a number of apparently secret rooms whose doors had not been properly shut. Sandro ran up to her now, as she had moved to the next room while he'd been filming an enormous walk-in closet filled with costumes. She was on her knees trying not to be sick when he reached her and laid a hand on her shoulder.

"What's in there?" Sandro asked, though he had a bad feeling he wouldn't like the answer. It took her a moment to reply.

"Remember I told you about Linda, the woman I came here with?" she began, and Sandro nodded. "Well, she's in there, and she's not alone."

Sandro grabbed the edge of the door. "It's cold," he said.

"It's a freezer," Tracey answered.

After he had turned away to compose himself, Sandro began to breathe through his mouth and started rolling the tape.

"Tracey . . . Allison, whatever your name is. Talk," he ordered.

She got up and wiped her mouth on her sleeve. She went into the freezer with him and began to narrate, pointing out Linda Metcalf among the two dozen or so ravaged cadavers they found inside. Many had tears at the throat, but a good number had double puncture marks, not only on their necks, but on their breasts, buttocks, penises. Some were savagely mutilated, others relatively unharmed. Tracey recounted the party she had attended the night before and pointed out a couple of people that she recognized from it.

"As I said earlier," she concluded, "the majority of these people came here of their own free will, as volunteers, aware of what awaited them. But from what we can see here, that in no way lessens the horror of what's happened to them."

The search of the house continued, though Sandro badly wanted to leave. He could understand now how Tracey had come to believe in these creatures, but he had been fascinated by crime all his life and knew how clever killers could be. He wanted to be out of there, to call the police and the network, but she pressed on.

He was surprised at how calm she was, considering what she'd told him had happened on these stairs. But they went up just the same. Halfway up the first flight, she stopped.

"Hear it?" she asked, and then he did.

The shower was running up on the third floor.

"I'm not going up there," Sandro declared with no uncertainty.

"I don't blame you," Tracey said. "Let's check this floor while the shower's still running."

He didn't want to, but they did anyway.

"I didn't think anyone was home," he whispered, aware now that someone else was in the house.

"Maybe they don't need the lights?" she suggested. "There's enough light coming in the windows to see by anyway, but if you didn't have that light on your camera, you could never catch anything on film. Maybe they see like it's light out?"

"Enough of that," he scolded. She was really starting to get to him.

In the second room, they found another body. A very pretty young woman was lying there under the covers of the bed, her bare shoulders and face as pale as marble in the weak light from the window and three deep scratches, like claw marks, across one arm. She wasn't breathing. Only when Sandro started to film did they see the twin punctures on her neck.

There were two armchairs by the window, and a set of clothes lay over each—one obviously the woman's, the other, including a pair of worn cowboy boots, likely belonging to whomever was in the shower upstairs.

The most surprising thing of all, considering what they had already found in the basement, was the open crate that sat up against one wall. In that crate, buried in layers of bubble wrap and packing plastic popcorn, were automatic weapons. At first glance it looked like there were several dozen. They noticed then that another gun, shorter than the others, lay in its holster under a balled-up pair of blue jeans with the cowboy boots.

"You wouldn't think the undead would carry guns," Sandro said quietly.

"It doesn't make any sense," she whispered angrily, "but I know what I know, and your sarcasm won't change that."

She picked up the gun from the chair. She didn't know if it was loaded, but she would have been willing to bet that it was.

"Put that down and let's get out of here," Sandro said, long beyond his fear threshold.

Tracey ignored him, though, and took three steps to the bed and sat down on its edge. She held the gun in her lap like a cup of coffee, and Sandro cringed at her carelessness. Then she touched the dead woman's temple—

he assumed she did so to be certain she was truly dead, though he himself had no doubt.

"I wonder who she was," Tracey said quietly as she looked at the dead woman.

He was about to comment again on their need to be going when a voice came from behind him.

"Meaghan Gallagher," the voice said, and both of them whirled around to see a handsome, dripping-wet man with a towel held about his waist.

"That's her name," the man said. "Mine's Will. Will Cody."

Tracey lifted the gun.

25

"AND THE ANGEL LUCIFER WAS DRIVEN from heaven because he tried to duplicate the works of his own creator, the Lord God. And Lucifer was placed in hell, where he lords over his twisted and darkly evil creations, and where he shepherds the souls of those who themselves *chose* to reject heaven, and attempts even unto this day to give life to worlds and beings which he hopes might one day rival the Lord's.

"It is for this purpose that Jesus Christ was born. To save the earth from such creatures and the human race from their temptations, to open the gates of heaven to us at the end of our lives, and to give us, while we live, a most important gift—the knowledge that allows us to enslave and control those dark forces, and nightmarish creations of Lucifer. Christ taught his apostles to ride herd over these creatures and, through their control, to protect the human race from their depredations.

"And we have succeeded. Upon a rock named Peter He built his church, and this church has controlled the forces of darkness, the minions of Lucifer for two thousand years. The human race now remembers such things only as myth, as legend, if at all. Even within the last twenty years, the rare instances of misbehavior among these dark hordes, their attacks on humanity, have been completely exorcised. Many of you are well on the way to completing your education in these disciplines, others are just beginning, but we shall continue to perform the functions with which we were entrusted by God Himself!

"Which brings us to our common mission this day. Of all the unnatural creatures born of the rift between heaven and hell, only one race has escaped our control. For this very same reason we call them Defiant Ones! Their origins are mystery even to us, for references to them in Christ's teachings have been lost since the time of the Apostles. Repeated attempts at purifying the world of these creatures have failed, but they *must not be allowed to roam free*! If they cannot be controlled, they must be destroyed. The fascination of our times with such creatures must be stopped before technology makes it impossible for them to remain in secret.

"Only the fact that they wish to remain unknown to the world as much as we desire it has kept them from being discovered before now. But as was the case before the Great Purge, their numbers have become far too many. They are unable to control their own kind. Reckless creatures are spawned who care nothing for their own society's rules.

"But the most disturbing reason which compels us to act now is that we have come to believe that the safeguards which were once firmly in place may now be slipping. Once this process begins, it will be similar to an avalanche. The Defiant Ones' knowledge of the church, especially that of the younger ones, is minimal. We are a small enough order now that if they were to concentrate their efforts on us, we could not long withstand them. Without the safeguards, so much the worse.

"The time is at hand, the Blessed Event is today, only hours from now. The world as we know it, as our predecessors have shaped it, hangs in the balance, based upon your actions today. You know your positions and your units. Departures will begin in thirty minutes and will move according to schedule until thirty minutes before dawn.

"I bless you in the name of the Father and the Son and the Holy Spirit. You are the Sword of God and, as such, can never be defeated. Amen."

They were ready. The Montesi brothers stood by Father Mulkerrin during his speech and swelled with sinful pride at his words. They were honored with having had a greater hand in the Blessed Event than any but Mulkerrin himself. And soon it was to begin.

The arrival of the Venice group had been handled swiftly, daggers and swords of silver given to each man and woman—the Roman Catholic Church had hoarded riches for two thousand years and there was little that money could not buy. Recently there had been problems acquiring funding, due to the necessity of keeping the pope in the dark, but the expensive stockpile of silver weaponry had been built up over centuries. As for such recent additions as flamethrowers, carried only by those both strong and agile, perhaps one in five, Garbarino had found a way. Now both problem and solution had been eliminated.

Sister Mary Magdalene undressed down to her waist without a care for those around her. None would dare to look at her or to question her actions except perhaps Father Mulkerrin, and he would see her faith clearly. She unsheathed her dagger and, pressing hard, drew a deep gash across her left breast. She did not cry out, but heard several others gasp despite their training as the blood ran down her chest to the waistband of her pants. Without any other covering, she pulled her shirt, sweater, and jacket on again.

The pain would keep her awake, the scent of blood would act as a magnet, drawing them toward *her* rather than one of the others. She intended to get more than her fair share. A warmth spread between her legs as she thought of it, and there was a tingling in her ruined and empty eye socket.

Isaac and Thomas went over the instructions a final time with the second in command of each unit. Each unit also had a Venetian guide handpicked from those troops only lately arrived, as well as a tracker—a novice whose studies had concentrated only on the use of magic to locate Defiant Ones, even specific creatures.

"Unit One will proceed directly to San Marco under command of Father Mulkerrin," Thomas Montesi began. "Unit Two will handle those few Defiant Ones expected to be found in Castello and then move immediately to San Marco. Unit Three will move on San Polo and Four and Five will take Dorsoduro and Cannaregio, respectively, and then move on to San Polo. Thereafter all units will converge with Unit One in San Marco, where cleanup and crowd control will be primary objectives."

"However," Isaac continued, "if there are complications, you will obviously be instructed on site by your commander or supervisor. Please note that the duration of this operation is intended to be four hours, beginning at noon exactly. Should complications arise, we must be certain to have nearly completed all exterminations by five P.M. at the latest, for obvious reasons."

"Finally," Thomas concluded, "let me say that there is a possibility that some of your targets may be aware of our plans and may have taken precautions. Be extra careful when approaching resting places and watch for human conspirators."

As the brothers were speaking, their youngest sibling had joined them. Robert listened as he polished their father's sword one final time. He wore two swords, one for battle and his father's, which was not to be drawn except to destroy the Montesi patriarch's own murderer. He smiled as he polished it, and many of the troops could not help but glance at him, the same way they could not tear their eyes from Sister Mary Magdalene's self-mutilation. Noticing he had their attention, Robert picked up where Thomas left off:

"This is a search-and-destroy mission. Chances are there will be *some* complications. In any war, some civilian casualties are expected, accepted within reasonable limits. You are doing God's work. If a civilian who is unaware of this threatens, purposely or accidentally, to interfere with this work, you must not shirk. You must eliminate that person or those persons. Time is of the essence. Our duty must be carried out,

"In the name of God," Robert said.

"In the name of God," the chorus came back to him.

"Form up," Sister Mary shouted as she and Father Mulkerrin approached the Montesis, and the troops moved into their units.

"We will disperse in groups of ten, units then forming up at the preassigned meeting places. I trust you all understand the instructions the Brothers Montesi have given you. When the operation is concluded, you shall return here singly and in pairs. Avoid contact with law enforcement or military officials, what few may then remain, and rendezvous here for further instructions.

"Now go in peace to love and serve the Lord."

"Jesus, Tracey, don't shoot!" Sandro shouted.

"He's one of them, dammit," she growled, not taking her eyes off Cody for a moment.

"Let's call the police," Sandro suggested.

"Cops can't do anything to this guy, Sandro."

Cody was amused, really. He'd only come back with the guns a short time earlier, and Peter had left him to watch Meaghan until the meeting had gotten well under way, hoping it would then be safe for him to show up there. At that point, Peter would send someone to relieve him.

It had never been Cody's way to stay back, safe and sound, in the shadows. But he remembered the old saying discretion is the better part of valor—and this one time he went with it. Besides, he'd had enough of leading as a scout and the owner of the Wild West Show. He remembered much more fondly his days with the Pony Express, buffalo hunting, and commandeering beer trains with Jim Hickok, old Wild Bill, whom he sorely missed. Nope, when he tried to be boss, he got screwed by the system. Now he preferred to work alone. He'd come to like being a rebel.

So he had only been there a short time when he decided to wash the grime of his black-market jaunt from his body. From the shower, he'd heard the woman scream downstairs and finished washing up, then left the water running and came down to see what was going on. Of course, he'd always had a soft spot for the ladies. This one looked mighty confused, trying to decide whether or not to shoot him. He didn't want to give her the chance. He hated to waste bullets and, though only for a moment, getting shot would hurt. As far as the camera was concerned, well, Cody had always enjoyed the spotlight. He was going to get a royal reaming from Peter and the gang, but what the hell. If a guy couldn't have some fun . . .

"Now, ma'am," he began, and Tracey flinched at his voice. "Why don't we discuss this? I've been aware of your presence since you got here, so why don't you just say what's on your mind?"

Tracey didn't know what to say. Among the things she had expected, this wasn't one. If the guy was one of them, he probably wouldn't be afraid of a gun, especially his own gun. But . . .

"Sandro, roll tape . . . okay, friend, who are you?"

"Colonel William F. Cody, at your service," he said, and saluted. He figured he might as well humor the woman. She was awful pretty and he'd hate to have to harm her.

"Colonel of what?" she asked.

"It's a long story."

"And this woman?"

"Meaghan Gallagher, a friend of mine."

"But you killed her?"

"No, ma'am I did not. And the fact of the matter is, she's not quite dead."

"She looks pretty dead to us," Tracey said, and Sandro swung the camera to take in the body.

Cody switched on the overhead light and Tracey almost shot him in surprise.

"Sorry, Thought it would be easier. Do you mind if I put some clothes on, darlin'? It's a mite embarrassin' giving an interview in my birthday suit."

"Just move real slow," Tracey said, backing off and steadying her aim, only the tiniest bit put off guard by his casualness.

"Now, what I meant to say is, that there girl is maybe technically dead, but not for long."

"So you're admitting it!" Tracey almost yelled.

"Admitting what?" Cody asked, almost innocently.

"That you're a *vampire*!"

Sandro cringed. He didn't want to hear the answer.

"Oh, yes, ma'am. If you'd wanted to know that, you should've just asked. And Meaghan's going to become one in a short time. Seems she was so in love with her boyfriend—that's Peter—that she asked him to do it. Kind of romantic, don't you think?"

"Prove it!" Sandro snapped.

"What?" Tracey said.

"I want him to prove it," he repeated.

"What exactly did you have in mind, friend?" Cody asked, and then he moved.

One minute he'd been standing in the middle of the room in socks and jeans, and the next he was behind Tracey with the gun in his hand. She barely felt it being ripped from her grip and then turned to face him, waiting for the shot to come. It didn't.

"How's that?" he asked, but neither of them spoke.

"Okay, I see this calls for something more drastic, how 'bout . . ."

His face changed. Over the space of several seconds it elongated. Hair sprouted and he drew back his lips to show terrible fangs. And then he was back to normal.

"I'd do the whole thing for you, but the process really is uncomfortable," he said, smiling.

"Why are you doing this?" Tracey asked, when she could finally speak. Sandro was still struck dumb.

"Doing what?"

"You're toying with us, aren't you? Are you going to kill us? Are we going to end up in that basement room the same way all those others did?"

Cody looked at her like she was crazy. Then it hit him.

"Hell no, I consented to this interview, didn't I? No, I'm going to give both of you what you truly deserve for having the gall to walk into this house and nose around like you did. It's gonna get me in deep shit, but that's no place I haven't been before.

"Forget this interview crap, I'm gonna give you a real story."

Standing before the crowd, Peter could not help but feel the confusion roiling among them. Here he stood, on the stage of the Venice Theater, with Sheng, Alex, Jazz, Ellen, and Rolf seated behind him, with Hannibal standing up next to him. Those who knew him at all knew he'd been a disappointment to Von Reinman and were none too happy with his actions themselves. Those who were politically aware knew too well how little Hannibal had thought of Karl and, therefore, his coven.

And yet there they were. Had Peter stood there alone, nobody would have listened. But Hannibal was the host of the Venice carnival—had been for several centuries—and they were all obligated to come. Even the great Genghis was there, in the first row, with several members of their race who were even older, many of whom Peter had never met. Hannibal had told him that as far as he knew, the oldest present was the Defiant One who called himself Lazarus, though he certainly was not the Lazarus of biblical legend.

Hannibal introduced Peter, with no attempt to hide his distaste, but in fairness, with an endorsement as to the truth of his statements. Any enmity between them would have to wait.

Peter began.

"My blood father, Karl Von Reinman, who also sired those you see behind us, is dead. Barbarossa is dead. Catherine is dead. Dozens of the eldest of our kind have been murdered. Each of you likely has a story of your own. Hannibal himself was the target of assassination, and eluded his would-be assassins by guiding them to Cody October in Monte Carlo."

There was a round of grumbling throughout the room. Of the hundreds of Defiant Ones in the room, few held any love in their hearts for Cody.

"Cody himself escaped, and has been instrumental in my efforts on behalf of all of us. What you probably are not aware of is that Marcus Aurelius is also dead, killed on the same day that Hannibal was targeted, though none of us were aware of this until several minutes ago."

The room was an uproar. Aurelius had ever been one of the most respected and feared of their kind.

"Why? That is the question on all of your lips. Second only to who. I have the answers to both questions."

The theater grew silent as Peter detailed Karl Von Reinman's interest in *The Gospel of Shadows,* familiar to many of them, as well as his own involvement beginning in Boston and leading to his retrieval of the book in Rome. When he told them he had gone into the Vatican, the place erupted.

"Impossible," Genghis yelled, coming to his feet, and Peter was stunned to see the elder so overwrought.

Others were yelling at him as well, and he looked to Hannibal for support.

"Genghis!" Hannibal broke in, just in time as far as Peter was concerned. "All of you. With all due respect, the Byzantine is telling the truth."

Silence reigned. They could not but believe Hannibal, and they were stunned. Finally, it was the one called Lazarus who spoke.

"Mr. Octavian," he said, surprising the room further, "why don't you tell us what is in this *Gospel of Shadows,* as you call it. That may clear things up for us, don't you think?"

Peter looked at him, and for a moment he thought he saw a shadow of a smile there, an imperceptible nod that might have said that Lazarus knew more than he was letting on.

"Go on," Lazarus urged. "If I'm reading you right, we probably don't have a great deal of time."

"Well, it's a very long book, and there are sections which were obviously removed from it at some point, early on. Other sections are completely indecipherable, though Hannibal has helped translate some if it just this evening.

"The book is composed of three separate documents. The first is made up of portions of the gospels of Matthew, Mark, Luke, and John, which the Christian faithful were never allowed access to. This material recounts certain of the teachings of Jesus Christ specifically relating the laws of the netherworld and the reality of demons and other creatures. Christ also discusses the origins of these creatures and the nature of Lucifer and the angels in far more detail than anywhere in modern Christianity's 'Bible.' Finally, though he has total mastery over these beings as a part of the divine nature which he claims, a human might acquire a similar control through lessons taught in the writings of his human father Joseph, to whom he had given these secrets when he himself was a young boy.

"The second document in the book is a collection of the writings of Joseph referred to by Jesus. A book filled with spells and instruction which will allow one to master sorcery. This section is extensive, and quite difficult to decipher.

"The third document is a journal, kept by the Vatican's master sorcerers since the foundation of the Roman Catholic Church. It recounts the tale of the church's total subjugation of all of the creatures of darkness, or 'shadows,' as they are often referred to in the text, with the exception of the Defiant Ones, which is where the term comes from. I'm very saddened to say the portions of this book which would detail the origins of the Defiant Ones, our own kind, have been expunged from the record."

He paused a moment to let that sink in.

"The subjugation of the shadows was an ongoing process; some of these beings, allegedly the twisted creations of Lucifer himself, were more difficult to control than others. Finally, early in the eighth century, there was a major effort to assert complete control, and it appeared that the majority of the shadows had been enslaved. Except us.

"The church attempted genocide, and eventually, only slightly more than fifty Defiant Ones were known to survive. These hid so well that they could not be found, and the church was forced to resort to the most profound and devastating magic ever used. They altered the very fabric of the supernatural realm that coexists with our own, what Jesus and many before him referred to as hell. This action was the true basis for the split between Eastern and Western Christians at the time. The Iconoclasm Debate was but a smoke screen for the church's followers, while the sorcerers argued whether their destructive methods would have been condoned by Jesus Christ, whether God would approve. After all, if they had developed the power to manipulate hell's borders, what of heaven's?

"Eventually, many of the fifty survivors were found, but when the church realized it could not possibly destroy them all, or stay aware of all possibilities of proliferation, it decided on a new course of action. Over the course of nearly two hundred years, the church tampered with the minds of those Defiant Ones it could capture. Eventually, they could make our kind believe whatever they wished.

"But they hadn't gotten us all. There were a handful of extraordinarily powerful members of our race who finally banded together and attacked the sorcerers. The sorcerers' magic had been stronger than any since Jesus had walked the earth as a human. They had entered hell itself, they had captured and brainwashed our kind, weakening us greatly. But they were together, and smug, and vulnerable. The attack killed all but one of the sorcerers, who managed to escape. He would later become Pope Benedict the Fourth. Details are scarce, but according to a record left by Benedict, all but four of those Defiant Ones with free minds were left to roam free, and the four seem to have all but disappeared from the records after that.

"Then, in 903, Benedict the Fourth was murdered by his apprentice, who would then become Pope Leo the Fifth. The same happened to Leo, who was replaced by Pope Sergius the Third. Benedict and Leo were the last sorcerers to have been involved in tampering with the netherworld, and Sergius was not a sorcerer at all, but a cardinal ignorant of the magic goings-on around him. Since then, the majority of popes have been used as puppets by the true rulers of the church, the sorcerers.

"By the end of the next century, the Defiant Ones, made somewhat less defiant, less of a threat, had propagated themselves once more. Though far easier to kill, our kind were still dangerous. Throughout the thirteenth century the church attempted to cull the herd, so to speak, by way of the Crusades. Though this practice continued afterward, it was never done on the scale of the Crusades again.

"Until now.

"Liam Mulkerrin is perhaps the most dangerous sorcerer the church has had since Pope Benedict the Fourth. He also has a number of apprentices and acolytes at different stages in their magical education. According to the final entry in this book by Cardinal Giancarlo Garbarino, made only days before the book was stolen by another cardinal ignorant of magical doings, technology and the media have combined with our own growing carelessness to make it virtually impossible for our kind to remain secret any longer. Though we have fought for such secrecy ourselves, it seems that what these sorcerers fear more than anything else is that a discovery of our existence would lead to the discovery of their existence as well. The power they have established over so many centuries would be destroyed.

"A purge is coming. What they consider to be the final purge, something they're calling the Blessed Event. They have every intention of destroying every last one of us, and we believe they will attack just hours from now, during the day, right in the middle of the major festivities of carnival."

Silence reigned.

✳

26

AS SOON AS THE MEETING HAD BROKEN UP, with Hannibal holding counsel with the elder Defiant Ones, Peter and Alexandra flew back to their reluctant host's house on Calle Bernardo. When they had reached the house and undergone the metamorphosis back to human form, Alex took his arm.

"Just a second," she said, looking uncomfortable. "This is none of my business, but I think you did the right thing with Meaghan. Bringing her to our life is better than losing her, and you know she's got too much sass not to make herself a target for these bastards."

"You're right about that," he said. "As far as the other, it's what she wanted, but I don't know if it's right. I don't know anything anymore."

"Join the club."

"And you're right about something else. It's none of your business."

Alex blinked her surprise, and was further confused when Peter gave her a big hug.

"But thank you for saying so just the same."

When he released her, she just looked at him, then smiled in a dreamy, faraway kind of smile. "You know," she said, "as mad as I've been at you, and as hard as it's been to understand you at times, I've never stopped thinking about all the good times. I've missed you."

"Yeah. We had it all, one time. Then we grew up, grew apart. I've missed you, too, old lady."

"Sez you!" She laughed, then stopped. The faraway look was still there, but the smile had gone. "I'm scared, Peter," she said, so softly he could barely hear her, though she stood right next to him. "I haven't been scared since I was first born into this life, but I'm really, really scared."

"Yeah," he said. "Me, too."

"Sheng's scared, too, only he's too proud to show it. And he's glad we're all together again, but he can't say it."

"He doesn't need to. Rolf couldn't say it if he wanted to, but I know it just the same. It's been too long."

"Now we're back together and it could be all over," she said, looking away.

"No," he said, suddenly harsh. "It may be the pot calling the kettle black, because I know that according to human standards, we *are* a truly monstrous race, but these people, they're human. What they do to their own kind, to their world, to the heavens themselves, is evil. As nasty and savage as our kind may be, we're not evil. Meaghan thinks we have souls, and I don't know if I could argue with her."

"You think all of it's true, then? Not just myth? You think there's a hell? I can't seem to get my mind around Lucifer and heaven and hell."

"Don't be blinded by Christian teachings. I've seen some of the 'shadows' they talked about . . . shit, I mean, we're real enough, aren't we? These are undefined things, not impossible ones. The church teaches now that hell doesn't exist, but heaven does. Did hell disappear? No; they're hiding it the way they're hiding us! I mean, Alex, think about it! They've been there! They've torn up the fabric of some alternate dimension filled with creatures even *we* don't know about. They've been in our minds as well."

"It doesn't seem like we stand much of a chance," Alex said, and shook her head.

"Wrong," Peter said. "That was a long time ago, when we were weaker and they were stronger. Even two days ago we would have put up a good fight. Now, though. Now we have a chance to win."

"That brainwashing is all so incredible. What do you think happened to the four that got away?"

"Four what?"

"In the book. Four of the ancient ones who hadn't been brainwashed, they took out the sorcerers and they got away. What do you think happened to them?"

Peter was quiet. With everything going on, it hadn't really occurred to him even to consider such a question. Though his mind had accepted the book as truth, his heart still considered it a bygone time, with only historical relevance for the present. But Hannibal and Genghis were among those brainwashed, and Aurelius, too. They were there. So where were the others?

Even as he and Alex entered Hannibal's house in silence, Peter's mind was whirling with the possibilities. They heard voices coming from the living room, and entered to find Cody seated on the couch, and the young woman they'd freed earlier on a chair across from him, while a man Peter had never seen before filmed them both.

"Howdy, folks!" Cody said happily.

"Oh, God," the woman said. "You scared the life out of me. I thought it was Hannibal."

Peter and Alexandra simply stood there, trying to make sense of the scene before them.

"What the hell are you doing?" Alex snapped at him. She may have resolved her anger toward Peter, but her grudge against Will Cody was not so quickly cured.

"What does it look like, darlin'?" He laughed. "I'm being interviewed for television! A showman once again, friends. Ah, it's been too long!"

"My blood! Are you out of your mind? Peter, we can't let him . . ."

She turned to him, but he was deep in thought. She looked back at Will, at the reporter—whom she instantly regretted freeing—and the cameraman, who looked like he'd just remembered he was supposed to be scared. The camera, that was what would have to go!

"Wait a minute," Peter said, just as she'd started to move in. Instead, he walked up to the young woman. "Who are you people?" he asked. It took the woman a moment to answer.

"I'm Tracey Sacco," she said, "I came here as a volunteer, supposedly to offer myself to your kind, the Defiant Ones. Actually, I've been working on this story for a long time, undercover, for CNN.

"This is Sandro Ricci," she tilted her head to indicate the cameraman. "I pretty much shanghaied him after you let me leave here earlier. . . . Thank you for that, by the way."

"You're welcome," Peter said, then turned and paced a moment. "Cody, how is Meaghan doing?"

"Well, she's still dead, if that's what you mean. But I'm sure she'll come around soon enough."

Peter continued pacing, but Alex glared at Tracey and Sandro with open hostility.

"Who knows you're here?" she asked them sharply.

"Alexandra," Cody said quietly. "Now, I know you mean well for us, but it's time now, don't you see? I mean, I'll go with Peter's decision on this, but as far as these people are concerned, I won't allow them to be harmed."

"If you think you—" Alex began, but Peter stopped her.

"Alex, what were we saying outside. Isn't it clear that they've wanted us secret as long as we've wanted to remain that way? I don't know if what Cody's doing is the right move, but I've never been entirely comfortable with the status quo. And if we fail, well, I'd like to be certain that the whole world knows who the ones who destroy us are and how terribly they've been manipulating all of us, human and immortal, over the years."

"Peter, what are you saying?" Alex asked, afraid she already knew.

"Well, you're going to stay here until Meaghan comes around, and then both of you are going to guard that book. Cody and I are going to take the guns back to the theater and distribute them to anyone who's willing to dare the daylight—every edge helps and those bastards will never expect us to have guns. Of course, all that can wait fifteen or twenty minutes, don't you think?"

She stared at him.

"Shove down," Peter said to Cody, then sat in the center of the couch and patted the empty space at his left. "Come on, Alex, sit down. We're going to be on the news."

27

CARNIVAL!

Costumes bright and clownish, or dark and elegant. Venetians and those tourists who came specifically for this event spared no expense on cloaks and hats, feathers and veils, and masks of every description, from the most pleasant to the most unpleasantly sinister. Literally thousands of people crammed the tight alleyways and filled the many squares of the city. Dark and evil costumes and those rich with plumage, all created with elaborate care, and worn with a pride and sincerity that might have been disturbing at a less festive event. Costumed revelers on stilts wore sun masks and white cloaks and leggings over their "legs", appearing more alien than anything else. Music blared from all over the city, carrying out over the waters.

For many tourists carnival was a new experience. They did not don costumes themselves. Rather, they wandered around Venice, enjoying the sights, the excitement, the romance. It was not always cold at carnival time, but this year there was no escaping it. Snow was a rarity, but it fell lightly on the crowd, the largest portion of which shouldered past each other in St. Mark's Square, the center of everything that was Venice. This year, as in past years, it was a claustrophobic nightmare, but the partygoers did not seem to mind.

Had they only known what walked among them, shoulder to shoulder. Vatican assassins, sorcerers, vampires, and human sacrifices—volunteers—perhaps they would not have felt so festive. Of the original group of *volunteers*, those who still lived had been quite disturbed by the cancellation of the previous evening's carnival festivities. They shared the day's sense of mystery and mischief with little enthusiasm, wondering what the night would bring. Though some still held out the hope that they would be chosen by a Defiant One, many of them had lost their nerve, and left Venice in a hurry.

Not that a volunteer had never backed out before. It was something that happened regularly, but far more so this year. Word had been passed down and had spread through the group that something terrible was on the horizon, that their faith and loyalty would be sorely tested today. Even those who stayed were afraid. The Defiant Ones were their gods, to whom they were more than willing to offer themselves. What could have *them* on edge?

By quarter to noon, all five units were in place. Unit One consisted of one hundred and twenty-eight men and women, total, while the other four units claimed one hundred each. Once within the district to which they had been assigned, each unit's tracker went to work locating the many dens of the Defiant Ones, in homes and hotels, in the basements of shops and restaurants. Then the individual unit was broken down into as many teams as necessary to cover all of the pinpointed locations.

The leaders each held a two-way with which he or she could communicate with any member of their unit. These radios allowed them to travel in small groups, thus remaining relatively inconspicuous; in the midst of carnival, getting lost among the costumed revelers was not terribly difficult.

Though they did not wear costumes, in most cases their uniforms were flowing and baggy to hide daggers and other weapons, and the scabbarded swords at their sides were sure to be seen as decorative. Many of them wore large packs that were actually flamethrowers. Only the crackling of their radios might draw attention to them, and these were used sparingly.

Mulkerrin's four acolytes didn't rely on such technology with their own superior. They had initiated a psychic rapport with Mulkerrin before the troops departed, and it was through that connection that the master sorcerer received a curious and disturbing piece of news. Unit Two's tracker had sensed only four areas where Defiant Ones were sleeping in all of Castello. Dorsoduro had only two. Cannaregio had none at all. Even San Polo had fewer than expected, eight total.

"Just what in the Lord's name is going on?" Mulkerrin said aloud, to which his guide responded with nothing more than a frightened glance.

Where are they all? he thought. Can it be that when warned, they were so frightened that they simply left?

But Mulkerrin could not credit such a thought. The Defiant Ones would never do such a thing, and even with the knowledge that could be drawn from the book, Octavian could never gather them all, convince them of its truth, and free them of their mental bonds in the time that had elapsed.

No, he decided, it must be that they have all gathered in one place for protection. Strength in numbers they believe.

"Tracker," he called, and Unit One's magical locator ran to him. The man looked very troubled, and Mulkerrin had already guessed why.

"They're here, aren't they?" he asked. "All of them. Most of them, anyway, here in San Marco?"

The tracker seemed surprised at his knowledge, but nodded. "Yes, Father."

Unit Five, he began, sending his mental message to Sister Mary and the Montesi in the instant his decision was made, *abort Cannaregio strike and move directly to assist with San Polo. All units proceed with caution, the hellspawn are certain now to be aware of our coming. Once targets are eliminated in your district, move immediately to San Marco and await instructions. Remember, none must escape, and we must retrieve the book at all costs.*

"Where?" he asked the tracker.

"All around us, Father. There are hundreds of them, but mostly they're in and around St. Mark's Square, the Venice Theater, and in between. Only a couple of blocks."

Mulkerrin smiled.

"They thought there was safety in numbers," he said to nobody in particular. "But they've just made our job that much easier."

Only then did he notice that the tracker was nervous, shifting his weight from one foot to the other and brushing the hair away from his eyes. The young man was their best, able to establish relatively close numbers rather than just locations like the others, and yet his skittishness was annoying Liam.

"What is it, man? Calm yourself."

"There's more, Father," he said, and bit his lip.

"What more?" Mulkerrin asked. "What is it? Come now, speak up!"

"Well, Father, it's only that it's daytime, and as I'm tracking . . . well, some of them are moving!"

"How many?" Mulkerrin asked, assuming it was only Octavian, whom he had already seen in the sunlight. Little good he would do them.

"There appear to be nearly twenty of them, sir!"

In Sandro Ricci's hotel room, overlooking St. Mark's Square, Tracey Sacco had finally reached Jim Thomas by phone. He had been unwilling even to listen to her when she started spouting bizarre stories of ancient warfare between the church and the forces of darkness.

"Listen, Allison," Jim barked. "I don't know exactly what you think you're doing, or what you think I'm paying you for, but I sent you out to get a story on cults and human sacrifice, and you come back with real vampires! Now, I think we'd better—"

"Jim!" Tracey yelled into the phone, shutting him up. "I can prove it."

He was quiet a moment. "How's that?"

"I'm sitting here with Sandro Ricci from the Rome bureau. He's here to get carnival footage. We've got it all on tape, everything from last night—the facts, the bodies, the house, even the transformations!"

She looked at Sandro while she listened to the sound of Jim thinking on the other end of the line. The cameraman still appeared to be somewhat in shock from the experiences of the past few hours.

"Look," Tracey said, "I know it's hard for you to believe. Don't you think it was hard for us? But you don't have to make up your mind right now. We're going to film it all. If what Cody said was true—"

"Who's Cody?" Jim asked.

"You don't want to know, hon. If what he said was true, the Vatican will attack within the next couple of hours or so. We'll get it all on tape and somehow get it to Rome, then we'll get it to you on a closed channel and you can decide what to do with it. Believe me, Jim. I've been through too much, been too close to death to have you give up on me now."

She was ready to hang up the phone when she heard his last words, a blessing. "Be careful," he said.

"Come on, Sandro," Tracey said as she put the phone down. "If this thing's going to happen, it's going to happen soon."

With a single, unspoken word, Father Liam Mulkerrin set his life's work in motion.

Go.

• • •

Mulkerrin had originally intended that all five units should move at once, but now he held back Unit One while the others attacked. In the first two minutes, he detected nothing amiss, and the reports his acolytes gave him were encouraging. They had met only the weakened, daytime resistance they had expected. Though they had but started, it appeared Units Two through Five would finish quickly and be joining up with his own group within the hour.

With renewed confidence, he turned to those men around him and gave the order. "Attack," he said, and his immediate subordinate passed the word by radio. He smiled to himself. What was the expression? *Like shooting fish in a barrel.* Even if some of them were moving about in the sun, they should be unstable enough to be easy prey.

"Father," his tracker said loudly, alarm ringing in his voice. *"They're* closing in on *us!"*

Tracey Sacco was staring out the window as Sandro Ricci picked up his portable camera and headed for the door. She had wanted to put the camera in the window. Peter and Cody had guaranteed that when it happened, St. Mark's Square would be the center of attention, and she figured they could safely catch the action from upstairs. But his fear notwithstanding, Sandro insisted they work on the street. If they were going to get this thing on tape, they were going to do it right. She was about to grab her jacket and follow him out the door when she noticed the group, all in black, suddenly converging in the square. With the thousands of people in colorful costumes and tourist clothing, the crowd of black-garbed visitors seemed to her a cancer growing on the happiness in the square. Perhaps it was only that she knew what was to come.

Sandro had opened the door when he heard her voice, low, respectful.

"It's starting."

• • •

"Where?" Mulkerrin shouted, angry.

"All around us," the tracker said, nervous. "I'm getting confused with all these civilians around, but they're here all right!"

"Converge to two groups," he snapped. "One on the theater, and one on me! Move to the center of the square."

Units Two through Five, he thought, *finish your assignments as quickly as possible, and keep your eyes open. It appears they're better prepared than we expected.*

The members of Unit One nearest the theater joined the team there, which was about to attack. All others, who had been assigned those targets in and around St. Mark's Square, now shoved their way through the crowd as best they could, amid cries of protest, and regrouped around Mulkerrin. He scanned the colorful crowd, attempting to find faces he could recognize as Defiant Ones. There were subtle differences he could easily detect, and yet the crowd was much too large for him to see any faces but those closest to him. And then, of course, there were the costumes.

"Of course," Mulkerrin said, cursing himself, then turned to his soldiers, *God's soldiers.* "Begin the attack; concentrate on those in costumes. Any who do not run are your enemies!"

They had gone north a block, then doubled back to come down Calle de Ascensione and into the arcade by the Correr Museum. Tracey had a large black bag slung over her left shoulder, in which she carried blank tapes and the one they had made earlier at Hannibal's house. As they rounded the corner she pointed to the knot of people in black moving into the crowd and the man who stood at the center of it all.

"Sandro," Tracey hissed, "roll tape. I'll bet money that guy is Mulkerrin."

• • •

They were ringing the damn doorbell. Alexandra couldn't believe it. Here they were, church assassins coming by Hannibal's house to kill whatever inhuman beings were hiding there, and they were ringing the doorbell like a bunch of Jehovah's Witnesses.

It was just too weird.

But what the hell? Go with it, right? She slid the window up and stuck her head out, grimacing in the sunlight. She was still uncomfortable, though it was getting overcast. It looked like snow.

"Can I help you?" she asked from the upstairs bedroom where Meaghan was soon to live again.

All of the men, and the few women, looked completely stunned. She judged that there must be more than a dozen, and she knew the last thing they'd expected was for somebody to respond to their ringing. They'd been preparing to shatter the first-floor windows just as she got their attention.

For a full half minute nobody spoke.

"Can I help you?" she said again, cross. "I don't have all day, people. What is it that you wanted?"

"Apologies, signorina," one of them finally said. "Wrong house."

Alex smiled and slid down the window, but stood back only a few feet and watched their confusion grow.

One of the men had pulled out a two-way radio and she could hear his voice clearly.

"Tracker," the man barked. "We're at the wrong house."

Alex couldn't hear the garbled radio reply, but then the man repeated himself.

"Wrong house!" he nearly yelled, then shook his head at the reply, motioning to the rest of them to draw back a respectable distance from Hannibal's house and wait. It appeared they were going to be having company very soon, and if they did indeed have a *tracker*, then Alex would have to fight. Her charm and good looks wouldn't be enough to keep them out of the house.

She turned and walked to the bed where Meaghan lay. Sitting on its edge, she touched the other woman's cool cheek. Alexandra examined the wounds on the woman's neck and the scratches on her arm, and wondered when she would come around. Peter had always had excellent taste in women, Alex thought, herself included, and the beautiful Miss Gallagher was no exception. Alex had never met a braver human.

As Alex pushed the hair away from Meaghan's face, she heard glass shatter on the first floor and knew that their reinforcements, and their tracker, had arrived. Sighing, she bent to kiss the dead woman's cool forehead.

Meaghan stirred.

Sister Veronica was leading the group of more than fifty that had converged on the theater, and she'd made it clear to those who had joined her that they would brook no interference by civilians. In fact, she'd made it clear that anyone who approached or questioned them during their attack, and anyone human found within the theater, was to be terminated immediately.

They might simply have set fire to the place, but like many buildings in Venice, the theater was made almost entirely of stone. After examining the entire structure and finding no reasonable access, they decided to burn the huge oak doors, and two men equipped with flamethrowers stepped forward at Sister Veronica's instructions.

Before the men were able to come within twenty feet of the entrance, the double doors were thrown wide, and two men emerged from the shadows. Sister Veronica barely had time to recognize the death that gleamed dully in their hands, and then the shooting began.

Something was wrong, Alex knew. *Everything is wrong,* a voice inside her screamed.

Meaghan had come back to life, the life of the immortal, with a sleepy smile on her face, as if she had only just woken from her life's most restful slumber. She looked up at Alex, then rested her hand on Alex's thigh. She opened her mouth to speak . . .

And then she changed.

Alex heard the pounding on the steps as the Vatican men trooped through the house in search of them. She knew she had to go, to protect Meaghan in this vulnerable state, but she couldn't tear her eyes away.

Meaghan's body appeared to melt away, her eyes staying relatively the same, locked on Alex's with a panic in them that was painful for the older woman to read. A bubbling began, as something happened beneath her skin, protrusions appearing all over and disappearing as quickly, the activity fast and furious.

Colors changed there, in Meaghan's flesh. Hair and fur grew, were replaced by scales and claws and fangs, portions of her body disappeared in a splash of water or a puff of mist, and were replaced moments later by something equally alien. Tough leather hide and cat's feet burst into flame and were snuffed out as quickly.

Only seconds after she'd woken, Meaghan had entered a state of flux, of constant metamorphosis, like nothing Alex had ever seen before. She didn't know if the woman could survive it, but she knew with certainty that they had to get out of the house or destroy the intruders.

There, on the bedside table, innocent as a King James Bible, lay the book that had started it all. That, too, must be saved. She picked up the book just as the door was kicked open, the weak frame not enough to support the lock Hannibal had installed. Somewhere in this house were Hannibal's secret quarters, though he'd refused to tell them where. No matter, she wanted to fight.

Just before she turned to face her would-be murderers, Alexandra Nueva took a final look at the woman she was charged with protecting.

Meaghan had stopped changing. On the bed sat an enormous wolf, whose eyes shone with a new intelligence and a look of hunger. The wolf leaped toward the home's invaders.

"Excellent," Alexandra said, and followed after her.

For the first time in decades, Rolf Sechs wished he had a voice. Beside him, Will Cody was whooping and shouting with every burst of lead from his gun, and Rolf wanted Will to know that he, too, was reveling in this slaughter. These humans had come to kill them, to massacre their brothers and sisters while they slept, as the Nazis did to Rolf's family, his great-grandsons and daughters. This time, however, he was there. He would not leave his people unprotected again, and he found a joy in their defense greater than any he had ever known.

The clergy had not expected them to have guns, had only blades and fire, and magic themselves, and this group didn't seem very well trained in that department. Several apprentices attempted to work spells off to one side, but Rolf strafed them with bullets, cutting them down before they could raise more than a single demon. And that single shadow creature ran amok without a magician to control it, killing several of the clergymen before scampering off along Calle de Verona.

By Rolf's estimation, he and Cody killed at least half of their attackers, including the woman who had apparently been their commander. Several times, humans armed with flamethrowers attempted to reach them, only to be shot. Two of the three were able to drag themselves to safety, where one of their fellows could take their throwers.

"Rolf," Cody said finally, when most of the surviving attackers were just out of range, behind buildings and around the corner. "When they come again, aim for the tank."

As difficult as it was to aim such weapons as Will Cody had supplied them with, Rolf did just that. The explosion was a monstrous thump that he felt go right through his body, and he shielded his eyes from the glare of the flame, nervous for a moment about the fire and the sun. He banished that dangerous thought from his mind and looked up to see black and burning body parts tumbling from the sky.

That would keep them from attacking for a while, he thought. His people would rest comfortably, though he doubted they were still sleeping through the sounds of battle. He knew from listening to Peter's conversations with Hannibal that there would be no attempt by the police to end the violence, and it would take the army hours to respond. By then it would be over. He and Cody would see to that.

No matter that the man standing next to him had been a rebel, despised by their whole coven. Today he had proven his true character to Rolf. He was a warrior, and that was the only language that Rolf could speak.

From where they stood in the center of St. Mark's Square, Mulkerrin's half of Unit 1 could hear clearly the sound of gunfire only blocks away. They had drawn their swords and attacked, and several civilians had gone down, bleeding onto the stones of the street. Still, there were too many people in the square even to notice what was happening. The gunfire changed all that. Immediately it did the job he had assigned the fifty-three men and women who surrounded him. The civilians were silent, listening, and when the gunfire did not let up, they scurried for cover. It took only minutes before the square was nearly empty, only a handful of civilians, mostly locals, wandering, wondering, and leaving their enemy exposed.

They were an even dozen, masked and costumed, in a rough circle at the perimeter of the square. At a signal from one, dressed in a long cloak and tricorner hat, all of black, with a white mask, they began to move slowly in, closing the circle. Several were dressed like the first, but others had more gaudily designed outfits. Harlequin costumes with ugly green monkey-face masks with hats, oversized cloaks, and painted faces of all colors and designs. One especially drew attention, a tall creature in all red, a red veil hanging over a white mask, a black tricorn hat topped with many-colored feathers.

"Stay where you are!" Mulkerrin ordered, not at the approaching creatures but at his own soldiers, who seemed about to bolt from the square. *"Octavian!"* he shouted, and the circle got no smaller.

The black-cloaked figure who had signaled their move took an additional step forward and spoke. "You can't win, Liam," Peter said loudly. "Too many of us have broken the bonds which your *church* placed on us those many years ago. And you certainly can't go back to Rome, not with the pope's death waiting to confront you. The whispers are already circulating about how so many clergymen could disappear at the same time."

"Octavian, you are children of the devil himself. You must be destroyed in the name of God! And we will have returned what you stole."

"You know far more of the devil than we," Peter answered, "but so be it! Any of you who wish to leave may do so without fear of harm from us, but Mulkerrin dies."

There was a terrible silence among the group, and many shifted their feet as though deciding whether they had the courage to leave, or to stay. Finally, one man made to move away from the group, and Mulkerrin lifted one hand toward him, muttering under his breath.

A huge shadow shape drifted up from the brick floor of the piazza, difficult to see in the daylight, though the sky was heavy with clouds. The mist-wraith darted from place to place, jumping in the air as if it were a kite in cross-winds, then dove upon the man as he stood and watched in terror.

As the man screamed snow began to fall, and the

screaming was joined by a brief burst of gunfire from the direction of the theater, and then the noise of an explosion. Mulkerrin turned his attention back to Octavian as the shadow thing made slurping noises nobody wanted to hear.

"Guns, Octavian? I'm surprised at you."

Peter took off his hat and mask, shook out his long hair, and smiled. "That was the general idea. It's a new age. A lot has changed."

Mulkerrin pointed at Peter and shouted a word no one understood. Apparently, however, the wraith did, because it got up from its feast and flew toward him in a flash of black mist. It looked as though Peter was simply going to allow it to hit him, but in the second before it reached him, Peter was gone, mist himself.

The white cloud that was Peter Octavian passed within the black, mixing with it, the two swirling together in a ghost war. Then they burst into flame, or rather, Peter did. The black mist became black smoke, and when Octavian's feet touched ground, the shadow called up by Father Mulkerrin was gone.

Mulkerrin was speechless, but his thoughts raced ahead of him.

Abort! he screamed in his head, not caring that the Montesis and Sister Mary must be doubled over in agony from his panic. *Abandon all other activities and join me immediately.*

Those at the theater could not hear his mental call, but he felt it best to leave them. He did not yet know the extent of the danger, or what they faced. As he spun, looking for a way out of the square, the snow falling harder limiting his sight. Mulkerrin witnessed half of the hellspawn withdraw guns from their own robes. Automatic weapons.

"Once again," Octavian said. "Do any of you wish to leave?"

"Get down!" Mulkerrin screamed to his soldiers, and all hell broke loose.

In the shadows of the Correr Museum, through the falling snow, Tracey Sacco and Sandro Ricci got it all on tape.

28

COSTUMES WERE IN TATTERS, STILTS WERE broken, masks were thrown off to reveal panicked faces. The people of Venice fled to their homes, and visitors to the water city, including those who had come to offer themselves to the Defiant Ones, took refuge anywhere they could find shelter. Hotels, restaurants, and bars took them in. Many, though, were more curious than frightened, and wondered if war was in the offing. If so, they asked, who was fighting? Discussing this, they stood in groups at the intersections of alleys and along the edges of the larger canals, and word spread quickly.

One man stepped away from his friends as a group of soldiers passed, dressed in black and carrying swords and flamethrowers, and held out a hand to ask what all the commotion was about. He stumbled back to his friends, screeching, as his hand was brutally thrust aside by the soldiers.

Who were they? the people of Venice wanted to know. Where were the army, and the police?

All over Venice, small fires became big fires. Throughout the city, the path of destruction left by the soldiers of the Vatican spread even after they had gone ahead at the summoning of their leader. Even those who had been in the midst of battle with Meaghan and Alex had fled, and left Hannibal's house burning from the inside. Not all of them had left, though. Between them, Meaghan and Alex had made certain that eleven of those who had attacked them would never leave the burning house again.

"What now?" Alex said, deferring to Meaghan's judgment without realizing it. Alexandra still could not drive from her head the images of Meaghan's bizarre series of transformations at the time of her resurrection. Her mind was racing with questions, but she knew they had to wait for the moment.

When Mulkerrin had issued his command to take cover and erected a sorcerous shield to provide his troops with that cover, he was still off balance slightly after the rapid turnaround in their plans. So were many of his soldiers, and only fifteen of them had been close enough to him, and fast enough, to get safely within his shield before bullets tore into the group. The rest of them had been spread out across the center of the square, and a number of them fell immediately under the gunfire. The rest ran—either in attack or in flight toward the arcades and alleys that led to relative safety. As Mulkerrin watched, several of the unarmed Defiant Ones broke away in pursuit. Many of those fleeing saw that they would not escape, and turned to face their attackers, drawing swords and brandishing flamethrowers.

One woman, who Mulkerrin knew was named Lorenza, battled valiantly, avoiding the blows of her brightly costumed attacker and slashing several times at its flesh with her sword. Safe for the moment behind his shield, Mulkerrin had time to wonder why the creature did not change, as Octavian had done, to a more powerful form.

And then the Defiant One did change, bursting into flame as Octavian had. And yet not quite as Octavian had. It took Mulkerrin a moment to realize that this was a different sort of flame. This was the flame of destruction, the flame of belief in the power of the sun that had been implanted in the creatures a millennium before. Clearly, many of these Defiant Ones were not as confident as Octavian himself. If he could make them lose their concentration, the sun might still destroy them!

He raised his hands and began to weave a spell of passage.

Ellen Quatermain was the first to notice the silvery shimmering of the air. Through the steady snowfall she watched as what appeared to be a mirror grew into existence just feet from where she stood, armed and ready. She had enjoyed their battle thus far, as it was largely one-sided, though she'd been saddened to see the death of the Defiant One who had lost his concentration, his faith. Pity, really, she hadn't even known his name.

She was watching the group of Vatican killers huddled inside whatever magical protection Mulkerrin had whipped up at the last moment. Then her attention was drawn to something else. This mirror thing, an oval shape hovering vertically, was growing roughly two feet from the ground. Though its edges were indistinct, it continued to grow until it was three times her height, and only when it had apparently stopped did her curiosity overwhelm her.

It had all happened in seconds. She looked around, but nobody was paying attention as of yet. Those with guns were still shooting at Mulkerrin, hoping he'd let his guard down. Those who had run were not pursued, but those who turned to fight had been killed easily and quickly. Peter had been clear about that. Many of these people were simply misled, and their hatred ought to be placed on Mulkerrin and his acolytes alone, though they'd yet to see these acolytes.

It occurred to her that this mirror must be so thin as to be almost invisible from many angles, and she approached it now, and reached out a hand to touch its surface.

"Shit!" she cursed and drew back her hand, sucking her fingers. Ripples spread across the mirror as though it were a calm pool of water, just disturbed. And indeed it was a pool of some liquid, though at scalding temperatures.

Ellen knew this must be some magical construct of Mulkerrin's. She had not survived this long without her wits. Yet she could not see its purpose. She looked at her reflection in the mirror-pool and touched it with the muzzle of her gun.

"Ellen! Get back!"

She turned at Peter's voice, alarmed and confused. Then she heard the roar of the approaching beast. She turned back to the mirror and the pool had become turbulent. She cried out as the scalding water splashed and burned her, though she healed almost immediately. Under other circumstances, she would instantly have retreated, metamorphosing into some other form to battle whatever was preparing to emerge, or into mist to escape it. But the events of the past few minutes had worked a terrible magic on her, one that had nothing to do with sorcery.

The gun in her hand had given her a false security, a terrible confidence. She took one step back and began to strafe the mirror-pool, even as the burning liquid bathed her. For one wonderful second she had the attention of all of her peers.

Then the thing emerged. The demon. The shadow.

Its huge head was covered with nubs and horns and spiny protrusions and its flesh had the appearance of an open wound. Blood ran from the red thing in profusion, yet at her first whiff of it, Ellen felt nauseated even through her fear. This was not the blood she knew.

She fired again, and was joined by gunfire behind her. Several of the bullets hit her, but she ignored them and silently thanked whoever had come to her aid. The huge shadow, at least fourteen feet high, which now stepped completely through the pool and into their world, did seem to be hurt somewhat by the constant stream of gunfire. Some—but not nearly enough. The eyes of the thing searched angrily for the source of its pain, and found her. While the shadow had seemed slow at first, its talons now swept down upon Ellen in a flash, lifting her to its clicking jaws.

Finally sensing the futility of her weapon, Ellen dropped it. She had little time to think, and her uncertainty of the sun might kill her even if she were able to shapeshift. Brute strength was her instinctive reaction. Pinned between the shadow beast's great claws, she kicked at the thing's left arm with sheer power that she had been given as an immortal. Its arm snapped in two with a sickening crack and the thing howled in a voice from hell. Still, it did not let her go.

Clamped in its one good hand, Ellen was shoved toward the huge mouth, the jaws closing on her left knee, biting clean through, her lower leg falling to the ground even as the thing gulped down its bite. Screaming, she struggled to keep away from the mouth, using her hands to snap several of the fingers on the hand that held her, and finally breaking free, only to fall across the thing's shoulder.

Her claws dug in, her fury at its peak, and her left arm drew back and drove forward, fingers stretching into claws themselves. The taut, needle-pointed fingers plunged into the thing's right eye, and her arm sank into the burning flesh of the creature halfway to her elbow. She withdrew it, screaming in agony and triumph, and barely noticed her charred flesh sloughing off the arm as she went for the left eye. But the creature moved, swallowing her arm as it shot forward, then biting it off.

Ellen was dropped to the ground and the thing bent over her, its jaws closing on her skull. Her brains sliding from its lips like spittle, it sat back on its haunches and howled again in pain, then fell to one side with a massive thud. In seconds it began a rapid dissolution that would erase all memory of it.

Peter stood by and watched it dissolve, holding at his side the silver sword he had taken from one of Mulkerrin's soldiers and with which he had opened up the thing's guts as it bent to finish off Ellen. He mourned her for a moment, but a moment was all he had.

"Peter!" A voice shouted, Lazarus's voice.

He turned toward the mirror-portal, and confirmed what he'd expected. The creature had not been alone. Glancing about, he saw other things forming, dark mist-wraiths that were Mulkerrin's favorite slaves, huge demon shadows appearing through the portal. He could see another portal shimmering into existence.

Mulkerrin couldn't possibly be doing all of this alone.

Peter saw past the creatures, to the hundreds of men and women in black, swords held high, who swarmed into St. Mark's Square. He saw several who must have been Mulkerrin's acolytes, for they, too, were weaving spells aloud, hands high.

"Damn," he said quietly. "Sheng," he yelled, and the man appeared next to him. "Go to the theater. See if you and Cody can't get a bunch of those cowards to tempt the sun. Hell, it's *snowing*, there's no sun out here anyway. Then get back here, and bring Cody with you.

"And all of you," he screamed aloud as he lifted his sword toward a demon, his eyes squinting as the piercing wail of the banshees began. "Get their silver. The swords and knives. The guns aren't worth anything now, only your own power and the silver."

Silently he hoped that Meaghan was safe.

Then they were the ones surrounded, and he found himself between Hannibal and Lazarus, preparing to bring down the largest of the demon shadows.

"You didn't say the acolytes were this powerful, to open such doorways!" Hannibal yelled.

"I didn't know!" Peter yelled back, to be heard over the wailing.

"Plan B?" Lazarus asked.

"Shut the hell up and fight!"

Sandro Ricci was roaming the arcades of Calle de Ascensione on the west side of the square. The camera was running as the first monster appeared, and Tracey asked him if he could get any closer.

Yeah, right!

"I'm telling you," Thomas Montesi was screaming to be heard, "my tracker, Pierre, was certain he saw the book at that house, at Hannibal's house!"

"Why did you leave?" Mulkerrin snapped, even as the two of them struggled to keep their spells intact, both offensive and defensive.

"You *ordered* us to!" Thomas said.

Mulkerrin grimaced under the strain of his magic, though he was able to take a breather for a moment now that the Montesis and Sister Mary had arrived with their troops. Unfortunately, the shadows were killing indiscriminately, and many of his own people were dying, but for the most part they were smart enough to stay out of the dark creatures' way. The Defiant Ones, on the other hand, attacked them directly, dominating their attention. Only nine of the vampires remained. After several moments he looked back at Thomas.

"Don't worry," he said with his first smile in several hours. "We're in control still. This should not take too long, and then we'll get that book, I assure you."

He surveyed the carnage in the square once more; many of the buildings around them had flames flickering at their windows. The corpses of several dozen civilians, martyrs in the eyes of God, had lain in the deepening snow, but now many were being eaten by the emerging demons. Smoke rose from the windows of the Doge's Palace, next to the Basilica, and Mulkerrin wondered if those venerable old structures would survive the day.

But no matter, victory was worth any sacrifice. In the distance, smoke rose from the purifying fires his soldiers had left behind. Of the Defiant Ones in the square, all but one had lost their hats and masks in the fighting. One dressed like a harlequin had taken on bat form and flown off; two were dead. Those remaining were in black, or harlequin costumes, save for the creature still masked, who was all in red with multicolored feathers in his hat.

Mulkerrin watched this one closely. He knew Octavian, he knew Hannibal, and several of the others were familiar to him from records and Vincent Montesi's reports. But it bothered him that he could not see the face of the thing in red, bothered him because the thing seemed familiar. His curiosity gnawing at him, he directed one of his mist-wraiths to attack the scarlet-garbed immortal and to rip off the mask. Such a simple thing, really, and when it was done, the creature's face was revealed.

Liam Mulkerrin knew him well enough. He had only seen him once, but his visage was forever etched in the priest's memory.

Montesi brothers! Mulkerrin thought, for he still had a psychic link with his acolytes. *The Defiant One cloaked in scarlet is the one! It is the creature who killed your father. I have fulfilled my promise to you, and I expect that you will fulfill your oath to him. Have a care, now. Only one of you may break off. We cannot divert all of our attention to this one.*

Mulkerrin had not expected a reply, but one came.

What is his name? Robert Montesi asked, his mental voice loud in Mulkerrin's head.

But Father Liam Mulkerrin did not answer, for he did not know.

Jasmine was dead. It seemed a simple thing, really. Though the wail of the banshees was not as effective outside, in the blowing snow, as it had been when Peter had faced them inside a Cambridge bookstore, when they got close, the noise was maddening and painful. Jasmine had been confronted by a demon, a huge shadow thing, and trapped in a corner by it and a banshee. While the screaming thing distracted her and blocked her escape, the huge, green-scaled beast took her down like a thing of the wild, disemboweling her and feasting on her entrails. It removed her head and held it high as a trophy. For the moment Peter didn't dare to go after it, as the wailing might be a fatal distraction for him as well.

Another of them, Opal, one of Hannibal's coven, had also been killed. Mulkerrin's creature was similar in appearance to a large firefly, and nearly invisible in the day. Had it not been snowing, Opal would not have seen it at all, but it was too late nevertheless. The thing flew into her open mouth and exploded with the concussive force and flames of a bomb. Peter's spirits were dropping dangerously low. Only grief and a terrible anger burned in him now; all else was forgotten.

Caught between shadows rampaging out of control and well-armed Defiant Ones, Mulkerrin's forces had been thinned by a quarter since their reinforcements had arrived. Some of the demons had simply run off, raging across Venice and destroying innocents wherever they found them—Mulkerrin and his acolytes could only herd so many of them at once. Still, the odds were decidedly against Peter and his people. He would have to even things out.

He cried out in sorrow and anger and pain as he mutated partially into his wolf form. He stood on his haunches and howled at the hellish creatures under the yoke of the Catholics. They were slaves, he knew, but to save his people, they had to be destroyed. Just before he leaped at the nearest creature—a blackish purple centaurlike beast with a huge bony phallus—he noticed that the mirror portals had disappeared for the moment. That the magicians were resting. This was the time, then, to fight the hardest.

He destroyed the centaur creature in seconds, leaping on its back and tearing out its throat in the blink of an eye. It didn't have a chance to react, never mind to attack him. Then he reverted back to his human form to shout a command.

"The sorcerers are resting. Attack now. Kill the magicians and we win the day!"

Peter had been born a warrior; it was a life he had given up long ago. And yet, for the first time since he had come to this life after life, he felt the excitement of the fight as he had so long ago behind the high walls of Constantinople, where he stood against the Turkish hordes alongside Carlo and Gregory and Andronicus. Then, they had no hope of winning, and he had left the city so that he might later exact vengeance for his friends. Now the odds were equally poor, but he felt strangely confident. He would not leave before Mulkerrin and his acolytes were dead, their blood melting the newfallen snow.

"More of them!" one of the Vatican soldiers yelled, and pointed to the sky.

As each group, killers all, followed the Vatican man's direction to gaze at the sky, Peter leaped in wolf form again on one of the acolytes. He knew what they must be seeing; Sheng returning with whichever of the sleeping immortals he had convinced to brave the sunlight and come to their aid. He was grateful for the diversion, for now he was upon the man.

Isaac Montesi looked to the sky along with the others and took in the new arrivals. Only two, he thought, and gave thanks to God. The two enormous bats were flying to join their comrades. Montesi turned to shout encouragement to his troops and saw the huge werewolf nearly upon him. Just before he was knocked to the ground, Isaac was able to retrieve the silver dagger from his belt. As the creature bit nearly through his left forearm, almost causing him to pass out from pain, he used his other arm to thrust the dagger deep into its belly.

Peter howled and fell over, wolfen paws reaching for the blade, which hurt terribly with its poison silver. He looked up to see Isaac drawing a silver sword, lifting the heavy weapon above his head with his good arm, and preparing to bring down the deathstroke.

The sword fell.

When it struck, Peter was no longer there, and the thud of silver onto brick was joined by the clatter of the dagger as it fell from the mist where Peter had been a moment earlier. Montesi whirled at the mist, swinging his blade at it, but it moved in and around him until he was nearly surrounded by it. Suddenly two hands appeared, one at his throat and the other clutching his sword hand, holding the weapon at bay. A second later the ghostly hands grew a body, and Peter stood holding Isaac Montesi with horrible strength.

"I've just had a revelation," Peter said loudly, snapping the acolyte's wrist and taking his sword—he'd had to abandon his earlier weapon when he shifted his shape. "I've just had the most amazing thought and I *know* it's true. You have names for us—Defiant Ones, vampires— you even lump us in with these *shadows*, but we're not. YOU HAVE NO IDEA WHAT WE ARE!"

He roared in Isaac's face, and then quieted abruptly as he felt the Vatican man's mind attempt to access his own. Peter's face went slack for a moment, and then his rage was back.

"You don't have any better idea than we do, and that's what scares you!" he yelled, then sank his sharp teeth into Isaac Montesi's neck, *taking* human blood for the first time in a century. It felt good.

He turned to see Sheng with the cavalry. The first two bats had been Cody and Genghis, who were arming themselves with silver weapons. Now Sheng had arrived with several others. With incredible speed only his kind could muster, Peter was at Cody's side in seconds.

"Buffalo were never this hard to kill," Cody shouted upon seeing him. "In a way I wish they had been. Of course, these bastards don't give me a moment's pause."

"Why'd you leave the theater?" Peter asked.

"Rolf is doing fine."

"How'd you get out?"

Cody smiled at him before a claw ripped through the old scout's face. For a moment Will Cody was all work, pissed off and slicing through the black-furred demon in front of him with a terrible hate, which Peter did not like to see on his face. When Cody had finished, he touched his hand to his cut cheek, but even Peter could see that the furrows ripped by the demon's talons were almost gone.

"We went out through the bathroom window!" Cody finally answered, and laughed to himself. "How we doing, boss?"

"One acolyte down, three to go. The two that look like brothers and the one-eyed witch. Of course, that doesn't count Mulkerrin! But we've got to shut those banshees up first. We can't afford to lose any more of our people from distractions."

Punctuating his statement, two of the new arrivals and another of Hannibal's coven went up in flames as they were being attacked by a banshee and five hellish things, not to mention the mist creatures. The things had made a concentrated effort, obviously led by Mulkerrin's manipulations. No wonder he'd closed the portals, Peter thought, if it allows him that kind of control.

Under Mulkerrin's direct manipulation, the same shadows had apparently become a "pack" of some sort. Together, they turned toward where Hannibal, Genghis, and Sheng were attacking a group of Vatican soldiers and two huge female demons that were protecting Thomas Montesi, the next acolyte to be targeted. Unfortunately, the creatures being directly controlled by Mulkerrin were about to make the odds decidedly uneven.

Peter and Cody would change that, or get themselves in the middle.

"Y'know," Peter said to him as they stepped into the path of the oncoming demonic horde, "a master show-man like you could've sold a lot of tickets to an event like this!"

"Well," Cody answered, raising his sword and mentally setting fire to his left hand, "isn't that what I did?"

Peter hadn't quite thought of it that way, but for the first time he realized what Cody meant. What they'd done, by talking to the reporter, Tracey, was give the world a show it could never forget. Mulkerrin and Garbarino, who he thought was most probably dead, might have figured out a way, whether magical or political, to keep the police out of it.

But the media? No way.

He and Cody had blown the status quo to hell.

Just as they ripped into the approaching demons, giving their brothers time to take out Thomas Montesi's protectors, Lazarus joined them.

"We can't do this forever!" he said to Peter.

"If we can kill the sorcerers, we won't have to," Peter replied. "We're still badly in need of an equalizer, though, something to turn the tide."

PETER!

The voice shouted in his head just as he was about to slice into the banshee, and he doubled over. Vulnerable for a moment, he was batted away by a huge fleshy shadow and slammed into a building before sliding down its side. He heard an unearthly scream and was satisfied as he opened his eyes to see Cody destroying the banshee. Will's fist was aflame, and he shoved it into the ghostly thing, which somehow forced it to solidify, to stabilize in order to combat the flame. Cody's blade whipped down and sliced a hole in the thing, and he was forced back by the wind that came from the banshee's wound.

Peter remembered the gale-force wind that had blown in the bookstore and realized that though weakened, the winds blowing the snow about had probably come from the banshees as well. This new wind was different, though, accompanied by a terrible noise, a howl of pain and dying that rose in pitch and volume until the banshee, flying in circles above their heads and screaming from its mouth and the tear in its body, flew out over the canal and disappeared.

One down, he thought. And now we know how to get rid of them, even if we can't kill them.

But whose voice was it that had distracted him in the first place?

MINE, SILLY!

Meaghan?

None other.

You're awake?

That and more, she thought to him, and he could sense irony in the words, but not their meaning.

We're coming over, Alex and I, she thought.

No, Peter answered, *you're not ready.*

I am ready, you'll have to trust me.

What about the book? Peter asked, slightly panicked now. Not only did he worry about Mulkerrin finding the book, but he didn't know if he'd be able to fight, with Meaghan to worry about. Even reborn as one of his kind, she had just woken. She'd be weak, in need of food. And the sun . . .

Don't be an idiot, her words came to him, and he realized their telepathy went further than he'd known.

You made me, she continued. *I don't have the constraints that the others do. You need me!*

Okay, maybe I do, but what about the damn book?

Send Sheng to guard it, you can trust him.

He considered for a moment, but then he was under attack again, and the decision was made.

Wait till Sheng gets there!

• • •

With Cody gone, Rolf had been left alone to guard the entrance to the theater. Though the job had become considerably easier—they'd killed more than thirty of their attackers—he reveled in it. He had been left with a great responsibility, a sign of respect from his people. The church was attempting genocide, and the majority of the population of his kind lay awake in the darkened theater, relying on his protection. He would not let them down.

The soldiers had begun to get imaginative, for they knew that he could hold out forever if they simply went for one failed frontal assault after another. Their numbers would dwindle until they were all gone. They'd tried to distract him to no avail. As a mute, Rolf had found learning a challenge, and his powers of concentration were based on a fierce, controlled attention.

A soldier bearing a flamethrower—Rolf imagined it to be one of few that remained—attempted a frontal assault just then, and Rolf cut him down with barely a glance. Yet that glance was enough to distract him for just a moment, and he was rushed from either side. Each man was armed with a flamethrower and a silver dagger, and blowing snow or no, Rolf didn't think he would stand a chance in the daylight if one of them got close enough to him. And he couldn't shoot them both at once.

Rolf Sechs was far more quick-witted than his coven had known, and ever calm in the face of danger, even when he'd been human.

He took one big step backward, through the door and into the foyer of the theater, forcing his attackers to come together in front of him. Crouched down as he was, two bursts of flame singed his wavy hair as he pulled the trigger, knocking both men off their feet, up and back quite a ways, only to land on the flamethrowers they wore. Rolf imagined that one of the two must have ruptured on the brick street, as twin explosions, one right after the other, rocked the entryway to the theater, and knocked him off his own feet to sprawl against the theater's inner doors.

He was up in a flash, though, and back at his post even as burning flesh and clothing rained from the air. He didn't think they'd try that again, at least for a while. He looked at the heavy sky, through the falling snow, and realized that soon they'd be getting desperate. It wouldn't be too long until dusk. Not long at all.

His eyes were torn from the clouds by the roar of the demon that charged him, the blood of churchmen decorating its mouth and claws.

They were desperate all right.

29

"NO, ROBERT!" MULKERRIN YELLED TO THE youngest Montesi. "We can't afford to break off now, with Isaac dead."

"I didn't ask *you* to stop, Liam. You'll have to make do without me for a few moments."

"Do not approach the creature personally! Use your sorcery!"

"No," Robert answered, dropping one sword and unsheathing another, far more ornate. "This sword is meant to spill the blood of the hellspawn that killed my father. And it shall!"

With that, he ran off toward the Doge's Palace, in front of which Lazarus was eliminating the largest demon they had yet seen, a twenty-foot monstrosity with what appeared to be vaginal openings covering its body. The ancient Defiant One slashed at the demon's legs and body, only to have the silver sword become stuck within one of its thousands of vaginas. Instead of fighting to withdraw it, Lazarus stuck the sword deeper, twisting and hacking, as the deadly metal cut through the thing like butter. The demon doubled over from the pain, and Lazarus drove the silver sword deeper into its abdomen, where he knew its hellish heart would be.

As Robert ran toward Lazarus a voice cried out in his mind, but this time, it was his own.

How in the name of God did he know where to strike?

Clearly, there was more to this Defiant One than even Mulkerrin knew, but Robert was not deterred. They all would die, but this one was his sole target now. His father's murder would be avenged. He raised high his sword as Lazarus turned to meet him.

Mulkerrin had worried for a time, especially at the death of Isaac Montesi, and then when the Defiant Ones had been joined by more of their kind. Though Robert's impetuousness gave him pause, he now realized he had been foolish to feel such concern. Their reinforcements had been even less confident about being out in the daylight than the previous group. Even though the sun was obscured by the clouds and snow, making it seem nearly night, its rays were still too powerful when combined with the suggestions long ago implanted in their minds. Though his group had taken severe losses both from the Defiant Ones and from Mulkerrin's shadow slaves, were in fact down to barely more than fifty, though he and his acolytes were feeling weak from both summoning and manipulating demons, they still had the upper hand. The newly arrived Defiant Ones had barely made a difference in the inevitable outcome.

Only five Defiant Ones remained in St. Mark's Square: Octavian, Hannibal, Cody October, Genghis, and the murderer of Vincent Montesi, whose name Mulkerrin did not know. One other, the stocky Asian, who had already once gone for help, had fled yet again. Mulkerrin wondered if it was for more reinforcements, or to protect those of his kind at the theater, whose numbers the trackers had estimated at more than three hundred. Also there were the two females guarding the book at the home of Hannibal, but even if night fell before they reached the house, two Defiant Ones would be nothing for his sorcery, even weakened, when he had his acolytes at his side.

They had been having trouble at the theater, but Mulkerrin had sent one of Sister Mary's own apprentices to summon demons to destroy the guardian there. According to radio reports, it was only one creature. Surely they could destroy one creature. They must, really. Dusk would not be long in coming now, less than an hour. But it would be done, he was confident. These five would be destroyed and the theater taken shortly, and then they could retrieve the book. So certain was Liam Mulkerrin of the inevitability of his success that he even took the time for a short rest. He sat and watched as several dozen shadows of all kinds and evils surrounded four of the remaining Defiant Ones, all but Vincent Montesi's killer, whom Robert was even now confronting, sword waving. Sister Mary Magdalene and Thomas Montesi would have no problem now. As many demons as these final creatures slew, more could be called up at any time.

In fact, he thought it best to go to the theater and ensure victory there so that the sleepers could be destroyed by nightfall. It would be disaster if this was not accomplished.

As he slashed at the demons, not daring to transform for fear of dropping his best weapon, the silver sword, Peter saw Mulkerrin stand with purpose. It had infuriated him to see the man just sitting there all this time. All they needed to do was hold out until dark, though he was beginning to wonder if they could do so. They'd made repeated attempts to kill the sorcerer and his acolytes, but the shadows were simply too numerous. Mulkerrin's mist-wraiths darted about the heads of Peter and the others, and though they wouldn't come too close as long as the immortals held their swords, the things still served as a terrible distraction. As Peter watched, Mulkerrin beckoned the wraiths to him.

He's leaving!

"Genghis," Peter shouted over the roar of the shadow

beasts, thankful that the other banshee had been terminated an hour before. "Don't let him go!"

He motioned toward Mulkerrin, and Genghis, covered
in burning demon gore, as were they all, saw the problem immediately. Neither of them was certain where the
sorcerer was headed, but whether to the theater or to
Hannibal's house, they had to prevent his departure.

Hannibal, Cody, and Peter all slashed in one direction,
making a deadly gauntlet for Genghis to run. That moment
was almost fatal, as a huge shadow grabbed Hannibal's
head from behind and began to squeeze, only to have its
hand cut off at the wrist by Cody's hacking blade.

The fight went on.

They all knew that their luck would not have held out
even for this long if Lazarus hadn't told them precisely
where to stab in order to destroy the creatures quickly.

Peter had to wonder how he'd come by that information.

"My name is Robert Montesi," the young acolyte said.
"For the murder of my father, I must kill you."

Lazarus only looked at him, unmoved and unmoving.

"Boy," he said. "Your father was a man filled with a
fanaticism more evil than the darkest imaginings of his
rabid mind. Prove yourself a better and smarter man. Go
away."

He knew he could have chosen his words better, even
have attempted to convince the young man he'd been mistaken. He could have. He did not. Lazarus watched as the
rage reddened Robert Montesi's face, as the man's eyes
widened with shock and fury. He shook his head.

"Take me then," he said. "I will not stop you."

And he could have. The hatred in Montesi made him
careless, and as he attacked, no magic save what little
existed in the poison metal of his sword, he left himself
completely open for counterattack. Even if Lazarus had
been a human swordsman of moderate ability, he could

have stopped Montesi, a dangerous man at any moment other than this, when he'd lost all control. The apple hadn't fallen far, Lazarus thought.

Then Lazarus was run through with a sword specifically chosen for that purpose. He bent over it, crying out and squinting at the poison magic of the silver, and Robert came in close to him, using both hands to ram the blade deeper, to the hilt in his belly. Lazarus threw his arms around Robert, and they clutched like lovers. Hands at the side of Montesi's head, Lazarus drew him close and whispered to him.

"Happy, boy? What a triumph for you."

"For my father, devil!" Robert shouted, his face red with effort as he dragged the blade up, widening the wound he'd made.

He began to draw back, to survey his work, perhaps to behead the murdering beast, but found he could not. What had seemed a weakened, dying gesture now stood revealed as otherwise. Lazarus's hands held tight to Robert's head and pulled him closer still. He struggled, forgetting his sword, kicking and beginning a spell to call shadows to his rescue. There was no time.

"Like you," Lazarus whispered, "your father knew less than nothing."

Robert felt cold lips on his neck, and icy teeth tore into his flesh.

Mulkerrin was preparing to leave, borne aloft by the wraiths so they might spirit him the few short blocks to the theater, when he saw Genghis running toward him. He thought little of it. The Defiant One would be too timid to transform, he thought, to shift his shape to that of a bat to fly in pursuit.

But, like his namesake, Genghis had been a warrior in life, and though he feared the daylight, had seen many of his kind killed by it since the battle began, still he would conquer it. And he did. Dropping his sword so as not to absorb the silver into his new shape, he became a huge, terrible winged predator, a black death. Of all the forms his kind traditionally took, he had always favored the bat.

Mulkerrin was surprised, but only momentarily. Swiftly he was brought back to earth, and the mist-wraiths turned on Genghis. Without his sword, and concentrating on his metamorphosis, he was easy prey. The creatures filled him, bloated him, destroyed him in a violent spray of innards. From the other side of the square a shout told Mulkerrin that Octavian and his monstrous allies were surprised. They ought not to have been, he thought, for they would be next.

He turned to his enslaved mist-creatures, preparing to leave once again, when he remembered Robert. He glanced over just in time to see Lazarus pull his bloody mouth from Robert's throat, dropping the young man's corpse, and lift his head. Mulkerrin was stunned. After his father, Robert had been Liam's best and final hope. None of his other acolytes or apprentices had the vigor, the courage, and the dedication of Robert Montesi. He might have wished all of them dead to bring Robert back to life.

And it could not be. Robert had driven the silver sword right through the creature. Yet now, as Mulkerrin watched, the monster drew the sword from its belly and lifted it high, a silent challenge to the rest of them. Even without the mental constraints the church had put on them, no Defiant One was *completely* immune to the poisons of silver! And this was the creature who had known just where to strike the demons.

He couldn't leave now, not until this one was dead. It was too dangerous. He would kill this nameless one and then move to assist his soldiers at the theater.

Thomas, he snapped in his mind as he saw the elder, the final Montesi running toward the thing that had slain his brother, *you must not attack that one. I will kill it myself. You and the Magdalene must continue your attack on the others, keep them in control. We can still win this!*

A real voice, that of Sister Mary Magdalene, safely surrounded by the surviving troops, burst into the air, a message, a warning to them all.

"LOOK!"

Even some of the demons followed her order, glancing skyward.

Mulkerrin began to smile. Two forms flapped toward them through the snow, already gliding lower to land by their fellows. But only two! If this was the best the Defiant Ones could muster, then they still might have a chance to win.

His smile stopped as Liam saw what Sister Mary had been shouting about. One of the creatures who now landed by the trapped vampires was not a bat at all, but the largest falcon he had ever seen.

"My God!" Tracey whispered. "Sandro, they're not going to make it, are they?"

It wasn't right what was happening. The world couldn't discover these wondrous and terrible beings and then have them destroyed before their eyes. She wanted to help, but she knew that she'd be killed in an instant. The irony was not lost on her as she hoped that Cody and Peter would be all right.

She and Sandro had settled into one spot, in the shadows of the arcade. The snow and the darkening skies made it difficult to get a clear picture of the action, but it was certainly clear enough to see the violations of nature that were taking place, the monstrous things of nightmare that slaughtered fighters from both sides. When this tape was broadcast from Rome, it would be like the creation of a new world.

From time to time, when the snow let up for a few moments, it was clear enough to see the transformations some of the Defiant Ones underwent, transformations that took Tracey's breath away.

"Tracey," Sandro said quickly, "how 'bout some reporting here?"

She stepped in front of the camera, Sandro making adjustments to keep both her and the action behind her in the shot.

"The battle rages on," she began. "It's difficult for anyone to understand the reasoning behind it, or to choose sides. Both forces have blood on their hands, though it would appear the more righteous of the groups is, surprisingly, not what you might expect. Still, no matter the outcome, it seems that the one benefit of this unnatural conflict is going to be something we've long been denied—the truth.

"Okay," Tracey said, no longer the reporter, "let's move up."

"Shit," Sandro said, but he moved up anyway.

Staying along the wall of the Archaeological Museum, he slid forward with his camera to his right eye, Tracey right behind him. The shoulder pad was ripped, and dug into his flesh, but he ignored it. They ducked into doorways to avoid being seen, and though the action was still far from them, Sandro knew that they'd be spotted, given time.

"That's far enough," Tracey said, but Sandro kept moving, and she kept following. His attitude had changed.

Tracey had talked about a story, and what a story this was. His career was already made, but if he lived through this, he'd be a hero.

They had almost reached the corner of the building, where a right would take them into the piazzetta and to the canal, and a quick, straight run would take them to the front of the Doge's Palace, where one of the acolytes had been slain just moments ago. But the way was clear now. From there they could make their way to Basilica San Marco, a perfectly ironic place from which to tape.

Sandro thought they might be safer there.

Running across the piazzetta with Tracey in tow, Sandro knew he had miscalculated. One of the demons menacing Cody and his friends had looked away from the bat and the huge bird that had landed and were changing shape into . . . something. It looked directly at him.

"Tracey," Sandro barked, "get the hell out of here."

She didn't argue. Sandro stayed put, and for a moment he was relieved when the thing kept its eyes on him and did not veer off to follow Tracey. Then the terror hit him. There was nowhere to run as the beast thundered toward him, its jaws split in what seemed like a hellish, slavering leer.

He'd fucked up, but he hoped at least Tracey would survive. She'd get the tapes they'd already made to Rome, and maybe the camera wouldn't be too badly damaged and she could get this last one as well. . . .

Sandro lifted his camera like a weapon, pointing it at the thing bearing down on him, and through the camera's eye he watched his salvation. Cody appeared out of nowhere, having leaped from the ground, and landed on the running thing's shoulders. Before the creature had a chance to try to buck him off, Cody had stabbed down through its skull, dropping the thing out from under him and tumbling himself into a roll that ended at Sandro's feet. Sandro had never felt so relieved.

Cody stood up, dusted himself off, and smiled at Sandro. "What a shot that must have been," he said loudly. "I made a film myself once, you know."

He flashed that smile again, posing in profile for the camera, then turned and ran back into the midst of the melee, almost slipping on the gore that covered him.

"Thanks," Sandro said weakly, then moved quickly to join Tracey in the deepening shadows at the front of the Doge's Palace. She threw her arms around him, then they both knelt down and stayed there. The camera was still rolling.

No way in hell was he moving again.

• • •

Lazarus had joined his brothers as they fought off the creatures that surrounded them. He only smiled as the rest of them looked upon the strange pair, the bat and falcon, with wide eyes and slack jaws. Peter and Hannibal kept stealing glances as they fought, and the two new arrivals transformed in their midst. The bat changed quickly, and when Peter glanced that way, he could see black flesh and knew it was Alexandra Nueva. The falcon, though, changed in a flash, and he had barely blinked away the lessening snow before he recognized her.

"Meaghan?"

"Peter!" she shouted back, but in warning rather than greeting. He turned just in time to fend off a strike by a tiny, vicious-looking shadow whose spidery limbs were like deadly spikes.

In a moment the thing had one less of those spikes.

And then Meaghan was fighting beside him.

"How did you do that?" he asked her.

"What?" she answered, picking up a stray sword.

"You were a hawk!"

"Falcon, actually."

"How?"

"Come on, Peter. The man I love is smarter than that! I told you I thought I knew more than the rest of you, and I do—not to brag or anything."

She broke off as she leaped above the spider shadow's reach and landed atop it, driving her sword down through its many-eyed center. It dissolved under her almost immediately.

"This is dirty work," she called to him.

"This is all part of it then?" he asked, a concept forming in his head.

"Yes!" she answered happily. "You're not as dumb as you look."

Hannibal had overheard them, but didn't understand.

"What the hell are you talking about?" he yelled at them. "Just kill these things."

"What she's talking about," Alex said, smiling as she defended Meaghan's back, "is that as much as Peter had figured out, he didn't go the next logical step. If we have the kind of control Peter has proved that we do have—"

"My blood!" Hannibal said at the implications, then turned to defend against a stinking, rotting attacker.

"We can be anything," Peter said, and Meaghan smiled.

Cody had run off to save the cameraman, and when he came back, he stopped several yards from the melee. He couldn't believe his eyes. Meaghan had changed again.

Into a tiger.

Mulkerrin watched in horror. . . .

Sandro swung his camera to follow the yellow-and-black streak. . . .

Hundreds of millions of humans would later deny the reality of what the camera showed. . . .

Peter laughed as Meaghan responded to his single request: "Kill the magicians." She sped toward the two remaining acolytes, Thomas Montesi and Sister Mary Magdalene, dodging the demons protecting them with incredible speed, tearing through the silver-wielding soldiers without a thought, settling upon Thomas Montesi before the man could utter a word or bring his weapon to bear.

Huge gleaming jaws of iron sinew and devastating hunger tore off the top of his head. Watching it, Peter felt elation, and was only brought back to his present, to his surroundings, by a nudge from Lazarus. He turned to the elder, grateful to be reminded of their immediate danger, and shapeshifted into mist, dropping his weapon, to avoid being thrashed by two deadly shadows.

Lazarus did not move. Rather, he stayed where he was and shifted into another form—that of a giant black bear, as big as many of the shadow demons attacking them. With its huge paws, the bear grabbed first one, then the other of the demons, ramming its claws through their middles and tearing out withered gray sacks of stinking flesh that must have been the creatures' hearts.

Then they were both in man-form again, and Peter looked at Lazarus in doubt, suspicions and questions forming in his mind, not as to the elder's loyalty, but his nature.

"You're a quick learner," Peter said as Hannibal and Cody protected them for a moment.

"Yes, I suppose I am."

Then Lazarus leaned in and spoke softly to him. "I'm done here, my friend," he said. "I'll see you again, sometime."

"Wait," Peter said, shouting as the snow blew up again, as he heard the wail of a new banshee begin. Mulkerrin was getting desperate now.

"You're one of them, aren't you?" Peter asked. "One of the four survivors, the ones who were never under the church's control?"

Lazarus looked at him kindly. "You're getting warm, Peter. Let me know when you figure it out."

"Let you . . ." Peter said, watching as Lazarus transformed into a bat, though he knew the elder could have chosen any form. "Figure what out?" he cried.

But Lazarus was gone.

Things had gone so wrong, so fast, Father Mulkerrin felt as if he would explode from the nervous energy building with every second of indecision.

What to do?

All three Montesis were dead, and the female Defiant One had become a tiger, something none of them ought to be able to do. And she'd been human just days earlier! Now the tiger was going for Sister Mary, and *that* he could not allow. Octavian, Cody, Hannibal, and the black woman were slaying their demon attackers easily, and many of the demons had wandered away. He was desperate.

"Un sptha pythfer, dothiende," he screamed, repeating the words several times, and a mirror portal opened in the center of the square, pouring demons forth. The portal would disappear when he left, and he could not control the demons with such a reckless spell, but he had no choice.

When he looked again, the tiger was mauling Mary with its claws, and one spoken word saved her life. Responding to Mulkerrin's call, creatures of solid power and complete darkness rose from the brick beneath the acolyte, carried the tiger hundreds of feet in the air, then let it fall.

Before Meaghan could complete her transformation to something with the power of flight, Mulkerrin and Sister Mary were borne aloft by the mist-wraiths, speeding west, toward the home of Hannibal, toward *The Gospel of Shadows*. Mulkerrin had failed to destroy the Defiant Ones, but with the book, he would be able to bide his time and return to finish the job.

Once he was airborne he realized that dusk had arrived. When the rest of the immortal creatures had woken, his demons would be easily overcome. From the sky he could see that the fires still burned, far and wide across the city, and he imagined that among the humans, many demons still roamed. Silently, he prayed for those innocents that the shadows might encounter. He would make certain their sacrifice was not in vain. God would provide.

"Where the hell are they going?" Sandro snapped at Tracey.

"How should I know?" she answered.

"Should we follow them?" he asked.

"Hell, no. We've got more than enough. It's almost

over, we know who won . . . and the streets are about to become even more dangerous.

"It's dark out."

The third demon that Rolf faced was the largest, and still he thought he might destroy it. He knew he had only moments before his task was complete, before the light was gone and his family could join the battle.

And then he fell.

The creature had overpowered him, tearing one arm from its socket, and now it bore down on him as he lay there. Still, he did not quit, tearing at it with his good hand in the gathering dark, and then changing, reshaping himself as a wolf. His arm was still gone, but out of the corner of his eye, even as he thrust his silent muzzle toward the demon's throat, he saw a miraculous thing.

His arm, too, had changed form.

He knew that his people had only just begun to understand themselves. He would not let them be robbed of that chance.

Rolf tore into the demon's flesh, and the boiling bile it called blood seared his throat and burned his lips. His tongue melted; useless as it had always been, the pain was still extreme. And then the soldiers were there, the clergy, and the burning flame from their weapons engulfed him and the demon both.

"Triumph," a man yelled, the same apprentice who had created these demons. His pride was immeasurable. "Quickly now. Inside before they rise."

"No," another yelled. "It is too late, we must flee."

"Coward," said a third, drawing his sword.

None of them saw the flames change, subtly, as if blown by an invisible wind, spreading across the ground to touch the hairy forepaw that lay torn on the street in front of the theater, engulfing the paw in a leaping flame, leaving at first smoldering ash, and then nothing.

Many of them started for the door of the theater, but jumped back as the fire flashed before them, ten feet in the air, blocking their entry before settling back down several feet.

To the height of a man.

They all saw it change, smoking, solidifying.

Rolf, still silent, ever-vigilant, had ignored the last seconds of the day, and put his faith in Octavian. He lived, and he was whole.

Raising a finger to his face, he waved it in front of them, admonishing them for thinking to enter the theater.

A moment later, as the men turned to run, the inner doors to the theater burst open behind him, and Rolf turned to see his brothers and sisters emerge, angry and hungry and bent on vengeance for the many deaths they felt in their sleep. In his homeland, the end of the Reich and its power-mad manipulators, its evil puppeteers, had come too late to save his great-grandchildren, and his few human friends. He had been powerless.

Never again.

As the darkness settled like the silent snow Rolf led his family into the night.

Miles away, Tracey Sacco and Sandro Ricci were on the road to Rome.

30

ALL THAT MATTERED NOW WAS RETRIEVING
that *Gospel of Shadows*. Father Liam Mulkerrin had
failed, and he accepted that. For nearly one hundred years,
his magic had kept him youthful so that he could fulfill the
mission given him by God Himself. And though he had
suffered a major setback, as long as he had the book, he
could start over. Their sorcerous order was the most direct
link the church had to the time of Christ. Perhaps he could
convince the new pope of the value of his mission.

Perhaps not. In any case, he would begin to proselytize
once again, gathering a new force of true Christians. Using
the book, he would train them as he had the others, and
with them he would continue the mission. Though sorcery
allowed him to postpone his aging and death, he was still
human, and would die eventually, inevitably. He vowed
to himself that before his passing, he would fulfill his
divine role.

Death—other than the Defiant Ones, the only thing his
magic could not master.

It looked as if it had come for Sister Mary. Rocketing
through the air, propelled along by mist-wraiths toward
the home of Hannibal, and the book, he took the time
to look her over. Sister Mary was badly injured, horri-
bly mauled by the tiger-thing that the Defiant One had
become. Her good eye had been torn away with a chunk

of facial flesh, leaving her completely blind. She would be next to useless now, but Mulkerrin wanted her with him. Not out of any sense of loyalty, though. Liam wanted Mary with him so that he would not have to admit total defeat. If she survived, somehow it wasn't quite as bad.

As they flew over Venice a pair of demons that had been indiscriminately rampaging through the alleyways below turned and sniffed at the sky, scenting the wraiths. They followed along below Mulkerrin, though he barely noticed.

Father Mulkerrin knew his enemies would be after him. Certainly it would take no more than a moment for them to realize where he was headed. But he had a head start, and they could not have left too large a force guarding the book. They would have needed most of their strength at St. Mark's Square. No, his head start should be sufficient.

Enough about defeat! He would do whatever it took to destroy them, even if that meant attempting spells he had never performed, spells he might not be able to control. He would be victorious even if he must tear asunder the gates of hell and let Lucifer himself free!

Less than a minute after sundown, the horde of Defiant Ones who had slept inside the Venice Theater had arrived in St. Mark's Square. Many, including Rolf, were disappointed by what they found. They had arrived just in time for the cleanup. The shadow demons that remained had gone completely berserk without any specific external control, but the gathered immortals had no trouble destroying them. To everyone's relief, Cody dispatched the remaining banshee.

Two minutes had passed since Mulkerrin had fled.

"Hannibal," Peter called to the older creature, "can you finish the cleanup here and then try to round up any stray shadows? We're going after the sorcerer."

Peter motioned to Cody, Meaghan, and Alex, and the three prepared to leave, but Hannibal stopped them.

"Why?" he asked.

Peter shook his head, angry. "Why? Look, I know you couldn't care less about these people. But the times are changing, brother, and you'd better change with them."

"What the hell are you talking about, lunatic? The humans are nothing to us."

"Wrong," Cody interrupted, knowing exactly where Peter was headed.

"Didn't you see the camera?" Peter asked, pointing to the shadows of the Basilica where Tracey Sacco and Sandro Ricci had stood, recording it all.

Hannibal shook his head.

"Everything that happened here today has been taped and will be broadcast around the world," Peter said, and smiled. "Nothing will ever be the same."

"You didn't!" Meaghan said, an astonished smile on her face as she hugged Peter.

"We did," Cody answered for him.

"The question for you," Alexandra broke in suddenly, pointing at Hannibal's chest, "is do you want to be hounded, hunted down by a world *filled* with humans as a creature of the night, an inhuman devil? Or would you like them to see us as unfortunate victims who triumphed over evil?"

"We could be their heroes," Meaghan said after a moment, and Hannibal looked at her with wide eyes, then up at the Basilica, where the secrets of the millennia had been put on display for the world.

Several times he started to say something, anger and confusion alternating on his face, then he turned away from them and walked several steps. After a moment he faced them again.

"You'd better catch that damned priest!" he said.

"We're gone."

The four of them were flying hard, and as fast as they could manage. Still, in falcon form again, Meaghan easily outdistanced them. They knew that under normal circumstances, Sheng would have been no match for Mulkerrin. They hoped that the priest's weakened condition would even the odds.

Shit, Peter thought, communicating his words to Meaghan, *we should never have left him alone. We should have had somebody else guarding that book with him.*

If it's anybody's fault it's mine, she replied. *I'm the one who insisted on coming up. Anyway, we never knew Mulkerrin could move this fast.*

They were all connected, really, in their minds. Cody, Alex, and Peter had all been of Karl Von Reinman, and therefore shared a psychic bond. And of course, Meaghan was of Peter. Yet the coven had denied both Cody and Peter, and their minds had been closed to each other. As soon as one of them realized the simplicity of it, it would be no problem to establish that rapport again.

Given the chance.

As they came in sight of Hannibal's house, the face of which appeared to have crumbled into the street, a scream ripped through all four of their minds.

It was Sheng.

En masse, they landed, metamorphosis bringing them all to humanoid form. What they saw as they changed left them motionless for a moment.

The front of the building was indeed gone, the roof destroyed as well. In the rubble stood Father Liam Mulkerrin, right hand held high while the left hefted the book of evil they had all dreaded. He was speaking, and yet they could not make out the words.

High above them towered a mirror portal of such huge proportions that they knew it had been what destroyed the house. Seventy feet or more in the air and as wide as the building itself, the portal stood. They could not see into the structure, for their sight was blocked by the mirror-thing. Even as they watched, the liquid surface of the portal began to bubble.

The worst part, though, was what they beheld in the rubble next to Mulkerrin. An unspoken dread had consumed them all when Sheng's mental cry had burst into their minds. Meaghan, for one, wished she had never discovered its origin. Sheng had been Alexandra's lover, and now her fury was preparing to overpower her reason.

Three shadows, demons of a middling size, who had either followed Mulkerrin or been made by him upon his arrival, were holding Sheng's limbs so that he was helpless before the attack of the blind Sister Mary. She swung the silver sword over her head and brought it down again, knowing from the smell where the death was. She chopped and chopped, and though *she* could not see her handiwork, the four Defiant Ones who had hoped to rescue their friend could not tear their eyes away from the scene, from the bloody pieces that were once Shi-er Zhi Sheng.

Still the sword fell, the words tumbled from Mulkerrin's mouth, and the bubbling at the surface of the portal became more violent.

"The three of you," Peter snapped, "get that crazy nun and those demons! I'm on that book."

"I do not want to see what's going to come through *that* hole," Cody added as he followed Meaghan and Alex toward Sheng's remains and his tormentors.

Meaghan had enjoyed the tiger form, and she took that shape again. Alexandra shifted into an imperfect bear. It would take practice, but she was destroying the bonds that had once held her mind captive. Cody, on the other hand, remained in human form, which he had always preferred.

As Meaghan leaped on one of the demons, the Alex-bear batted Sister Mary away from Sheng with a cracking of bones and a shriek as claws tore across the nun's flesh. Cody was surprised the nun was alive at all, but he doubted that was still true. On the run, he picked up her fallen sword and used it to attack a second demon, and Alexandra faced the third. A scream brought Cody's head up and he saw a chunk taken out of Alexandra's furry side, but she ripped into her enemy with even more ferocity and he was forced to assume she was all right. Talons raked Cody's skull, taking half his face with them, and he fell to his knees in pain and shock.

Peter ran at Mulkerrin, who seemed to be ignoring him, and when he was less than five feet from the man, ten from the portal, he dove for the book.

And passed right through the figure, screaming as he landed and his left arm pierced the sulfurous, burning liquid portal. He pulled back his arm to find that halfway between elbow and wrist, it was aflame. Pain and anger filled him as he turned to look for Mulkerrin and saw him several feet away, closing the book. The sorcerer turned, finally acknowledging their presence, as the turbulence of the portal worsened.

"You saw a reflection of me. A good spell, is it not?" the priest asked.

"What the hell are you calling up, you monster?"

"Monster? Surely evil is also insane," Mulkerrin yelled, over a wind that had sprung up.

Peter noticed for the first time that the snow had completely stopped.

"And it's not what I'm calling, but what I've called. Beelzebub himself, the first of the shadows created by Lucifer the Fallen. And you, Defiant One, are to be his first meal on earth."

Mulkerrin put *The Gospel of Shadows* under one arm as if he were a boy walking home from school.

"Once before, with the sorcery in this book, the followers of Christ tore a hole into hell itself. Not some limbo where demons could be found, but *hell,* where the souls of the damned suffer eternity at the hands of Lucifer and the First Order of Shadows. Now I've done it again. Only this time I've called *him* across!"

As he was splashed by the burning liquid only feet away, fear overcame Peter's confusion, and an anger he'd never known possessed him. "Your madness has no end!" he bellowed, teeth baring and claws stretching from the flesh of his fingers.

His voice became a growl. "You could have taken the book and gone! Instead you call something to our world that you have no hope of controlling!"

As Peter leaped for him Mulkerrin held up a hand and spoke three words aloud: *"Ladithe, rothiel, urthoth."* And Peter stopped in midair, and fell like a brick.

"I *am* leaving, Octavian," Mulkerrin said. "But I must see this, God's final justice, before I'm on my way."

His smile was mad, his eyes wide with awe and insanity.

It wasn't that Peter couldn't move, but he moved so painfully slowly that it seemed as if he made no progress at all. The spell had not been meant to kill him, only to prevent him from acting before the creature emerged from the portal. As he looked up at Mulkerrin he saw that it was already too late.

What appeared to be a hand was slowly pushing through the portal, tugged at by the liquid around it as if it were the last sign of life from a thing drowning in quicksand. Only it wasn't drowning. It was crossing over!

Each finger was the size of a man, gnarled like a tree, but a deep red and pulsing with obscene life. The claws of the thing were shining and came to a razor point. Peter did not want to see the rest. The hand descended, slicing down through the portal. In pain Peter turned his head to see its destination, though he'd already guessed what it was. The hand closed around Cody, and lifted him from the ground.

"Peter, are you all right?" Meaghan yelled to him as the wind picked up.

The spell was wearing off, though Mulkerrin had succeeded in draining much of his power. Peter could see that Alexandra, though injured, had finished off the last of the shadows, but he wondered where the wraiths had gone. Above them, Cody was screaming. He had to find a way to stop Mulkerrin, to prevent Beelzebub from coming through and to save Cody.

"Help him," Peter screamed to them, and Meaghan immediately transformed, leading Alex into the air, racing up the monolithic creature's body. They tore into the demon's huge fingers, attempting to loosen its grip on Cody.

"Get this asshole off of me!" Cody yelled, his face tight with pain as he tore into the fingers himself.

Turn to mist! Alexandra's voice filled his head.

"I can't!" he yelled in a panic. "I don't know why, but I can't change at all!"

Mulkerrin was summoning the mist-wraiths, which were gathering about him, as he prepared to take his leave. Above them, the gargantuan demon's face broke through the portal, and for the first time Peter believed it might truly *be* Beelzebub.

Unlike all the other demons they had seen, the ugliest, most disgusting, and perversely constructed creatures a mind could imagine, this creature terrified Peter Octavian. It looked down upon him, its face a crimson ruin, with furrows and rocky growths, two horns on each side of its head, eyes bright with a light reflected from nowhere, and he met its gaze. For a moment he felt as if Mulkerrin's spell had not faded, for he was frozen solid by his terror.

What frightened Peter, what made *this* creature so different from the others, was its intelligence. Eyes, nose, and mouth, where many of the other creatures had none. Personality, character, where the others were mindless savages.

And it smiled at him.

Not an evil smile, though the face was evil incarnate, but a knowing smile. A nudge, a wink, a nod that said, *Yes indeed, thing of the world, everything and nothing is true. Wouldn't you love to know what I know?* Peter could almost hear the words in his head.

Perhaps he did.

"I called him to me and he came!" Mulkerrin shouted as he was lifted from the ground by his wraiths. "HE CAME! WHAT POWER!"

Peter moved. Above him the second hand came through, struggling still against the pull of the other side, the other world—against the hold that hell had on the demon. The rest of the head was emerging and he could see what looked like another horn, halfway between the ground and the creature's head. It might have been its phallus.

Peter heard Meaghan scream at Alex to shapeshift into flames. His friends were going to be killed.

Bolting to where Sheng's remains lay, Peter picked up the silver sword Cody dropped when the demon had grabbed him. He had always wondered at their vampiric metamorphosis, at how they could incorporate clothing and objects into their physical forms, and then shift back perfectly, shirt still buttoned, gun still loaded. He had never even considered what might happen if he absorbed silver in his shifting. A foolish question, for silver was poison. Silver was pain.

Silver sword in hand, Peter changed and the sword melded into him. He became something new, forged in pain, a creature with wings and claws and fangs. A griffin, perhaps, or something that only lived in his mind, but his mind created the form he needed.

Then he was beyond pain, beyond rage, beyond fear. He shot into the sky toward the fleeing sorcerer and struck out at the wraiths that carried him with claws laced with silver. The mist-things reacted instinctively and fled, shrieking, while Mulkerrin and the *Gospel* fell the forty feet to the stones below.

A huge hand reached for him, closed around him, and for a moment he despaired. But then it was gone, and only action remained. Peter tore into the giant hand with hands and teeth, with razor-sharp extensions of himself filled with silver. His own pain was a terrible static filling his every nerve with hissing, steaming heat. Silver was poison to anything not of the earth, not of their plane. Perhaps because they had once been human, his kind could withstand the pain, overcome the poison.

There was so much they didn't know.

The thing was bellowing pain, and Peter was free. He looked up at the head, bending toward him, and the smile was gone, replaced by a terrible, grim satisfaction and the certainty of triumph.

Peter! Meaghan's thoughts broke through the chaos in his mind. *How?*

Clear out! he ordered, ignoring her question. *We'd all be dead without you, but get back or you'll be killed.*

Cody! Alexandra balked.

I'll take care of Cody.

As Alex and Meaghan backed away, barely escaping the swat of a huge claw meant for him, Peter swooped in to where Cody fought, blood bubbling from his mouth and shoulders. Peter realized they were broken. He lashed out with his silver claws, but the hand did not let go. Cody was still trapped.

Cody, make the change!

There was no response. Somehow this thing had prevented Cody from changing, but now Peter couldn't even be sure if Cody was conscious, or alive, to make the change.

Peter dove in again, stopping this time and digging his talons into the demon's flesh, scraping and cutting with the silver deep into the creature's hand. The fingers tensed up, crushing Cody further. The shadow bellowed above them and its other hand came down to bat Peter away . . . but the fist in which it held Cody relaxed.

C'mon, Will, make the damned change.

Cody was burning, the fire that he'd become engulfing the demon's hand. And then he was falling, and Peter could do nothing more for him as he regained his normal shape and hit the rocks by Mulkerrin.

What Peter had thought was the creature's penis was actually a bony horn protruding from its left knee, which had now come through along with the foot. They could see much of its chest and shoulders. From the waist down, except for the lower left leg, it was still invisible.

But not for long.

Peter landed near Alex and Meaghan, who had dragged Cody's form out of range of the creature, at least for the moment. Cody was not moving, but Peter could see that he was healing rapidly. The creature he had become disappeared in flame, and then Peter was there, hand on his belly, doubled over as the silver sword clattered to the ground.

Meaghan rushed to his side and helped him to his feet.

"I'll be okay in a second," Peter said.

"Do we have a second?" Alexandra asked as she tended Will Cody's wounds, and they all looked up at the face of hell, towering above them.

Hannibal's house was a ruin. Ca Rezzonico, next to it on the Grand Canal, had one wall destroyed and was burning from the inside out. Peter could see that many of the other Defiant Ones had started to arrive on the scene, but did not know what to do any better than he.

"How do we stop it?" he asked, to nobody in particular.

"Where's the book?" Meaghan asked, turning his face so that he could focus on her. She could see that he was baffled. "There's got to be something in it that can help us!"

"Mulkerrin had it when he fell," Peter answered, then looked back at the demon.

"What is it, Peter?" Alexandra asked him, waiting for Cody to open his eyes. "What is that thing really? All these things? Demons, or something else? And why does silver affect them all the same way it does us? Are *we* demons, Peter? Did we come out of hell like that thing?"

"NO!" Peter yelled, more to the hellspawn itself than in answer to Alex's question.

But then he did answer her.

"We're nothing like these other things, like this thing," he assured her, seeing how deeply the questions disturbed her. "There is humanity in us, no matter how deep we have to go to find it."

HAH!

The booming voice came from above them, and they all looked up again. The demon was leaning forward, putting its weight on its left foot, on the rubble of Hannibal's house. Only its buttocks and right leg were still trapped, and its face was tight with the effort of pulling free. With the grip it now had on their dimension, the shadow's flesh was emerging faster than before. Still, it looked at Peter.

It spoke to them. One sentence only, after the huge, rumbling laugh that had drawn their attention. Ca Rezzonico crumbled to the ground as the words became tremors. The ground shook, and flame, of a color they had never before seen, shot from deep in its throat.

YOU HAVE NO *IDEA* WHAT YOU ARE!

Those were its words, and the pain in them, for Peter, for all of them, was that the words were true.

Peter felt like he had woken up from some complacent dream, a dream where he'd rested after saving Cody, where he simply waited for Beelzebub, or whatever it was, to emerge into their world. But he dreamed no longer. He didn't know if he could prevent it, but he wasn't about to let the invader violate their world without a fight.

In less than a second Peter was at Mulkerrin's side. Though he could barely believe it, the sorcerer was alive. Near him lay the body of Sister Mary Magdalene, her corpse torn open by Alexandra's fury. Peter looked up for a moment and saw his own reflection in the shimmering mirror surface of that portal.

There is something human in there! he thought.

Two paces away, he saw the book. Grabbing it, he knelt at Mulkerrin's side and slapped him awake, not trying to be careful.

"Priest!" he said, then got no response and began to shout. "Mulkerrin. Liam Mulkerrin. How do I send it back? How do we close the portal?"

The sorcerer did not respond, and Peter slapped him again, looking up to see that Beelzebub's foot was only yards away. If he were not straining to pull his other leg through, he could surely have stepped on Peter where he knelt, or at least have made a grab for him.

"Damn you!" Peter screamed at Mulkerrin's prone form, slapping the book against the earth. "You wanted power? Here it is. You called it and it came to you, you said. Well, do you have the power to send it back? You called it and—"

I called it and it came to me.

That's what Mulkerrin had said.

"Meaghan," he yelled, and in a breath she was by his side. "Take this." He handed her the book.

"What? What are you going to do?"

He ignored her as he hefted Mulkerrin off the ground, placing him on one shoulder. The priest had to be dying because he was aging in front of them. He looked more than eighty years old now, and Peter realized that magic had kept him young. While the creatures he had so hated were given the gift of immortality, Mulkerrin had used his powers to steal a little bit from the things he most despised.

Peter turned toward the demon, and Meaghan grabbed his arm.

"What are you going to do?" she said again, and he whirled to face her.

"Our world is one of order. According to our legends, hell is a place of chaos. But over here, we have rules. We have a lot of them. If we didn't have them, these spells, the magic by which the church has held demons in their control for so long, would be nothing but words. The silver, that's another thing. Somehow, whatever put together this world gave it rules—natural or supernatural, whatever. And one way or another, everything abides by them."

He looked around and saw his people, several hundred beings whom legend had dubbed vampires but who he knew were so much more. They were watching, waiting, as the terrible wind battered them with the stench of brimstone. The door to hell had been opened. Who could say that once this creature, this Beelzebub, was through, it would close?

"PETER!" Meaghan yelled over the sound of the wind, clearing his head. He looked at her and saw she didn't know what he was talking about.

"Mulkerrin called it and it came to him. *To him!* Do you understand? He said it like it was important, like it was part of the spell. Maybe, if he's gone, it won't have an anchor here!" Peter responded.

"HOW IN HELL CAN YOU KNOW THAT?" she screamed.

Peter saw the pain in her face and he felt it, too. For them to lose what they'd found in each other, after what was really no time at all, especially for an immortal, it wasn't fair.

"I can't," he answered, almost too low for her to hear.

"Fine, then just kill him."

"I don't think that will be enough."

"My God, Peter," she screamed, and he sensed the reaction of the others nearby, their astonishment that the name of the Almighty could roll so easily off her tongue, an invocation they'd believed fatal to their kind. "You can't mean to go through . . ."

He put Mulkerrin down and took Meaghan in his arms, the book pressed between them. They kissed, but unlike any they had previously shared, this kiss held not a trace of the desire that had once driven them. It was a sad, pure gesture, and when Peter drew back his head, he could see that Meaghan was crying, tears of blood.

"I love you," he said.

"I love you, too."

Peter looked up to see Alexandra helping Cody to his feet, and he felt better knowing Will was going to be okay. Together, the three of them would have to deal with the new order of things. It was going to be a new world for them.

"Come back to me," Meaghan said.

Peter nodded yes, though he knew it couldn't be. He didn't even know for sure if what he was doing would close the tear that Mulkerrin had rent in the fabric of their world. But in his heart, Peter felt it. Something spoke to him there, urged him on.

He turned toward the portal, where all that held the demon back was the pull of its own world on its right leg, just at the knee, and its huge tail, which they had not seen before. On its face were the signs of its struggle to break through, its concentration utterly and completely on escaping into this new world. And then what? Peter had to wonder, and the thought chilled him.

He went to lift Mulkerrin again. . . .

And the priest was gone.

"NO!"

"Above you!" Meaghan yelled.

Peter looked up to see Mulkerrin, broken and twisted but alive, borne aloft by the mist-wraiths he had dispersed before.

"Keep the book safe," he said as he changed, and then his thoughts took over as he flew after them. *You may need it very soon. Just get out of here, as quickly as you can. Get them all away. Use that book! Find out what we really are!*

Meaghan ran back to where Cody and Alexandra were standing. Rolf and Hannibal were there, too, and many others. She held tight to the book and watched the sky, the terrible sky from which hell was emerging, and where the man who had remade her—even before she'd been reborn—into a new being, a being with a destiny, was fighting to save a family that had denied him.

The griffin-thing again, but without the silver claws, Peter attacked the wraiths in flight, one talon latching onto Mulkerrin's arm while the other tried to bat away the wraiths. Abandoning their master to Peter's grasp, they attacked him as was their nature, seeping in through his eyes and fanged mouth, filling his body. From where she was, Meaghan could see Peter become bloated, as if he would explode, and then he burst into flame. Black smoke that might have been the wraiths seemed to stream from the fire, almost as if it were escaping. But the fire leaped over it, and the wraiths were gone.

Peter had destroyed them, but not without a cost. Mulkerrin was falling, and if what Peter said was true, his death could undo all that they were attempting. Meaghan prepared to rush to catch him, but stopped herself as she saw Peter.

Half flame, half griffin, or simply a creature on fire, Peter screamed in agony as he beat his wings after Mulkerrin's falling form. Only seconds before the priest would become a part of the rubble that had been Hannibal's home, Peter was there, straining skyward, breaking Mulkerrin's fall. Or trying. They both hit the ground. Meaghan wanted to run to him, but Alexandra grabbed her and hugged tight.

"You can't!" she said. "Look!"

Above them, the demon had pulled its right leg through. It set its foot down now so that Peter and Mulkerrin lay between its legs. Only the creature's tail held it back, and it relaxed a moment. It looked at the immortals gathered around, and Meaghan thought the face looked confused.

It must be wondering why we haven't run, she thought.
And then it looked down.

"PETER, GO!" she screamed as the demon raised its newly freed foot, a three-toed doglike haunch with tufts of black hair crowning each digit. It would crush them both. Peter might be able to change and get away, but Mulkerrin never would.

Peter had only one move, the one he'd planned. It was no longer a matter of choice.

GO! She screamed in her mind.

And he did.

Under Mulkerrin, he returned to his own form, to the face he'd worn at the fall of Constantinople, when Nicephorus Dragases became immortal. With the speed of his heritage, he threw the sorcerer over his shoulder and leaped toward their mirror image in the portal, headfirst.

Mulkerrin's feet went in first, and from unconsciousness, the pain of the passing brought him awake, screaming, as the demon's foot slammed down, cutting off the onlooker's view of the scene.

The ground shook with the footfall, drowning out the priest's wailing, but Meaghan knew they were gone.

It began. As slowly as he had extricated himself, bellowing all the while, scrabbling and clawing at the earth, tearing up the street, the demon was drawn back to hell. Where it belonged.

I COULD HAVE TAUGHT YOU! it yelled. YOU MIGHT HAVE RULED THIS WORLD IF ONLY YOU KNEW YOUR TRUE SELVES!

But mostly it saved its breath for the effort to escape.

Peter had followed his heart and found the answer, Meaghan thought. Farther along the devastated Calle Bernardo, they all watched as the thing's hands were drawn into the portal, which, when the demon was completely gone, seemed to melt, or flow, in on itself until it had disappeared.

Meaghan turned to them. Blood streaked their faces and she could see that they, too, had been crying.

"What now?" Alexandra asked her.

Meaghan smiled, feeling suddenly brave, and hopeful. "I think Cody knows the answer to that," she said, looking at him expectantly.

He was back to normal, though slightly weak, but it took him a moment before he got her meaning, and when he finally did, he laughed out loud. "Now," he said to Alex, "we get to deal with the press."

"Reporters?" Her eyes went wide.

"Darlin'," he said, "it's a brave new world, and an old showman like myself can't turn away the spotlight once it's shinin'. Besides, Tracey and Sandro are probably halfway to Rome by now. We don't have much of a choice."

As they spoke Meaghan let her gaze wander back to the ruins of Hannibal's house. Many of their kind had started to wander toward the mess, lost in Cody's "brave new world."

"Will," she said without turning, and the tone of her voice quieted them, "one thing. They've got to know we were human once. It's in us. That's what Peter's actions have always meant."

She faced them, then, and her eyes were sad but strong. "Never let it be said that we have no souls."

Epilogue

"MEAGHAN, HONEY, WAKE UP. YOU'RE GOING to miss your plane."

The insistent nudging, both physical and vocal, finally roused her from a much-needed sleep. She stretched and yawned, then turned onto her back and looked up at her lover. Both of them were naked, and the room still smelled from their lovemaking of several hours earlier. Sleepily, Meaghan reached up for a hug, and when it came, she pulled Alexandra down onto the bed with her, their breasts pressed together and their mouths meeting in a hungry kiss.

The sun shone through the wide windows of their bedroom, one of many in the antique house they now shared. They rolled around playfully for a few moments, hugging and enjoying the moment, the little time they had to be silly in their lives.

"Get in the shower," Alexandra said to her. "You're going to be late."

"Come with me," Meaghan answered.

"Oh, good. Then you'll really be late."

Meaghan made a sour face, gave her lover's breast a final, friendly squeeze, then was up and on her way to the shower. "You know what today is?" she called as she made her way to the bathroom.

"How could I forget?" Alex answered. "Wait till you see the *Globe*'s headlines."

"What's going on?"

" 'Hearings on UN Membership, Land Grants for Vampires Begin Today . . . First Anniversary of Venice Jihad Leaves Many Questions,' " Alex quoted, reading from the *Boston Globe* they had delivered to their doorstep. The paper girl still stood several yards away when tossing the paper on their porch.

"Shit," Meaghan said. "Tell us something we don't know. When are they going to do something about the Vatican?"

"I wish I knew, sweetheart."

The phone rang, and Alex went to pick it up. "*Will?* Where are you?"

"Where do you think I am, darlin'? I'm all over the damn place. There are more of us than we ever realized, and they're coming out of the woodwork."

"You were supposed to be here today."

"I'll meet Meaghan in New York tomorrow," Cody answered. "I thought I was close to finding Lazarus, but my lead dried up."

"You better be there, *Colonel* Cody. Meaghan needs your backup, and then I've got another lead for you."

"You haven't seen the news, have you?" he said.

"What are you talking about?"

"Put on CNN."

Alex grabbed the remote and tapped the power on, jabbing in the channel command for CNN. On the screen was Allison Vigeant, better known to them as Tracey Sacco, who'd become a major force both on the air and behind the scenes at CNN in just twelve months. She was considered the world media's number-one authority on the Defiant Ones.

Alex turned up the volume.

". . . has announced that the president has pledged to use any means necessary to back up United Nations resolutions regarding the Venice Jihad. The announcement comes after months of church interference in the ongoing UN investigation into possible Vatican involvement in the Venice Jihad and what has been called 'attempted genocide' regarding the so-called Defiant Ones. The press secretary implied that the White House refused to rule out the use of military force at this time."

"YES!" Alex shouted, dropping the phone as she ran to the bathroom door, banging for Meaghan to hurry so they could share the news. When she came back into the room, she reached for the phone but was drawn again to Allison's words on the television.

". . . sad note, one of the people indirectly responsible for the 'new order' we find ourselves in today, as well as one of the spearheads of the UN's Vatican investigation, is dead. Former Cardinal Henri Guiscard died last night, apparently of natural causes. While thousands of people have pursued the possibility of undergoing what is being called the Revenant Transformation, and many others have volunteered to be blood donors, Guiscard was reportedly *offered* the transformation dozens of times, and obviously refused.

"By all accounts a man of great wisdom and courage, Henri Guiscard will be missed."

Alex was quiet for a minute, the phone held loosely against her face. She shook her head sadly, and then heard Cody's voice on the phone.

"Alex," it said, sounding far away.

"Damn," she whispered, then put the phone to her ear again. "I can't believe nobody's called us before now. I mean, the news knew before we did. That sucks."

natural causes

"Listen," Alex said, "you don't think . . ."

"You have to wonder, though, don't you?" Cody said, and he was as serious as he ever got.

"See you tomorrow," Alexandra said.

"You're coming, too?"

"I am now."

Alex hung up the phone, mind racing with terrible possibilities. Didn't they have enough to worry about without this? The whole UN thing, the Vatican investigation, volunteerism, combating both human and inhuman predators, and the obvious and understandable fears and prejudices that faced them; weren't all these things enough?

Find out what we are!

They had vowed to themselves that Peter's last request would be fulfilled. They had all loved him, and respected him. Alex and Meaghan had been his lovers. The question he died asking was still the number-one question on their minds, and on the minds of governments, scientists, and just plain people all over the world.

What were they, really?

She and Cody and Meaghan had dedicated their lives to answering that question. Finding Lazarus would be the first big break, if they could find him, but there seemed to be so many things that took precedence.

Not the least of which was analyzing *The Gospel of Shadows,* learning as much as possible about the magic in that book. There had to be some control over the shadows, and nobody but the Pentagon thought that the American military should have that power. Alex knew it had only been left in their hands because nobody had gotten brave enough to try to take it from them yet. Still, who better?

So many questions. So many responsibilities. And now another dead friend and more questions.

Meaghan stepped out of the shower, still rubbing vigorously at her wet hair. Alexandra couldn't help noticing how beautiful she looked naked, drops of water still beading on her breasts and belly. She loved Meaghan more than she had ever loved anyone or anything, a difficult thing after so many of their friends had died. But they had power and, with it, tremendous responsibility, a lesson even Hannibal and his followers were beginning to learn.

Alexandra didn't know if they'd ever have time just for each other.

But they had forever to find out.

Dr. George Marcopoulos sat in his rocking chair smoking his pipe. He'd never thought of it as smoking, really, more like relaxation. Few people knew he smoked. His wife, Valerie, knew, of course, and some of his family. Nobody at the hospital, though. These days you got a hard time about smoking wherever you went, and that was for regular folks. If you were a doctor, someone who ought to know better, well, then you were truly the lowest form of life.

He rocked just a bit, back and forth, slow and methodical, the way he knew an old rocker like that was meant to be rocked. The rocker had once belonged to his uncle George, after whom he was named and who also smoked. It was the wonderful smell of his uncle's pipe that started him smoking, and perhaps rocking, and convinced him that a pipe wasn't like real smoking no matter what the surgeon general said.

He alternated looking out the window and looking into the fire as he puffed on his pipe. Sometimes he tried to read himself to sleep, but too often the insomnia took on a life of its own and he found himself rocking and smoking and thinking. He thought a lot in that chair in front of the fire.

Peter Octavian had also known that he smoked. They had shared all their secrets like little boys in a tree house or in the blind darkness of a sleepover night. Of course they'd been far from little boys, he an old Greek and his friend far, far older and for all intents and purposes the last ruler of George Marcopoulos' ancestors.

Most of the time, when he couldn't sleep and he rocked and smoked and thought, and gazed alternately out at the windy dark or in at the flickering blaze, it was Peter he thought about.

He puffed the pipe just to smell that wonderful pipe-smoking smell and set to rocking again and thought about friends that had left him. First Peter and now Henri Guiscard. Both men of great personal strength and intelligence, with whom he was proud to have been associated. He had not had much time to know Henri, and he felt some guilt at his death. In a way he had blamed Henri for Peter's death, but he'd known that was foolish.

What happened was destined to happen, and he was sure that Peter had been destined to be a part of it. Even if Octavian had lived, their friendship would never have been the same. The new world order controlled every moment of the lives of his new friends, the lives of Meaghan Gallagher, Will Cody, and Alexandra Nueva. Peter's life would have been affected as well. Nothing would ever have been the same.

It had to do with sharing secrets. Knowing another's secrets was a power few could wield, a difficult burden to bear. A great power, which carried with it a great responsibility. Friendships were built on such power, and the closeness that resulted from it. Nations were destroyed by it. The intimacy of secrets was the basis of love, and friendship, far more than simple fondness had ever been . . . and all the secrets that Peter had shared with George had now been revealed. Everything Peter Octavian was had been violated, and yet he had freely chosen this revelation for a greater purpose.

Sharing secrets is never easy, George Marcopoulos thought as he rocked slowly and puffed long and lovingly and watched sparks fly on brick.

He was broken out of his reverie by the sound of his wife's voice calling his name. His gaze turned from the fire and there she was, shuffling into his study in the wee hours of the morning, his beautiful Valerie come to find her bed-furnace of a husband who ought not go off in the middle of the night leaving her to freeze.

He doesn't have to tell her he can't sleep, she knows

already. She has seen him this way many times, smoking and rocking and gazing out at the night or into the fire. He doesn't have to tell her he'll be right up. At their age and after forty years of marriage, there's little need for talk. She bends painfully, the cold does that to Valerie, and kisses George on the head, then shuffles back toward the stairs, which she'll take quite slowly.

The fire is dying anyway, he sees, and the night is beginning to brighten a little.

The rocker stops, and he taps out his pipe in the ash-tray.

Though he is saddened by Henri's death, it is Peter he thinks of. Always Peter. He misses their conversations and the excitement of living vicariously through Peter's adventures. He misses his visits and his humor, which few people had truly been able to appreciate.

He's been told what Peter went through, his passage into *somewhere else,* and he wonders what he might have found on the other side. He's also been told of the questions that haunted him at the end. Questions of nature and origin.

Find out what we are, he had instructed his people.

George could have told them, for all the definition anyone might ever need was to be found in the grief of a loving heart.

Peter Octavian had been a man.

His friend.

And he was truly missed.

ABOUT THE AUTHOR

CHRISTOPHER GOLDEN is the bestselling author of such novels as *The Myth Hunters*, *The Boys Are Back in Town*, and *Strangewood*. He co-wrote the lavishly illustrated novel *Baltimore, or, The Steadfast Tin Soldier and the Vampire* with Mike Mignola, and the comic book series spin-off. With Tim Lebbon, he has co-written the Hidden Cities series, the latest of which, *The Shadow Men*, hits in 2011. With Thomas E. Sniegoski, he is the co-author of the book series *OutCast* and the comic book miniseries *Talent*. With Amber Benson, Golden co-created the online animated series *Ghosts of Albion* and co-wrote the book series of the same name. He is also known for his many media tie-in works, including novels, comics, and video games, in the worlds of *Buffy the Vampire Slayer*, *Hellboy*, *Angel*, and *X-Men*, among others.

Golden was born and raised in Massachusetts, where he still lives with his family. His original novels have been published in more than fourteen languages in countries around the world. Please visit him at www.christophergolden.com

The Shadow Saga

Of Saints and Shadows
(July 2010)

Angel Souls and Devil Hearts
(October 2010)

Of Masques and Martyrs
(December 2010)

The Gathering Dark
(February 2011)

Waking Nightmares
(May 2011)